NEVER WALK BACK

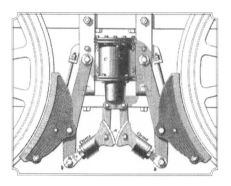

Adam J. Shafer

AN OUTLIER BOOK
from
ALLIUM PRESS OF CHICAGO

Allium Press of Chicago
Forest Park, IL
www.alliumpress.com

Outlier Books are novels without a Chicago connection
that will appeal to those who've enjoyed other Allium Press books.

‹ ›

This is a work of fiction. Descriptions and portrayals of real people, events, organizations, or establishments are intended to provide background for the story and are used fictitiously. Other characters and situations are drawn from the author's imagination and are not intended to be real.

Book and cover design by E. C. Victorson
Cover image: adapted from
Albert Bierstadt, *Figures in a Hudson River Landscape*.
Title page image: air brake detail, adapted from *A Treatise on the Locomotive and the Air Brake* (Scranton, PA: The Colliery Engineer Company, 1900*)*

Library of Congress Cataloging-in-Publication Data

Names: Shafer, Adam J., author.
Title: Never walk back / Adam J. Shafer.
Description: Forest Park, IL : Allium Press of Chicago, [2020] | "An
    outlier book" |
Identifiers: LCCN 2020025222 (print) | LCCN 2020025223 (ebook) |
ISBN 9780999698297 (trade paperback) | ISBN 9781734801705 (epub)
Subjects: LCSH: Railroad stories.
Classification: LCC PS3619.H329 N48 2020 (print) | LCC PS3619.H329
    (ebook) | DDC 813/.6--dc23
LC record available at https://lccn.loc.gov/2020025222
LC ebook record available at https://lccn.loc.gov/2020025223

To Emily, for keeping the horse alive past the first page

I am a slow walker, but I never walk back.
—Abraham Lincoln

adapted from *Westinghouse Automatic Brake Catalogue*, 1886

PART ONE

June~September 1865

1

Near Chattanooga, Tennessee

Shooting at wild elk with a small caliber rifle called for a direct hit through the head or lungs, and Ruth Casper wasn't sure she was up for either.

She'd wandered toward Citico Creek looking for wild turkey, not expecting to come across the last elk gang for fifty miles. A thousand times she'd crossed the river to Missionary Ridge without ever seeing elk. Not at Cummings Gap, or Lookout Mount, White Bone, Chickamauga, or Forest Hill, either. The best she could hope for around here was a band of lackluster coyotes or a few wild turkeys. They made her nervous, the elk did. All that meat. It wasn't normal and she was sweating as a result.

About fifty head had stopped to graze the wild strawberry field. The red-freckled grassland stretched two miles, the only break coming from the East Tennessee Railroad, which split through the field's middle.

The sun had just buried itself in Arkansas, which made sighting the beasts troublesome. It didn't help that her knotted hair had come loose from under her slouch hat, distracting her. She tied the hat to her saddlebag. The brim bothered her aim. She dismounted and lay flat on her belly, sixty yards downwind. This kept her scent, and that of her sorrel mare, unnoticed. The horse, who answered to Wimp—which was an apt name considering her sagging back and ambling gait— stayed put behind Ruth, head bent low, teeth jutting, nibbling on the wild berries.

Ruth exhaled a long, nervous breath. This was the first elk ever centered in her sight and the thought of all that meat unsteadied her hand.

Her stomach rippled loud enough to remind her how little was in it. It had been two days since she'd last eaten and that was only a groundhog, just enough to provoke her appetite rather than vanquish it. She swiped the sweat from her sharp, unflattering cheekbones and tightened her grip on the rifle. Her arms were ropy from hard work and struggle, her every muscle tensed.

She lined up. The first shot had to be perfect, the next shots just had to be close. The lung, she decided, would be easier to damage with the small caliber.

She sighted an elk with its head tilted skyward, listening to the wind for its fate. Its massive summer antlers sprawled heavenward.

Ruth's finger rested against the curved trigger.

A locomotive climbed the bluff and frightened Wimp with its high-hiss whistle just as Ruth squeezed the trigger. The spooked horse nickered and kicked in front of Ruth and forced her to roll. The rifle's brass butt plate recoiled into her clavicle and popped the bone. The bullet hit the ground ten feet ahead and split open the earth. Red and brown chunks went airborne and rained down heavy. The grouping of elk tore away from the sound of the shot. She heard the drumbeat of hooves. The pain in her shoulder didn't impress right away. She'd been preoccupied at first by the rumble of stampeding elk and a spooked horse. The gang sounded like rolling thunder. The sensation of quaking earth dazed and frightened her. It was twice as dark as it had been the minute before, and she didn't know if the gang was charging or fleeing or what had happened to Wimp.

When the pain arrived in full, she rolled on her back holding her shoulder, grunting and cursing. It felt like her entire neck had rearranged itself under her skin. She dropped the rifle and pushed herself up on her elbows, squishing flat the strawberries, her dark blue calico blouse and skirt made purple by the juice. She felt the exclamation of pain in her shoulder, made more injurious by the fact she hadn't put down a single elk. She'd been the only one who'd come to any damage, in fact.

Ruth weighed whether to continue the hunt or to go home and tend to her shoulder. Either way, she'd need Wimp. Ruth clucked her tongue and called the horse to get her to double back. She'd been good and spooked. Ruth knew it would take some more urging before she returned.

Tom-toms of pain beat in her shoulder. When she lifted her arm, she heard the grinding sound of peppercorns in a mill and she groaned as she lowered it.

"Wimp!" she said, shambling toward the horse. "You dim-witted nag."

The horse lollygagged nearer, lacking any grace in so doing. When the two reunited, Ruth gripped the saddle horn and tried to remount. She hooked her strongside foot into the stirrup, but Wimp took a careless step forward. Ruth stumbled and reintroduced a sting in her shoulder sharp enough to cure her desire to ever mount a horse again. Despite the pain crackling along her collarbone, she imagined how she might fire on the elk again without hurting herself further. She dared not return home empty-handed and one less a bullet. She'd taken with her the few hunting tools Henry owned. Took the rifle and the skinning knife and left him a hatchet no sharper than its own handle. Henry had his bear trap, but she couldn't count on it doing what it was supposed to do. God help any critter caught in that damned thing. And God help Ruth, cursed with few bullets, poor aim, and now a stove-up shoulder. Guilt had pushed her onto this field and guilt would keep her out here until she killed something worth skinning.

The guilt hurt more than her shoulder ever could.

She'd fallen into the sulks years ago. After the babies had all slipped away and Henry enlisted, she sank into melancholy. She wouldn't move for whole days. When she did leave the bed, nothing useful came from it. Solitude had given way to loneliness and loneliness had given way to despair. She hadn't realized how important Henry was to her state of mind. It wasn't Henry, exactly, but just someone. Anyone. With Henry away, she was forced to reckon with her own mind. She was stuck imagining her babies until she ached. Day after day stolen from her as she'd hid inside her own mind. It was like she'd fallen in a pit and hadn't the strength to do anything but stare at its dark walls. By the time she'd found grit enough to claw back into the living world, months had passed. She still wasn't certain how she'd spent up all that time. The planting and sowing seasons came and went without the fields having been properly seen to. The plow lines were shallow, the seedlings too close together or too far apart, not tended enough to save. The whole damn homestead looked to have been hewn by thumbless, brainless animals. All that time in the pit, the land had gone to pot. She'd not prepared for next season. Her bones had been made too prominent by hunger. And if she was the reason they were starved, then, by God, she wouldn't leave this field until she had some damn dead animal with her.

She grabbed the reins and led Wimp back to the rifle, still squinting through the darkness in the elk's direction. She sensed motion up ahead, but saw only dark shapes amidst darker shapes, none of them moving.

The wind carried distant sounds nearer, announcing the low clatter of a train coming from the southwest. Ruth was about two hundred yards from where she thought the elk had run.

Ruth couldn't see the trunk class engine until it arrived hurtling up the slope. The driver's whistle had sent the brakemen out, but they moved too slowly. A frantic squelch rose from the train. Lanterns threw a conniption of light along the cars.

"Jesus," Ruth said into the wind.

Dozens of elk littered the track, still moving away from Ruth. The brakeman had locked the lead brake. The train jerked, fighting against its own momentum. Ruth saw one of the brakemen, saw him locking the brakes of the second car, saw the train heave, saw him lose footing. Then she lost sight of him.

The train wasn't slowing fast enough. The locomotive's lead lamp illuminated the horror. There was no doubt the cowcatcher, fixed to the front like the tip of a spear, was going to clip its fair share of elk. It pierced the first beast quickly. The elk didn't even shuffle its feet before its joints came apart and jellied up the tracks. It made a raspy honking bellow that Ruth had never before imagined a beast could make.

The second and third elk got their legs swept out by the husk of the first. All three were chewed up between wheel and rail. Sparks and ballast made fast arcs into the earth while the front of the train loosened from the rail. Thump. Another elk. Thump. And still more. Thump, thump,

thump. Each one fell like grass before the sickle until the derailed train crashed into the fleeing majority. The noise and sparks spooked Wimp all over again and she snapped Ruth's grip and scampered away. Ruth had lost count of all the struck elk. The train spun them around like weathervanes in a storm as it skidded to a stop. What remained of the gang scattered further ahead into the darkness. Most of the train's connectors had come undone. Gravity got the best of the rear car. It rolled lonesome back down the shallow slope in the direction it had come. She watched the mess a while longer before clicking at Wimp and double-timing it toward the massacre, closer to the moaning of dying elk.

The train's pistons popped and hissed in a loose symphony. The cowcatcher had been wrenched loose and sizzled among the blades of tall grass. The engine cabin was empty. It wasn't until Ruth dropped back to the third car that she found the driver and his second passing a stubby flask of ammonia under the fallen brakeman's nose. He wasn't moving.

The driver was a ruddy-faced man with tinted spectacles and unkempt side-whiskers poking out from underneath his hat. He stood over the brakeman with a determined expression pulled tight across his face. "Jeremiah," he said, and slapped the man across the jowl. "That was some tumble, you old handler. Now open them eyes." He gave out another smack.

Ruth could see the brakeman's left arm and leg were bent in the opposite direction nature intended. It was a grotesque kind of splay. "His left side's broke," she said from out of the darkness.

It startled the driver and the second. The driver spun around and aimed a tin lantern at her. "Christ, woman," he said. "Announcing yourself like that's a good way to get kicked in the cunt."

Ruth looked at the driver, wanting to make sure he wasn't going to come down off that train and do what he'd said. He didn't move, so she continued. "His chest don't rise, neither."

The driver shot her a hard stare. He seemed as unnerved by her words as by her surprise appearance. He knelt and put two fingers under the unconscious man's nose, felt his chest and came away with a less determined look, as if a tension had been released.

"Man's dead, ain't he?" Ruth asked.

"Who are you, madam?"

"I'm a hunter," she said and lifted the rifle off her good shoulder as proof.

"What are you doing out here?"

She shrugged as if the answer was obvious. "Hunting."

"A lot of good you did us," the driver said. "Don't know if you noticed, but every goddamned elk in the state gathered right in front of you."

"I ain't the one popping 'em off the track like kernels from a corncob, sir."

The driver looked her over—conduct to make any woman nervous. "You out here alone?" There was malevolence in his voice.

"No, sir." She considered lying but saw no way of keeping it up. Instead, she pointed back into the darkness and said, "I'm here with my horse." There was no evidence of a horse behind her.

"Why're you bloody?"

"Sir?"

"Look at you. You're bleeding every which way."

Ruth remembered that the flattened berries had colored her in violent red splotches.

"Just before you bucked the gang, my horse wandered in front of me. Had to shoot cockeyed to avoid her. Shooting cockeyed left me mashed in strawberry." She decided against confessing her shoulder injury for as long as she could avoid it.

The second brakeman gripped the dead one's broken arm.

The driver shouted, "What are you doing?"

"Snapping his bones back in place," the man said, his voice shaky with grief. "He won't fit natural in a casket with his limbs akimbo."

"Don't touch him," the driver snapped. "There's going to be an investigation and I don't want nothing to point to us as derelicts." He returned to Ruth, looking down on her from the platform.

Ruth knew there were already plenty of signs pointing to the man being a derelict but decided against saying so.

"Can you believe it?" the driver said. "Wasn't that long ago there were a million elk in this land. Like poppies in a field. And these elk here, these last few, survived ten generations of Shawnee and four years of war, only to meet their fate on a railroad track in the goddamn dark." Ruth did not know what the dark had to do with it but supposed the man's upset state had confused his tongue. He hopped down the train car steps and studied the strewn and dripping elk fractions. "Lord almighty," he continued.

"I didn't know the Eastern was hiring again," she said.

"It ain't. I owed a favor."

"You usually take a Mogul full steam over a blind like that?" she asked.

"Ain't no usually for me. This is only my third run."

"Probably your last," Ruth said. She wished she hadn't. It slipped.

The driver shot her a glare. "What you know about trains?"

"My husband's a driver. Used to be."

"That makes you an expert?"

"Compared to you, maybe. A good handler knows not to take for granted the top of a slope. Not with the brake time needed to stop four cars. No way can a brakeman save the gore under the circumstances."

"No way of guessing there'd have been eighty elk waiting for me."

"Don't that just prove my point?" She couldn't help herself. The man was arrogant. And dim-witted. "These slow-stopping trains don't allow for chance. Someone comes up a hill that speed, you'd need a brake clamped around the wheels like a bear trap."

She stopped. A thought had overtaken her. An idea, like a bolt from Zeus on high. The driver was speaking. She could tell by his tone he was asserting his manliness, but she wasn't listening. She was trying to keep still the idea bouncing around in her mind like a loose greased hog.

"…so you can just keep a quiet tongue about the way I handle my damn train," the driver finished up. "Go disappear into the shadows or wherever you came from."

"I was hoping you might help me tie some of this meat onto my saddle?" Ruth said. It was indelicate, but then, so was the situation before them. "Tie me up a leg or two and I'll be on my way."

The driver set his jaw and inhaled as if readying to blow fire. "Drag 'em away yourself."

Ruth shot him a sharp look that got lost in the dark. Another misfire on the night. "I can't," she said. "Will you at least have your brakeman help?"

"No, ma'am. We've got a long damn night ahead of us and I'm in no charitable temper."

"Sir," Ruth said, "I want you to look at me. I'm starved and injured. Is an uncharitable temper all it takes to refuse me a hand in cinching these loins to my saddle?"

He hawked in her direction and shook his head. "You got a field full of strawberries. Cinch *them* to your saddle."

Ruth imagined forsaking all this meat. It made her head whistle in hot hate. She called for Wimp, then aimed the rifle at the driver. "If you don't help me, I'll report your reckless driving to the railroad and that brakeman's death will be on your head. And, before you get any ideas about threatening me, you ought to know that I know you've got a railroad-issued six-shooter and rifle in the engine cab. You ought *also* to know I won't let you anywhere near it until I've got meat on my saddle. You think your night's long now, wait until you make a break for those stowed guns and find a bullet spins your knee the wrong way."

The driver regarded Ruth as if she was something a dog had vomited. His hands went to his hips and he hawked off the side of the train again. "Shrew."

She ignored him and searched the field for Wimp who had not responded to her first call. "Damn fool nag." She whistled again, then once more without patience. "Wimp!"

The driver was confounded. "You said your nag just upped and wandered in front of your gunsight?"

Ruth stopped. "She does that."

"Does what?"

"Wander."

The driver shook his head and leaned down to start dragging away elk wads. "Is it wandering or is your mare just trying to get away from you?"

2

The massive gathering of Baltimore mourners waited in a line wrapped around Gay Street before they finally made their way into the Merchants' Exchange. There they entered a queue that moved first in one direction and then snaked back the other way for as many rows as the Exchange's great chamber could accommodate. The domed room had been stripped of every decorative flourish except its wall and ceiling frescoes and the mosaic floor. The air was thick with sweat and body rot, and the latter not all from the corpse.

Each mourner was allowed a brief moment to climb the steps to the marble pillared dais, where they could view the catafalque of Leopold Windom before exiting. Space had been reserved around the perimeter for people to stand and view the railroad magnate from afar.

Augustus, a boyish-looking man of twenty-six, sat beside his dead father, looking pale and grim in a black serge suit and plum paisley vest, disassociated from the sea of aggrieved. *These people are more oglers than mourners,* he told himself, equal parts embittered by his loss and resentful of having to suffer it in public.

Standing behind Augustus was a well-trimmed, brick-headed gunman named Uriah Rathbone. Behind him stood a bent old maid named Beryl Gerry, who had attended to Leopold's affairs for years. She shed no tears, but a deep set-in glum darkened her features.

A man whose silver mustache connected his side whiskers removed his topper and held the brim with both hands. He wore a defeated expression as he mounted the short riser. His mood seemed in competition with Augustus's.

"I stood at this very spot two months ago to the hour," he said, referring to President Lincoln's funeral procession. "I wept then for the country's fate and I weep now again…that our Lord might deprive us of two great men."

The gentleman's words arrived to Augustus's ear from a great distance, as if corked in a bottle, thrown to the ocean, and discovered years later. It had already been hours of this. Hours that felt to Augustus like weeks.

He hadn't the faculties to do anything but cradle the gentleman's clammy hand while the man awaited a comforting sentiment. Augustus wondered what, in this stranger's estimation, made his father so great. The gentleman was neither rough nor bent like true railroaders were. His clothes were well tailored, and his hat was a slick beaver skin. The man was wealthy, and it was likely that Leopold Windom had set him on the path. It was even likelier that what the gentleman truly mourned was the dried flow of his own particularly prosperous spigot.

Leopold Windom had been a brakeman before he'd been a corpse. Long before. As a young brakeman, he'd improved a series of signals to help men function atop the train and sold his ideas to the railroads. And then, when he'd done all he could with the brakemen, he'd started advising the train owners how to better design their railcars and, later, their method of manufacture. And then he'd channeled this expertise in train manufacturing into his own firm, the Windom Locomotive Works.

Augustus's mother had described Leopold as a man who saved the cracked skulls, legs, elbows, backs, and lives of a thousand men. It was something she often told her son. Augustus had lived out his childhood with only the version of his father that his mother wanted him to have… and he believed it. After all, his father was rarely present. Augustus's mother had described a man who became so influential that locomotive manufacturers sought his counsel on every little matter until there was nothing for him to do but create his own engines. At first, only railroad men knew of him; to them Leopold was a miracle maker. But he soon found renown among men who cared nothing for railroads.

Men, Augustus believed, like the gentleman standing before him now.

That our Lord might deprive us of two great men, this one had said.

Augustus snapped to and revealed two impressive rows of picket fence teeth. It was a soothing smile, enough so that it seemed to unburden the stranger. "That He blessed us with two great men for any duration should warrant our gratitude."

The gentleman nodded and slid to the casket for a final moment with the deceased.

Augustus was a man whose every wink put others at ease while it also concealed a hundred violent thoughts.

A wide woman in an unflattering cobalt dress struggled up the stairs. She was breathless when she reached Augustus.

"Allow me, madam," said the gunman, Rathbone. He held out his hand in case she required extra support.

She ignored Rathbone and fixed on the young man before her. She was short, eye-level to Augustus despite him being seated, and extended a covered hand to him, her fat fingers testing the strength of her gloves' threading.

"I loved your father." She sniffled and dabbed a white handkerchief at her nose. "And your father, young man, loved me in kind for a time."

Augustus warmed her with another smile, as if the sentiment meant a great deal to him. But he was finished with her. He looked to the head of the queue and beckoned for the next person to approach, waiting for the woman to move along.

The woman stayed in her place.

"No, young man. You don't understand. Your father and I were in love. *Before* your mother. Before I abandoned him. Left him heartbroken and ripe for the pickings. It was my mistake to leave him to her, fine a woman as I'm certain she was. And now he'll never know my regret for having done it."

Something rabid replaced Augustus's empathic expression. She was an absurd fool. Must have been. He had never known his father to have romantic inklings but, if he had, he would not have stooped to this low creation. She was homely and hadn't the carriage to have ever been delicate, even in her youth.

11

His mother had been delicate. And fair. She had high cheekbones, wide-set eyes, and a button nose that turned upward as if proud of itself. She was courteous, proper, and contented by housework. If she had thoughts to the contrary, she kept them to herself. Indeed, there was little about which she expressed opinions, including her own son. She neither complained about mothering the boy, nor gushed over him. He, too, was housework, and she took as much pride in the boy's upkeep as she did anything else, never allowing any hired governess to look after him. She'd always insisted she do it herself.

As an infant, Augustus doted on his mother, cooing in her direction, crying upon the rare occasion she put him down to rest her arms and back. He carried on this behavior well past the age other children stopped. He would not cooperate when a wet nurse cared for him. He demanded care from his mother. When he was old enough to toddle about the house, he never strayed far from her. He flipped through picture books, happy to be at his mother's feet as she cleaned. He insisted on napping beside her like a cat, rather than in his own bed. There was no end to his studying the delicate lilting way she glided about the house. Her movements were like dance steps. He mimicked them, teaching himself to move about a room with grace.

When Augustus was seven, his mother developed stomach pains and took sick. When overcome with a heaving stomach, she vomited just beside her bed so that it would land on the carpet. Not knowing how else to help, the boy laid beside her sucking his thumb and holding her sweat-sopped hair.

Leopold had hired handlers for his wife and child, but those he hired were fearful of upsetting any of the Windoms. They did not act quickly enough to keep the woman's sickness from worsening. When they did alert a doctor, they did so with timidity, improperly expressing the woman's dire need for medical attention.

One evening, Augustus had fallen asleep holding his mother's warm hand and awoke holding cold fingers. She'd died without having said her farewells to the boy and without the boy having said his. When Leopold returned to the news of his wife's death, he did not slow his business pursuits long enough to mourn in any meaningful way. He left the funeral arrangements to others. When he finally sat with Augustus, he did so for only the briefest of moments. He assured the boy he would not grow sick like his mother had and that she loved him with the summation of her being. "Your mother made you a *good* person," he told Augustus. "I'll make you a *strong* person."

Once satisfied the ends of his wife's passing had been knotted, Leopold returned to his work, now taking Augustus with him when the mood suited. At first, the son altered his father's life no more than the addition of a small portrait to a crowded museum wall. There was nothing of obvious importance to Leopold Windom other than work.

He was not a man to have been in romantic love. He certainly was not a man to have squandered time lamenting the loss of a woman—as the portly preening fraud in front of Augustus imagined he might have. She would not budge from Augustus's station. As if before an altar, the old stuffer waited for some semblance of esteem from Augustus. Instead, he leveled a glare at her that could bore a hole. He would not comfort her the same way he had comforted the man before.

"Would you wish to speak to my father once more?" he asked her.

"Oh, I would, indeed."

His smile seared with anger. "Then continue lingering there, woman."

She looked to Rathbone for some confirmation that she had just been threatened. When he offered nothing, she hurried along.

The mourners continued. Each glance toward the entry discouraged Augustus, as the line never appeared any shorter. He imagined sitting there forever listening to limp bromides, war stories, Lincoln comparisons, declarations of love, or advice on the Windom company's future. A bronze plate would be placed on the floor below where he sat. It would read: *On this spot, the son of Leopold Windom died upright in his chair after greeting every man, woman, and child to ever have met his father.* It was a selfish but forgivable musing. The unending day had beleaguered him.

Augustus had been a wealthy boy and now found himself an even wealthier man. For nineteen years he stood as an only child at the elbow of his father, primped and prodded into the position as heir to the Windom empire. How he would command that empire, Augustus was less certain. He was not his father. Even on the day of mourning, there was no shortage of men offering Augustus their condolences and services in the same breath. Or if not services, their knowledge, time, capital, whatever would take them from this encounter to another.

He couldn't think. Another forty people passed. Each offered remarks without exciting more than a nod or murmured "thank you" from the young man.

A man with long legs and uneven eyes ascended the riser with a single high step. He said nothing and offered no hand.

Augustus recognized him immediately. Leopold had amassed a tremendous amount of capital and influence selling his ideas to other locomotive companies. More than once, his say-so halted improvement plans to a manufacturer's fleet. Now and then an irritated railroader took issue with his power.

One such incident occurred at the Windom home when Augustus was eight years old. A local machine shop engineer named Caldwell Begone confronted Leopold. He'd been incensed by Leopold's suggestion to recast the train gullies with more durable iron plating. Caldwell believed Leopold had made his recommendation out of spite and turned frothy by the wronging. He shouted at Leopold—cursed him—on Leopold's own property. None of it excited a response from the elder Windom. Leopold was a startling tincture of mettle and detachment. He rested his hands on Augustus's shoulders and offered no counterthreat. Set off balance by Leopold's dispassion, Begone filled the quiet with his own aggressive yammering.

"It's lucky that boy stands between us," Begone said.

Leopold pushed open the gate. "Go inside, Augustus."

And thus ended the man's luck.

Some boys would have asked to stay, to watch, to help defend their father's honor, but Begone's irate bearing had frightened Augustus, and he did not hesitate to break into a run. He was happy to escape inside, off to the safety of the first window allowing a view of the proceedings.

Augustus watched from the vantage of the solarium's jutted window. He could see his father standing with his hands behind his back, Begone rushing into punishing distance. Even to a boy, it was clear Begone meant to harm his father and that his father had not positioned himself to defend against it. Begone never threw a punch. He'd stopped head-on in front of Leopold, hand raised like a clock about to strike twelve, but no ringing had occurred. His face had softened, the anger pruning as if left out in the sun too long. Confusion lingered. Leopold had not moved, had not unclasped his hands from behind his back. Augustus could not hear him through the window, nor could he see his father's face. He could only see that something vital had left Begone and that, whatever it was, Leopold had taken it. At eight, Augustus had barely known his father. He'd known the version his mother had given him. But she had not told him of her husband's punitive nature. She, perhaps, had not known it.

Just as one might experience thunder, the incident shook Augustus in a way he felt more than he observed. Something more devastating than violence had happened, though he knew not what it was. He'd witnessed something grotesque and elusive, something that had not ended a life, but removed its luster. It sickened Augustus that one man could hold complete dominion over another, even if that man was his own father. He sensed Leopold must hold such dominion over *him*, too. And once the thought occurred to him, he was immediately diminished by it. He was an intelligent boy, but soft. He watched his father with fear. Other boys would have recounted the confrontation with pride. They'd have seen themselves in their fathers, but Augustus saw himself in Begone. He felt as if he, himself, had been attacked.

Begone had not returned to work at the machine shop the next day or any day after. The Windoms had never heard from him again. Until now, when he stood before Augustus at Leopold Windom's funeral.

"Are you here to ensure he's truly dead?" Augustus asked.

Begone nodded, the muscles in his clenched jaw flexing. "You remember me." He said it as if confirming a suspicion.

"There is quite a line," Augustus said. "You must have waited a long time."

"You've no idea."

Augustus could not help but feel sorry for him. Even after all these years, he felt a kinship. As if his father had harmed them both in some equal measure that day years ago. "Have you landed on your feet?" Augustus asked.

"I practice law now. For your opposition, as a matter of fact."

The jab was warranted. "The only thing more abundant than lawyers are men who oppose my father."

Begone nodded. "It is true. More than a few people were disappointed not to see him get the lash." He took a step toward Leopold's casket before thinking better of it. "There *is* some catharsis, though. Knowing I draw breath still and he does not."

The sympathy drained from Augustus. "Yes, but your breath is of no consequence." He pointed back toward the front of the mourners' queue. "Go back the way you came." At once, the entirety of the gathering had quieted and looked upon the two men. Begone paled. Augustus lowered his voice. "You will not disrespect my father and then stand over him."

The man appeared to be calculating the weight of Augustus's stricture. Rathbone stood over Augustus's shoulder, waiting, a swallowtail coat wrapped around his square middle. He was perfectly postured, his hands fitted into tight leather gloves.

The man stole a glance at Leopold's old secretary and then the open casket before retracing his steps and exiting amid a breeze of gossiping murmurs.

"Shall I follow?" Rathbone asked.

Augustus shook his head only once.

The next woman in line stepped up with caution. She'd seen lightning and readied for thunder.

Rathbone whispered to Augustus, "Having been at your father's side for the better part of a decade, I can say with certainty the world adored him, even his competitors. That man there does not reflect the masses."

This caused Augustus to steal a glance at Leopold's secretary, Beryl, standing in the wings, her head low. Augustus kissed the next mourner's hand, preoccupied now with a halting realization—after all these years, he still felt a confusing kinship with Begone's attitude toward his father.

3

It was slap dark now. The soft jangle of a saddle and the clopping of tired hooves was the only company Ruth and Wimp had on their way back to the cabin. Her muscles were tight, and her jaw hurt from extended clenching. The rank salt stink of her body cut through the thin summer air like twine through a cheese wheel. Her gums stung at the nerve. She was bone tired, and her eyes ached and thumped inside her skull.

Wimp's head dipped with every footfall. The galumphing nag made a damn racket as they drew closer to home. Even if Henry had fixed a trap, Wimp's clanking would scare off anything nearby.

Ruth halted Wimp at the edge of the overgrown meadow. The amount of time she'd spent staring along that expanse, she'd come to memorize every yard of it. She knew the dead spots among the tall grasses, the rabbit dens, the rich soil and the dry. She knew where the rains pooled after a storm, knew the name of every weed and the patterns in which the wind spread them. She knew which birds preferred which trees. She'd planted all her thoughts into this place, though nothing had grown from it.

Nearby, in the center of their land, was Henry's horrible contraption. It was an oversized bear trap, two feet wider and twenty pounds heavier than even the Newhouse brand #6 model. Henry had spent three months designing and building his trap to be powerful enough to stop whatever might trigger it. It was massive, too heavy for anyone to open with his hands, and so he connected the leaf spring to the rotor of a stationary steam engine. The engine would do the work of prying open the jaws so that Henry could pin it open. When it snapped together, it did so with the heavy *screechbang* of a slammed prison door. The problem was its power. As tightly as the jaws had been drawn open, whenever they snapped shut, closing at a height of over four feet, they tended to explode an animal's neck, chest, or head rather than simply keep it pinned. It was a hellish kind of butchering that would turn the toughest stomach. And if the animal had not been gored into an agonized death, the trap simply closed above its body, missing it completely. Even Henry had conceded its invention was a mistake. He cursed himself for time spent building useless things.

The cabin's front door banged in rhythm with the wind. Ruth arrived at the porch and found Henry asleep in a rocker. His Confederate blanket was draped across him low enough to only keep his knees confidential.

He'd been born with a slight frame, not a pinch of fat. His whiskers filled out the hollows of his cheeks some, but his eyes, when open, were sunken and blue as a June sky. As was the style among Confederate soldiers, his hair was long and raggedy, down past his shoulders.

They hadn't any soap to wash and settled for cold rinses in the nearby Tennessee River. Ruth had often repeated how thankful she was not to have anything reflective in the house that would show off her disheveled appearance. The last time she'd said it, Henry nodded and told her, "You should be." It was a full day before she spoke to him again.

Now before him, just off the porch, Ruth gave the leather cordage a tug. She let fall the sixty pounds of elk chunks the engine driver had been blackmailed into tying to the saddle. It landed with a tender thud and woke Henry. He turned the kerosene key up on the lantern to get a better look at the lumps on the ground. Squinting past the porch into the darkness, he called out to her. "Well, now, where've you been?"

"Feels like Hell and back," she said. "My shoulder's cracked." She waved for him to open the front door. "My struggles weren't for naught, though. Clear a path."

He moved to the door and held it open. "And what are you covered in?"

She looked at her own shirt, having again forgotten the strawberry blotches along her front. "I got bunged up along Stringer's. Misfired the rifle shooting at elk. Broke my shoulder or thereabouts."

"Elk?"

"I didn't believe it at first, neither. Figured it was my hungry stomach making a maniac of me. Counted more'n fifty head. One of which I brought home with me." She kicked the meat the way you would rouse a drunk.

She gripped a leg and lugged it up the cabin steps, the elk's muscles scared stiff underneath its short fur. "Help me inside with this leg, will you?"

"I thought it was your *shoulder* needed help." He smiled at his own joke.

He propped open the door with the lamp and grabbed the leg's heavy end. Together they dragged it inside to the butcher table, where the smell of their sweet honey poplar planking reintroduced itself. The embers pinging off the inside of the stove sang the cabin's only song.

"My errant shot scared the gang," she said. "Antlered twits went running onto the track. Train smacked 'em dead and derailed. One of the brakemen got killed."

Henry's mouth fell open, but no sound followed. His eyes examined the splotches along her front with a fresh horror.

"This ain't blood," she said. "Them elk were in the strawberry field past Stringer's. I laid down to aim, then rolled around to agonize. But never mind about that." She returned to the meat pile outside, grabbed a smaller shank, and added it to the leg. "I had a notion while I was out there."

Henry knelt down to inspect the meat. "It's covered in grit and the like."

"I said I had a notion. Your bear trap might have a better purpose."

"You had this idea out there in the berry field?" he asked. "With your body cracked in two?"

"Listen to me. Steam opens that trap out there. An animal steps on the trigger, the steam bladders empty and the trap shuts. That right?"

"You've learned it well," Henry said.

"What if we fit the same idea to train brakes? The same apparatus, even. All the parts are sitting right out there."

"What parts?"

"For a new train brake. Something different than every locomotive's got now."

"You want to switch out a bear trap for a train brake?"

Ruth shook her head and pulled the lantern away from the door. "Train brakes are open until you close them, right? A brakeman's gotta exert effort to close the brake, otherwise the train keeps rolling."

Henry nodded. "That's right."

"Well, what if we reverse it so that stopping a train is easier than letting it roll?"

Henry nodded again. He'd always busied himself building impractical contraptions that served little purpose. And, in the beginning, Ruth enjoyed understanding how his contrivances worked. Often, she'd seize on an idea and offer up a way to improve it. But three lost children, war, and hunger had slowed her willingness to take part in his hatchling ideas, until this elk massacre had rekindled something in her.

"Force the brake open instead of forcing it closed?" Henry asked.

"That's right. Same as that bear trap out there. Same parts, too. Steam engines and air." Ruth moved in closer. "Your bear trap closes easy; it's prying the damn thing open that draws a sweat. Change it so the effort is in opening the brakes, not closing them, it'd make a train stop faster. The driver could do it on his own. You don't massacre a herd of buffalo, or miss a broken turn, or overshoot a stop."

Henry smiled. "Or decouple from the cars behind, or grind up the track for a mile, or flatten a clumsy brakeman."

They shared a smile before Ruth pushed on. "So, you think you can build that brake?"

"The way you described it," he said, "it's already built." He thought further. "I'd have to puzzle out how to reconfigure it exactly and connect them across every wheel. But we already know it works. Already got the parts we need."

Ruth turned and leaned against the wall, staring at Henry. She readied for his mood to darken at the next bit. "This one we patent," she said. "If it works, we patent it. That's how it's gotta be."

Henry tensed. "Your shoulder's all mangled. Let's take care of that before we—"

"You'll need to draw up exactly how it'll work," Ruth said, ignoring him. "Remember? Like we talked about with that oil-burning iron you made? You started drawing up how it would work."

Henry nodded absently. His unpleasant expression suggested a storm of thoughts had overtaken him. He was not a man who enjoyed the company of strangers.

"We'd have to build it," Ruth continued. "Test it. How would we do that? We'd have to get a train on loan. I don't know what happens after the patent. We sell it, I guess."

"License it," Henry said, without enthusiasm. "But I don't think we can do it."

"What's keeping us from trying?"

"I'd like to. But…but, it—"

"I won't hear any buts. I won't have you treat another contraption of yours like something frivolous. You blow too damn many of your ideas off like hot scurf from the forge."

"Scurf?"

"Scurf," Ruth repeated, then said it louder. "SCURF." It angered her when Henry didn't focus. "If we can build a train brake to beat all others, why wouldn't we?"

"I didn't say—" Henry shook his head. "Why are you riled?"

"Because you'd just drop it, wouldn't you?"

"What?"

"Another keen idea won't no one know we had."

"Keep the field fertile, Ruthy. How's that for a keen idea I had? Keep us in crops to live on. Planting season's a fine time to fall into fits of melancholy. We're out here hungry as hell and you're breathless over an invention I don't know nothing about."

A vein throbbed down Ruth's neck. She didn't suffer guilt gracefully and rarely accepted condemnation. "We're talking about our names, Henry Casper. Yours and mine. We're talking about a reason for being. We're also talking about how easy it is for you to leave it be. You'd give me a bunch of buts and let someone else make a life from it." Ruth shook her head. "You don't take credit for nothing." She flung her good arm in the direction of the bear trap. "You already invented the damn thing! All you have to do to make it sing is fiddle a little."

"It ain't about credit," Henry said. "I ain't in this life for the glory."

Ruth slammed her hand on the table, toppling the piled elk meat. "We ain't barely in this life at all." She sat down in front of him. "What if, for once, we did something for the glory of it, is my point." The lamplight illuminated the tears filling her eyes. "How 'bout that? Instead of letting the idea die on the vine, why not pluck it for the juice? Just once. Or give me a good reason not to."

He could see how upset she'd gotten. A sick look crossed up his face as he stared through the window out into the pitch dark of the meadow. "They burned the Richmond patent office," he said. "We'll have to go north."

"Then we'll go north."

"Also, we have no locomotive."

"You got any friends left at the East Tenn Railroad? You said they ain't hiring, but maybe they'll loan you a train after hearing what you plan to do with it. Might give it to you for a cut."

"I...there's a lot of uncertainty. You know I get nervous when there's uncertainty."

"I know it. When your spine goes limp, I prop you up till it straightens out again."

Henry smiled even though Ruth hadn't meant it as a joke.

"So you'll go talk to someone at the Eastern?"

"There are abandoned Confederate depots up and down the E.T.," he said. "Might could find a working locomotive inside any number. I'll do that."

"What's this 'I'?" Henry's face had been scrawled with torment. Ruth saw it. It concerned her plenty, but she was smart enough to know not to bring up new troubles when there were plenty at the fore already. "Now, Henry, you know damn well I'm coming with you, don't you? This is mine as much as it is yours." She pointed in the direction of Chickamauga. "How many soldiers died or went missing not four miles over them trees? The sky ain't been clear in two years on account of all the ash. I hate it here, sleeping in this living grave. This Hell without the heat. There ain't nothing sorrier than a woman from a defeated country. I tell you, I hate it here." She flicked the meat with her finger. "Wouldn't bother me if I left here tomorrow and never came back."

4

The viewing was over. Rathbone escorted Augustus and Beryl Gerry along Lombard Street to the Windom mansion. Augustus was first into his foyer, eyes low. He slipped off his topcoat and upturned his hat. He handed them both to the footman, a big-eared jake named Jefferson. Jefferson took the garments, but remained close, looking upon Augustus with pity. The sight of it angered Augustus and he might have said something had he not then realized that his entire staff had filed along either side of the polished mahogany rail, all wearing Jefferson's same pitying expression. Thirty-three breathing bodies in the foyer. The only sound was the house clock tic-tocking on the second-floor landing.

His father was gone. It was sudden. What else was there to say about it? Augustus looked to Rathbone first, then to the throng, suspicious of their somber expressions. He did not consider they might be concerned for him and saddened by the loss of their headman. He assumed they were only concerned for their jobs. The staff could expect some quantity of dismissals, as the number of residents in the house had been halved.

"The day has been arduous," he said. "I return without sentiment or comforting words or any desire for chitchat." He met the eyes of everyone along the staircase. Each pair seemed desperate for him to slake their sadness. Augustus exhaled. "My father believed the fight continued until there was nothing left of his opponent. They may think the fight is over now, but I look forward to stamping out that belief." The expressions of his staff suggested this was not the rousing summation of his father they'd expected. "Thank you for this gesture of concern," Augustus continued. "Please retire for the night. I require nothing more of you."

The staff turned away with some hesitation before Beryl, still at the stair bottom beside Augustus, called out to the gathered, "It was an admirable turnout." This stopped the staff's retreat for a moment. "Befitting, I mean."

Augustus nodded, though the woman drawing attention to herself irked him. "A respectable counting of heads, yes," he said. "However, there was some question of quality." He looked at Beryl, who nodded and knew to follow him. The two of them, along with Rathbone, moved to the rear of the house where Augustus kept his office.

Bowed windows along the far wall dominated the room. A heavy desk and thick Oriental rug monopolized the room's center. A pair of damask settees and wall-to-wall shelves toppling with books provided enough dark to counter the windows' light. Augustus had decorated the mansion walls himself with gilded framed portraits of his mother, tintypes of his father, and quaint watercolors of trains. He'd selected the paper for the walls and the fabric for the furniture. When an armrest frayed or a slat split, he did not repair or reupholster them, he replaced them outright.

Leopold had not been a fashionable man in anyone's interpretation. It was Augustus's duty to persuade his father that appearances mattered. Augustus sold his amusements to his father, sold them as strategies to help Leopold's pursuits. It was a manipulation of Leopold shrouded as a manipulation of future financiers. Augustus rather enjoyed convincing his father of things. It made him feel capable and necessary when little else did.

He fell into his wingback as Beryl took a short step inside. Rathbone placed himself between them on one of the settees. He set his hat beside him on a cushion.

The secretary wasn't much for conversation but give her a finance ledger and she'd follow a dime around the world. Never once had Leopold asked her to redo expenditure tabulations or to organize client books more thoroughly. She was anticipatory and efficient and seemed to enjoy working in general. Also, she seemed grateful to Leopold. She was the only woman in such a lauded position, often the only woman in rooms of men. None accepted her, but acceptance wasn't a requirement for Leopold's masterful find. She'd been plucked from the Gerry Foundry, where Leopold's representatives were continuously coming up short in negotiations for new castings. After an extended interval of defeat with the foundry, Windom, not used to losing negotiations of any proportion, graced the Gerry establishment to understand for himself the whys and wherefores of the constant losses. What he found there was a doddering old man and, at his ear, his adult daughter whispering quick figures and complex payment structures that gave the foundry the profit advantage. Within the hour, Leopold Windom had bought the foundry from the old man, providing a guarantee his daughter would remain richly employed. What Windom kept hidden from both Gerrys was the admission that the daughter was the only part of the purchase that truly interested him. "What a lucky strike it was," he told Augustus later, "to have as qualified a person beside me to whom absolutely no one will pay any mind. She is a stealth weapon." Leopold was generous with Mister Gerry up to and upon his passing, and Beryl remained grateful. There had been an obvious dreariness in her composure since Leopold's death.

"You respected my father," Augustus said.

"Very much, sir."

Augustus nodded. "He was a sneak. Did you know that about him?"

The secretary blinked, perhaps deciding between a number of responses. "I guess he was crafty, yes."

"Did you converse much with my father?"

"I listened, mostly."

"Did he ever offer you his opinion of me?"

Again, she weighed possible responses. Augustus respected this penchant but found it troublesome just now. That she had to stop to evaluate her responses suggested she had reason to lie.

"He loved you," she said, finally.

"No." Augustus put out his hand to stop the words from reaching him. "Don't do that. He never once told you he loved me."

"I could tell nevertheless."

"I'm interested only in what he made explicit. About me." She hesitated. "Go on," he said.

"Is this a test, sir?"

"It is always wise to assume *everything* is a test."

"He believed you to be more…" She tiptoed. "…blunt than he."

"Oh? How so?"

"He once said the difference between the two of you was that when *he* hit a wall he'd dig underneath or leap over it."

"And me?"

"He said you would have people remove the wall and convince them it was their idea to do so."

A surprised laugh bounded from Augustus. It was sour, curdled as it came out of him.

"He said that keeping the wall where it was maintained order. Removing it invited chaos."

It felt like a side-winding slap from beyond the grave. "When was this?"

"After Rochester."

Augustus frowned, only remembering the incident in dribs and drabs. "Remind me. What was it? Was it that we were delinquent on delivery?"

"Yes, sir. You had me send four wires. The first was a command to send out an empty train to Rochester. The second went to our northern foreman ordering him to derail that train. The third went to several newspapers with your statement on the marauders who'd derailed and robbed your train. And the fourth to—"

Augustus nodded. "The fourth went to our Rochester client, explaining my decision to delay shipment and keep his trains safe upon word that marauders derailed a Rochester-bound convoy."

"Yes, sir."

"Sent out a team of Pinkertons to capture the criminals. Came out a hero. Rochester extended me another month with relish."

Beryl nodded.

Rathbone shook his head. "I'm not hearing this. Especially the portion about you misusing the agency."

"Your *former* agency. Allan Pinkerton should thank me. It bolstered his business as much as it did ours." He looked up at the ceiling, smiling. Recalling the minor triumph in his mind's eye. "I don't understand how my father could have disapproved of that."

The secretary nodded. She'd been gazing fixedly at his desk, but now met his eyes. He didn't know what was in her mind.

"I did a damn good job on that man in Rochester."

"Yes."

"But he didn't agree?"

"The man in Rochester?"

"My father."

She shrugged and shook her head. "He said you burned too many favors on that one."

Augustus sighed. "How would he have done it?"

"I never asked," the secretary offered as softly as she could while still being heard across the room. "I am tasked only with figures."

Beryl was small in the doorway and forlorn. She shared the same pitying expression Jefferson had earlier. They'd all had it, the expression. He imagined the look to be doubt. No one believed Augustus could lead in place of his father, including the secretary.

He lifted a ledger and held it up, gesturing for her to walk across the room and take it from him. When her little feet had pitter-patted to him, he lowered his voice. "I know you're uncertain of your position here," he said. "I'll mince no words. You're a fine secretary and I mean to keep you. You were the secretary to the company president, and you will remain as such." He released the book and scooted a nib pen toward her. It was her pen. She preferred the old-fashioned instrument to the newer fountain models.

"I'm quite glad," she said, nervously scratching the edge of her metal nib across the spine of her ledger.

"I hold you in higher esteem than my own secretary or else I would have switched your positions. That I didn't should give you all the confidence you need as to my trust in you."

"Of course, sir."

He looked upon the rest of the stacked ledgers and contracts waiting for him on his desk. "These were not here this morning."

"I moved them, sir. From your father's desk."

He opened the ledger at the top of the stack, flipped through the first few pages before addressing Beryl.

Beside her was a salon-style wall of woodcuts, lithographs, copper engravings, and a daguerreotype of the company's first warehouse. Centered among them was a large framed portrait of a seated Leopold Windom, which hung from a hook off the crown molding and commanded attention from the rest of the framed decorations. The angle suggested he was scowling down at his son.

"Why is it," Augustus asked Beryl, "joy moves in seconds, but sorrow moves in hours?"

Her response was demure. "It only feels that way, I'm sure."

"It's all I can do to make it to the end of each day."

"Well, then," she said, feigning cheer, "here it is at the end of another one. So far, so good."

"So far, so good," Augustus repeated. He rubbed his face. "A bell ringer slips from the church tower and plummets to certain death. He's falling but he's still alive. And in that moment, having survived the fall up to that point, he tells himself, 'So far, so good.'"

His little story pulled a melancholy smile from her that left as quickly as it arrived.

"We were all unprepared," she said. She meant it to be something comforting but, instead, it was something grim.

"Well, that's damned unhelpful, unless one of the ledgers figures the cost of unpreparedness."

She stalled in the doorway until Rathbone permitted her to leave with a nod of his head. She exited, having said nothing further.

Augustus listened to the scuffling report of the secretary's feet shrinking down the hall. He'd become transfixed by the eyes of his father's portrait, the shivering blue variants of oil paint falling into the black blotch of the pupil. Augustus had an ache deep inside his belly as if bullets were lodged there. Bullets would be merciful. At least then he could know what ached. Augustus would now have to fend for himself in the guise of a person he was never comfortable being—a glutton.

He unbuttoned his vest. A light-headedness came over him. Sparks sizzled in his vision. He closed his eyes, but the sparks followed. He panted.

"Steady, son," Rathbone said.

Augustus leaned on his desk and wept in full. His shoulders heaved and his throat made a clacking sound as he shuddered to himself. The day's strain, the moment's gravity, hitting him all at once. Finally, he cleared his throat, made rough glottal sounds that returned his composure. He gathered himself, looking on at his father's portrait.

"Did he ever blubber in front of you?" he asked Rathbone.

Rathbone did not answer. Instead he asked, "May I inquire, Augustus, why it is you shed tears? The two of you did not enjoy each other's company."

Augustus nodded. "And now we never will."

Rathbone did not inquire further.

"I cannot do this," Augustus said.

"You can."

"How? I'm no diplomat. You heard the woman. I flip trains and avoid repercussions. That's who I am."

"Be *that*, then," Rathbone said. He nodded to ensure Augustus heard him. "Be *that*."

Augustus stared at the oil smudges creating a likeness of his father from across the room and considered the agent's advice.

"Very well," he said, finally. "Then I have something I'd like you to do for me." Rathbone awaited instruction. "I'm not going to keep Miss Gerry. I've changed my mind."

"I see."

"Please relieve her." It was a command rather than a request. "She may draw her pay for the full month, but she'll need to find new lodgings tomorrow."

Rathbone's expression carried with it no smidgen of surprise, though he asked Augustus why he'd changed his mind.

"She looked at me with scorn. I'll not have my father's ghost lingering in the eyes of others."

Rathbone nodded slowly and rose to his feet. "I've known...knew your father for thirty years," he said. "Was in his employ for ten." He studied Augustus. "Do ghosts linger in my eyes?"

Augustus searched Rathbone's face for signs of temper. He found none. "The secretary hasn't seen a fraction of what you have. Your ghosts are justified."

"It's in you," Rathbone said, "to prove you have no betters. Prove it to every last bastard who doubts it." He inhaled as if readying to say something else before deciding against it. Instead, he offered only, "Good night, Augustus." He left without receiving a reply.

Augustus sulked and continued staring at the portrait. He was not the man his father wanted him to be, though he'd forged a close enough likeness to make do. Once a quiet boy who did his best to care for his sick mother, he had now ripened into someone else. He meant only to inhabit this skin until he deciphered a clean way out. He told himself it wouldn't take long. He wouldn't be this other person long. He would not lose himself to the contemptible man made in his father's image. He would not lose himself to his father's treacherous business. He would not lose himself to anything at all. Augustus would never share his father's dreams. He repeated it over and again and then repeated it less. Then not at all. Then he forgot it was something he'd ever told himself.

5

It had been four weeks since Ruth mangled her shoulder and used an empty grain sack to sling it up. While she convalesced, Henry sketched out engineering drawings of the brake as best he could. He'd first dismantled parts from the big bear trap and reconfigured as much of the air brake as possible given their limited tools. He loosened what could be loosened and banged together what could be banged. Some pieces would need a forge and they wouldn't find one until they moved eastward, something which Henry remained in no hurry to do.

While Henry sketched, Ruth grew restless. After a week, she made herself useful by yanking many cords worth of wood off the barn, until the structure was skeletal—like a gale had ripped it open. She'd placed each six-foot board on the chopping stump and snapped it in half with her foot. Then she carefully plucked the flat head nails from each board in order to use them again, often bending back her own fingernails in the process. By the end, the thumb and forefinger of both hands were numb and pulpy with blood. She piled the wood—enough to fire up a small steam engine for a hundred miles—onto a short-sided wagon, all with only one good arm and a bottomless well of pained grunts.

Some days the two barely spoke. Henry remained inside drawing or setting the cookstove to fix more of the elk meat. It irked Ruth that the only time he'd come outside was to steal some of the barn wood to heat the stove. Then he'd return inside having spared no conversation.

After a week of gloom and moping, Henry woke Ruth, his chest full, his eyes bright, his voice having regained some life.

"We can't go," he said.

"Why not?"

"Because a patent costs thirty-five dollars to file and we ain't got it."

She sat up and looked out the window toward the river, disbelieving they'd gotten this far without considering the price of filing a patent. "That a flat cost, you think? Is it negotiable?"

"You wanna try negotiating it down to nothing?"

Ruth rolled her eyes. "Do we have to pay it right away, is my meaning."

"Not right away," Henry said. "Just as soon as we arrive."

Ruth sat up and stared hard at Henry. "We're going, Henry. That's just all there is to it."

"With what money, Ruthy?"

"I didn't spend the week pulling up that wood, rubbing my fingers down to nubs, to stop now."

"Well, it's always something."

"Something, I can handle. It's the nothing I can't stand."

They'd packed everything they could onto their rickety wagon. It had belonged to Henry's parents and should have found its end when they did. Wimp was bedeviled by the heavy load of brake parts and wood. The pile of parts sunk the wheels into the ground, making them stubborn to turn in mud. The weight dragged on her harness and pulled the loin strap into her hide. Henry had rolled up two blankets and wedged them between the saddle and her flank. It eased the raw rubbing but did nothing to halt her from gnawing at her thigh sores and slowing her already lazy gait. Henry was careful not to overtax her. He made frequent stops to let her graze and watered her every couple of miles using his own canteen. Two normal horses pulling the wagon could cover forty miles a day, Wimp could only cover ten.

The plan was they would search every train shed between here and the Atlantic Ocean until they found a working locomotive. "It's only a couple more miles," Ruth would tell Wimp, though she didn't truly know how far it would be.

The world had gone wet. Ruth untied her slouch hat from the saddle, where she kept it most of the time, and lowered it just above her eyes to keep away the side-slicing rain drops. It also shielded the wind from the lit match she'd struck against the bowl of her meerschaum pipe. She puffed the tobacco alive as she shook the match dead and shrank under the dampness. Her shoulders squeezed against her ears. Her arms prickled with duck bumps as she waited in the wagon for Henry to finish grazing the nag.

The earliest suspicion of dawn kindled just below the horizon. What looked from a distance to be a field with row after row of four-foot cornstalks revealed itself to be roughly cut and twined wooden crosses. Ruth guessed that buried below each one was a dead Confederate, but she knew that not every secesh had been buried and not all the buried had been planted in one piece.

They'd kept near the East Tenn track. It ensured they'd stay on a more or less direct route but had so far steered them clear of farms. Since leaving Chattanooga they'd approached very few other homesteads, most at a considerable distance away. Until now.

Ruth squinted hard into the distance at a squared, two-floor house. A remuda of riled horses pranced inside a picket pen. She pointed toward the house. "That's where we're gonna get our thirty-five dollars."

Henry twirled around to look where she pointed and studied the house before turning back. "How you know he's got it?"

"He's got two dozen stallions running around out there. What's he doing with 'em all? He's breeding and selling 'em, is what."

"Think a man like that's prone to goodwill?"

"You bring Wimp back here to the wagon and we'll find out."

The trail dust powdering their faces had turned to streaking mud in the rain. They did their best to wipe it off before greeting whomever lived in the house. Then they drove the wagon up to the wrap-around porch, hitched it to the railing and climbed the steps.

A perched quintet of mourning doves cooed at them from the barn roof. Henry interrupted the coo chorus by rapping the door with more clatter than he intended. The doves fluttered in the distance, off the barn and underneath the house's overhanging roof, where it was dry.

Despite the falling rain, Ruth could still hear the report of approaching footsteps from inside.

An old man opened the door, blinking hard as if not yet aware he was awake, a constellation of sun-scorched freckles across his face. "Yes?" he said, bending the wire frame of his spectacles around each ear.

Ruth looked at Henry and urged him to talk first.

"Hello, sir. Sorry to trouble you."

"You woke me."

"Did I? Well, I am sorry," Henry repeated.

"All that banging, I thought someone had been kilt or worse."

"No, sir. No one's died, Heaven forbid. Not yet, anyhow. You see, my wife—this is my wife." He gestured to Ruth, who nodded and smiled. "Her name's Ruth, mine's Henry Casper."

"Brewster," the old man said, without offering his hand.

Henry smiled. "Glad to meet you, sir. We're on our way north to Baltimore." Ruth gave Henry the skunk eye. He'd never mentioned Baltimore to her. "Been riding four days already. Tough. Hard land. Came up on your place and, well, you can see we're pulled by a busted little mare there—"

The old man straightened. "Ninety a horse. Not negotiable."

The interruption surprised Henry. Ruth, too. They exchanged a questioning glance.

"No," Ruth said. "We don't need a horse. We come to—"

"From the looks of that hobbler strapped to your wagon there, I'm certain you *do* need a horse," he said. "I'm in the horse business. That bent-back nag of yours won't get you out of the county."

Already, Ruth wanted to take the buggy whip to old Brewster.

A brief silence made its way between the three of them.

Henry cleared his throat again. "Well, that's nice of you to offer, sir," he said. "Truly. But, just the same, we're not here for a horse."

"What then?"

"Just a glass of water for us, if you can spare it." The old man looked them over as Henry continued. "We'd be obliged by your generosity."

"People say they're obliged," the old man said, "but they never mean it."

He turned and ambled back into his house, leaving the door open. Henry looked at Ruth, inquiring if he should follow the old man. Ruth shooed her hands at Henry suggesting he should.

They stood in his parlor. It was spacious and spared of any decorative flourishes—only the most necessary furniture, bare floors, and empty walls, save for a framed tintype of a woman with saddle jowls. Ruth guessed it was the old man's dead wife. He returned with a glass in his hand—a single glass—for Ruth and Henry to share.

Henry raised his eyebrows. "Oh," he said, receiving the tepid water glass. "Yes. I see. For the both of us. Thank you."

"Why dirty two glasses? You're married, ain't you?"

Henry smiled at the old man and then at Ruth, though the two smiles did not hold the same meaning. He watched the old man watch him sip. When he passed the glass to Ruth, the old man watched her sip, too. No one made any attempt at conversation. The old man seemed bored, as if passersby were as common as a clock's chime.

The house was ghostly silent, except for the water bobbing down Ruth's throat and the raindrops slapping against the windows. It occurred to Ruth that rapping on the door as hard as they had most certainly would have been a clamorous agitation in this tomb. She finished the glass and handed it back to the old man with a smile.

"That it, then?" he asked.

"I thank you, sir," Henry said. "And my wife thanks you."

"That it, then?" the old man repeated.

Ruth took a half-step forward. "Pardon, sir. I'm afraid we're in a bad way. We hope not always to be so but, right now, that's just the way it is."

The old man blinked. "You asking for more water?"

Ruth smiled. "No, sir. We're wondering if you have thirty-five dollars."

"For what?"

"A fee on a patent we're holding," Henry said.

"I meant, what do I get in return for giving you thirty-five dollars?"

Henry smiled. "That's a fair question, sir. I'd guess the same thing you got for that glass of water."

"I got nothing for it."

"Not even a warm flicker in your belly from having done something nice?"

The answer was clear to Henry before he'd even asked it. But, having asked it, Ruth and the old man looked at him as if he'd gone delirious.

"We'd hope not to ask for charity," Ruth said. "It ain't our way, you see. We can't promise to repay the loan, but we can promise to try."

"I ain't a bank."

"No," she said, "I know you ain't, but—"

"I ain't a bounty man, neither. Hunting you down in Balt-*i*-more and the like."

"You wouldn't have to chase after us," Henry said. "We're honorable."

Henry figured he ought to shut up. This was why he wasn't much of a talker. He was smart, but he wasn't clever, and his word meant nothing to this old man.

Ruth cut in. "I grant you've no reason to believe us. What'f I left you my wedding ring?"

Henry frowned at her. She'd not mentioned that part of the endeavor.

The old man looked at the ring on her finger and shook his head. "S'not worth thirty-five dollars."

"It's worth a great deal more than that to me," she retorted.

At this, Henry eased a bit.

"I don't have thirty-five dollars to give you anyway. Now, I'd like you both to leave me be."

"Sir, what's the real reason?" Ruth asked.

"Huh?"

She smiled and shrugged ever so lightly. "You do have thirty-five dollars. I'm sure of it. Just give us the real reason and we can come to some sort of—"

"I don't want to give you money because I can't be sure I'd get it back."

Ruth bristled. "The point isn't getting paid back. The point is doing a favor. Christian charity. You've got a pen of expensive horses, a big ol' house with nothing in it, and you're already a step in the grave, would it be so bad if you never saw us again?"

"Never seeing neither of you again would suit me just fine."

Ruth landed her hands on her hips and aimed a tight smile at the man. No teeth. She turned heel and left the house, hopped down the stairs, and fetched the rifle from the wagon boot. Henry followed her out.

"Ruth!"

She ignored him and fired the rifle in the air. A warning shot proving that her anger was to be believed. What Ruth had not intended was to hit two of the doves with the shot. Both fell in the horse pen and riled the stallions. She heard the flapping of the remaining birds rise above her head as she returned inside. The cooing doves eulogized their sisters from the safety of the barn.

The old man's eyes widened behind his spectacles, but he didn't move. "I wasn't lying to you, madam. Ain't no money to offer. I trade in horses."

"Then we'll buy a horse."

"How you plan to buy it?"

"On credit. Our words don't hold no water, mister, but I'm still promising that we ain't thieves. As soon as we can, we'll pay you for the horse. It just ain't gonna be today."

A storm clouded the old man's features. He was not a member of the willing, but he made no motion to put up a fight.

Ruth lowered the gun. "And I'm still leaving my wedding ring."

6

Two years before Leopold's death, discussions bubbled around the construction of a railroad that would connect the Atlantic Ocean to the Pacific. President Lincoln organized a committee to decide the railroad's path, including the eastern terminus. Hearing of the committee's formation, Leopold traded in multiple favors to ensure his inclusion.

The Transcontinental's most likely starting points were Missouri and Iowa. The former would benefit Windom, as his trains were contracted to route through the Kansas portion of the Union Pacific, whereas the latter would benefit the Fairbanks Locomotive Manufacturing Company, a middling operation out of Rhode Island whose trains had been limited only to the northern lines.

"It's going to be quite a chore," Lincoln told Leopold, "for you to convince me to start the track in a state that suits your purposes."

"All the better then that I have no intention of doing so, Mister President." He was eager to impress Lincoln and show he was a trustworthy ally. "This country has suffered enough disruption without my additions."

"Pity," Lincoln said, a smile lifting his sagging face. "Seeing you make the attempt was my cause for inviting you."

Leopold remained true to his word. He did not push for a Missouri terminus, going so far as to urge the president to start the rail on the Iowa-Nebraska border. Leopold had a second strategy at play. He'd been angling to dismantle Fairbanks for a year. Now, he'd finally found a way, using the closed doors of the president to do it.

Upon his return to Augustus, Leopold described Lincoln as "too distracted by the doings in Gettysburg" to consider the gravity of the endeavor. Had Lincoln been focused, he'd never have allowed Leopold on the committee. On matters not pertaining to the war, Leopold found the Republican president unguarded and pliable.

"Well, if Lincoln won't question you, I will," Augustus said. They were in Augustus's office, but it was Leopold seated behind the desk, feet propped. "Why did you squirrel your way onto the committee just to hand the Transcontinental to our competitor?"

"What do you mean?" Leopold's smile shriveled into a leer. "Our stock is up."

"It's up because everyone, including me, believed you'd persuade Lincoln to decide in your favor. When they find you didn't, our stock will plummet."

Leopold raised a finger. "Ah, you hit upon it, haven't you? *When* they find out. Do you know when that will be?" Augustus shook his head. Leopold added two more fingers to the one already raised. "Three months. And that, dear boy, is where you come in. You are correct. No one should believe I'd fail. The announcement of my involvement with the committee might as well have been an announcement of Missouri being the Transcontinental's eastern terminus."

"That was everyone's thinking," Augustus said, still incredulous.

"All I ask is that you not correct that thinking. Say nothing. Admit nothing. Act pleased."

Augustus studied his father. "What are you brewing?"

Leopold lifted the folded newspaper on the desk in front of him and tossed it at Augustus. "Our stock is up. It's up because people already believe the lie we never told. Now I want you to notice something on that page, boy." He leaned forward and pointed to the Fairbanks company's stock price. "The Fairbanks stock is falling at the same rate ours is rising. And it's happening because people believe the lie we never told. A lie that will last another three months. It's a lie, boy, that will sink Fairbanks's ship. Sink it low enough that we can buy it outright for pennies on the dollar. We'll own every train running west of the Mississippi. That, boy, is why I handed the Transcontinental to our competitor. So that, when this is finished, we'll have no competitor." Leopold snapped his fingers, proud of his own deceit.

Augustus did not believe the scheme would work. He'd thought his father had finally made the blunder his detractors had long believed was inevitable. His father's hubris had strangled his good sense. But, in those important three months, Augustus did nothing to defy his father, which was all Leopold wanted.

The Fairbanks Locomotive Manufacturing Company's stock saw thirty straight days of decline before Leopold approached with an offer. And, when he signed the purchase agreement weeks later, Augustus was there, standing over his father's shoulder watching him absorb a company at a tenth of the price it was worth.

It was Leopold's largest victory, and it was not lost on Augustus that it had happened without his help.

The Orange Street Club was the grandest meeting place in Baltimore, quite possibly the country. When Augustus ascended the building's stone staircase, a valet with a thin waxed mustache and horseshoe of black hair was there to open the door.

Augustus handed him his topper.

"My condolences to you," the valet said. "Your father was a colossus."

Augustus nodded and struggled out a smile that gave him the appearance of someone having detected a flat note in the orchestra. He reconsidered the valet's expression as it disappeared into the coatroom. Perhaps it was not one of respect at all but of pity. Since his father's death, those pitying glances followed him everywhere and he'd grown intolerant of them. He despaired. His face bent like dented tin as he stepped into the populated parlor.

Taper lights sent shadows dancing in jangling rhythm. Club members sat in heavy, tufted furniture. Blue-gray tobacco smoke canopied above them, cloaking the tin ceiling and the multitude of smoking pipes hanging from small metal hooks. The pipe stems, hundreds of fragile ribs, dangled free. The churchwarden-style pipes of club members past and present were stored on the premises for convenience, the thin stems otherwise so easily snapped in transit. The tiny glow from their pipe bowls and cigar butts—which resembled fireflies—was the only way members could be located in the secretive confines of the club.

Augustus moved into the chestnut-paneled hall, which was lined with baroque-framed oil paintings of fox hunters and their hounds. A fiddle and spinet duo played a cheerful tune in an oval galley off to one side. On the other was the wide, gilded tippling room.

At the hall's end, behind heavy purple curtains, was the club's board room. Above the room's French doors, printed in gold leaf on a wooden plaque, were the words "Regency Room." Augustus took short steps. He wanted to appear relaxed and unflappable. He slipped behind the anteroom curtain, where he relished near silence. Standing before the Regency's closed doors, he took in a deep breath.

His succession into his father's vacant board chair was to be the grandest of moments, one that would dignify him in the eyes of his father's peers. *His own* peers, now. They were not forty miles from the White House, but it was in Regency Rooms all over the mid-Atlantic coast where the real business of governance and deal-making took place. His father had been one of thirteen board members and, today, Augustus would be sworn in to replace him.

"I want to thank you gentlemen," he whispered to himself, imagining the grandees of every stripe seated on the other side of the doors, "for, though all men are created equal, we do not stay that way. My father believed no men outside this room could equal those inside it."

He considered his practiced words and decided they struck the proper chord. He gripped the carved doorknob but hesitated, compelled to stillness by the chattering sounds within. Light punched through the keyhole.

The sinister nature of private conversations attracted him. The seduction of prying had been too potent for him to resist. He savored hearing and seeing and knowing what was not intended for him. He cherished these increasingly rare moments, as it had already become difficult for him to go anywhere in secret.

Voices of board members simmered from the door's other side. Augustus hovered close to hear. He was careful to stay undetected outside the room, figuring even a light footfall could be heard by men inclined to listen for it.

He squinted through the space in the door. He could only see the oval girth of Broussais Kimball, the lawyer who had taken Leopold's seat as board chairman. This action was both figurative and literal, as Augustus spied Kimball sitting in his father's chair. While anyone else in the room garnered the attention of most, Kimball garnered the attention of all. He spoke always to an undivided room. Here, Augustus had caught him mid-soliloquy, which was not uncommon.

"The boy's character is the issue. That is what we're evaluating here, isn't it? Far too often his character has danced with the likes of disrespect, bullying, charlatanism, immorality, and indecency." Kimball let his last statement settle before stirring up another. "How many families pulled up stakes and left their homes because of those Transcontinental rumors? Settlers and farmers and homesteaders and miners uprooted from good land to settle westward. They uprooted on the promise of prosperity. And it was Windom who whispered that promise in the public's ears."

Kimball had rarely aligned with Leopold on public matters but had given him begrudging respect as a man of vision. He did not hold Augustus in the same regard.

Another voice interrupted. "There is no certitude that Augustus knowingly lied. It's slanderous what you're saying."

"Is it?" Kimball asked. "Because he is either clever enough to have executed a ruse on the entire country or so dull a weapon that his father chose not to wield him." He was rolling now. "It must be one or the other. And, if he is not a swindler, it means he is a dunce, and that's all the reason I need to keep him off this board."

The room crackled into a series of suffocated titters, which surprised Augustus.

Leopold had been explicit for years about his wish for Augustus to replace him when he died. These men, gibbering about him on the other side of the door, had never outwardly opposed the desire and yet here they were now discussing a reversal on their agreements.

The cowards.

"Is it possible, Broussais, you're sulking because the Windoms fooled you, too?" someone asked. "You were just as much on the blind end of the Transcontinental bargain as the rest of us."

Kimball gave an arrogant smile but said nothing.

"Never mind the rest of it," another voice said. "I want to know what the boy's done. What do we know of him other than he's his father's son?"

"I agree," said a new voice. "Familial lineage doesn't necessitate a place at this table."

One voice said, "I am certain none of you gained your seats by recounting to others the many intricate steps that brought you your successes."

Kimball tisked. "None of us gained our seats by having our father bequeath it to us, either." No one refuted this. "We may privilege the board by making their unexamined offspring *club* members," Kimball added, "but we've never made them *board* members without proper review."

"It was Leopold's wish."

"And he's dead."

"His *final* wish, then. We agreed to the sum and substance of it."

"The boy's a snoot," someone scoffed.

They went on to say worse things about Augustus, and so he stepped aside and sat nearby staring at the velvet privacy curtains.

He hadn't wanted this. Any of it. Leopold wanted his son to replace him on the board. Augustus blanched at the gravity of doing so. He didn't care about succeeding his father or about rejection from the board. What he cared about were the sons of bitches on the other side of the doors defiling his name without the sand to do it in his presence.

He stood and straightened himself and, in so doing, caught his silver cufflink on his watch chain. It ripped wide the eyelets of his cuff and left the link dangling. It appeared unrepairable. He considered exiting the club and retreating the three blocks home to replace his shirt but thought better of it. He might roll up his sleeves and risk comparison to a common butcher. Or he might favor one arm over the other and keep the tattered sleeve secluded from view to stave off embarrassment.

He pushed the door inward, forgetting it required pulling. The doors rattled against the jamb and halted the conversation inside. Augustus twisted the knob again, this time pulling it open.

The grandees turned together toward the disruption like a chorus of marionettes attached to the same strings. The room was intimate, all twelve men crowded into the airless space. No more than ten feet separated the wall from the sitting members' seat backs. It was stifling hot and carried many odors, none of which were pleasing.

Kimball was the first to speak. "My lord, Augustus." He smoothed his long, oiled side whiskers and looked around the room. "Worth a wagonload of gold bricks, yet the function of a door eludes him."

The room's collective snickers made a slow crescendo, each laugh its own unique instrument in the symphony of Augustus's embarrassment.

"Forgive me." He exhaled his way to calmness as the men quieted. "I see you've taken my father's seat."

"Indeed I have," Kimball said. "And indeed I shall."

Augustus did not quarrel with Kimball being named chairman, nor had he assumed that he, himself, would arrive to the board and immediately advance to that post. But he did quarrel with the usurpation of his father's favored chair.

"There seems to be no open chair for me."

Kimball nodded. "Also correct."

The seated men had become a study in bashfulness. Some averting their eyes, others watching Augustus as if he was the last beast of its kind. Discomfited by the situation, they bit their bourboned lips and nervously ran their fingers along the table's shallow grooves.

A moment ago, the room had been awash in noise. Now, only the muffled sounds of clinking glass and the low thrum of the musicians down the hall rippled the quiet air.

Augustus cleared his throat and began speaking with a steady calm that was not in his heart. "I had prepared to thank you gentlemen," he said. "Instead, it seems my time would be better spent reminding you who I am."

A water-eyed drunk, who'd known Augustus from birth, scoffed. "And who are you?"

"I'm the one whose engines will take you from one ocean to the other. That's who I—"

"No, no," Kimball interrupted. "The railroad, the Fairbanks purchase, those were your father's efforts, my young popinjay. We are asking about *you*." Kimball had always been careful to dishonor the younger Windom by doggedly dismissing him. Augustus would have to be cautious not to lash out too harshly at him, for he was a man who returned punches with an anvil's force.

"I find it rude, sir, your disparagement of my efforts."

Kimball did not answer right away. Instead, he pressed more tobacco into his churchwarden and resurrected its smoke. The effect his dawdling had on the room did not concern him. Big men always relished opportunities to show themselves.

"Well, anyway, I'm sure you've prepared a puffy speech to put us all in the weeps, but…" He shook his head, annoyed. "Let's come off it, now, young Windom. I sat with your father and understood him to be a man of clever strategy. It was he who set the course of the Transcontinental grift, not you."

"Sir," Augustus countered, calling upon his smile to widen without cracking, no matter what this room hurled at it. "It was not a grift."

"What was it then that weakened Fairbanks?"

"For us, it was good fortune."

"And, again, I say your fortune was borne from your father."

Augustus stepped further into the room. "My father was flush with ideas and plans. It discredits me, however, to pretend I was not responsible for implementing them."

"What's done is done," said another member. "Augustus was integral to the doing."

"Well, but the doing isn't the challenge," Kimball said. "The challenge is having the idea."

"You underestimate the difficulty of the doing," Augustus replied.

Kimball took a long drag from his pipe and grinned before speaking again. "When Gutenberg invented the printing press, he didn't build it alone. But can any of you name one man who helped him?" No one could, of course. "To know who built it," Kimball continued, "someone would've had to care. And no one did. No one cared who built the thing. Only who dreamt the thing up."

The ridicule nicked Augustus, though he'd sooner somersault back through the parlor bare-assed than admit it. He employed a glare upon Kimball he wished would puncture the fat man's skin.

"You don't hide your feelings very well," Augustus said.

"I hide them exactly as well as I care to." Kimball returned the pipe to his mouth, a curl at either end of his lip. "But since we're speaking now of candor, allow me to continue in kind. You are not becoming a part of the board today. Unless a majority opposes me." He looked around the table. No one spoke. "Yes, then. So it is."

One of the softer, smaller members held his arms out at either side as if trying to separate the two men. "Today," he said. "You'll not be a member *today*. Perhaps at a future date."

This was meant to soften the blow but having another come to his defense so woefully made Augustus feel more wounded.

"The majority opinion," continued the merciful member, "is you've not proved yourself to the extent required for a chair at this table."

Augustus swallowed hard and let his hands tremble at his sides. "I am the president of the largest locomotive manufacturer in the country." He spoke with caution, fearful a jostled delivery would detonate his words. "I am worth more than any pair of you."

Kimball swatted this aside. "We're all moneyed enough. In this room your wealth provides you nothing that ours does not. What you require is influence." He urged his pipe. "I want you to notice now two things, young man. The first is that you are, at this very moment, floundering. The second is that you are alone as you do it."

"He isn't alone," said the merciful member.

Two others mumbled, "Hear, hear."

Kimball raised an eyebrow. "Fine. You've the backing of three." He emphasized the last word as if it were the plural of buffoon.

"We're no longer discussing my election to the board?" Augustus continued. "Very well. But I'll not stand before your discourtesy."

"Well, then, you'd better stand here no longer. I don't see any end to our discourtesy."

"I require only that you extend to me the same respect you showed my father."

"You are not him," Kimball said.

"Everything I've done has been successful. What else do you call for but success?"

The merciful member smiled. "Something unmistakably yours. Of your own accomplishing." God bless him, he was trying his best to navigate Augustus through this drubbing. "Unmistakably yours and unmistakably, er, *proper.*" He leaned on his last word as if it was code for something else, a synonym he was uncomfortable saying.

"Proper?" Augustus repeated.

"Lawful." Kimball hurled the word from across the room.

"Are you suggesting the Fairbanks merger wasn't lawful?"

Kimball inhaled from his pipe as if preparing to convert it into a cannonball and blow it at Augustus. "There are six lawyers in this room. Do you really want us to dig into the suggestion that it *was?*"

"The merger was lawful."

"The merger was an invasion. An assault orchestrated by your father. Furthermore, I believe the best you have to offer—the *only* thing you have to offer—is your having piggybacked on his trickery."

"You potbellied bastard. My father had you cowed for fifteen years and you think flogging me is going to make up for it?"

Kimball smiled. He was a man who enjoyed a good scrap. "You'll want to dull your sharp language, boy, before you trip and impale yourself."

Augustus crossed his arms. "Never in my life have I seen the equal to this room's gall." He straightened his back and flung his arm out toward the men sitting in judgment. He'd forgotten himself. Forgotten his torn sleeve.

Kimball pointed at the tattered cuff and smiled wider still. "Is this not your day's first skirmish, popinjay?" He spoke now to the members seated around the table. "He's worth more than any two of us and yet cannot keep the muskrats from besieging his wardrobe." More laughter rippled across the room.

For twenty years, Augustus stood at his father's side watching him battle men like Kimball, watching them chuckle as Kimball had. Never once had any of them laughed for reasons of joy or humor. They laughed at unjust things and combative things and offensive things, but never a jest. It was as if men like Kimball had misunderstood the intention behind laughter. When Kimball laughed, it was for his own reasons.

Augustus examined his sleeve as if only now discovering the tear himself. It awakened something in him. A wild rampancy. He leaned against the table and pointed at Kimball, the torn cuff dangling. "Call me popinjay again, you'll find things go damn hard for you after."

He'd taken leave of his good sense. He was now a great distance from the earlier version of himself that had pretended wide smiles. Had his threatening words been insects flitting out of his mouth, he'd have clapped them dead before they reached anyone's ears. But he had said them, and fate would take control now. He would not back away from the words. He'd spoken them and they would inform the trajectory of Augustus's days. He was not a man who would fear Kimball, but one who would fight him. Win or lose, fate had made Augustus a man who battled.

Kimball removed the pipe from his mouth. "If you're threatening to bring violence to my door, boy, rest assured I will leave on the lantern to light your way." The men were soundless, looking from Augustus to Kimball and back again. "Public threats demand action," Kimball said. "So you'll speak apologetically, or I'll see to it you never speak again."

A new Augustus had already begun wriggling out from the dead skin of the old. He'd be damned before he'd be apologetic.

Augustus snorted forth a bulge of slaver and spit it on the floor. It landed with a wet smack and exploded in every direction, after which the starburst of hawked disgust remained still as if in shock at its own existence. Augustus had nothing more to say.

Several board members called out in surprise. Someone admonished Augustus's action by declaring, "Lunacy!" But not Kimball. Kimball smiled.

Augustus's mind vibrated as he rushed back through the dark parlor. The fragile pipe stems set upon him from the ceiling like the pointing fingers of damning angels.

Keep moving, he told himself. *Keep moving and give them nothing satisfying.* Rathbone's words from the previous week returned to him. *Prove to all the bastards you have no betters.*

This may have been the mission of a man with a false sense of the world, but no matter. This was the mission Augustus would ride into Gehenna if it meant righting the day's wrongs.

Gawking stares lashed him as he emerged from behind the anteroom curtain, surging toward the respite of a cool night, leaving behind his hat. The only sound he made was the squeak of the club's loose floorboards, bending under each heavy step.

7

Ruth and Henry fixed the stolen stallion to the spare wagon traces beside Wimp and were able to halve their time crossing into Virginia. In the two days since they'd robbed the old man of his horse Henry had gone sullen. Ruth hadn't conferred with him, hadn't warned him, hadn't even apologized after the fact. She couldn't bring herself to do it. Henry had a way of mashing her nose in her own mistakes whenever she admitted to making them. Made it so it was easier on her conscience to pretend she'd been right than to accept more punishment than she was due. She told herself Henry was too soft and that they'd pay the Virginian back as soon as they could, which would be a lot sooner now that they had a stallion to sell.

"The old man can do with one less a horse for a spell," Ruth said. "A man who sleeps past seven ain't chasing us into north country. And, anyway, we left a good faith token behind."

"Your wedding ring ain't some token."

"Oh, ease up, Henry. It's not like we're the Great Western mail robbers." She chased it with a laugh. "If you'd a better idea, you certainly kept it to yourself, didn't you?"

Ruth's ire was ready to come rattling out of her at the slightest response from her husband. He wisely held his tongue.

The rain fell heavier as they reached Ingles Bridge over the New River. The bridge had remained intact despite two attempts by the Union Army to destroy it.

"Thank the Lord," Ruth said, as Wimp plodded over.

Henry veered the horses off the overland path at Bugtussle Fork.

"Why we heading this way?" Ruth asked. When he didn't answer, Ruth spared a glance in his direction. He was silent, drooped with the heavy expression of worry. His heart gave enough thump to flutter his shirt and vest. "Henry," she said again, "why're you redirecting us?"

"Because we need to get to where the rail gauge changes so we can find a train that'll roll on the narrow Yankee tracks. We'll get to such a place sooner if we head this way instead of aiming for Richmond." His voice shook. Flapped like a kite in the wind. If he was telling her the truth, he was careful about hiding something else.

"Something wrong, Henry?"

"Nothing ain't already been discussed."

"You seem anxious."

"I *am* anxious. Nothing about this expedition is tranquil."

"All right, Henry. All right, now."

She let it alone and Henry closed his eyes. After another quiet minute, he seemed relieved not having to speak on it further.

Ruth had been wearing Henry's black, wide-brimmed slouch hat since he'd gone away during the war. Even with Henry returned, and her own bonnets and field hats better guards against lice and vermin, she preferred stuffing her knotted hair up into the old slouch. The brim extended past her nose, leaving the water to drip onto her knees instead.

They stopped to feed Wimp, who required less frequent stops aside the stallion, but still more than a reliable mare. The stallion, by comparison, ate and drank when allowed, rested when Wimp required it, and was otherwise sturdy in duty.

"If I thought we could get more than a shinplaster for Wimp," Ruth said, "I'd sell her instead of the other'n."

Henry drew up a smile, but otherwise they went another few miles in silence until he couldn't keep himself quiet any longer. "I'm sorry, Ruthy," he said. "For the rain and a million other things." The wagon bucked and rolled.

"Fold up your sorries and keep 'em." She hovered over her meerschaum like it was a precious gem. It struggled to light.

"Well, if the words don't matter," Henry said, "let their intention mean something."

"Blessed Lord," Ruth said. "Kind of man apologizes for the weather?" Though she knew he wasn't apologizing for the weather, she couldn't figure what he was apologizing for.

The air smelled ripe and wounded, and the trail had been little more than one long mud puddle. A week after leaving Chattanooga—wagon sleeping or hiding in storehouses along the way—they arrived in the town of White Cake, sopping and glum. They entered under a sign propped ten feet in the air by two sunken posts. It said:

> *White Cake, Virginia*
> *95 miles E to Richmond*
> *115 miles NE to Front Royal*
> *170 miles NE to Washington*

Behind them, a black range disappeared behind low clouds and colorless hills. They'd just journeyed through a week's worth of God's own vast nothing—winding, jagged brush and coulees that stretched from the Tennessee-Cumberland confluence to the Appalachian Plateau.

The two horses marched into the emptied camp town along the thoroughfare, nodding their heads to release the bit's tension. The late hour mingled with the storm to create a sight of glistening purple darkness. The ghastly stench of shit and rot fought through the rain to offend the nostril.

A water tank anchored the south end of the street. Next to it, sinking into the soil, was an outfitting house and a machine shop with its sides scored and fallen away. A warped and splintered carved replica horse had been set ambitiously high in the air on a stilt to draw attention. An uneven duckboard walkway extended along the fronts of the buildings. Freighting materials had been abandoned in piles along the length of the street. To the north, a tent advertised wine and liquors. Beside it, a clapboard tobacco house rose from the muck, then a dry goods stall, a lean-to grocer, and sleep quarters for the timberers who'd once worked the hills.

Save for the storm, and the claps and creaks of their wagon party, there was no sound. Battle had run off everything and everyone. The mud street had been well-smoothed by months of undisturbed rains. By the appearance of the camp, no one had been present for months.

Henry pointed into the distance, following a spine of blue rail that ran to a triple-sized barn. The weathered engine shed sat at the runoff of a wide bluff. The blue slatted sides had been weathered into the dirty gray color of sheep.

"See there?" he asked. "There's our next shed. Could be our locomotive's in there."

They rode the horses past a brick forge and up to the engine shed. Ruth dismounted, careful of her still-tender shoulder, and sank ankle deep into the mud, her footprints leaving shallow graves in which the falling rain was laid to rest. She hiked her dress to a clearing height. When Henry climbed down off the wagon the wet ground swelled up around his boots. They stood, letting their muscles reform into their natural positions before moving toward the shed's doors. Every step made a wet sucking sound.

"No locks on the doors," Henry said. "Either there ain't no owner or the owner don't care."

"Ain't there, don't care," Ruth repeated. "Oughta be the new hymn of the Confederacy."

The two of them split open the heavy twin doors and went inside. It was a yawning space with barrels and pack crates stacked along the wall. Pieces and parts had been left for the ghosts. Three staging tracks merged into one connecting rail at either end of the barn.

The outermost tracks hosted a jumble of ragged freight cars but, in the center, there stood a Mogul-type 2-6-0 locomotive, with one lonesome boxcar attached. *Windom Locomotive Works* was painted along the boiler.

"Where do Windoms come from?" Ruth asked.

"Baltimore."

She scrutinized the engine, recalling that Henry had mentioned Baltimore to the horseman, Brewster. She thought it was odd then, and damn coincidental now. "That's lucky, I guess."

"How's that?" Henry asked.

"Us needing to file the patent in Washington and Baltimore being less than a day away. Engine could've been made in Providence and then where'd we be?"

"We'd be in Providence, I guess."

She looked at him closely. Watching for a twitch or squirm. "This locomotive taking us right where we need to go is providence enough, I reckon."

They stared at it, letting the water trickle from their mud-spattered clothes and form puddles at their feet. Ruth climbed the engine cab and tapped the gauges, kicked an old pair of gloves left on the floor, pulled open the squeak-hinged tender hatch.

"You gonna inspect the thing with me?" she asked. "Make sure it runs?"

He pointed at the wheel, having spared only a cursory glance at it. "We're lucky. This here's a standard gauge wheel like I'd hoped. Should run fine."

"All the way into Washington?"

Henry gave the ground a thoughtful stare before sucking the side of his cheek. "We can't run it straightaway, no. Even if the Alexandria rail wasn't war-ravaged and ripped apart in some places, we still would only get ten miles south of the capital. The thing doesn't go through. And even if it did, the two of us ain't gonna be allowed to ride up the middle of it like it's normal for us to be there." Henry's certainty about the problems made Ruth believe he had a solution at the ready, but he stopped talking. He rubbed his neck and took a squat.

"So what then, Henry? You're saying there's no way into Washington on this train?"

"On *any* train. They unload freight in Alexandria and move it over land into the capital. But we can ride into Washington on horseback and file the patent. Where I struggle is getting this train past Washington into Baltimore where Mister Windom is."

"So what then?" Ruth was agitated by having to ask twice. And also for not having an answer herself. "Tell me something pretty."

Henry was wrestling with an idea, trying to get both of its shoulders pinned down. "We can go the long way. Swap the mainline tracks for feeder tracks."

"Them little dinky lines?"

"Dinky lines still have all their rails and ties intact. We'll take the Alexandria north to Charlottesville, then take a feeder west to Rockfish, then north to Manassas Gap. Manassas can get us to Winchester where we can move through Harpers Ferry. Once we're at Harpers Ferry, we'll be fine. Plenty of feeder lines and small trains moving in and off the B and O. It'll be a long ride, but quiet at least."

Henry had a miraculous mind for pathways and routes, but even being impressed with him annoyed Ruth. Everything was a reminder of what he was capable of doing if only he gave a damn. "So it's a working engine, then?" she asked. "You can tell that standing over there?"

"I know my engines. This one's a worker. Long way or not, she'll get us there."

That, Ruth reminded herself, is what Henry sounded like when he was telling the full, God's honest truth.

They'd toted several large sheets of metal from Chattanooga still in need of bending and upsetting to fit into the braking apparatus. Henry had enough understanding of blacksmithing to shape the crude pieces into what he needed. He stretched his back while bending a rectangular sheath of metal. It felt good to stretch for longer than it took Wimp to swallow a muzzle of creek water.

Ruth had spent an hour moving the barn wood from the wagon to the tender and another few minutes feeding some of the tender's contents into the furnace. She tossed the furnace pick to the other side of the cab, then snatched up the firebox gloves left on the ground. She slipped one on and stopped to examine it. It was oversized. Thick around the fingers. Her heart sank.

Most firebox gloves were made of a single layer of tough cowhide, but these were triple-layered. Cowhide outside an insulating layer of tincal to prevent burns, and another cowhide layer on the inside to protect the hand from the tincal. She'd seen these tri-layered gloves before. There was only one pair like it in the world. Henry had invented these gloves. She left the door to the engine furnace swinging and turned to see Henry outside under the smithy staring back at her. She leapt off the train and rushed him.

"Shit," Henry said, louder than he probably intended.

She slapped the gloves down on the anvil face as the full force of Henry's comeuppance stood before him. "That horseman back there," she said, "you told him we were headed to Baltimore when you introduced yourself."

"Did I?"

"You coulda said anyplace. You said Baltimore. Now how the hell did you know where we were going?"

Henry set down the tongs and stepped back. His face paled and his shoulders drooped. He'd moved out from under the smithy's roof and let the rain pummel him. It was nothing compared to what Ruth felt she might do to him.

He had told Ruth the Confederate paymaster hadn't paid out the last five months of his service because the war was nearly finished and the Rebels nearly defeated. The truth was—and he confessed it to her now—he could not be sure whether the paymaster had the funds or not because he'd fled a week before they were due.

The Rebs had stolen a Union supply train outside Appomattox. Henry imagined the Yanks, having erred so spectacularly as to let their provisions get taken, would go about recouping their train with a reckless desperation. Desperate men are the most dangerous kind. The problem was multiplied by the fact that Henry's first lieutenant had ordered the theft without a plan of what to do once they had it. Given the difference in width between Northern and Southern rails, a stolen Union train couldn't ride past Lynchburg on Confederate rail. Then what? Poison the food? Dump it in a creek? Blow up the train itself? Henry puzzled over these questions from the cab of the locomotive as the numbers of his troop dwindled.

His first lieutenant ordered the train stopped while the thirty-five-man troop tried to detonate the trestles of a bridge to keep the Yanks from crossing it. They hadn't the explosives to do the job and, in the attempt, the Union had caught up to them. Within three hours the troop was halved, then halved again—all while Henry waited with the first lieutenant on the idling locomotive. He'd suggested to his first lieutenant that they surrender the train and themselves in the process, but the first lieutenant called Henry a "chicken-heart cocksucker" and ordered him back to the front cab, with no better outlook than when he'd started.

What happens in a losing battle, when men die around you, you stop looking around. You assume the worst and desire no confirmation of it. So you keep to yourself. You survive as long as you can. This was how Henry's troop lost sight of the larger picture.

He'd only been alone three hours on the train, but each one was fraught with paranoia. All he had was his Enfield rifle, a pair of cockeyed revolvers, and anything else on the train he could throw or stab fast enough to take a Yankee life. As he sat on the cab floor, rifle in hand, thinking about the battle at High Bridge, Henry could feel the heat rise in his ears. The fear and the guilt, the panic. They'd crossed the bridge but failed to hold back the Yanks. It would not be long before they stalked over it like hungry wolves.

He would not be around to see it happen. Somewhere in the slap-dark, after the first lieutenant left to join the remainder of his troops a mile behind, Henry conjured the idea to unhitch the supplies and escape with the engine. They'd leave the locomotive if he left them the supplies. He figured, too, there'd be no Rebs left alive to chase him after the Union made its next push. He'd forfeit his wages but keep his life.

As the remaining regiment fought into the night, Henry unhitched the cars from the tender. Amidst the shrieking fury of rifle blasts, he fired up and rolled forth before the shots faded, disappearing to an eastern track outpost along the Blue Ridge Mountains in the ghost town of White Cake.

In White Cake, he'd taken all his belongings with him except a pair of firebox gloves he'd made himself. He'd forgotten the fucking gloves.

He stopped only after there was nothing left to confess. When he finished, Ruth didn't move. Somewhere in the middle of his retelling, she'd shut her eyes. The telling of his story, along with the driving rain, had appeared to tire him. He waited for her to open fire.

"I'm glad you're alive, Henry. What some might describe as failings in your nature, may damn well have kept you alive. But listen here." She pulled Henry back under the smithy roof by his collar. She did it slowly and gently. It was almost kindhearted, but then she gripped his collar tighter and it became altogether more threatening. "It's time you understand. You have an idea. It's yours and no one else's. And I need you to see it through."

"I always see—"

Ruth interrupted. "No, sir, you do not. If you did, we'd be someplace else doing something different. I'm saying this one's got to stick. This time you don't run." Her hands trembled, and her jaw jutted. She feared she'd rupture at the slightest nudge.

The water beaded on his wet lashes. He fluttered under the rain and he suffered from a slight shiver. His mind riffled through a series of responses before settling on, "Of course, Ruthy."

"No." She shook her head and let him go. "Not *of course*. I can't count on you for nothin'. You're just as likely to run away from an idea as you are from a fight. How many other doodads you make before these gloves?"

"Now we just don't know what would've happened, Ruthy, if I'd patented those other gewgaws."

"That's right. We just don't know."

"Ruthy—"

"But I know someone with these gloves could stick her hand in the mouth of Hell and come away without a scorch. You think anyone else might want a glove could do that, Henry Casper? Because I sure do."

"Ruthy—"

"I didn't know you deserted, but it's no surprise. You're a runner, by God. You're a runner. You'd let us die right along with every idea you ever had."

"Ruthy—"

"Shut up, you goddamned sluggard. I've dragged you through Hell's Half Acre just to get this far, so let me say my piece. I know why you ran. I ain't mad. I can stomach it. I can stomach you running from death, but I can't stomach you running from life. We already lost too many chances. We can't run from the ones left."

He propped his hands on his hips and looked around his feet. For what, Ruth couldn't guess. A good excuse, maybe. Or a place to crawl in and die.

"I've lost things, too, Ruth."

Ruth lowered her voice. "I lost more." It was the sound of a slammed door. "This brake of yours is different and I need you to be mindful of it. If you don't put your name on it, someone else will. Then you'll have nothing. You'll have *been* nothing. And *I'll* have been nothing. And we'll die as nothings. And our time alive will have been for nothing. And it'll be more tragic than all the other nothings because we can be more than nothing. I need you to be more than nothing for once." She'd run out of breath. "You're a marvel when you've a mind to be. I have no earthly understanding why you're not a mind to be more often."

He would've explained it if he'd known the answer. "There was a time you could spend a kind word without drawing blood," he said, instead.

"There was a time I respected you more than I do now."

He watched her face for a sign of regret. She was careful to ensure her expression held.

The air was a fragile egg.

She'd never spoken to him like this. She nagged, plenty. Groused.

But this was different. Her guts were open. Pain had come scratching out. Their eyes met and she knew he'd be the first to look away.

"I lost so much time because of you, Henry." Her frustration welled. She was being cruel. Worse than cruel, she was being honest. "What I'm telling you is, we need to see this through. Promise me." Her face hardened like clay in a kiln. "Promise me, Henry. Promise me you won't run."

Henry looked down at the pieces he'd molded. He probably considered defending himself. As usual, though, he refrained. "I promise."

The storm surrounding them had grown in intensity. Ruth and Henry had been spared its violence standing under the smithy roof.

"I'll finish these pieces," he continued. "While I do that, keep an eye on the steam gauge. When it points straight up, it means it's time to go."

Ruth was torn between being satisfied with his answer and skeptical of its authenticity.

Henry watched the storm. Barely above a whisper, he added finally, "This is the best I can do."

Ruth gave no quarter. "This damn well better not be."

It was another hour before they loaded the train with the brake parts. They'd cannibalized the wood from the wagon and tossed all the planks into the tender. When they finished, all that remained were the wheels and traces.

Henry built a slapdash ramp and cajoled the horses aboard the train. The stallion dutifully climbed the steep incline, but the skittish nag wasn't as obliging. Henry led her up the plank, tugging the reins in a coaxing fashion, her rapid breaths visible from flared nostrils. She went slow, legs wobbling, head bobbing, mincing until she stood sideways in the boxcar. Her rump and tail poked through the barred window. She could not have been comfortable in that orientation and, yet, she never made any attempt to shift.

"I'd-a never stolen a horse if I knew you was a deserter," Ruth said, as Henry closed the boxcar and boarded the train. "You're a deserter and I'm a horse thief. Ain't we both gonna be on some list? How we gonna file for a patent if we're on some list?"

Henry gave her a hurt look, like a scolded child. "We might not be on any list."

"Might not. But might so, too."

"You said yourself no one sleeps in is gonna run down two horse borrowers."

"That was before I knew you was already a criminal, Henry."

"Well, shit, Ruthy. So what? You want to go home? I'm happy to go home."

"No, sir. We're to continue on. But it's going to make for a damned more fraught ride, knowing we're both malefactors now."

Henry readied himself to answer her but thought better of it as the locomotive snorted to life like a sick Goliath.

Ruth tapped the steam gauge and said, "It's pointing straight up." She turned the steam valve. The engine lurched and threw them against the boiler. After one more strong jerk, the shed exhaled them out. They were on their way.

Henry opened the brake and they moved faster. The engine lumbered over the switch track and the rain blew in sideways. They were soaked all over again. Wimp bucked and whinnied from inside the boxcar. This was going to be a galling expedition for her. For them all.

8

A hullabaloo greeted them along the streets of Baltimore, even in the early morning hour of their arrival. The chaos of activity reminded Henry of Chickamauga or Fort Cass. Only the sweet, licorice smell of black-eyed Susans overpowered the decayed stink of horse pies and rain rot.

They stored the Windom locomotive just outside the city at the Elkridge Landing railroad depot. They sold the Virginian's stallion to the foreman and got in return the thirty-five dollars they'd need for the patent fee, a place to stow the train, and a hundred yards of track to test the brake's function. They set up camp in an empty boxcar nearby after clearing away spiderwebs and offal from the grimy interior. This was to be their home for as long as it took the patent to transpire.

They soon learned they'd underestimated the time that would take.

It was thirty miles south into the capital. They left before daybreak, riding Wimp at half-speed into the city limits about ten hours later. Henry's directional knowledge stalled at the border. Neither Henry nor Ruth knew where the U.S. Patent Office was and made themselves look a sight foolish in asking for the location of a building that took up a full square block. They came upon it suddenly, reaching the corner of Seventh and G Streets to see the building stretching before them. A proud leviathan. It was as if they'd been asking for directions to the ocean while standing on the shore. By the time they finally reached their destination evening had descended, accompanied by the close of posted business hours. They'd have to wait until the next day, so retreated several blocks to a stable on Third St. and sheltered with the permission of a sympathetic head groom.

In the morning, they beat as much filth from their garments as the threads would bear. Trail dust had crept into their haversacks and carpetbags and coated everything. They wore the same duds they had in Tennessee. Every mile had greeted a more tattered version of the pair, every fray a little more prominent, the rings of salt sweat a little farther down their seams. Henry's jacket, once black, had lightened to gray from several coats of chalk soil. Ruth's hat and netted hair kicked up a dust cloud whenever she swung her head.

They left Wimp earth-dirty, mane crusted, hide dull. "A little mud is a natural bug repellant," Henry said, trying to make them both feel better about it. Their own grime had been endurable when they thought they could change into something more proper, but it looked now as if there was no escaping their filth.

Once they'd made their way into the Patent Office they were faced with lines of Yankees in waistcoats and striped trousers, a prospect to make any poor southern rebel nervous. Each minute beset upon them a new struggle, first with where to stand, then with whom to speak, then with how to file.

Waiting to see an examiner, Henry fell asleep beside Ruth along a pew. Sleeping with perfect seated posture was a common skill of soldiers. On Ruth's other side, a dour woman in a worn black dress tucked her small hands in her lap and stared straight ahead, unblinking, not altogether dissimilar to Henry. Her eyes were open, his were closed. She looked calm to the point of boredom, which Ruth found reasonable considering their current environs. There was something about the rheumy-eyed woman that set Ruth at ease. She wasn't friendly or lively in any way. She was alone. They were the only two women in the building. This woman, it seemed to Ruth, had no man beside her. The oddity of not only their presence in a place like this, but their proximity to one another encouraged Ruth to speak.

"Ever done this before?" Either the severe woman did not realize Ruth was speaking to her or didn't care. She made no reaction and continued staring ahead. Ruth leaned a bit closer. "I say, pardon me, madam. You ever done this before?"

The woman did not move her head, but eyed Ruth sidewise. "Done what before?"

"Mark a patent?"

"Many times."

"Many, you say?"

She nodded. If Ruth wanted more details, she was going to have to pull them out of the old woman one by one.

"What's the nature of your business?"

"The dead," the old woman said. "I'm an undertakeress."

Ruth reared around to glance through the window at the stable across the street. She remembered seeing a glass-sided funeral carriage and two posted horses. Lettered in charcoal paint on the glass was:

E. C. Blighton
UNDERTAKER
Baltimore, Maryland
Manufacturer of Rest & Comfort
Mattresses, Spring Beds, Husk & Sea Grass Fiber
Old Furniture Repairs

"You're E. C. Blighton?" Ruth asked.

"Etta Claire Blighton. Yes. But I prefer just Blighton. Simpler."

"The undertaker?"

"Undertakeress."

"Your wagon says *undertaker*."

"There were no remaining funds to repaint the sign once it'd been incorrectly painted the first time."

Blighton appeared unbound by the confines of proper decorum. Her dress betrayed the dust and dirt of her work, her hair spilled from her bonnet. The only accessory garnishing her person was a folded patent application secured on her lap. She had little femininity to her at all, which struck Ruth as a pity because she was striking. She was older, but her skin was free of liver spots. Her lips carried a defiant curl that suggested blood still pumped heavy in her. Ruth tried to imagine this old woman younger. That she appeared utterly without a woman's touch and comfortable that way impressed Ruth. She continued squeezing the conversation, determined to get from it every last drop.

"Your carriage says you build mattresses on top of burying the dead?"

Blighton's face wrinkled in confusion. "On top?"

"In addition to, I mean."

"I started building coffins. Then moved on to shorter rests." The woman missed Ruth's smile. "Someone you know recently die?"

"Why do you ask?"

"People only ever have one reason to talk to an undertakeress."

"No one's died, madam. I'm sorry."

"I've never heard anyone sorry for the good health of their friends and family."

A gap-toothed man as wide as he was tall appeared from behind a marble colonnade and motioned for the next person in line to follow him. They disappeared and the line scooted down one seat. Ruth tapped Henry on the shoulder to scoot along with everyone else, which he did before continuing his upright nap.

Ruth returned to Blighton. "What are you here to patent?"

Blighton side-eyed Ruth once again. "I'm not in the habit of talking about my ideas before they're officially recognized as mine. And only occasionally after."

"Will you speak on a previous patent then?"

Blighton thought a moment. "Ever heard of the diamond coffin?"

"No, ma'am."

"Most coffins are built with six points. Gives the head a nice bit of room for presentations. But since the war, we've been getting men in no shape to be presented and no need to be presentable, if you take my meaning."

"Yes, ma'am."

"I removed two points from the coffin. Began building them in a top-heavy diamond-shape. Four points. For them who wanted a proper burial, but no visitation. Saves my costs, too."

Ruth nodded. "The diamond coffin?"

Blighton nodded. "The diamond coffin."

Ruth found she quite liked the woman's manner once she got a handle on it.

"Anyone help you? You have apprentices or assistants or the like? You're all alone?"

"You aim to rob me?"

"What?"

"Because if I tell you I can't afford to repaint the sign on my carriage you should assume I haven't anything worth robbing unless you have a peculiar interest in four-point boxes. Otherwise, why do you want to know who else helps me or if I'm alone?"

"I meant no offense," Ruth said. "I meant the opposite, in fact. I'm envious of any lone woman with her head above water."

Blighton rolled toward Ruth and frowned. "Well, what in the hell have you got to envy? I bury the cripples and the crazies, an occasional Chinaman…only them what got no place else to go come to me. No one is ever going to see my story sung at the opera, I assure you."

"I envy any woman content in her solitude, is my meaning."

"Well, don't. Solitude and loneliness are neighbors and the path between them is short. You ever been so lonely you start telling stories to the air because you haven't said a word out loud in days?" Ruth had, but she didn't want to admit it. "I lose track sometimes of how to speak to the living," Blighton continued. "Being in the trade of the dead, there's no one to talk to."

"You deal in mattresses, too," Ruth said. "Not just the dead."

Blighton grinned. "Yes, well the mattresses don't talk enough." She made a dry sniffle. "I've got an honest lawyer I talk to when I need it. About the patents. Don't know how good any *honest* lawyer can be, but he's doing well enough. Used to be friends with my pap. Takes me on for a favor." She returned to staring straight ahead. "The gentleman to your left looks less lively than the folks I put in coffins. Is he the reason you envy the solitary?"

Ruth considered this. It sounded cruel coming from the old woman, but not altogether mistaken. She searched for the right response.

Blighton didn't give her the chance to utter it. "You want some advice. Don't compare yourself to other people. Especially not women. You'll never get anywhere or *do* anything. My grandpap was an undertaker and he passed it down to my pap, who had no choice but to pass it down to me. Pap said, 'Etta, you just learn the trade. Get good and proper at it and word will get out. If you get good and proper and walk into every room like a gambler with a full house, you'll be just fine.'"

"Was your daddy right?"

Blighton took a deep breath and let it go slow. "Well, I'm still here." She let another grin get away from her. Her hands had been resting right over left. She changed them left over right as if in preparation for something. "I can give you his name, if you want."

"Your daddy?"

"The lawyer. The honest one. If you need it."

The gap-toothed examiner reappeared and motioned to the next applicant. Everyone slid down one spot closer.

Ruth nudged Henry awake. They slid down, then Blighton. The only two women in line, both inching closer to the end of it.

"We come alone," Ruth said. They had not yet sat. The examiner eyed her up and down.

"That's fine. I don't usually have a crowd in these types of exchanges, ma'am."

"I mean, we have no financial backers. We've got enough to pay the file fee and no more. So don't try to squeeze us for more than we got 'cause we ain't got it."

"How might a patent office squeeze you?"

"If you were to ask me, I'd say the fee you charge is high."

"Ruth, honestly." Henry sat first. His fallen arches made it so he didn't abide standing. Which was too bad for him because a sitting man had a hard time browbeating a standing woman.

The examiner raised his hands in front of him in a show of peace. "It's fine, Mister Casper. Really." He motioned toward the empty chair in front of his desk meant for Ruth. "Please, ma'am. Do sit. I should explain that the fee pays my wage, in part."

"And that's fine if you grant us a patent. But, if you don't, you still keep our fee and we'd be out money we might need. More than ever if we ain't holding no patent."

"You have an accurate accounting of our operations here," said the examiner. "And, as such, I can assume you know the part you both are to play. Namely, providing me with a proposed item to patent. I'd like to see it. I'd like to grant you a patent. I take personal pride in so doing and will do all I can here to see it out the way you'd prefer."

He smiled. He seemed amused by Ruth. And so she sat, feeling comfortable in his presence. He was an affable sort.

"Will you refund us the patent fee, sir, if your findings don't work out the way we'd prefer?"

The examiner sat back, all four chair legs creaking under his shifting weight. "Do you have reason to believe they won't work out?"

"Yes, sir," Ruth said. Henry looked at her with the same confused, knotted expression as the examiner. "By virtue of nothing having worked out for me and mine so far. A woman's got to consider her past when thinking about her future."

"There's a word for people like you, Missus Casper."

"Is that word unmistaken?"

The examiner let out a laugh that surprised even himself. He nodded. "Okay, let's let it lie there. What have you brought?"

Henry leaned forward. "A train brake."

"They already make those," the examiner said, chuckling still. "Little joke. I say it all the time." Ruth and Henry sat blinking at him. "Yes. Well. A train brake, you say?"

"Stops trains in a quarter of the time."

"A quarter, you say? How's that?"

Henry unrolled his parchment and laid it flat across the man's desk. "Air's what does it. Instead of the effort going to closing a brake, I swapped it so the effort went into opening them up."

The smile had left the examiner's face as he leaned over the drawings. He frowned and blinked and leaned forward more. Got so close, Ruth thought he might have died without pronouncement and was wilting in front of them.

The examiner sat up and looked at Henry as if trying to determine if he was real or a figment of his mind. "This works?" he asked. "You know this works?"

"I have no working model, of course. But I do have the parts. Additionally, I was an engineer for more'n ten years. I do believe it works, sir."

The examiner tilted his head to one side and smiled in reverence. His hands folded easy-as-you-please over his belly.

"We have no permanent home," Ruth said. "Nor money to pay past the fee. It ought be said outright and you ought believe it's true."

The examiner removed his half-moon spectacles. "Did you know that the granting examiner is named on the certificate and other pertinent documents? This gives a lineage to an examiner's efforts. Connects him to his work forever and always. I hope you will believe me when I tell you it would be an honor to connect myself to an apparatus such as this one. With a lineage such as it has." He smiled. "Only a third of the applications that come though this building are granted patents. But I pledge you this," he leaned forward in a gesture of conspiracy, "I will take special interest in overseeing this particular patent. I have great empathy for a dark horse. A week from today, I'll have the necessary patent amendments for you. Then I'll hurry along the patent prosecution. It normally takes several months, but I'll see it goes much faster for you if I can. If this does what you say, I have no doubt it will go quick enough." He leaned back and smiled again, likely certain he had made the couple sitting before him the happiest two people in Washington.

Henry only nodded. He'd been dragged this far, no reason he'd get excited now. Ruth didn't smile, either. By the expression on the examiner's face, the Caspers had not been as appreciative as he assumed they might. He looked from Ruth to Henry and back again, then sat up in his chair.

"Missus Casper, if the patent is not awarded, I can agree to return the application fee. Will that suit you?"

Now came her smile.

Henry paid the thirty-five-dollar fee and shook the examiner's hand with vigor as they left. Even Ruth, often distrusting of men in suits, smiled and hugged the round little man. His shape suggested a lackadaisical life of sitting and poring over people's hopes, doing his best to make something out of them.

It wasn't exactly sundown yet, but the boxcar they'd called home for several days blocked all the light. Ruth and Henry spoke few words. They moved around one another in the careful choreography only years of hard marriage could allow. It wasn't anger that quieted them, but alliance, neither obliged to entertain the other. They'd brought their two wool blankets from home. Ruth lifted them toward Henry.

"You take these. Your weary bones are in need of saving. I get hot at night anyhow."

"I can't take the blankets from you," Henry said.

"You ain't taking them. I'm giving them."

"I can't abide you *giving* them either."

She turned her back to him. She could be stubborn, spiteful even. If she turned around and found the blankets unmoved, she'd toss them outside in the dirt or ball them up to stop the wind whistling through a chink in the boxcar slats. When she turned her back, it meant she'd made up her mind. She wouldn't use those blankets. Not because she was overheated, but because she'd gotten it in her mind not to.

Henry put his hands on his hips, searching around the dark boxcar for a reason not to take the blankets, but gave up and wrapped himself fully, then laid down. He stared up at the darkened roof. A whisper came out from under him. "Good night, Ruth."

Ruth, too, lay down, wrapped in the woven horse blanket. She meant to answer. In her mind she'd told him 'Good night,' but she'd gotten distracted thinking about the last time she was happy. The thought took her all the way back to the first time she'd seen Henry. She remembered their wedding and the pastor who married them at the edge of the Tennessee River. Instead of saying 'Good night,' Ruth kept all these recollections to herself and left Henry in the dark alone.

She'd almost drifted off when he spoke up again.

"Answer me true," he said. "Why did you marry me?"

Ruth's answer had been waiting for him. She did not know how long, but it had been set for a while. Locked in the breech, ready for firing. Aimed at his heart if he chose to ask her the very question he just had. "Because," she said, "I thought you were going to be something, Henry Casper. And I wanted to be something, too."

9

It was closing in on eleven at night. The faction in Augustus's office—three engineers and the handler, Rathbone—had been sequestered there since six. The intention was to conjure ideas on how to improve the company. In five hours, they hadn't even come close to this goal. Increasing the production of engines, raising prices on future contracts, or expanding into other machinery were ideas too risky to hazard while the company continued adjusting to life without Leopold.

The engineers, being engineers, suggested avoiding risk by changing nothing. The Transcontinental's construction was enough to keep the stockholders happy. Why push it? They reasoned it was best to stockpile profit while showing the world the company would not fall apart in Augustus's care. It was safe and smart.

Rathbone kept his mouth shut. His counsel was better suited in private.

Augustus had forgotten himself. He'd shed his necktie and let split his pomaded hair into two swooping parts that resembled water buffalo horns. "We have nothing," he said. "We don't leave until we have something."

The company's head engineer, Frank Marcy, a bald, bearded man with his sleeves perpetually rolled to the elbow, spoke with reserved agitation. "We *do* have something. We have a plan to stay the course."

Augustus shook his head as if ridding himself of a fly. "Your plan to do nothing is not something."

Another engineer said, "Think of it as keeping the ship level until the passing of choppy seas."

Augustus squinted. "The passing of…choppy…seas?" He repeated the man's words slowly to stress his annoyance.

The engineer did not catch this unsatisfied tone and nodded with pride.

Augustus continued. "Ships pass in choppy seas or the sea itself calms, but the sea is where it is. The sea doesn't pass."

Now the engineer understood the error of the metaphor. "Yes," he said and gave a throat clear. "Well… but…you take my point."

"I don't take it. I leave it to wither right where it is. I want a plan of action. I've offered up idea after idea and you've slit the throat of each one."

Marcy stood. He was exhausted and looked the part. "You wanted us to tell you what's possible and what isn't. We told you." He spread his arms in exasperation. "You're the boss. You want your ideas done, then do them. I'm going home." He tucked his spectacles in his waistcoat pocket, retrieved his jacket and topper from the rack, and made his exit.

The other two engineers did not hold the same vaunted position within the company and were less inclined toward defiance.

It was Rathbone who stood next to relieve the pressure. "Let's all retire, then. Sleep would do us good. Wake up with a fresh feeling and carry on from this point tomorrow."

The second engineer nodded in agreement, slapped his hands on his knees, and pushed himself to his feet. He said, "Tomorrow then." He and the third engineer fetched their vestures and left the chamber before putting them on.

Augustus did not care to watch them leave, preferring instead to stare out the window behind his desk, his own reflection the only thing he could see in the glazed glass.

Rathbone was much slower in his preparations to leave, slipping his coat over his thick arms as if every part of him was tender. He buttoned each strained brass button and placed his hat atop his head without speaking.

With nothing else to adjust, he said finally, "I suspect you've still got Broussais Kimball in mind feeding your frustration." Augustus tensed but did not answer. "To this I urge you to think of nothing but your business."

"You may leave," Augustus said, still staring out the window. "Close the door behind you."

Those were direct orders. Rathbone obeyed them as such. Augustus appreciated his obedience, though never enough to tell him so.

10

1850

On Thursdays, Ruth's father and younger twin brothers had taken the wagon and the week's harvest of onions, rye, and barley to sell to neighboring counties. If they returned with seven dollars, Ruth's mother would be happy. They harvested at least ten dollars' worth of crop on any given week, but Ruth's father never brought home that much. Father did his selling during the day and would spend a portion of the onion money on whiskey at night. He'd send her brothers off to sleep in the wagon during the summer, or the backroom of a saloon during the frost, and drink until his head got too heavy to hold up.

Ruth counted herself lucky in one respect—though her father drank, he wasn't violent. He was lazy but never careless. Mother had said many times that he was careful in order to manage being lazy. He knew how much drinking money he could spend without Mother making a fuss about him spending it. He was a shrewd negotiator and if he could earn an extra handful of cents per peck and bushel, well, then all the more whiskey for him. If he couldn't negotiate high, he'd tell his wife that conversions had shifted out of favor and forced the price low.

It was a lie they both could live with. To her father's view, this was a lie told out of necessity. He loved his wife and never wanted to be the cause of her ire, but he cherished little in this world more than his Thursday benders. That he came home with any money in his pocket relieved Mother. Had she gotten on him about the drinking, she feared he'd flash a mulish nature and spend more, out of spite for having been scolded.

Ruth's brothers were happy with the arrangement, too. No matter how much Mother needled the boys, they never confessed to knowing about Father's doings. Every week they'd provide some cover excuse about camping or a hotel stay. More than once, they confessed to having fallen asleep early. This, Ruth believed, was true more often than not. The boys were still small. When it came to their energy, they tended to burn bright, but only briefly.

Ruth was jealous of them all. She imagined it being nice to have a place to go to shout about the world right before you laughed at it. A place where the people inside brightened a little at the sight of you.

The family still managed to save some money, but if a tool broke or there were poor crop yields Father's whiskey money was never the victim of it.

Ruth's only purpose, as far as she could figure it, was to look after her mother and to help her with chores. Mother had been born weak. She never grew past five feet or one hundred pounds. She was a plain woman with a tiny nose and close-set eyes. She shivered, even in warm weather, and ran short of breath without exertion. Death was always a thread's width away and living had grown exhausting.

"Your mother's twice as strong inside as the rest of us and twice as weak outside," Father had told Ruth many times. "Watch her close." But he never gave clear instruction about what, exactly, to watch close for.

While the males in the family worked the fields or bartered around the county, the two women remained within the farm's sixteen-acre fence. They had little to discuss except which chicken's eggs had been collected, the cleanliness of their habiliments, what work needed doing around the farm, the state of the fields, what needed tending for supper, and the like. They did everything with dull-eyed efficiency. They never left the farm. Any disturbance excited Ruth. Once or twice a year, a stranger would pass through, or the weather would play havoc. Every day she longed for something different, for the wind to blow in a new direction. She didn't know she was bored, exactly. She thought she was evil, welcoming the prospect of her mother falling ill so that she might save her. It was something to break the monotony she craved. She wanted a reason to exist. Mother was sickly enough to require Ruth's company, but nothing more.

Mother often said, "There are fifty ways to die from one day to the next and somehow none of them have taken me yet." But she never said this with a smile. It always came out of her like a damnation, something to repeat like a cursed incantation.

Some lived each day as if it was their last, Mother lived as if she hoped it would be. The nature of her frail body and harsh work made it so she always looked harried and strained. Ruth was young, but even she could see how much energy it took to get through.

Every supper contained onions and both women chopped them as a matter of course. Mother had taught Ruth early to dunk them in water to take out the sting. "Wet the onions," she'd say, "not your eyes." As Ruth became old enough to understand how poleaxed her mother had become, she noticed her mother no longer dampened the onions. She'd let her eyes redden and fill and told Ruth never to mind about it. In addition to swollen eyes, her mother had taken to sniffling and drawing short breaths. She'd angle her body away from Ruth, then return to facing her with several chopped onions and a face twisted in sadness. She'd blame the onions for it all.

Father lied to Mother about whiskey. Mother lied to Ruth about onions. For all Ruth knew, every family lied as a matter of course.

By sixteen, her mother's gloominess became too much to endure. But she could not feign ignorance of her mother's frailty. She suspected one day—unnamed as it may have been—if she left long enough, something bad would happen. Her mother's condition had neither worsened nor bettered. Every time she saw her mother grip the workbench to steady herself; saw her glassy eyes when she came in from outside; heard the soft groans that followed every few steps; saw her staring at the floor after she finished scrubbing the dishes, hands dripping off the side of the wash basin, Ruth thought, *Is this the end of it?* She thought it more than once. In fact, she thought it the very day her mother fell. She shook it from her mind. There was something out there and she wanted to see what it might be. Wanted it bad enough to ignore the possibility that her mother would need her, and she would not be there. She'd been there for years. It was time to be somewhere else.

On Thursdays, while the boys were gone, Ruth started venturing away from the farm to clear her mind and to satisfy her need to see a world past her sixteen acres. First, she ventured over the fence to climb the near tree. She'd be gone a few extra minutes, her mother never the wiser. Then she'd linger for longer stretches of time, climbing higher, able to see further in the distance, gazing out toward the orchard or along the creek, wondering how far she could follow it. Then she followed it. Kicked along the creek, lost in the copse of cypress. A quarter hour would pass. A half hour. She became more careless in her absences. She knew she'd made a terrible mistake the day she returned to find her mother naked in the tin tub, scrubbing mud off her legs with a brush and cold water, her cough wet and loose.

Ruth's family kept five hogs in a slatted pen, which is where Mother had found herself when she got lightheaded and collapsed in the slop. The sun was high when it happened, the hogs had all been let out. By the time she came to, it was dusk. She roused, thankful at first not to have drowned in an inch of pig shit but, by the time she found her feet and took an accounting of her muddied dress, she'd turned irate at her sixteen-year-old daughter who was nowhere about.

When Ruth finally turned up, Mother greeted her with disdain. "She returns. Back to double the offense by staring at my bruises with indifference."

"Where are you bruised?"

"Let me first wipe away the pig shit that's dried on me from having fallen unconscious in the pen all afternoon, you goddamned devil. Maybe then my bruises will out."

Ruth took a step closer. "I'm sorry, Mama."

"Fold up your sorries and keep 'em. Where were you?"

"Mending the fence by the creek."

"Two posts needed mending. That's a quarter hour task at most. I wager I walk out there now, them same two posts are as broke as ever."

Ruth didn't believe her mother had the strength to walk out anywhere but held her tongue—in case she was wrong, and her mother had at least enough grit left to rise from the tub and smack her across the mouth for being so sass-lipped. Instead, she looked at the ground and avoided the topic of where she'd been. "You said you fell?" she asked, barely above a whisper.

"I don't know what happened. I was in the pen and it was day and I was fine, then suddenly it was dusk and I was prone."

"The mud's soft at least." It was the thinnest of silver linings.

"The mud's muddy, too. And mingled with shit, old corn cobs, and who knows what else. It was in my mouth, girl. My hair. Inside my ear. Soaked in my goddamned skin. And you were off somewheres pretending to mend a fence while I laid rotting in it."

"Anything broke?"

"Everything's broke."

A sunken feeling weakened Ruth's knees and she slid down the wall until she was sitting. Guilt overcame her. "I wanted to know what's past the orchard. I went walking and lost time." Her eyes filled.

Mother stopped rinsing her back. She rested both arms on the lip of the tub. The only sound was the dripping bathwater falling from her bare arms to the floor. She spoke in low tones and slower than normal. "You went walking?"

Ruth could not stand to look her in the eye, but she did examine her arms. Even in the flickering apricot mantle of the lamp light, she saw the bruises and welts. Her mother was so fragile.

"You went walking," Mother repeated. "Into the orchard?" Repeating it made it sound worse.

It was selfish and dangerous. A girl didn't need to be out in the forest herself, especially if she didn't know what she'd find. Her shame had become an oversized beast that stomped around the room and shook the plank boards.

"Yes, Mama. I was curious. I curse myself for it."

Her mother coughed again. Neither of them knew then that the cough would remain long after most of her mother's other qualities had abandoned her. Her hair, her coloring, her sharp tongue, her ability to do chores. The cough outlasted it all.

Mother stared a hole into Ruth before she pointed across the room at the boys' shuck pallet on the floor and the books stacked on either side. Two sets of stacked volumes each topped with a bent tin candle holder. "Let's see how far your curiosity takes you with those."

Ruth followed her mother's pointed finger, not certain if she meant the mattress or the makeshift tables or what.

"Take one of those mildewed old books," Mother said, clarifying her intentions. The books had been in the house as long as Ruth could remember and had never before registered as anything but tables. "Go on," her mother urged her. "Or has all your curiosity left you? Your father thought he might be curious one day, too. Which is why he thought it a smart idea to trade a harvest of barley for an incomplete set of encyclopedias."

Ruth approached the books the way a child's tongue approaches a swallow of medicine—slowly and with little optimism. The merlot leather spines were embossed with the gold foil title *The Encyclopedia Americana*. The subjects contained in each volume had been organized alphabetically. Four volumes on the right side of the bed and four on the left. Ruth placed the candleholder on the floor and opened Volume 10, *Penance* to *Retina*. She felt her mother watching her turn each brittle page and did not understand what was expected of her in so doing.

"Have you read these through?" Ruth asked. Mother sniffed at the idea but didn't answer. "I don't know these words," Ruth continued. "I can't hardly figure all of them."

"Well then thank Lord you're curious. Might mean you have a hope of figuring it out before you give up. You want to know the world, girl?" Mother flung her arm at the books. Ruth felt errant drops of bathwater land on the back of her neck. "There's half the world, right there. Didn't do us no good. Maybe you're different." Ruth had assumed her mother was taunting her, suggesting in an angry way that Ruth certainly wasn't any different and hadn't any hope of ever being. But then she curled up in the bathtub and spoke quieter than before. "I think maybe you are."

Ruth turned to see her mother, to match a vision of her with the soft words just spoken. The small woman dipped below the tub's lip, only the top of her undone hair was visible, mudcaked still and thick like broom whiskers. "What, Mama?"

A long moment passed before her mother spoke again. "I don't begrudge your curiosity, rest assured of that." Not knowing where else to train her eyes, Ruth reviewed the encyclopedia page on which she'd stopped. *Punishments, War* it read. Mother continued. "I'd-a liked to have gone with you. Maybe next time you're feeling curious, you'll ask for company."

The confusion of the moment halted Ruth. It had never occurred to her that they could be allies. That her mother had yearnings, too. Her brothers had covered for their father, why couldn't she have covered for their mother? All that melancholy and pain, by God, there was still a beating heart in there. Each venture outside the farm, Ruth had managed to abandon her mother twofold. She said she was sorry, begged for forgiveness, and then said nothing for the days that followed.

Mother's fall had jarred something loose. Her cough worsened and produced blood. Her bruises spread. And her body slowed as if in need of a proper winding. A darkness came over the family that was unique in each member but sprung from the same source. It was as if whatever scant traces of love had existed within the family before were disappearing with the speed of Mother's declining health.

Two weeks after her fall, Mother set down her cut onion and closed her eyes for the last time. Ruth would never know if the final tears squeezed from her mother's closed lids were the result of a strenuous life or a single onion.

They buried her at the edge of the property using three smoothed wood slats as a grave marker. Etched below her name was a passage from Matthew 24:44. *Be ye also ready*, it said. It was as much a threat to Ruth as it was good advice, especially when considering it came from her mother.

Ruth had never forgiven herself, made worse by the fact her own father had not forgiven her carelessness, either. When Ruth tired of flagellating herself, she turned her ire to her father. His Thursday bouts of whiskey drinking kept on, and Ruth was now the homestead's lone caretaker. Her only escape, under the weight of the constant choring, was the facts and ideas listed alphabetically in the forgotten volumes beside the boys' bed. The entire world started with *Cathedrals* (for they did not have the first two encyclopedia volumes). In her solitude, she read about *Sulphur, Falsetto,* or *Venial Sin,* while also wondering what the set's missing volumes held. The world, even summarized and stacked on the floor beside her, remained a frustratingly incomplete mystery. Curiosity was a cruel affliction for a girl like Ruth to suffer.

Three years passed in which Ruth and her father barely spoke. He became desolate and distant until, one day, all that whiskey caught up to him. Went to sleep one night and never woke up. Ruth and the twins had to lift him into the wagon and ride him to the town doctor twelve miles away. His liver had long given out by the time he was examined.

Ruth was old enough that the court granted her guardianship over her brothers, a responsibility she did not want but could not refuse. She hadn't had freedom before, and still didn't. Instead, she had responsibility to her kin, herself, and the farm. There could be no more exploring the cypresses, nor anything else.

The boys were some help to her, demonstrating as best they could the way Father had sold their crops. For a while, she let the boys handle things while she watched. What she saw was a world of men giving no quarter to the poor boys. They took no pity on the twins. Her family, it seemed, appeared to the world an easy mark. If she and her brothers were going to live, they were going to have to prepare more, stand straighter, hold firmer, and assume everyone was trying to get one over on them. They would upset the customer's equilibrium and injure the means by which they sustained themselves. (Ruth, in her growing embitterment, had taken a particular interest in Volume 12's *War–Strategies* section.)

Ruth stopped going to the men altogether. No more general store owners, mercantile providers, no more saloonkeepers, no more traders. Ruth would not speak with them until she'd struck an understanding. She rode into town and approached the wives. Spoke to them about the stews that wouldn't taste right without onions, talked to the patrons of the drinkeries who were looking at a beer shortage if the barley didn't arrive to the brewmasters. She hoped they would join in on the nagging. No one respected her, but maybe the wives and patrons could talk sensibly to their insensible folk. For several days Ruth spoke to everyone in every town *except* the men her father had once sold to.

And then she and the twins went home. They rationed the canned food they'd saved, sacrificed a hog, and harvested what little they could. They planned to wait a month before returning to the towns. She needed everyone across five counties to believe she was capable of turning her back on their business. And to be able to make them believe it, she had to do it.

Ruth did not have to wait the full month. A wagon carrying a half-dozen customers trundled up, a week after her gambit. The men aboard threatened to rip Ruth's crops from the ground themselves.

She passed a glance over the lot and smiled. "If you're all planning to keep your businesses open *and* reap our crops, I guess that means you've forsaken sleep from now on?" The men realized the flaw in their threat as Ruth continued. "What you men bought from us—back when you was still allowed to buy from us—was the work goes into bringing you the crops. This ain't an apple you pick off the tree and bite into. But, if you think you can steal from us, I invite you to try. We could use some amusement."

A fatgut with a rope belt and one long eyebrow pulled a pistol from his britches and aimed it at her. "Maybe we come here once a week to make sure you've got our fortifications."

She stared into the gun's barrel. To this day, she could draw it from memory. The cartridges peeking out of the chamber, readied for harm.

"No," she said. She could not hear her brothers' obnoxious, open-mouthed breathing behind her on the porch, which meant they were holding their breath. "If you don't pay for the labor, we don't labor."

"That won't be good for your health."

Ruth stopped passing over the faces of the group and focused on the one doing the threatening. "Look at me, mister. What good is health when everything else is a toil? Pay us fairly or do your worst to me and mine and be known statewide as the man who killed three orphans because they wouldn't let you rob 'em."

The silence didn't last long. The elder saloonkeeper had no patience. He pushed away the fatgut's pistol and said, "We'll pay your father's prices and no more."

"And no less," Ruth said. "I'll ride in next week."

The elder saloonkeeper asked, "Can you provision us now? Even just a little to get us going?"

"No. You get going without my help." She turned away from the gaggle and shooed the boys back in the house. She grabbed the rifle inside and cocked it just in case, but the tiny mob hiked themselves back up on the wagon and rode off. The next week they grinned at the sight of her, paid her a fair price, and spoke nothing about their sudden change in attitude. They just wanted the goddamn shipment.

There were lean times even after that. Ruth had to pay for field plow repairs by selling the wagon. When the time came to carry the goods into town, she fashioned a platform on the plow only big enough to carry half what the wagon could hold. She'd raised the plow blades high enough not to slow the horses and resolved to make twice the trips—the plow wagging wild, left and right—around the circuit with half the load.

It was embarrassing at first. People snickering, or assuming she was too backwards to know the difference between a plow and a wagon. It also drew the attention of the curious and industrious. After a while, it was a reason for people to talk to her. Ask her about the contraption and if she was the one who thought it up.

This was how Henry found her. To hear him tell it, he'd seen her out riding the re-jiggered plow enough times to draw it out and improve it from memory. Even bought the parts before ever having spoken a word to her. When he introduced himself, he did so by complimenting her craftiness then offering his suggestions on how to make it craftier. He said, "I can help you with that plow buggy," and Ruth laughed a little at the ridiculous phrase, then composed herself and shot him a playful skunk eye. "Help ain't something ever comes for free," she told him, "and I ain't interested in paying."

But she was twenty by then. So, when he asked her to marry him for the third time, she said yes because no one else was asking. And because she wasn't sure anyone would ever ask again.

The boys were old enough to fend for themselves. She had looked after Mother and then the twins, never herself. Henry seemed capable of taking care of her. She married him hoping she could rest.

11

It took two full days for Henry to dismantle the braking apparatus from the Windom locomotive. Breaking the welds took the most time. He needed to ensure the welds along the brake block broke in the right places so as not to damage the wheel treads or himself. They could use the linkage, pins, and brake wheels for the new system along with the parts they'd removed from the bear traps, but there was no room for error, so Henry disassembled everything slowly. He needed every scrap of iron. There would be no pieces left over. If he miscalculated the steam intake and blew the bladders, he didn't have anything with which to replace it. The steam pressure couldn't be too weak, either. It had to be enough to force open the mechanism so that the brake pads lifted off the wheels—the entire function of his design. They'd come too far to squander their chance now. A patent was necessary but wouldn't serve their full purpose. What good was a brake patent if no one wanted the brake? What good was it if the brake didn't work? They would have to show investors what it did. They'd start with the Windom Locomotive Works. It was the largest manufacturer of trains but, even more important, it was the manufacturer of *this* train. And if they were going to get Windom to license their patent—or even better, buy it straightaway—they'd need more than drawings and claim papers. They'd need proof.

So, while the patent examiner bent a groove in a cane chair reviewing their application, Henry tore down a locomotive only to build it up again into the most advanced engine in the world.

While Henry toiled away, Ruth rode Wimp south in search of enough food to fill their bellies. Even fifteen miles outside the city in Anne Arundel County, the pickings were limited to birds and rabbits, neither of which were worth the expense of a bullet—ambitiously assuming Ruth would only need one shot to drop two of the fastest creatures a person could hunt. Rather than wasting the rifle's cartridges, she thought it smarter to barter them for food at the first merchant who'd entertain them. She returned north along Stoney Run and returned to Elkridge Landing.

She'd found a scruffy hotelier who had a need for a rifle and didn't mind it being Confederate issue. She made a deal to trade Henry's Enfield, and the cartridges that came with it, in exchange for a pair of meals twice a day for a month. She didn't relish trading away their only armament, but she relished starvation less. She shook the hotelier's snaggle-nailed hand and helped herself to a ladle of rabbit stew and hardtack before telling Henry what she'd done. The decision sat well with him and they spent the next day eating two meals between bouts of deconstructing the spin-wheel system.

Several days later, they rode Wimp into town and inquired about the whereabouts of Augustus Windom's home. His mansion crowded out an entire block along Charles Street. They switched up and down the street, watching the comings and goings, until they set eyes on Augustus Windom himself.

"He's a boy," Henry said.

"And puny," Ruth added. "Don't look able to hold up a buggy whip without tipping over. How's he manage to hold up a company?"

They watched him climb into a coach and rattle away in the opposite direction.

"I seen my share of young grandees in the army," Henry said. "Think their rank makes them a different species. I worry a boy like Augustus Windom has the same thoughts in his head."

"He might not cotton to us no matter what we offer up."

"So we don't go at him softly?" Henry kicked at Wimp's haunches and set out for the depot.

"No," Ruth said. "We ought not go at him softly."

A week in, Ruth gathered discarded wood from the train yard. She rummaged through hollowed tinder boxes, storage cars, underneath cobwebbed tracks, stacked crates, broken rain barrels, and anywhere else with loose wood. Anything she hauled went into the tender.

Meanwhile, Henry and Wimp ventured back to Washington and the Patent Office. He waited an hour before the gap-toothed examiner pulled him aside and told him how impressed he continued to be with Henry's application.

"Most patents," the examiner said, "require some revision. They need clarifying or further work. After reviewing yours with the meticulousness of a starved mouse in search of crumbs, I cannot claim to find anything requiring your redrafting."

Henry told Ruth this was bittersweet news. It meant they had at least another week of sleeping in the mildewed train cars of the Elkridge Landing depot.

It took them most of the next week to get the air brake in place. And, when they did, they planned to leave the train yard and move the refortified locomotive into the middle of French country near the Guilford switch for high-speed testing. They eased out of the depot's gut, checking for the first time the new system's effectiveness. It took fewer than twenty yards to discover the new brake had no effect. Henry rolled to a stop another twenty yards on. This puzzled him for two more days before learning the angle fittings for the brake pipes weren't sealed. Once he closed the pipes, the cut-out nuts all fell off and scattered along the track. This sawed off the rest of the day, as they searched for every last nut.

The air had farther to travel on the train brake than it did on the bear trap. This forced the bladders to loosen and bang against the track. If the train gained speed, they'd come loose completely, and the train would be without brakes. Tightening one part inevitably resulted in something else loosening. It was like trying to build a house of cards by removing the bottom layer and re-stacking it on top. This required three more days of low-speed tests before Henry straightened it out.

A patent drawing explained how an apparatus worked. It did not, however, explain how it would fit with other apparatuses already in existence on the train. That would be for Henry to learn hour by hour for weeks. He'd finally gotten the brakes to grip the wheels properly and decided it was time to run further tests in the open country. They cajoled Wimp onto the train and rode out. Each pull of the brake came partnered with a deafening screech that frightened anything within earshot. Once outside the Elkridge depot, the sound had gotten worse and sent Wimp fleeing the area. It cost them an hour just to corral the nag and another four to put an end to the squealing bleat.

Through it all, Ruth said little. She wanted neither to confess her flagging faith in Henry, nor lie about it. She was fighting against her belief that his bite exceeded his chew. When he looked at her, she knew that only a tired map of wrinkles and creases looked back.

They failed a few more tests, and had to sleep two nights on the train, but on the third day out on that prairie path rail, the air brake stopped the train cold. It made no more noise than any other train, it emitted no strange overheated odors, and shook only to a manageable degree. Henry increased the speed to twenty miles per hour without hardship and decided he'd have to push it to forty for the final test. He hit forty and yanked the brake valve. Sent the train sliding and screeching. The engine bucked but remained on the track. It stopped exactly where Henry wanted it to and in a fraction of the time.

They'd done it. The air brake had stopped the train in a third of the normal time. Damn thing stopped like an old heart.

There was no questioning it now. Ruth was moved to the point of giggling and spinning out a little curlicue dance right there on the track. Henry sank to his knees aboard the train and laid his forehead on the floor. He closed his eyes and said nothing.

It didn't matter that they'd slept sixteen days stuffed in a boxcar, or that they were still near starved on stew and lump biscuits, or that without soap or shave blades they were raw as ripe hell. The brakes worked. Nothing else mattered.

They'd smell of lilac and honeysuckle soon enough.

PART II

October~December 1865

12

Six of eleven chimes from the foyer's grandfather clock made their way to Augustus's ear. The rest were overpowered by the sound of mingled voices down the hall. Three voices, to be exact. One was his footman, Jefferson. He moved closer to the door but did not recognize the other voices. (Was he doomed to forever listen in secret on the other side of doors?) The sound at the end of the hall started as a hushed exchange but grew in volume and obstinance.

Finally, he opened the door and traversed the hallway to wonder no more. He reached the grand foyer to find Jefferson halting the unfamiliars from entering.

"Who is it, Jefferson?" He thought better of the question as he neared the front door and addressed the vagrants directly. "Who are you?"

A man with sallow cheeks and a sunburnt nose met his eye. "Sir," he said. "I'm Henry Casper and this is my wife, Ruth." He motioned to the hardest looking woman Augustus had ever seen. When he'd first glanced at her, he'd mistaken her for a small man. "Our apologies for coming at a late hour," the man said. He carried a bent roll of cartridge paper poking out of a haversack. "The windows were alight."

The two of them were depressing to look at and depleted the last of Augustus's energy. He was tired and fraught and did not care to make this couple feel comfortable in their imposition. "Have the pair of you just escaped a hogpen?" he asked. He felt himself inhabiting the manner in which Kimball had jibed him about his torn cuff. It still rankled him, and it felt good to give it back to someone, even if it wasn't Kimball he was giving it to.

The couple looked themselves over. The man answered, "No, sir. Just a long engine ride to see you."

"Well, the night is upon us—the time I feel my least tenderhearted. So, good night." He noticed a look pass between the couple before continuing. "And don't return tomorrow hoping for a different outcome." Jefferson had fallen away, his gaze low, no longer standing between the couple and Augustus.

The woman moved into the foyer. "Sir," she said to Augustus, "we understand you're the manufacturer of locomotives?"

"Not me personally, no. I employ warehouses full of men to do it for me." He rubbed the bridge of his nose. A headache was flourishing behind his eyes.

"But you own them?" the man asked, still outside the doorway. "The trains smacking into all the migrating buffalo out west are Windom trains, correct, sir? And harsh stops are what's causing your trains to rip up all that rail? Or am I wrong?"

"My trains are not to blame for shoddy rail."

The man (*What had he said his name was?*) shook his head. "That wouldn't be fair at all. But, just the same, sir, it's your engines on the rails, no?"

"Perhaps you do not receive national news where you're from, or know how to read it, but the locomotives belonged to my father up until his death four months ago."

"My sympathies, sir."

"*Your* sympathies." Augustus looked at the man as if he was a kitten who'd claimed to be a tiger. Augustus cleared his throat. "My patience has worn as thin as the threads in madam's dress." He turned into the hallway and retreated toward his chamber, calling over his shoulder to Jefferson. "See them to the street."

"No." He was halfway down the hall when he heard the woman shout, "No, sir. We've come all this way and I ain't withdrawing after such a mild overture."

Augustus completed his tromp back into his chamber. He listened for Jefferson's appeasement. His footman was no stranger to apologizing for Augustus's rudeness or making some other excuse for him. No matter. As long as they—

"Is that door locked?" he heard the woman ask from down the hall.

She must have been a madwoman to linger still. He heard Jefferson assure the couple the door was locked. It had little effect. The determined clatter of small boots came nearer, followed by the scurry of the other two sets of footsteps—each growing louder. Then came the yawn of his unlocked door opening wide. The woman had evidently felt compelled to settle the matter herself. She scuttled right on through, greeting Augustus with a put-upon scowl. "Now listen here," she said.

Augustus opened his desk drawer and retrieved a small pistol, the type that fired loud and spread messy. Cocked it. Aimed.

The surprise firearm slowed her, but didn't compel her to raise her hands, or crouch out of range, or call out to her husband—who had just now reached the entrance himself. To Augustus's point of view, she hadn't even looked at the damn thing, only at *him*, as if she'd expected a gun to enter into it sooner or later.

"Is your aim with that thing to kill me or just frighten me away?" she asked.

"Remind me of your names?"

"Ruth Casper, sir." She gestured back at the man. "Henry Casper."

"Ah. Well, Ruth and Henry Casper, do leave and don't return."

The woman lowered her hands and held them out. "Now calm it down. If you shoot me dead, you'll have to rid yourself of my mangled body and you already said you ain't got much steam left tonight."

Augustus had never heard a woman speak with as much mettle as this one had already done. It was off-putting. He was unaccustomed to the end of a pistol having so little effect. Perhaps he could reclaim some semblance of control by sitting in his chair.

The woman waved her husband into the room. "Mix in here, Henry. Don't force me to talk by my lonesome." She returned to Augustus with an unappealing smile. "Henry gets nervous."

"I ain't nervous," the man said, stepping forward and muttering to his wife.

"Whatever it is you hope to sell," Augustus said, "trust me, tonight is not the night I'm going to buy it."

The man, too, stood against the gun without looking at it, which suggested he'd been a soldier at one point. Experienced soldiers never looked at a gun. They'd seen enough of them in their time. Looking at a gun didn't change what would happen. Looking at the man holding it might. And that's where the man was looking when he opened his mouth to speak.

"I'm sorry for our imposition, sir. No one of proper mind would arrive to your door unannounced, intrude like we have, and expect to fall into your good graces."

"Then you can fucking leave and take with you the lessons of your error." His words did nothing to slow the couple.

"We come from Tennessee with a proposition," the woman cut in. "And if we weren't certain of its interest to you, we wouldn't waste your time with it."

"I don't care about your certainty." He had no curiosity for the pair. They soured his stomach. He did not like people trying to seduce him. More specifically, he did not want to keep company with people who thought he could be seduced.

The woman took a step forward and sank into the chair in front of his desk, a maneuver so brazen it stunned Augustus to see it unfold. She seemed inexplicably comfortable. Was she daring him to pull the trigger? If so, he thought it on account of his age. His youth had a way of urging out the rudeness in other people. They watched each other a moment before Augustus leaned forward on his elbows, happy to spell his arm from the full weight of the pistol.

"I don't have to fire this," he told her. "It works just fine as a bludgeon."

"Why don't you indulge us first and maim us after? That way, you'll never wonder if you made a mistake."

"My mistake is letting you spoil the air in this room with your putrid fucking body stink."

This quieted the woman, and Augustus was pleased to have gotten through to her. Sometimes, a bullet whizzing by a person's ear fixed the problem better than one buried in their skull.

"We've discerned, Mister Windom, sir," said the man, "that it's no easy task to get a man of your caliber to listen to people like us. So our patience is abundant."

"*Your* patience." Augustus was genuinely amused now with the gumption of these two.

The woman shot a glower at her husband and restated his sentiment. "We've prepared for resistance, is his meaning."

"Well, you arrive unannounced at a late hour, resistance is exactly what you'll find."

"I know, sir," the man said, "and we are most sorry. But we brung you something that requires a late hour to show off properly."

Augustus looked from the woman to the man and back again but kept the gun leveled on the woman. "Exactly what are you selling?"

After an impatient urging from the woman, the man slid into the seat beside her. "The Casper Air Brake, sir."

The woman added, "Patent pending."

"We've made brakes that stop trains—your trains—in a quarter of the time. Hundreds of yards sooner." The man spoke quickly, as if his success or failure was measured only by the speed with which the message was delivered. "You'll chew up less rail, won't drop as many wild animals, won't need brakemen, you can clip your payroll and add cars. A train with the Casper Air Brake would—"

The woman interjected again. "Patent pending."

"—would make the owner of it mighty wealthy."

"What is that to me? You're the owner."

"It would make anyone with that brake on their trains wealthy."

"I'm already wealthy," Augustus said.

"You won't be," said the woman. "Not if you shoo us out to go someplace else. Fit our brake over someone else's trains. Henry, what's harder to fathom—*gaining* ten million dollars or *losing* ten million dollars?"

The room was pregnant with silence awaiting Augustus's response.

"Losing, probably. To fathom losing ten million dollars, you'd have to fathom having it in the first place."

The woman nodded. "That's what we're selling, Mister Windom. Skirting the unfathomable."

The sand of these two.

They did not interact with each other the way Augustus imagined two married people ought to do. The pair in front of him seemed somehow distant. Perhaps they were swindlers engaged in a poor pantomime of marriage. He'd seen gamblers, politicians, desperate paupers, and men with moral sicknesses all abandon decorum in hopes of profit, but never before had he seen it to the extent of two cracked pots begging for his time only to tell him it's running out. It was enough to threaten the sobriety of even the most temperate of men.

"You're just about the goddamned spiciest tongued woman I've ever met," he said. "I don't relish conversing with you."

The woman chuckled. "I take that as a compliment."

"Then I said it wrong." His attention returned to Jefferson who clung to the doorway awaiting instruction, unsure what he should be doing. "Linger outside the door should I need you," he told the footman. Jefferson turned to leave. "And please, for God's sake, answer the front fucking door no more tonight."

With the footman gone, Augustus felt a change in the room. The air had shifted. He was outnumbered. But that was not his greatest concern. He was having a separate problem—in the last few minutes he'd turned curious. It irked him that he was no longer willing to dismiss these interlopers outright. They were having a different conversation now than the one they'd been having a moment ago. It felt like a defeat.

"How'd you come to Baltimore?" he asked.

"Windom train, sir," the man said. "Not far from here, we brought it to you."

"Brought *what* to me?"

"Your train."

"On the B and O track? Are you aware how many laws you're breaking?"

The woman chimed in. "Are you aware how serious we are?"

"You fortified one of my trains with your contraption and rode it into the city?"

"Yes, sir," said the man.

Augustus set the gun on the table. "You invented the contraption?" he asked the man.

"Yes."

"Not her?" He nodded in the woman's direction.

"No."

"Yet here she is. Part of the endeavor."

"Yes."

"What is her part, then?"

"Well…" A confused expression crinkled the man's face. "She's my wife."

"My part was to get us through the door," the woman said.

It was hard to argue.

"I could have you thrown in jail," Augustus said.

Both nodded at this. It, too, was hard to argue.

With a resigned sigh, Augustus asked, "What makes the brake superlative?"

The man pulled the paper roll from the bag he'd been holding at his side, loosened the twine and unrolled it onto the desk. Measurements and calculations peppered the mechanical drawings of a train and its isolated components. "Air, sir."

"That's why it's called the *Casper Air Brake*," said the woman. "Patent pendi—"

"Yes, yes. Patent pending. Patent pending." Augustus was too tired to mask his aggravation. "I'm under no illusion they granted your patent in the five minutes we've been sitting here."

She shrugged. "If you went through what we went through to get a pending patent, it would be every other phrase out of your mouth."

"We've trialed the brakes," the man said. "All with success, all on a Windom 2-6-0 Mogul."

Augustus's eyes traveled across the heavy paper, not quite sure what he was looking at.

"How did you come into possession of a Mogul?"

"Uh," said the man. "Well…"

The woman swung her meaty hand down over the drawings. "Can't allow you a lengthy lingering, Mister Windom. I don't know if you've heard—" She grinned. "—but the patent on this is *only still pending.*"

Her sass sent Augustus back in his chair.

"I apologize if I am misunderstanding your intentions here. How am I to evaluate my interest in your contraption if I cannot see it or know how it operates?"

"That's just it," the woman said. "We *want* you to see it. We *want* you to know how it operates." She pointed out the window. "That's why we brought the wares to you."

Augustus watched her collect the drawings and pass them to the man to finish rolling.

"You want me to board your train?"

"We do," the man said. "Though, to be precise, it's *your* train."

"I still wonder how it is you came into possession of it?"

"Cowardice and panic, mostly," the woman said. The man set his jaw. "The rest was luck."

"And you've come here, you dumb rubes with your boldness and grit, hoping to charm me into what, exactly?"

"Firstly, just getting you on that train, sir." The man leaned forward. "Showing you what it is we believe you'll want to see."

"And then?"

The woman smiled. "And then we'll negotiate a price to license what you saw."

Augustus studied them both, then returned the gun to the desk drawer. "Okay, Ruth and Henry Casper. Show me."

13

Augustus followed Henry Casper and his wife down the street toward the train and the Camden depot they'd kept it in. A small crowd of night laborers had suspended their activity to look upon the looming, still hot, Windom locomotive, out of place and hogging a main track.

The closer Augustus got to the depot the more murmurs of recognition followed alongside him. When they came upon the locomotive, it was clear they'd refortified it. "You're fortunate no other train rolled this track," he said.

The Casper woman was the first to climb aboard. "I guess that makes you fortunate, too," she said. "Seeing as how one day you'll tell stories of this night."

Henry climbed on next, while Augustus remained on the ground inspecting the bulky brake apparatus.

"Jesus." Faced now with evidence they were telling the truth, Augustus found it harder to contemplate. "You've really...Jesus," he said again. "You really fortified this locomotive with a different brake?"

The gathered crowd had increased by the minute. The train had become flypaper. No one who walked toward it walked away. Even passersby without any business at the depot stopped. Most passersby out at midnight hadn't anywhere that required their immediate presence.

As Augustus climbed onto the cab, Ruth fed wood into the furnace and shouted over the engine's panting. "We planned for this late hour in hopes of avoiding a crowd. They came by their own curiosity. We ain't used to so many gawkers. In Chattanooga, a man's full acreage could go up in a brushfire and he'd be the only one to see it."

"Are you an engineer?" Augustus asked.

Henry called over his shoulder. "Used to be. Engined the East Tenn Railroad before the war. Then the South Side Railroad during it." He pulled the choke chain on the train's whistle out of habit and let the beast bellow. Then he turned and pointed to the tender's crossbar behind all three of them and told Augustus to hold on to it.

"Why?" Augustus asked.

The train lurched. They were rolling forward.

"Because the demonstration's begun, sir."

Ruth leaned over the side of the lookout while shouting back to Augustus. "What good's a brake demonstration on a stopped train?" Her ragged hair had come undone from its netting and spun in strands around her shoulders.

Usually the engineer or the handlers had to loosen the brake wheels before the train started moving. All the Caspers had done was heat the furnace. But a larger concern had pushed aside the oddness of the train's start.

"You can't canter a horse in this town without a fine," Augustus barked. "Do not take this train past ten miles per hour." In truth, his concern was his own safety, not city laws.

They'd exited the depot and moved south along Howard. The train's noise made it so shouting was the only way to be heard.

"Just passed five miles per hour," Henry yelled.

An uneasy gurgle formed in Augustus's stomach as the smattering of onlookers below slid by quicker and quicker. "Where is your brakeman?" Augustus was equal parts agitated and concerned. "I said where's your—"

"Don't need one," Ruth shouted over her shoulder, too focused on the track ahead to do anything else.

Augustus called out, "This is reckless!" The train lurched again and advanced speed. The motion jerked him forward. He lost footing and was on one knee. He recovered and held onto the bar Henry had asked him to find a moment before. "Stop this goddamned train."

"Oh, we will." Ruth whooped.

Augustus realized what was happening. He was being kidnapped. He considered jumping off the locomotive, but it was picking up speed and the moonless night shielded him from the mysteries below. "Stop, goddammit!" He leaned forward to kick Henry, but his grip on the crossbar restrained him and he missed his target by several feet. Missed by so much neither Casper even noticed.

The train had turned on Putnam and was heading north, making a wide circle around the western part of the city. Henry called out that they'd reached twenty miles per hour.

Augustus's hat had taken flight into the darkness and away forever, leaving nothing between his hair and heaven. He was mortified. "Brake, you bastards!"

He'd never been on a train going faster than thirty and, in those instances, he hadn't been standing in the engine cab exposed like this. His face tightened. He did not want to admit he was powerless to stop what was happening. Not only had he been duped into his own kidnapping, but it was aboard a locomotive boasting his own name.

He stood like a newborn fawn, legs splayed and shaking. He was pale. "Where are you going?" he screamed. No answer. He went wild eyed. The panic was made plain on his face.

The wind slapped them around. Augustus bent his knees and widened his stance and held tighter to the crossbar, hoping they would not collide with anything along the track and, if they did, that their deaths would be immediate. He did not know where to focus his eyes or if he should close them. He desired to be shut of the horrible vision of his own death, but those visions were contrived from within. To close his eyes would mean giving his imagination the stage unobstructed. He was a well-known figure and it would not do to appear so cowardly. Although, if this speeding train ended up slaughtering the citizenry and taking his own life in the process, it was best to appear in protest of it all.

He only had a vague sense of location. It was dark. The train and the wind were the only sounds he heard. He listened for a scream or meaty thuds or an explosion. There were half a million people in the city proper and if any one of them wandered onto the track at the exact wrong time it would be disastrous.

Henry pulled on the train's whistle chain, maintaining a firm grip so the ten-ton iron banshee screaming into the Mt. Clare Station would not take any stray rail hands by surprise.

One last curve and then they went shooting on a long straightaway down Pratt. Henry shouted, "Forty per!"

Unable to see past the train interior, Augustus focused on the Caspers. They were both reveling at the whooshing world before them like two pups lapping up wind drifts from a hill.

"Please...stop," Augustus screamed, breathless.

"Coming up on the Falls turn," Henry yelled.

Every uptick in speed felt to Augustus as if it would cause his heart to burst from his chest. His eyes had become dry. He felt his pomaded hair tighten at the hairline, the wind yanking at the roots. His face burned.

Henry gave the whistle one last blow as the train made the turn and sent all three of them swinging to the right.

Ruth gave Henry a signal and shortly thereafter the wheels underneath them clacked. All other sound drowned in the squelch of careening metal. Something pumped underneath their feet. A hissing chorus of released air followed. The report inside the cab had become deafening as it slid along the metal rails.

Augustus's head dropped. He felt sick. He had become too frightened to call out. Flashes of imagined massacres circled his mind. A cart. Horses. Driver. Splashes of blood. Threads of tendon. The train would send the pulpy carnage hurtling through the street. He could no longer keep his eyes open. He screamed again and continued screaming. Had he not curled his arm around the crossbar he surely would have gone tumbling into infinity. He had no awareness of what was going on around him for a long while until a rough hand rested on his shoulder.

He opened his eyes. His head was pounding but lacked the disturbance of sound. Had he gone deaf? He looked up to see the woman urging him, it seemed, to uncrumple and stand up.

Moments ago, a hot, gray maelstrom had swallowed Baltimore. Now it was calm. Augustus's hearing returned and he loosened his grip on the crossbar enough to ensure he would not fall face first onto the cab's grimy floor. The world had returned to him and, with it, the realization that he had not died, nor had anyone else.

He looked to Henry and found him leaning against the storage pan, a pleased look on his face, cockier than the king of diamonds. The urge to knock the teeth out of his skull was overwhelming. The jaw was a fine target, jutting away from the face as it did. Punch a man in the cheek or ribs, the puncher's hand might fracture. Punch a man in the chin, it was the surest way to put him on the ground without employing bullets or sharps.

Augustus had never struck another person before, though he'd often fantasized about making good, square contact with the cap of someone's jawbone—a fantasy that had bitten him since he was nine, after his father shattered the will of Caldwell Begone on the lawn of their home. What would have happened if Begone continued his path and walloped his father? How would fate have differed? The jaw Augustus had targeted most in his fantasies had always been his father's.

Something twisted inside Augustus now. It admonished him for being too weak kneed and urged him not to repeat the mistakes of his past. He was outside himself. Beside himself. The feeling joined with other lingering resentments and wrongings. It joined with the memory of Broussais Kimball manhandling him at the Orange Street Club, and his engineer Frank Marcy walking out on him, and a lifetime under Leopold Windom's thumb. It felt as if every slight ever imposed, whether imagined or not, had journeyed from his mind, his heart, his balls, and his throat in that moment. They'd all united in his fist.

The swing came flying out of him. Wide. Loose. Poorly aimed.

Henry was too slow to avoid it, though, and the shot caught him in the neck. His Adam's apple pushed against his windpipe. Collapsed him. He retreated. Eyes bulging. He held his throat and made a choked honking cough that rose above the steam sounds of the settling train.

Ruth moved between them without thought for her own safety, but the fight was well over. Henry's expression suggested he'd been struck dumb. Augustus, meanwhile, did his best to shake away the pain zinging up his hand. All the fight in him was gone.

The woman came into focus. He'd forgotten about her.

She faced Henry, asking if he'd be okay. He was coughing and water eyed, but he nodded that he'd live. She returned to Augustus. "Do you see, Mister Windom?"

She gestured over her shoulder to Lancaster Street, overlooking the Mathews Shipyard. It was a busy location, but everyone had stopped all activity in the locomotive's screaming wake. The docks were silent now. Aghast. The laborers had dropped their crates and riggings and sidled toward the train. The gathering crowd was bigger than the one that had watched them leave. Deeper and more curious. Sleepy priests from the Church of St. Luke, mechanics, messengers making late deliveries, shipmen, and freighters, all shouldered together, every one of them having suspended their comings and goings to gape at the locomotive just yards away from the track's end.

Augustus watched the crowd approach. He misread their excitement for anger and readied for riot. The clamoring factions grew, and he realized they were not the sounds of hisses but of cheers, each one addressing the train and its riders as wondrous heroes. Tamers of runaway dragons.

Henry had regained control of himself but remained bent over, rubbing his throat.

Augustus, too, hunched over his sore hand, rubbing the bone. Ruth leaned down to where he'd wilted. She asked again if he saw where they'd stopped. He straightened and looked about, realizing just now where they were.

Those in the vicinity had clumped together into small pockets of gossipers recounting to the late arrivers the feat they'd just witnessed— that a locomotive traveling faster than a fired cannonball around the Falls Street turn had come to a full stop one hundred-fifty yards later.

A hissing sound bellowed from underneath them, which Augustus guessed must have been the air brake system that had both saved all their lives and put them in jeopardy to begin with.

Ruth reached for him, grabbed both of his arms and gathered him up. "Are you impressed?"

He did not like to be touched, but he was too distracted to warn her against touching him. The answer to her question shot through his center and rattled around his bones. It surprised him.

Yes.

Yes, of course he was impressed. And furious. And frightened. It altogether hollowed him out until there was no distinct singular feeling present at all. But he did not respond in kind. Instead he asked, "Were we truly traveling as fast as you say? Were we traveling forty?"

She shouted over the general ruckus, "No, sir. I'm sorry to say we were not." She gripped his shoulders. "We were traveling fifty."

At two in the morning, several hours after the "Run on the Rails," the Caspers followed Augustus from the docks to the City Hotel where he rented them a room. It was a high-toned spot on the second floor, a balcony suite overlooking Calvert. Neither Ruth nor Henry spoke to Augustus until they'd arrived in the room—holding the belief, perhaps, that he was under a spell and to speak would break it. He'd paid for the room for the next three months, through the New Year. Arranged for two meals for the both of them to be included each day.

They tromped up the stairs behind Augustus, all three windswept and wide eyed. He showed them their room. The finest decor and ornamentation in the city greeted the Caspers as they looked on in gape-mouthed awe. They pawed at the velvet drapes and the brass bed's satin sheets. Teardrop crystals hung from the chandelier. Damask ottomans sat obediently at the foot of four matching chairs. Augustus felt the outside breeze whisk his cheek as the Caspers gawked at the activity still happening below their balcony at this hour. There were not one, but two wash basins, which Ruth eyed excitedly.

Augustus let them enjoy themselves for a moment before explaining what he expected in return for his hospitality. "You've brought me this magnificent machine, and I aim to do business," he said. "But you've surprised me. You've come unannounced and I cannot simply toss you all the money in the world on a whim."

Ruth was not satisfied. "Mister Windom, I was under the impression you were one of the few people in this world in the precise position to do exactly that."

"No," he said, trying to keep his annoyance from rupturing in full. He still did not like these people, didn't care to be in their company, but they'd given him an unassailable reason to keep them close. "I cannot simply pay you and be done, unless you aim to accept only a pittance of what the apparatus is worth."

"No, sir. But I'd like to know what you think it's worth."

"I certainly haven't decided that just now."

"Maybe it's not you doing the deciding."

A tray of crystal decanters awaited their attention on a marble center table. Each decanter brimmed with liquids in various syrup shades. Augustus helped himself to a glass and poured himself a drink. He held the glass up to the flickering light from lamps set around the room's edges. "Thrice distilled," he said, proof enough of its quality. In one swallow, he finished the glass and returned it to the tray before continuing.

He picked up the conversation right where he'd dropped it. "It truly is a miracle, your brake. I could not have imagined it before this night and therefore I have no figure to offer. But we will work something out, Caspers. I am certain we will."

There were no sounds except for the clomping of hooves outside until Augustus inhaled deeply and smiled at Ruth. "How this will work is, you'll stay here for as long as is necessary," he said to her.

"Necessary to what?" Henry asked.

"To determine how I am to go about fitting the brakes onto my trains. I aim to act quickly, but I cannot work overnight."

Ruth nodded. "It's nearly three. You're not far from working overnight."

Augustus shot her a needlegrass glare. But, in truth, the late hour was an excellent excuse for him to leave. "I'll send my man in the coming days. He'll discuss the brake further."

"In the coming days?" repeated Ruth.

"Correct."

"And once the day comes, what's your man gonna say that you can't say right now?"

Augustus opened both arms and gestured to the luxuriant room. "Are you in a hurry, madam?"

She straightened her back. "Look here, sir, we've given you a train that stopped quicker than Lincoln's enjoyment of the theater. Now I *am* grateful, but gratitude rides only so far."

"My, but you *are* a church bell, aren't you?" He squared on Henry. "She ever stop ringing?" Henry didn't answer. Just skimmed his hand along his wife's back to calm the messages of death written across her face. "I can't tell you what I don't know," Augustus continued. "In the coming days I'll know more. And so will my man."

"Your man have a name?" Ruth asked.

"Uriah Rathbone. He's my aide-de-camp. He's also a former Pinkerton."

"You're sending a lawman?" Henry looked distraught.

"Former lawman," Augustus said. "These days he's a private enforcer only."

"Why won't you be the one we see in the coming days?" Ruth asked.

Augustus leaned against the doorjamb, making clear his exasperation at explaining himself to this pair of rubes. "Every man who works for me has orders he is to follow for the next six months. I have to go to the stockholders, distributors, foremen, engineers, stevedores, rail agents, and the like and tell every one of them that not only has the plan changed, but it's changed drastically. In three hours, your train is going to be on the front page of every newspaper in the city. And then the country. The world is going to tilt, you understand? And, because of that tilt, I cannot remain here. I must be out there ensuring your brake appears on shipments sooner rather than later."

Ruth swallowed hard. "A million dollars."

Augustus believed he knew to what she was referring but would require her to expand before reacting in full.

She continued. "I know you have a number in your head, Mister Windom. So do we. You can license the brake from us for a million dollars. You said it yourself. The world is going to tilt."

"And you want to make certain you catch every coin that falls out of it?"

"Yes, sir."

He shrugged. "All right. I'll not push you on price, but you mustn't push me on time. I'll send my man in the coming days."

Ruth nodded. Taking a cue from his wife, Henry nodded too.

Having nothing more to say, Augustus turned and left them to wonder if he'd have agreed to an even higher number.

The night's recounting ran on the front page of every morning paper, including the *Sun*.

WINDOM TRAIN RACES TO HARBOR
INDUSTRIALIST STUNT THRILLS CITY POPULACE
Baltimore, Wednesday, October 4—1:30 A.M.

A six-wheeled locomotive rolled at high speeds through the city last night. Manned by Augustus Windom, president of Windom & Fairbanks Locomotive Works, it appeared uncontrolled for almost a mile until sparking to a sudden halt at the Lancaster docks.

The train reached Perry Street within two minutes of its launch and rounded the B&O circle to move eastward. Witnesses described no evidence of braking as it came around the Falls Street turn. Those in the vicinity scattered hither and yon to escape the train's path, its plunge into the river seeming, at that moment, an inevitability. Within a matter of 200 feet, however, the locomotive made a dead stop. The excitement that followed was of the wildest description. The throng burst, abruptly chanting "Windom! Windom!" into the night.

After taking several minutes to confer with his engineer, the locomotive magnate emerged from his train and shook hands with the midnight populace who had no interest in returning to the nearby steamers. Mister Windom made no formal statement.

SECOND DISPATCH
Baltimore, Wednesday, October 4—7:00 A.M.
The secret to the stop is the Windom Air Brake. Augustus Windom, having reboarded his "Waterfront Miracle" after a half-hour of glad tidings from the area's dockworkers, stated his company had been developing a revolutionary braking system able to stop quickly, safely, and without additional cost to the rider. He went on to describe the stunt as the brake's introduction to the world.

The lingering crowd interrupted the statement for over a minute with applause and revelry. When Windom continued, he said he expects to fortify every one of his trains with the "new Windom Air Brake," including those trains set to embark west to help in the building of the Transcontinental Railroad. He did not provide details as to how the train was able to stop with such precision, stating, "Ours is to labor. Yours is to enjoy the fruits of it." The locomotive will remain at the dock end of the tracks for a public viewing Friday.

Paper after paper offered the same excited front-page praise. They called it the "Pratt Street Sensation" and "Supernatu-rail." Not a single word written mentioned the Caspers by name.

14

It had been Augustus's finest hour, but it confronted him with the tricky position of now having to behave as if *he* had created the brake, despite having no knowledge whatever of how it functioned. And having thus acted, without forethought to the consequences of his claims, all the next day he retreated from his home and work, where the public eye could follow, and into the relative privacy of the Orange Street Club.

He and Rathbone hid on the second floor playing gin. The game was meant as a distraction, but their continued talk around the previous night's event ensured no distraction was to be had. Augustus would have preferred they not discuss it. Not now. Not until he could wrestle his mind around what it was he had.

Rathbone, contrary-wise, saw the evening's doings as a flaw in their professional arrangement. He'd left his man for the night. It was in his leaving that the Caspers were allowed to abscond with Augustus. "I don't have to be in your pocket to keep you guarded," he said. "If I'd remained close, they'd never have spirited you away."

"Quiet your voice."

The agent looked around, as if to question the purpose of speaking in hushed tones. They were tucked into a corner table of the club's grand ballroom, out of sight of the dozens of others present elsewhere in the building.

"You've got a foul disposition," Rathbone said. "You'd do yourself a favor to be rid of it."

Augustus had read the descriptions of himself in the day's newspapers and did not recognize the man described there. He felt no confidence, no triumph. He was not amidst a moment of celebration. He felt only the increased gurgle of red-hot anger in his belly. It was as if the newspapers had validated his feelings about himself and, instead of enjoying the adulation, it only reminded him of those who would deny his brilliance. To be validated only made the denials more offensive to him. Leopold Windom had intimidated men like Broussais Kimball, and now they all had the indecency to take that intimidation out on Augustus. He was not excited by his good fortune. Rather, he was excited his good fortune would taste bitter in the mouths of his detractors.

"Where are your abductors, anyway?" Rathbone asked. Augustus sighed like a child, frustrated by having to converse on the topic further. He stalled, swapping a few of the playing cards in his hand with the cards piled on the table. Rathbone changed his own subject. "Your father hated all your secret keeping."

Augustus waved this away, as if rejecting its very notion. "They are at the City Hotel. In a room I've rented for them." This instigated a raised eyebrow from Rathbone. Augustus shrugged in defense. "I offered him a job. He accepted. We discussed no terms. It was late."

"It's unusual to ignore terms, no matter the hour."

"That is unusual," Augustus agreed and drew his pipe. "It's also unusual to leave a train in the open where my engineers can inspect how it functions. Wouldn't you agree?"

Rathbone was dubious. "They're just sitting in a hotel room? Waiting?"

Augustus nodded. "And we are picking over their creation right now, as I sit here speaking to you." He puffed his pipe. "They have nothing. They're nobody. They will wait until the heavens fall."

"That's quite a big gamble from a man discommoded by risk."

"What risk? They've arrived to me unprotected and I aim to show their folly in having done so."

Rathbone leaned in. "So the brake is real?"

A thin plume of smoke swirled from the side of Augustus's puckered lips. "You're concerned it's a trick?"

Now it was Rathbone's turn to shrug defensively. "I've seen an escapist in wristlets free himself from a locked trunk. Now, I don't know how he did it, but I don't believe his bones are made of sealing wax. What I'm saying is, if the brake *was* a trick, I'd be curious to know how you did it and I could help keep it secret."

"Not telling you would also help keep it secret."

"So it *is* a trick?"

Augustus leaned in and whispered. "It's not a trick. Added to which, I suspect you've overestimated my level of distraction." He fanned his cards face up in front of him. "Gin."

Rathbone fell back in his seat. The gloominess of losing had come over him. Augustus gathered the discarded deck, riffled the stack a few times, and dealt again, tossing the cards higgledy-piggledy in alternating piles between them.

When the silence wore out its welcome, Rathbone leaned forward. "How do you know the two Rebs aren't swindlers?"

Augustus nodded. "I considered that. That's why I'm having Frank Marcy pore over the locomotive."

"And if your engineer verifies it?"

"Then every train I own is going to have one of those goddamn air brake systems on it."

"You're gonna pay them the million they asked for?"

Augustus leaned away. "I didn't say that."

"If they're smart enough to build the thing, then aren't they smart enough to keep you from stealing it?"

"We'll see." Augustus shook his head. "I'm going to Washington in two days."

"What are you doing there?"

"I'm patenting my new air brake."

The look on Rathbone's face was a tincture of delight and caution. "You little charlatan."

"If you are to be a help to me, you best be a charlatan, too."

"So you *do* want me to help you?"

"I need you to keep them happy while I'm away. It won't be difficult at first, but they'll wonder soon enough where I've gone."

"How long will you be away?"

Augustus shrugged and shook his head.

Broussais Kimball suddenly appeared with three snub glasses of whiskey and ice. When Augustus and Rathbone had been alone in the wide chamber, it had felt small and safe. With the addition of a third, the room appeared altogether cavernous and cold.

"There you are," Kimball said to Augustus. "Hidden from the warm flicker of public attention. It was a nice touch, young Windom, decorating that train with bunting for the public viewing."

Placing the draped cloth over the train was one of the first things Augustus had his staff do. Kimball's mention of it was unnerving. The lawyer was such an astute antagonizer, Augustus assumed whatever attracted his attention was a foolhardy maneuver. If Augustus could have snapped his fingers and, a mile away, the bunting would disappear, he'd have done it that very moment.

"You *are* fond of displaying your paragons to the masses, aren't you?" Kimball asked.

"Pardon?"

"First your father and now this locomotive. You're keen on grand displays, are you not?"

Augustus shook his head. He was in no mood. "A friendly game of gin needs no third, Broussais."

Kimball ignored the hint. "You've got the rabble climbing the surrounding rooftops to get a better view of the thing."

"People always clamor to glimpse the future." Augustus was careful not to cross his arms or bob his knee or signal in any other way how uncomfortable Kimball made him feel.

The lawyer set down the three glasses and pulled up an open chair. "I come to drink with you, young Windom." He scooted one glass toward Augustus and another toward Rathbone, lifted his own whiskey and swigged. He licked around his lips and looked at Rathbone, who appeared coiled. Not agitated, by any means, but ready to find his feet. "That's your drink, friend," Kimball told Rathbone.

"That is not my drink and you are not my friend," Rathbone said, locking a firm scowl on Kimball. "You spent up four words and three of them were false."

Kimball chuckled and pointed to Rathbone with his thumb. "Now there's a man who wants to wallop me," he said to Augustus before retrieving the morning edition of the *Gazette*. He read aloud. "'It is a testament to the growing popularity of rail travel—and also to Windom's evident ingenuity—that he has emerged from his father's death not only one of the wealthiest men in the country but also one of its greatest visionaries.'" He scoffed and returned the paper to the pile as if it had left a residue on his fingers.

"I know how you see me," Augustus said. "No need to belabor it."

"Let's remove all doubt on the matter." Kimball halved the remaining portion of his drink in one hard swig. "I see you as a vile coward. I'm quite certain you're too much of a cowheart to have intentionally put yourself at risk. So I was surprised to read the illogical reports of your having planned something both brilliant and brave." He clinked the edge of his glass with the one he'd brought for Augustus, still on the table where he'd placed it. "This is why I've come, boy. To congratulate you on fooling them all."

Augustus smiled and continued rearranging the cards in his hand. He was doing his best to weather Kimball's henpecking.

"No response?" Kimball leaned on his folded arms and studied Augustus, like a bear sniffing for food. "You bring that lie into my club and then haven't the sand to defend it when it's challenged?"

"*Your* club?" Augustus asked. "What of it do *you* own?" He hated the waver in his own voice.

"A club is not made by walls and floors, but by those who populate it. As long as I populate it, you're sitting in *my* club."

"I won't be baited."

Kimball laughed. "That's what a coward would say."

Rathbone slid away from the table.

Kimball rolled his head in an exaggerated motion toward Rathbone and then back again to Augustus. "The thug's presence by your side doesn't exactly refute my claim of your cowardice, does it?"

"If you want me expelled from the club, Broussais, the board will have to vote on it."

Kimball lit his tightly packed churchwarden. "Have your vote, popinjay. I'll enjoy seeing it go my way."

Augustus gave the table one quick, flat whack. It caused the ice in the glasses to clink. "Broussais, be honest. When it's dark and you are alone, you know, don't you?"

"Know what?" Kimball asked.

Out came that curdled smile of Augustus's. "You know your wife died so's to escape another day with you?" Augustus surprised himself to have said it.

Kimball's face sobered. He leaned over the table and slapped Augustus across the mouth. Struck him hard enough to split his lip and clack his teeth. The sound bounced around the high-ceilinged ballroom, then retreated like a tattling child.

Rathbone stood, planting his feet like a dropped bag of flour. His breath was steady, his hands hovering near his holstered pistols.

Kimball squared up on Rathbone, fists balled. He drawled, the pipe bobbing between his teeth. "If he's going to choose those words and that tone with me," Kimball warned the agent, "next time he better have forty of you standing behind him when he does it."

Kimball was a good six inches taller than Rathbone and outweighed him by a hundred pounds, but Rathbone had two pistols at his hips and extra men outside in carriages.

Oh no, Augustus thought, *everyone in the club must have heard that slap.* The pain and indignity of being struck by a Kodiak bear did not come into play until several seconds after the shock subsided. It felt more like a punch. Kimball could do more damage with his thick pork chop of an open hand than Augustus could do with two closed fists. He hadn't moved or made a sound, though his cheek was screaming. It was an uncooked meat shade of pink where Kimball's palm had met him, and a dribble of blood appeared on his lip.

"And you will take it," Kimball said to Augustus. "Because, if you open your mouth again, you know I'll put my boot in it." He took a long, final swallow of his whiskey and upturned the glass on the felt. "If I ever see you in this building again, I'm going to throw you off the balcony and I'll have a smile on my face while I do it. All in favor? Aye." He looked from Augustus to Rathbone and back again. "All opposed?" No one played along. He shrugged. "The ayes have it." He straightened his jacket and tottered back downstairs.

Rathbone waited until Kimball was out of sight before returning to his seat. "Are you hurt?"

Augustus ran his tongue along his back teeth. "That remains an open question."

"He is not a man quick to combat. Why couldn't you hold it in?"

"I *have* held it in. My whole life has demanded I hold in one thing or another." He licked at the blood sliding down his lower lip.

"Well, you just burned that bridge."

"Fine by me. I never wanted to be a member here." He was in a daze. "I don't care what happens to this place."

The glass that Kimball had left for him remained at Augustus's elbow. He leaned forward and pushed it off the table's edge with his forearm. It shattered. Rathbone watched him do it but made no effort to stop him. His concern was larger than spilled whiskey and broken glass.

"There are two ways off a burning bridge," Augustus said. "Jump off or hope for rain." He pulled a pair of double eagle coins from his vest. "Help me leap off this burning fucking bridge."

Rathbone took the coins, inspecting them for answers to whatever madness had bitten his man.

"Find two cook maids. Downstairs. Any two. Doesn't matter. Give each of them one of those coins and tell them it's from me. Tell them to rush the hallways yelling fire. Caterwaul. Make a ruckus. Make certain they get everyone running. Empty this place out. Tell them there will be no repercussions." Rathbone nodded. "Have your men help in the endeavor. When everyone goes running, be sure your men are holding them out there." Rathbone remained seated, searching for absent words. "No dawdling," Augustus said, and waited for his agent to disappear down the grand staircase.

It happened in less than three minutes. Augustus remained seated listening to the clatter explode from the floor below. It started with an undefined crash and then the clearer sounds of two women banging pots together screaming *Fire! Fire!* Then the more authoritative gunmen's voices commanding everyone to leave.

Augustus did not move. He waited. And he listened. The heavy thrum of worried club members hurrying through the exits sounded like charging buffalo. He listened to the burst of panicked commotion go out the front doors as the cook maids continued their fracas from the back. Augustus tingled. If he had quills, they'd have pointed straight out of his body.

The banquet hall was still. Only the gentle rise and fall of Augustus's chest animated the room. But, below, a crowd had bloomed in the street. He stood and moved to the balcony connected to the banquet hall by a pair of French doors. The bolt holding closed the doors was stuck. He gave it a few artless swipes with his fists before jarring it loose with some resentment.

He flattened his jacket to his chest and approached the stone ledge like the lone remaining God on Olympus. He looked down at the evacuated. They huddled in packs below. Flecked among them were Augustus's hired guns, Rathbone guarding the front entrance. The members were restless and confused, two states most unfamiliar to them. They stood in the chilled air, coattails wagging, and, for some, hat brims gripped to keep them from tumbling away.

When Augustus appeared at the balcony's edge, every man looked upon him in offense. Some had started leaving the grounds but stopped. The scene had gone quiet except for the cleated flags on either side of Augustus snapping in the breeze.

"You've all made a terrible mistake," he bellowed, still rubbing at the grease spot on his hand where he'd banged the door bolt. "You've overestimated the amount of discourtesy I'm willing to endure." He paused to wet his lips and regain enough saliva to keep his tongue from getting thick. "From now on, you'll either tender courtesy to me willingly or have it wrung out of you like dishwater from a dirty rag." He stood above them, pouring out his ire like red hot lead over the castle wall.

For the second time in a week, a great number of onlookers had stopped to witness a public Windom spectacle. The club was an alluring Second Empire-style building that would have attracted the attention of anyone passing by even without the crowd out front. Indeed, no one on the street could ignore it. Several club members looked to see Kimball's reaction, but he only squinted up toward the balcony, blankly registering the situation.

Augustus had grown emboldened by the audience. He was no longer planning, no longer reasoning, no longer hoping for rain. He would bring the rain himself, even if it meant standing above and spitting.

"My father would have been proud to someday see my pipe behind the glass cases of this club, but…" He waved his hand at his side as if discarding a rough draft of that life. "…he would have been prouder to see me burn it to the ground for all the disrespect its members have shown us both." He said it, but he was uncertain his father would have agreed. "Setting fire to this place would not change how you estimate me. Understand me—you will sway by my rhythm or you will be flung to the fucking heavens." His voice rose and rebellowed off the grand club's walls behind him before rolling through the wide street. It was a big, pleasing sound. "So buck up when you find yourselves around me, men."

The men looked to one another for some sign of what to do next.

Kimball gazed upward, untroubled. His hands were behind his back as if waiting for his carriage to arrive. "You've no authority," he called out. He was speaking just as much to those surrounding him as to Augustus. "You've worked us into a panic under false pretenses and now you threaten us with expulsion from a club of which you are no longer a member? You're no more than a louse."

"Oh, but I *am* more than that." Augustus reached inside his waistcoat and pulled out a folded document. It came unfurled with some difficulty in the wind, but he endured and held it out for those below to see. It was a symbolic gesture. Fluttering in the wind at that distance, no one below could have authenticated it. In actuality, it had been a letter draft to the Baltimore Police Commissioner apologizing for the air brake stunt and offering a generous donation to the department coffers.

"This is the deed to the building and the land upon it, gentleman. I'm your new landlord. And, as such, I'll honor few previous tenant agreements. I'd as soon write them away with a swipe of my pen and replace them with new ones. Starting with this one, Mister Kimball. No fat sacks of pompous fuckery allowed on the premises as long as I draw breath."

Kimball nodded, then said, "He speaks from a distance, knowing that, if he came any closer, I'd rip out his throat." This was Kimball's true gift—bending any scenario to a view that made him appear stronger than he was. He continued. "Is it really your aim to return inside, having abandoned everyone out here at the doorstep?"

"Not everyone, Broussais. Just you." Augustus leaned over the balcony in search of Rathbone. He hadn't moved from his front door post. "Mister Rathbone," he said, "fetch this man's topper, please." Rathbone looked up at Augustus from under his bowler. "You'll recognize it," Augustus continued. "It's made not only from the finest silk and beaver, but also from the *most* silk and beaver, what to accommodate that fat fucking head of his."

This seemed a good enough description for Rathbone who disappeared inside. The committee members shuffled in place, murmuring to one another.

"Do you believe this will end here, Augustus?" Kimball asked, his tone alluding to his own answer.

Augustus spoke to the remaining agents. "That man is no longer welcome in this building," he said, pointing to Kimball. "If he tries to enter, shoot him for trespassing."

The herd of club members took several subtle paces away from Kimball. They did not acknowledge this move and, in fact, tried to hide it. But, from Augustus's vantage point, the migration was clear.

Augustus called down to one of his men and told him the others were free to return to the building. He leaned forward, feeling cocky. "I want you to watch this, Broussais. I want you to watch as each one of your friends abandons you."

Kimball did, indeed, watch. It was not dissimilar to a funeral march, each silent man filing in with his head buried in his chest.

"And now I want you to notice, old man, that you are alone. Do you see it down there? Do you see it as clearly as I do up here?" Kimball's face was clear of expression as he stared at Augustus, not acknowledging his peers leaving him. "No rebuttal? You threaten and belittle me not ten minutes hence, you call this place yours, and now you haven't anything further to say?" The moment gratified Augustus. It satisfied some sunken fathom of his soul. For a moment, he felt like his father.

Kimball stood before the club, not as a man expelled, but as an ogre preparing to storm the building. He gritted his teeth and reared back three steps like a bull before reaching into his coat pocket for the revolver hidden within. His maneuver was clumsy and, before he could complete it, the agents had trained their own pistols and froze him in place. A half-dozen barrels pointed at him. The still-gathered crowd along the street cried out.

"Assume these men will not act in half measures," Augustus called down. "Their contract stipulates they are to be paid in full at year's end with a hefty percentage forfeited if I am harmed before. You strike me down, they don't get paid."

As Kimball slowly unhanded his waistcoat, Rathbone emerged from inside with the man's hat. He carried it down the steps before flinging it the rest of the way. It landed near Kimball's feet, blowing cobble dust out from under it. The agent faced Kimball, hands on both holstered pistol grips, daring him to try for his revolver again. Kimball refrained. Instead, he cast his eyes down at his discarded hat. His thick thatch of hair clung to his head, slick with sweat and pomade.

Kimball's soft words to Rathbone carried in the wind. "If you were going to shoot, you'd have done it upstairs."

"You didn't make a play for your gun upstairs."

"Well, then, why don't we both drop our weapons and see if you're still inclined to treat my wardrobe like that."

The agent shook his head. "If we dropped our weapons, you'd overmatch me by a hundred pounds. I prefer overmatching you by six shots."

Augustus could not see from his angle, but he was sure the rest of the members were all peering out from the windows, each of them watching Kimball just as Augustus had watched Caldwell Begone fall to his father those years ago.

Augustus called down. "Mister Rathbone, make sure he leaves before you."

Rathbone nodded once in acknowledgment. Nothing moved along Orange Street. Even the breeze seemed to have held off. Augustus turned and went inside, shutting the balcony doors behind him. He took one last peek as Kimball bent to fetch his hat and withdrew into the slackening crowd. Inside, Augustus's shoulders drooped, and his hands shook. His lip was damp underneath his mustache despite the cool day. He descended the main staircase, at the foot of which stood the dazed club members—chattering in hushed groups or staring out the windows. They had reddened amidst their fury, or the chill outside, or both. The gunmen all remained near the front door awaiting commands like obedient mutts. The confused staff loitered along the edges of the great room and the parlor.

Augustus spoke as if still in open air. "Do any of you protest?" He waited. Looked at every man who stared back. "Well bless you all for cowering."

He moved to the Regency Room, closing himself in and stopping to listen at the door, curious what might happen now that he had removed himself from the rabble. Another instance of pressing his ear to a door. The absence of noise tempted him to return to the parlor. He imagined them all still standing in unspeaking clumps like dim children. He thought better of it and instead found the chair at the table's head and eased into it, careful not to pollute the silence with sound. He watched the door, awaiting a reckoning for what he'd just done. Surely someone would object. Someone would counter. Someone would show him a flaw in his hasty calculation.

No one came. Not Rathbone or the remaining board members, or the club staff. He sat staring into the middle distance, allowing whatever spirit had taken hold of him to leave his empty body behind. A snuff of laughter left his nostrils at the sight of blood. In his haste and fury, he hadn't noticed the cut trickling from his hand after having punched open the balcony door bolt. He gripped the armrests and watched the door in front of him, ignoring the fact that of everyone in the club, the only blood he'd drawn was his own.

15

Neither Ruth nor Henry knew how to spend each day. They were anxious to see Windom again and had become terrified by what could happen next. It was as if they had only just now considered the stunt they'd pulled. Adrenaline had carried them this far, and it had now bucked them off and returned them to the earth.

Augustus had been a sour man in his treatment of the Caspers, right up until the moment he understood there was money to be made. It was enough to put Ruth and Henry at a slight ease—they'd both had the most restful sleep in either of their memories the night before—but they both remembered how he'd treated them when they first approached. They woke up remembering. Woke up remembering the former Pinkerton, too, who would come a-calling soon enough. There was no telling exactly what kind of outlook that former Pinkerton would bring with him. So they waited.

They had no proper clean clothes and spent the first day in the room awaiting their laundry. Henry had marched downstairs in his over shirt and long johns, handing a pile of putrid vestments to the washer woman who held her nose and suggested he see about a bath. He nodded and flashed a reflexive smile. She would return the clothes clean in two hours, or clean and dry the next morning, depending on his preference. He said clean was more than he deserved and decided there were worse ways of spending a morning than by staying in a high-falute's hotel room. He grabbed two biscuits and a pair of apples left momentarily unguarded on the restaurant's display table and moved quickly upstairs.

It was an odd feeling, beset by luxury without a penny to their name. There could be no relaxing, no appreciation. They were interlopers. Stowaways to an enriched life neither Ruth nor Henry believed, truly believed, they were meant for. Those who belonged, dined as if they belonged. They sat in the restaurant and paid for what they ate. They received no bathing instruction from washer women, and they had more than one proper change of clothes. They'd come all this way, and nothing felt in their control. Augustus Windom decided whether to pay them and how much, the Patent Office decided if they had anything to sell, and some former lawman would arrive any moment, maybe while they remained without proper outfits, to tell them what would happen next.

While Henry was downstairs, Ruth sat in the silence of the opulent room. It spoke to her. Gave her a warning—something was coming. Might have been chasing her or waiting for her, but it was nearer to her now, she was sure of it. All that had happened in the last few months— the war, the train, Henry—something bad was closing in, all right. She knew the sound of thunder. Knew what happened if you ignored it. From grass to hay, life wasn't pretty. She had long ago lost hope of coming out of it clean. She knew now. There would never be a rest. Never. This is what happens—she would never stop running. Even in rooms like these made for respite.

Her only hope—the only hope she had left—was to savor one victory before the end, one moment of providence to have made life worth living. The world would not swallow her up before she left something to remember her by.

The afternoon breeze was nippy and blew through Ruth's thin travel duds as she stood perched like a gossiping crow over the railing on the balcony connected to their room. The air had an invigorating effect as she imagined every hale hatted man approaching the hotel to be the lawman.

When the lawman finally appeared, it was by curtained coach just before sundown on the second evening after the train stunt. He stepped from the coach and tightened the glove leather in between each of his fingers. He looked up, meeting Henry's eye first and then Ruth's, as if expecting to find them in exactly that spot. He called out, "Mister and Missus Casper?" It was a formality. He knew it was them. Knew exactly the room they were in.

Ruth nodded in the lawman's direction. Henry did the same and said, "And I gather you're the man we've been waiting to see? Mister

Rathbone?" Henry sounded more confident than Ruth knew him to be. It more surprised her than impressed her. He'd never be able to keep it up.

"The very same," Rathbone answered. He gave one last tug of his leather gloves. "With you in a moment." He disappeared into the hotel.

"Man's built like an ox," Henry said.

Ruth turned away from the street and straightened her dress front. "Everybody's built like something."

Henry moved toward the entry before Ruth gave a sharp little hiss that stopped him mid-step. "Don't you open that door. Not until he knocks. We don't want to seem more eager than we are...or eager at all, in fact."

Henry pondered this angle but was interrupted by the lawman's knock before he could decide how he felt about it one way or the other. He looked at Ruth for confirmation that no further games with the door need be played now that a knock had been presented. She gave a little *scoot* motion with her hands to urge him along.

When he answered the door, the squared off brick of a man stood before them, not with warm greeting, but with bedraggled exhaustion, as if the Caspers were the last stop on a long route. He looked for one of the two of them to speak first.

"Won't you come in, Mister Rathbone?" Ruth called from deep inside the room.

Henry stepped aside and smiled to assure the lawman that she spoke on his behalf, too.

"Thank you, madam. Thank you, sir," Rathbone said. He took exactly three steps in and removed his hat. "Forgive me, won't you?" He looked around the room as if expecting them to have redecorated it. "I am a liaison to Mister Windom in all matters of the train brake."

Ruth wanted to ask him if he'd seen the train himself or was familiar with what they'd done, but Rathbone made himself clear before she had the chance.

"More than a liaison in all matters of the train brake, I am Mister Windom's adjutant." He looked first at Henry and then to Ruth for a reaction. "His aide-de-camp, if you'd prefer." Henry nodded slightly. "His general counsel. I had been in his presence not a half-hour before you spirited him away on that train. And had I been there, you'd not have done so."

"You're here because he's grateful for us having done so," Ruth said, moving closer into the room.

"I'm here because he's interested in your contraption. He is not—and I am not—grateful for the manner in which you showed it."

"We had no intention of hurting him," Henry said.

"And I had no intention of him leaving his house after I left his company. And this is my point, sometimes things happen despite our intentions. Which is another reason I'm here—to minimize the impact your intentions have on Mister Windom."

Ruth and Henry shared a glance. They were thinking the same thing— Rathbone's words were as forbidding as his gloves.

"Where's Mister Windom now?"

"Attending to other business. A number of other opportunities have developed in addition to your train brake. When he sees to those, I suspect he will return to the matter at hand and update me accordingly. And then I will return to you in kind."

"Thank you," Henry said.

Ruth shot him the same look of contempt one might serve to a schoolhouse bootlicker.

"You're very welcome," Rathbone responded. He returned his hat to his head and took two steps toward the door before Ruth spoke up.

"Mister Windom says you're a Pinkerton?"

The question slowed Rathbone but did not stop him. He reached for the doorknob and opened the door. "I was."

"Not anymore, though?"

The question seemed to agitate the former lawman. "Not anymore. I serve only one client now."

"And if he doesn't pay off," Ruth said, "you've got nothing?"

Rathbone trailed away from her scorching stare and looked at Henry as if pitying him for being bonded to her. His face betrayed that of a guilty survivor of this woman's presence, knowing Henry would have no such providence. "If Mister Windom doesn't pay off, it will be you with nothing."

"We three, then, are paddling in the same direction. I just want you to keep that in mind going forward."

"Going forward, I will absolutely be keeping you in mind." Rathbone maintained focus on Henry. His expression had shifted now into something much colder. Something suggested it was in Henry's best interest to silence Ruth. Rathbone returned to her now. "This was simply an introduction, madam. Nothing more."

"So...so..." Henry fumbled for an appeasing note. "He mentioned what's next the night before, Mister Windom did. He'll be in Rhode Island first, talking to other manufacturers who might build the brake. Then Ohio to figure how to change the production orders? Is that right?"

Rathbone nodded.

Henry, normally a sloucher, stood straight. "Well, what's he out there telling them? Only *I* know how the brake works."

Rathbone nodded again. "Yes, well..." He cleared his throat. "It'll take time to stop the current run. He wants to secure the stop, and then I'm sure he'll return and have you meet with his engineers to untangle the rest of it. I was under the impression Mister Windom mentioned at least some of this."

"He did," Ruth said. "In fact, you haven't told us much more than he has. When do we discuss pay and timing? I thought that's what you were here for."

"Likely soon, that will be true. But not today. Today Mister Windom simply wanted us to make acquaintances. And now we have. I'll message you when we're ready to meet again."

"One week," Ruth said.

"Pardon?"

"Return here in a week. Sooner is fine. Not later."

"I have no quarrel, madam, but I wonder why you demand it?"

"Because if a week goes by and nothing's been accomplished, it's going to upset us. We spent every last cent to get here. And, while the hotel is nice, it's not as nice as doing business. So you come back here in seven days or we leave in eight."

"Is that a condition you really want me to bring to him?"

"Yes, sir."

"For two people who spent every last cent to get here, is that a condition you can afford to uphold?"

Henry looked to Ruth. Ruth, having no answer, studied Rathbone silently.

He looked displeased but bit his tongue and nodded. "Mister Windom has graciously ensured your room includes two meals downstairs in the restaurant each day. Gratis. He also asked me to forward you this cash." He laid a small stack of bills on the table. "He begs you to bathe and buy yourselves a clean set of clothes so that he may not be offended by your odor the next time you consort."

Neither Ruth nor Henry acknowledged the gift.

When he left, Henry looked crossly at Ruth over the risky negotiation.

Ruth was not having it. "Was 'thank you' really the best you could muster?" she asked.

"One of us needed to find our way into his good graces."

"He can like you for the both of us, then. That squared off bronco says he'll be keeping me in mind."

They both instinctively returned to the balcony.

"It's all right, Ruthy."

"It isn't all right. I don't know what it was, but it wasn't all right."

They watched Rathbone return up the single wobbly step into his carriage. The driver flung the horsewhip and they were off without the former Pinkerton ever returning an upward glance.

Ruth continued. "Why do you suppose he put on his gloves before he came up?"

Henry spit off the side, careful not to dribble in anyone's path. "A refined man needs to show off his refinement. Or else how would anybody know?"

Ruth didn't answer. She had no answer to give. Just a feeling. The same feeling as before. Something damned ominous was coming.

16

Augustus sensed his own internal shifting. Something inside him had become unmoored. He did not believe himself to have fallen into hysterics. In fact, he felt calm and quite attached to his senses. It had been a day since Kimball's ousting. Augustus had spent most of the previous afternoon in the First National Bank. Today, however, he would find himself inside George Townshend & Company's American Land Agency.

The tinkle of a weak bell over the door announced his arrival. A lanky scarecrow of a man sitting behind a polished mahogany desk hadn't yet risen from his seat before Augustus was upon him, hefting a leather case onto the desk. "Mister Roland Townshend," he said, as the sum total of his greeting.

Townshend was fair skinned, fragile, and pretty. His blond hair was a bit overgrown but parted, pomaded, and smoothed into stern grooves from a comb's teeth. "Mister Windom," he said, but he did not have the chance to offer more pleasantries.

"Mister Townshend, this hardside valise is for you. There are a substantial number of bonded bank notes inside it I intend to exchange for the title of property deed on the Orange Street Club."

Townshend squeezed his neatly knotted bow tie and took little nervous gulps of air. He looked out the window as if checking to ensure the Orange Street Club hadn't pulled away from its foundation and journeyed alongside Augustus. "You want to purchase the Orange, sir?"

"Is it not under your company's private control?"

"Sir, to be quite honest, we have no intention of selling the club. It's been—I'm sure you understand—quite lucrative."

"I understand." He slid the case between them. Still closed. Still clasped.

"And even if we could be compelled into such interest, it is not a decision I would be able to make alone."

"No?"

Townshend continued glancing out the window. "No, sir. This is Townshend and Company. *Company* means I have partners."

"*Company* means you have unnamed partners. This outfit might as well be called the Townshend and Lesser-Thans Corporation."

"That name would have been a hard sell to the others."

"Roland." Augustus leaned on the case, now just a foot away from Townshend. "You know who I am."

"Yes, sir."

"I've not come here curious about the normal doings of your business."

"Yes, sir."

Augustus popped open the case. It opened facing him. "In fact, I've not come here to ask anything except the amount that, if placed in front of you, would salve your partners' burn of not having been consulted on the matter." He removed a thick stack of $500 notes from the case and placed them within easy reach of Townshend.

"Yes, sir."

"Roland, that requires an answer, not an agreement."

"Yes, sir," Townshend repeated, eyeing the stack of notes in front of him—so far amounting to forty or fifty thousand dollars. His expression remained thick with distress. "Sir, pardon my presumptuousness but... has something happened at the Orange?"

"Indeed it has, Roland. Now, what price would compel you to transfer the responsibility of that happening from you to me?"

"Mister Windom, sir, I cannot simply—"

"It cost you thirty thousand dollars in '58 to purchase the land, raze the building occupying it, and construct the Orange from the ground up. I'll triple that, plus some. One hundred thousand." He set out a second thick stack beside the first one.

"Sir—"

"Two." Out came two more stacks of bonded notes.

"Sir—"

"Three, then." Townshend looked too scared to speak. "Roland, do not make an enemy of me." Augustus slammed another stack on the desk between them. "My next offer will strike you as considerably less favorable than this."

"Is that a threat?"

"Threats don't come to fruition. Warnings sometimes do. Now, will you take four hundred?"

"I thought you said three."

"All right then. Three hundred it is, but you have a damn irregular way of bargaining."

"One million," Townshend blurted out. "If I secure one million dollars, I can assure my partners will be satisfied."

The thought of the Casper wife demanding the same figure from him, not three days prior, took residence in Augustus's mind. He stepped back, admiring Townshend the way one might behold a fine portrait. "Well, that would make me the owner of the most expensive piece of real estate in the city, wouldn't it?"

"And me the man who sold it. The price would have to be gargantuan, sir. I'm sorry."

"Don't apologize." Augustus collected the stacks of money and returned them to the leather case. He closed it, clasped it, spun it so the handle faced Townshend, and pushed it toward him.

Townshend looked from the case to Windom and back again. It appeared he had summoned all his self-control not to pounce on the elegant Goyard hardside.

Augustus betrayed the first inkling of a grin. "And, please. Do keep the valise."

Augustus had not announced himself, not made his presence known. He had not sent a messenger to speak to the gap-toothed patent examiner, nor to fetch him and bring him to the mansion. He wanted to find the man in his own environment, sitting in his own chair. Augustus wanted him comfortable. He found this to be most effective. The patent examiner was his partner now, whether he knew it or not. One feigned respect for business partners or they wouldn't tend to stay business partners long.

So he spent a morning waiting in line at the Patent Office, sitting between two bald men with spectacles. Everyone near him wore spectacles, and they were all at least ten years older than him. It was as if everyone around him was placing their last bet. If their number didn't come up this time, that was it. They were sleep strained and forlorn. Looking around, Augustus did not see men pursuing success but men in desperate avoidance of failure. How many sad bastards did these examiners have to sit across from each day? Each year? Augustus dealt with his fair share of desperate persons but, in his coterie, even the saddest mope still knew he'd eat next week.

He was short on pity. For these people to wager everything this late in life on a bauble, a device, was irresponsible. It was ignorant. Tinkering was for those with the means to make mistakes. These people had let down their guard. They'd failed to protect themselves from a hard world and so the hard world would teach most of them a lesson. They would serve as examples for others. Don't become this. Don't expose your soft underbelly. For the few who got lucky, who struck it rich with a patent, Augustus saw it as due to devil's luck. They would not be able to keep their strike paying out and it would crush them. They'd fall. Most men who did not find success early, or were not bred for it like Augustus, would not do well to find it later in life. It would bend them all up until they were worse off than they'd been before.

Sitting on these worn pews, amongst these embattled inventors, it felt to Augustus as if he was seated in a graveyard. He should have brought flowers to hand to each of them.

When it was his turn, the place had figured out who he was. They'd read the articles about the miracle train. A few even had the sand to tell him how glorious the train's description had been. Compliments begat questions and questions begat inquiries and soon Augustus asked to be left alone. The room had become pregnant with unasked questions and unspoken plaudits. A slender examiner with a long sloping nose that gave him the air of a flamingo called Augustus to his desk. Augustus refused him. He pointed to the gap-toothed one still speaking to some poor dead bastard and said he'd wait to speak to him.

When the gap-toothed examiner was available, Augustus did not wait to be summoned but walked toward him, hand outstretched, noticing the weary expression on the man's face.

"Hello, sir," Augustus said.

"Mister Windom."

They shook hands.

"You know me?"

"Everyone knows you, sir."

The examiner led the way back to his desk and offered Augustus a seat.

"Do you know why I'm here?"

"I assume you have an invention you want to protect."

Augustus sized up the man and smiled. "In a manner of speaking. Yes."

The examiner was not cowed by Augustus. "Well, what is it you want patented?"

"An air brake."

The muscles in the examiner's face tightened. Muscles always gave away the man. He nodded. "You want to patent an air brake?"

"You've read a newspaper in the last day, haven't you?"

"I have."

"Then you know exactly what I want to patent."

The examiner nodded again. "I would've thought anything on the front page of a newspaper would've been patented long before. Do you have patent papers? Drawings?"

"I can get them."

"I'm certain you know how patent reviews work. I cannot simply grant you a—"

"Stop it." Windom let the air turn cold between them before continuing on. "I came here to speak to you specifically. You know why."

"Sir?"

"Decline the patent." As he spoke, Augustus made a show of inching his chair toward the examiner and leaning his elbows on the man's desk.

The examiner leaned back, as if an iron bar ran between his chest and Augustus's. Any movement Augustus made, the examiner made the opposite. "Decline what patent?"

"Henry Casper's brake patent."

"Is there a reason I should?"

"Many reasons, yes."

"One valid one will do."

"Infringement for one." Augustus sat back. "I'll provide patents to prove my claim."

"Do so and I'll review them."

"But, for now, I'm asking you to decline the patent."

"Before you provide proof?"

"Do you mean more proof than my train having made national news?"

"That proves only that the device exists, not who created it or who owns it."

"I'm trying to save everyone from future aggravation."

"Oh?"

"You and I both know where this will go if you grant him the patent. I will waste valuable time and resources suing him, he will be unable to defend himself, I will easily win the decision, and you will look foolish for not having done your due diligence enough to know I already own patents on the brake. Do you not think it coincidental that Mister Casper was sitting in this very seat not weeks before my train took flight? Did you not wonder where such a man came from?"

"I did not wonder."

"Whatever documentation he showed you, it was not his and, if you grant him a patent on it, I'll pull you right into the legal suit as a willing accomplice. Decline the patent."

"Sir, the patent is still under review. If you return tomorrow with proof of patent, I'll be happy to fold it into my review. But you've provided me nothing but your word to go on and I'm afraid that just isn't sufficient."

"Ah." Augustus smiled. It was a tight-lipped, knowing smile. "I see."

"Nothing nefarious, I assure you. I simply need more."

"You make, what? Three dollars a day? Am I close?"

The examiner grimaced. "Sir?"

"Three dollars a day at about three hundred days a year, that's nine hundred dollars annually. What if I gave you a thousand dollars right now to decline that patent?"

"I was not angling for money, sir."

"And yet here money has presented itself to you." Augustus reached onto the man's desk and lifted a pencil nub, worn down from constant sharpening. He wiggled it between them. "Money that would keep you in full pencils." He dropped the pencil where he'd found it. It landed with a definitive clack.

The examiner looked at it. Augustus was confident he was considering his offer. It took a little longer than he'd hoped, and he'd hoped not to have to pay, but it would be worth it.

"I use these pencils down to their stumps because I don't like waste, not because I can't afford new ones. The government provides us pencils." He opened his desk drawer, pulled out an uncarved fistful and dropped them on top of the old pencil. "Are you going to have me killed, Mister Windom?"

Augustus was breathless. "What did you ask?"

"You didn't send someone else to wait in this office for an hour. You came yourself, which suggests you want as few people involved as possible. You came with an offer of money in place of proof. This is important to you. I believe you to be a man quite used to getting his way. But I cannot grant you what you are asking for in the manner you are asking for it. And so I say—assume I am immovable."

"No one is immovable."

"Assume I am immovable *on this*. Assume I watch poor men sit in the very chair in which you're sitting and lay before me their toil, torment, risk, and blood. Assume I did not question where Mister Casper came from because I see far more Caspers come through here than Windoms. Assume my father was poor. Assume I value grit more than riches. Assume I, too, am a product of toil, torment, and risk and that I want more Caspers in this world than Windoms. Assume it's easier for me to believe you are stealing an invention than that someone has stolen it from you. Assume there isn't one part of me that would allow your thievery for a thousand dollars or a million if I can help it. Assume you walk out of here having faced far less success than you planned. Assuming all that, Mister Windom, will this end with one of your men killing me?"

Augustus studied the examiner. He'd greatly misjudged the man's contempt and had been sent on his heels recalculating the play. He reached for the pencils. Gathered them one-by-one in his fist. "I'll take as many things from you as I have to, until I have my way."

The examiner was sober, enjoying no moment of this. But he did not budge or blink. "I see," he said. "I'll make a note of that in Mister Casper's file."

When Augustus left, he took the bundle of pencils with him and tossed them in the gutter.

17

The Caspers had taken to long strolls to Franklin Square in the mornings and the Patapsco River Basin in the evenings, both after a meal in the hotel restaurant. They were restless and anxious and increasingly jittery with every hour. It had been just five days since the Pinkerton's visit, but already Ruth and Henry had grown tired of their hotel and weary of Windom's promises.

For those walks that were not experienced by the two of them in silence, the majority of conversation between them consisted of Ruth giving voice to her fearful imaginings. Maybe Windom had found a flaw in the brake. Maybe the brake had been invented and patented elsewhere already. Maybe the Confederate Army had gotten to Windom. Maybe Windom had lost interest. Maybe, and this was more likely, it was something they'd never fathom in a century of trying. Or maybe it was nothing at all.

"We'll just have to wait and see," was Henry's near-constant conclusion. "We've done what we can, and the rest is out of our hands." And while nothing was a poor plan in Ruth's estimation, she couldn't conjure up anything better, either. They would go around and around, the two of them would, until they'd talked themselves tired and retreated for the rest of the stroll into silent contemplation. This usually lasted until they returned to the hotel where Ruth would stand on the balcony watching the world pass by while Henry read a book in the tub.

And this is exactly how it went the morning of the sixth day. They returned from Franklin Square to find Rathbone, hat tipped forward, gloves squeezed around his fingers, standing just beside the twin-door entrance to the hotel.

"You've returned," Ruth said.

"So have you," Rathbone shot back, his response spiced with annoyance.

"Long walks help us think," Henry said.

"And what have you got to think about?"

The Caspers had stopped at the hotel's first step. Rathbone remained unmoved on the second.

"What we'd do if you didn't return to this hotel," Ruth said.

"I guess my presence here now means all your thinking was for naught."

"We'll see," Ruth said.

Rathbone smiled. "Mister Windom isn't ready. He says he will pay you the money he agreed, but cannot do it yet, nor will he be able to do it in one lump sum."

"I see," Henry said.

Ruth looked at him crossly. "Well, *I* don't. Where's the holdup? The man's wealthier than William the Conqueror, ain't he? He can bend any man to his will, can't he?"

"Not *any* man, no."

Ruth rested a boot on the second step, from which Rathbone still had not budged. She noted his immovability and supposed maybe he meant her to understand he was one of the men Augustus could not move. At any rate, he appeared to be a man *she* could not move. A tinge of worry prickled her: Might he have been sent to block their re-entry into the hotel? "Simmer down and be patient," she said. "Is that what he sent you to tell us?"

"Mister Windom acknowledges the inconvenience of this interval and asks that I remain in your service for the duration of it as a personal courtesy to you."

Ruth and Henry looked at one another, trying to read the other's face for clues as to what "in your service" might mean coming out of the mouth of the former Pinkerton.

"If you require a carriage someplace, I can transport you. If you feel unsafe, I will have my men guard you. If your stay in this hotel becomes untenable, I will see to improving it and the like." He gestured ahead at the coach stopped a few feet away. "My coach will be here for your use. Rap on the door whenever you like at any hour. I will be in it most of the time, if not in the hotel. If not me, one of my men. You'll never be alone. This was at Mister Windom's insistence."

"You'll do everything except what it is we most want to do, which is get to business-making," Ruth said. Her words were loud, and Henry glanced every which way taking stock of who was listening, nervous she was offending perfect strangers.

"For what it's worth, Missus Casper, I'd prefer this go quickly, too. I side with you. Mister Windom sides with you. That is why I'm here. To make you as comfortable as possible while you wait, because today we cannot set forth with any business."

"So we get a guardian and he gets all the time in the world? Did he tell you how long you'd be completely useless to us, Mister Rathbone?"

Rathbone seemed to have held his breath and stared at Ruth. He was still and silent, and his stillness and silence tipped into menacing.

"My, how he must be galled," Ruth continued, "to be a man of such versatility, now relegated to nursemaid." She was doing what she always did when she felt ambushed and manacled, she barked like a mad dog. And if Augustus Windom aimed only to send his man to them, she'd bark at the man until the noise of it made its way back to Windom. But in so doing, she'd made a mistake that she heard immediately and hoped to hell Rathbone hadn't. She'd acknowledged that Windom was, for now, both an adversary and a gatekeeper. By asking what Windom said and when he'd be ready, she'd sent Rathbone a none-too-subtle signal that the Caspers were prepared to wait, that they weren't planning to leave Baltimore and try their luck somewhere else. And she knew, just as anyone would know, that those with the upper hand weren't the ones waiting.

She had one card up her sleeve and she let it peek out from under the sleeve of her garment. "Oh, look somewhere else, you gawk-eyed fool. You come here to tell us there's nothing to tell and expect us to fall down and kiss your boots?"

141

Rathbone continued staring into Ruth, waiting for her to finish her mad gibbering.

She moved her foot off the second step and puffed loud from deep in her belly, then shook her head. She wanted to say more but was scared the damage she'd do.

Rathbone remained a pile of bricks a step above the two of them. Henry wagged a finger playfully in his direction. "I see why Mister Windom relies on you. You're not a man to be hectored."

"I'm not a man who bends to the will of others."

"That too," Henry said. "I believe it."

"Does *she*?"

"We both do," Henry added.

Rathbone took a half-step down and was within teaching distance of Ruth. He shook his head once. "*Do* you?"

"You're here on the say-so of someone else, ain't you? With the order to do what we tell you? Ain't that the definition of bending to others' will?"

"Augustus Windom has asked that I correspond with him every evening when he is here in Baltimore and weekly via couriered letter when he is traveling."

"Weekly?" Ruth blurted.

Rathbone ignored her outburst. "If the next time he hears from me I tell him you were, the both of you, trampled to death by a coach-and-four, he would believe me. And upon the delivery of this news, he might return with a number of questions, but do you know what question he wouldn't ask?" Ruth and Henry weathered his rhetorical question. "He wouldn't ask if the coach belonged to me. And I mean to tell you, future talk in that tone and aimed at me will get you run the fuck over. If you only know one thing about me, know that I don't bend to the boy's will. Now turn around and take another long walk to help you think about that."

Ruth searched Rathbone's face to gauge the seriousness of his demand. The man's jaw set, and his eyes had gone dead like a blown candle. He meant for them to go walking once more. He meant to show them he could bend them to his will. The bastard.

"Who are you to talk to us like that?"

Rathbone's shoulders rose slightly in an insignificant shrug. "Who are you to ask?"

Days had turned to weeks and Augustus Windom had disappeared. Uriah Rathbone, however, had not.

During the long weeks of waiting, Ruth and Henry's walks became something altogether more productive. To beat back boredom, they'd varied their routes and destinations, sometimes longer, sometimes shorter, but always involving someone or something new. Today they might stumble onto Green Mount Cemetery, tomorrow, Locust Point or the shot tower. The most fulfilling strolls for the Caspers, however, were the ones that led them not to a place but to a person. Finding a coachman with a busted wheel or a short-handed hostler they could help scratched Henry's itch to tinker and fiddle and, for Ruth, she tingled with a nasty little joy every time she offered her help and, when accepted, whistled for Rathbone to take up her portion of the effort. To add sour lemon to it, she'd taken to puffing her pipe while Rathbone worked.

It was damn unclear to the citizenry involved in these Samaritan efforts who the third man was or why he was with the other two. When questioned about it, Rathbone always had a snippy retort. He'd say he was their disappointed cousin or a most skeptical probationer, or the owner of the livery from which the woman had escaped. It made for a patter that left bystanders confused and unwilling to question them further but kept both Ruth and Rathbone mildly entertained.

During this time, the patent had cleared. The gap-toothed examiner had made good on his promise and seen to the patent's early completion. On the occasion of their receiving the certificate, Rathbone had been eager himself and in relatively jolly spirits when Ruth and Henry boarded his coach-and-four to travel to the Patent Office. Windom's man had often waited in the coach but asked to accompany them this time to revel in their good fortune. Immediately, Ruth sensed something was wrong.

First with Rathbone's demeanor and then with the manner in which they were greeted by the patent examiner. He seemed spooked by the sight of Windom's man as he presented them with a beribboned and wax-sealed certificate. Ruth snapped it up and inspected it with a hunger saved for starved wolves. Rathbone, too, peered at it from over her shoulder.

The examiner leaned in close to Henry under the guise of congratulations and warned him quickly and quietly of the visit from Augustus Windom. He detailed the industrialist's aim to stop the patent and the attempt to force the application's rejection.

"I am sad to tell you, Casper," the examiner whispered, "yours will be the last patent I grant. I believe Augustus Windom saw to punish me for standing my ground."

"He had you tossed out of this office?"

"I believe so. I believe doubly he won't stop at that if I care to push it further. Though I can't prove a lick of it."

"I don't know how to thank you for what you done," Henry said, matching the man's low tones. "I don't believe there's a proper way to thank you."

The examiner nodded in Rathbone's direction. "I hope you're appropriately weary of that one. I'd suggest you rid yourself of him, then take your patent and sell your brake elsewhere."

In the brief interval between leaving the Patent Office and remounting Rathbone's coach, Henry relayed to Ruth what he'd been told. She stood just outside the coach door, understanding that this was the reckoning she'd felt in the pit of her belly. Something was coming—or, if the examiner was correct, it had already come. The coach ride back to the City Hotel was damn unbearable.

"May I see the certificate once more," Rathbone asked, his hand extended toward Ruth who had unconsciously been hugging the leather cover to her chest. Her instinct was to deny him, to sass-talk him like she normally would. But he appeared different to her now. Rathbone was no longer Windom's assistant, he was his spy. She felt foolish for ever seeing it any other way. She'd been walking on air and only just now realized she was plummeting to her death.

She swallowed hard, the putrid burn of bile at the top of her throat, and handed over the certificate for fear of reprisal if she did not. "Be careful with that," she told Rathbone.

"I'll prize it as if it were my own." He did not look up from the certificate when he said it. Ruth and Henry traded glances, doing their best not to make the exchange evident. Rathbone ran his fingers across the parchment and sighed deep, as if remembering a long-lost thought. He closed the cover and kept it on his lap a moment, long enough that Ruth thought he might just keep it. "No matter what else," he said, "let nothing strip your pride of having won this patent."

He handed the certificate back to her. She thought she detected a smirk on that square fucking head of his.

"We *earned* the patent," Ruth said.

Rathbone nodded once and looked out the window as they rode the rest of the way to the hotel in silence.

18

Augustus *had* been away. This much was true. He returned to Baltimore weeks later, greasy and irritable. His trip to the capital had taken as much as it gave. Armed with a posse of engineers, he'd gone to Washington to file false patents. It had cost more money and time, but he'd secured the filings. He'd arranged for numerous meetings in secret offices held in remote corridors within the Patent Office. When he needed assurances of absolute discretion, he held private meetings with more influential patent lawyers at the Willard Hotel. The effort amounted to paying his patent lawyers and examiners to back date and bear false witness to the documents. This gave him, not Henry Casper, overriding rights to the air brake. In so doing, he'd also defanged the gap-toothed examiner prick.

He'd done it before, learned from his father.

Upon his return, though, he'd thought of his mother. He considered how she might look upon him now. He feared his boyhood essence had dwindled until there remained no real part of it left. A man whose behavior was at odds with his essence was capable of shame beyond belief. He could not imagine his mother would feel pride in him. Embarrassment, maybe, but not pride. Had she felt pride in Leopold? Had she known of his swindling nature? Was it possible to know him? And might someone ask the same question of Augustus? He was acting out his destiny…or was he not? Who was a man to serve if not his own legacy and heritage? Had he not more to lose than the Caspers? If Henry Casper fell, he was low enough for it to make but a whisper across the glen. If he, Augustus Windom, fell, the drop would shake the core of the earth.

His hair had gone without pomade for days, his cheeks without a shave for longer. His gait had slowed. He was curt with people, even those in his favor. When he returned to Baltimore, he sensed his staff was doing its best to stay out of his way. They'd condensed inquiries, contracts, and bills to limit the number of interactions they were forced to have. His servants cleaned when he was away or tucked in his office. Rathbone had become the only person he communicated with and, even then, only through exchanged letters.

It was Christmas Day. He'd purchased no gifts, nor had he received any. He trudged down the staircase and into the banquet room of his mansion. There were less formal spaces to eat but, tonight, something had taken hold of him. Perhaps it was the insistent, purveying specter of his father always on his mind. Leopold had often eaten alone in the banquet room, always at the head of the thirty-place table.

Augustus seated himself in his father's chair and rang a handbell resting on the table. After a long minute, a hunched maid toddled in from the kitchen.

"Mister Winnum," she said in greeting, but kept her eyes aimed at the floor. Augustus, uncharacteristically, was doing the same. The maid waited as the silence expanded in the room like a balloon. "Thought you might eat elsewhere tonight. On account of it being Christmas."

Augustus didn't move, didn't even acknowledge there was another person in the room with him.

"Mister Winnum?" the maid repeated, leaning over to see his face. Checking, most likely, to see if he'd fallen asleep sitting up.

"What was he eating?" Augustus reached out for the woman's hand and held it. "The night he died?"

She studied him. "What's that now?" Her voice was deliberate, perhaps deciphering why he was asking.

He kept ahold of her hand. "Will you fix me his last meal? Will you do that for me?"

"Your father's last meal?"

"Yes."

"The one he choked over?"

"Yes."

"Pardon my asking, but why you want that? Wouldn't you prefer a nice turkey leg and candied yams? Slip in a slice-a cherry pie to cheer you up? It's Christmas, after all."

"No," he said. "I'd like to finish what he started."

The woman tensed and slipped her hand from his. "I can do that," she said and hurried away.

Thousands may have paid their respects at Leopold Windom's funeral, but it had taken an hour for anyone in his own home to find him face down in a pork loin. His heart had stopped. The cause had been left to gossip. Some believed his quest to topple Fairbanks had resulted in his working himself to death. Conversations about what it was that killed him never escaped the jest that—whether it was from his company's rapidly doubled size or from choking on his dinner—Leopold Windom had bitten off more than he could chew.

Augustus had been away on business the night of his father's death, just as his father had been when his mother died. And, just as it had been with his mother, Augustus was again denied the opportunity to say goodbye. There were no deathbed oaths, no mournful confessions. There was nothing. Just a body in a box awaiting his return to the city.

Jefferson entered the dining room to announce the arrival of Rathbone, who treaded in with confidence, spinning his hat in circles between his fingers, his wool Kersey coat and matching cape hanging open. Jefferson offered to relieve him of his outer wear, but Rathbone waved him away.

"Uriah," Augustus said, by way of unenthused greeting. He was born cautious, but his caution lately had degenerated into paranoia. He believed it possible Rathbone was there to warn him of a pending arrest. Maybe Rathbone had trapped him, fixed him against his Pinkerton friends. Augustus never believed a man was ever fully out of the Pinkerton Detective Agency. It was foolish, of course, given what Rathbone had done for his family. The violence. The intimidation. Rathbone had given his father similar notices upon occasion. It felt inevitable the same would happen to him. This was the terrain on which his family trod.

Rathbone cleared his throat. "In July, a Virginian hired the Pinkertons to track and arrest a horse thief. Two horse thieves, actually. A married pair." He waited, watching Augustus as if deciphering how he was made. "Besides what the Virginian could describe of their appearance, he only had their last name to go on. That and the understanding they were headed for the Patent Office."

This got Augustus's attention. He gathered himself up as Rathbone sallied forth with the explanation handed down to him by his Pinkerton friends.

"They're horse thieves, Augustus. Not only that, I followed that train back as far as I could—all the way to the Confederate Engineer Corps. Mister Casper is a deserter from the Rebels. And I'm certain no cheap southern militia would unhand a full locomotive to some wobble-kneed corporal."

Augustus sat thinking. "The Pinkertons told you this?"

"Yes, sir. Plus dribs and drabs I've picked up being in the company of the two of them all these weeks. And I must confess I've been remiss in not telling you sooner."

"Why didn't you?"

"My aim was to save you from distraction. Added to which, I didn't know if you had further use for the Caspers."

"You're making an argument for telling me, not secreting around without my say-so."

"I've not been secreting. You've not made your whereabouts clear."

"Why are you telling me now?" Rathbone gave another throat clear and fiddled with his hat. "Mister Rathbone?"

"I've erred, Augustus. I can admit it."

"How?"

"If the Caspers return to Virginia, they'll sit before a judge."

"Yes. And they'll be found guilty and hang."

Rathbone nodded. "Yes, but not before they have their say in open court and, once there, you can't control what they air out. I don't believe you'll want them spouting honest about their expedition. How they came to that train. How it is they've been holed up in the City Hotel for three months but can't afford to pay the price of a horse. How the patent examiner missed your patents. That gets aired in court, someone will look into it. It's messy."

Windom stared into Rathbone. He was correct about two things. The first was that he did not want the Caspers speaking in court. The second was that his most trusted man had erred monstrously. Rathbone had enjoyed complete trust in Leopold, never asked him twice about anything, nor gave a second guess. The same wasn't true for Augustus. He was once again reminded that he was not his father. Neither in the eyes of strangers nor old friends.

"You should have told me, Uriah."

"I know, Augustus. I come to you to make it right."

"Oh?"

Rathbone nodded. "The Virginian would consider twice the value of the horse as recompense for the theft. One hundred and eighty dollars. I tell you because you should pay it."

Augustus inhaled and stared into the table in front of him. His drawn-out silences were common. Rathbone did not seem discomfited.

"Please," Augustus said to Rathbone, "have a seat."

Rathbone sat as far removed from Augustus as it was possible to be while still at the table. He understood he was not invited company. "If you pay the Virginian, the Caspers won't appear before a judge."

Augustus considered this.

"The Pinkertons…why haven't they come to arrest the Caspers?"

"I asked them not to. Not just yet. Called in a few favors. Gave the agency my word I would keep everyone close."

Augustus tapped the table impatiently with his finger. "Everyone but me." Rathbone did not answer, so Augustus went on. "Your word was enough to keep the Pinks from arresting the Caspers for months?"

"No, sir." Rathbone stilled his face. His expression implored Augustus to use his imagination as to what else might have compelled the detectives to stall.

"I see," said Augustus. "How much did you say I'd pay them?"

"Fifty for every week that goes by. It stands at four hundred currently."

Augustus closed his eyes and shook away the thought of it all.

"Forgive me for saying it, Augustus, but you seem unwell."

"Everything makes me so very bitter, Uriah. Have I an ailment that makes me this way? I cannot figure it. I can only feel it."

"That's unsurprising. The ordeal seems to be wearing them thin as well. The husband's restless and the woman festers."

Augustus scratched his chin as if his very skin annoyed him. "Tell me, have the Caspers persuaded you to oppose me?"

This surprised Rathbone. He considered Augustus before answering. "They're good people. The wife can be a trial, but the husband is upright. It's wrong what we're doing. Getting too wrong to live with."

"I can live with a monstrous amount of wrong."

They both turned at the sound of the swing door and the servant woman approaching with supper. She set the food before Augustus and turned toward Rathbone to ask if he would like anything.

Before she could get out the words, Augustus said, "That will be all, thank you." He did not touch his plate until she was gone and the door to the kitchen had stopped swinging. He declined to continue his train of thought, simply cutting his pork into bite-sized chunks.

"Do you remember your mother?" Rathbone asked.

Augustus answered before he finished chewing his first bite. "Every ounce of her."

"You've forgotten how you were with her. You were kind. And thoughtful. You pulled out chairs for her—chairs taller than you were, weighed more than you did. You would dance near her. Did it until she praised you. Her opinion meant quite a lot to you. You loved her."

Augustus bit off a chunk of biscuit and chewed it.

Rathbone continued. "Now you don't love anything."

Augustus shrugged. He had intended to chew and swallow and finish the meal his father had started. The act was not meant to be morbid. But the first thing he did, after he'd finished cutting his pork, was to eschew all silver and use his fingers like an animal.

"Your younger self loved deeply," Rathbone continued. "I wonder, where it is you've hidden him? Because she would not recognize you."

Augustus continued shoving food in. He was not swallowing. He was merely chewing and adding cargo to what was quickly becoming an overstuffed trunk.

Rathbone continued. "Am I alone in feeling regretful? I don't think I am."

Augustus started breathing heavily. He could barely close his lips to chew. Gobs of wet meat abandoned the ship of his mouth and splashed down on the table in front of him.

"Augustus," Rathbone started. "I fear these woes of yours..." He caught himself. He watched Augustus gorge and spoke no more.

Something had changed in Augustus. Something gruesome. Loathsome. He appeared no longer hearing, his eyes no longer seeing. He emitted grunts as he packed in the morsels. It was vulgar.

Rathbone could only stare.

In all his life, Augustus had only wanted the good opinion of brutal men. He was too grateful for their approval. He never ceased rubbing against his betters. But the more rubbing he did, the more rubbing he needed to do. He was thirsty for praise, but it was saltwater in his mouth.

He understood now that it would never be enough. The thirst would never slake, and he would die of drinking. It had already killed his father and it was killing him now, six months later.

After stuffing the last fistfuls of pig into his gaping maw, he moved to the asparagus and fit it in. His jaw now a jammed vice unable to close or mash within normal range. Air was scarce. Gobs fell down his straining windpipe. Still he did not stop, all the flavors and juices mashing in one chunky slurry.

Rathbone sat rapt, an expression of revulsion fixed on his face. "Augustus, stop it already."

Tears filled Augustus's eyes. He looked to the ceiling, choking now as the food expanded past his tongue and palate. His stomach lurched. Wet hunks of partially chewed meat capped his esophagus. The air in his lungs had no exit. A tightness seized his neck in a red wringing. Veins bulged in tight ropes from his temple.

Rathbone eased back into his seat. If Augustus was serious about choking on his own sickness, he would do nothing to stop him.

Augustus noted Rathbone's apathy. Then he looked down at his empty plate, gagging and thinking of his father. No one had been there to help him, either, when he died. Was this how it felt at the end? Did he think about his son as, in this moment, his son had come to think of him?

He heard the thumping of his own heartbeat from inside his skull and began retching. It all came up. Pulpy and gray. Coated in slick foam and tendrils of red. The noise of it was of a man having a leg removed with dull instruments.

Rathbone stood and walked the length of the table to the handbell beside Augustus, picked it up with his thumb and forefinger, and gave it a dainty little shake. The echo of its ring stopped immediately upon its return to the pillow on which it rested. Rathbone retraced the path back to his seat. He crossed his legs and waited for the staff to come running.

The wet, gagging wheezes from Augustus were the room's only sound.

Jefferson hurried in from the foyer and the huddled maid came in through the kitchen to bear witness. They each stopped cold, unsure what had happened.

Rathbone looked from one to the other, nodded toward Augustus and said, "He's choked himself on dinner."

From the looks on the servants' faces, this did nothing to clarify things. They both rushed toward Augustus to help, regardless. Halfway there, they stopped as Augustus vomited again. Hard and fast. It came gushing from down deep onto the plate, the silver, the table, the floor, his pants, his shirt, his hands, his shoes. What spewed out of him was triple what he'd put in. It was as if his soul had escaped right along with supper.

That he did not die may have been an accident. Slumped there, froth dripping from his lips, he could not be sure if he had meant to choke or simply meant to hurt.

He sat without moving, Rathbone and the appalled staff standing nearby. Everyone breathed heavy except Rathbone. He glared at Augustus as if watching a child in tantrum.

Augustus turned toward the maid. "I'm good and finished. No dessert for me."

The maid didn't move. She didn't look away. She stood behind him, mouth agape at the foul mess Augustus had created.

"Arrest the Caspers," he said to Rathbone. "Tonight. See they're hanged. Give the devil his due."

Rathbone didn't move. It was his way of asking *Are you sure?*

The room hung suspended as the two stared at each other.

"How about now, Uriah?" Augustus asked, dregs smeared over his face like a baby. "Would my mother recognize me now?"

19

Ruth, taking in the frigid air from the balcony, watched the snow settle on the cobblestone street, then melt under the commotion of carriages and boots. How nice it must be, she imagined, to have someplace to go and someone expecting your arrival. Christmas had long been empty to her. Every year there was something missing or someone. Some hole too big to fill. Too wide to bother trying.

At best, the day itself had consisted of her father and brothers taking the horses and wagon out for a jaunt. It would be the only time they hadn't had to load it with crops before moving it. There had been one year it snowed in Tennessee on Christmas. She and her brothers had damn near cleared the field of its powder, throwing snowballs one scoopful at a time. Otherwise, the day had always passed without anyone acknowledging it. Christmas had long been Ruth's quietest day of the year. She had always featured herself buying fruits and trinkets for her children, maybe decorating her door with a holly wreath, but, of course, had never done so.

It had been a week since the patent examiner's warning had dug itself deep in Ruth's gut. They had no rifle, no wagon, no train, and nowhere to go and every reason to believe someone or something would lay siege on them both at any moment. Her nerves had swollen in full and she'd become snippy at all hours. Henry was her primary target. She'd become afflicted with his penchant for musing instead of taking action.

"We oughta demand to speak to his engineers," Ruth said, shouting across the room while Henry drew a bath. She would not go over to him. Would not sit with him. Even the thought of doing so had brought her closer to the memory of her sick mother scrubbing away the pig slop all those years before. She draped a leg over the arm of a chintz wing chair.

"To what end?" Henry asked, scrubbing himself with a brick of soap.

"To the end that they'll make it clear whether the bastard has truly been swindling us or not." She dropped her leg from the chair's arm. "Or maybe we force that Pinkerton to take us to the warehouse where they're readying for to make our brake. Or force him to sit us in Windom's study until his return. Or to do something other than let us go to flower in this hotel."

"I don't believe we can force Windom's man to do anything he don't want to do already. I think Windom told him to play nice and he's going as far as he can, but no further."

"I don't hear you coming up with any better idea."

"We could go back to that horseman. Offer to work off the horse we stole and get your ring back." Henry dunked his head under the water as if anticipating Ruth's reaction and wanting to avoid being hit with it.

She waited for him to reemerge. "How you suppose we get back to him, Henry? On Wimp's back? With Rathbone trailing us the whole way? And what else? Just let Windom have the Casper brake?"

"Better than sitting here, ain't it?"

"A fine statement from a man floating in bubbles like a prized princess." Ruth didn't have a more suitable reply for him, so she left it at that. "Or we go sit in a lawyer's office. Pour him out all the mistakes we made, including sitting here like a pair of dolts."

"If Windom is angling to swindle us, you think we got a chance of stopping him?"

"Not unless we try. Now, what's your point? You said you wouldn't run. And here you are plotting your way out. I can see it in your eyes, Henry Casper."

Henry squeezed his eyes shut. "Ruth—"

"You'll want to pitch that tone and try again with a new one."

Henry slapped the soap against the tub. "Smoke and oakum, Ruthy! You'd have us stay in the house of a swindler? Ignoring danger ain't the same as being safe, and sometimes running is the safest choice. Better than waiting here for the horseman, the Virginia marshal's service, the city government, Augustus Windom, or the Confederate Army."

"I don't want nothing in this world but to make a name from that patent, Henry."

"Ain't it something that we got the patent in the first place?"

"No, that's part of something. *Part* of it. Not all of it. The patent ain't the end. The patent is the beginning. You're quitting at the start again."

"I'm not quitting."

"Well, my mistake. I couldn't decipher your struggle what with your fresh bath and bubbles."

"I didn't want to be here," he said. "I don't care about none of this. I ain't looking to make a name for myself."

"So, if *you* won't advance your name, give way and let *me* make something of it."

A knock on their door circulated the stale heat in the room. Henry came slipping onto the floor, dripping half the tub's water around him. He pulled on his britches and shirt, glowering at Ruth as he did it. The knock came again. Harder, less patient. When Henry answered, it was Rathbone, holding a shotgun. It rested against his shoulder.

Ruth gave a curt little nod from the far end of the room as she returned to the wing chair. "Merry Christmas, Detective."

"Merry Christmas to you both," Rathbone said, still avoiding their gaze. "I've come bearing bad news," he said. "News I'd have preferred to save for a less revered day than this."

"Go on," Ruth said.

Henry stepped aside. Rathbone interpreted it as an invitation to enter, which he did. He took a moment before speaking. It was a long enough silence that Ruth knew something was wrong. Terribly wrong. "I'll ask you to stand up, Missus Casper," he said. "And for you both to get dressed."

Ruth looked at Henry and she at him. Henry came around to face Rathbone. "Has Augustus returned? Has he given you bad news?" he asked as he buttoned his shirt.

A thought stung Ruth—the bad nature of Rathbone's news was awful enough that even someone as dulled to a person's signals as Henry had detected it. It was a childish thought, but it came to her, nevertheless. And, nevertheless, there was some truth in it.

Rathbone's jacket fit tight around his squat frame. It was cut with an inexact relationship to his dimensions. The outlines bending his coat made clear he'd come armed with more than the shotgun.

"Well, out with it then. What'd you come for?" Ruth asked.

Only the man's eyes moved as he completed a reconnaissance mission from Ruth's head to her feet and back again.

"Hike your dress," he told her.

"Pardon me?"

"Hike it to your knee."

"I will not."

He took the shotgun off his shoulder and cradled it loosely in both arms.

Henry squeezed into his boots, the floor all around him slick with bath drippings. He stepped toward Ruth.

Ruth, for her part, looked at the shotgun with skepticism. "You must be a poor shot to need a scattergun and two pistols in a room without anyone aiming back at you."

"Lift it just enough," Henry told her. "He ain't looking for thrills."

"Henry, if this man asked you to floor your pants and show him your pecker, you'd at least take a long pause before doing it. Don't rush me. I ain't the one being improper." She lifted her dress to the tops of her shoes, keeping eye contact with Rathbone the whole time.

"Higher," he said.

She exhaled and hiked her dress to the knee. "I'll lift it no higher. And should I have a pistol stowed at my thigh, you'll just have to hope not."

Rathbone moved closer to her, examining her legs, his hands cradling the shotgun.

"You go rooting in your hooch for a manstopper," he said, "I'll shoot you before you get there."

She supposed this was likely true and flattened her dress with her hands. Though he cut an imposing figure, Rathbone was short in stature. Ruth found that when she looked him in the eye, she did not have to angle her head up to do it.

"For weeks now, all we been saying is we want to do business. Why, all a sudden, are you nervous about us shooting holes through things?" Ruth asked.

"A Virginian says you stole his horse months back."

"You've seen our horse," Henry shot back. "That look like a nag someone would chase us across state lines to recoup?"

Ruth guessed Henry had thought up that response weeks ago and had been ready to use it ever since.

"You've been tracked from the old man's ranch," Rathbone said. "I know about the wedding ring, the patent, the depot, the stallion. I know it all."

Ruth watched Rathbone's face. Tried to read it for answers. Had he always known about them? From their first meeting? Had Augustus? Now that he knew (or was willing to make it plain to them) what did it mean?

"I'm afraid Mister Windom can no longer do business with you. I'm doubly afraid he wants to see you answer for your crime."

"Which crime?" Henry asked.

"Horse thieving." Rathbone thought more about it. "Was there another?"

Ruth clenched her jaw, praying Henry would shut up. Rathbone hadn't mentioned knowing anything about the stolen locomotive or the army. A chill came over her at the thought of Henry unwillingly confessing to something not already known.

Ruth interrupted. "Windom's gonna give us over? Just like that? If we pay the horseman for the stallion, it ain't theft. He'd rather us hang and him lose the air brake?"

Rathbone looked upon her softly, resisting the explanation she was seeking. The grandfather clock marked the passing of time from behind Ruth. She looked from Rathbone to Henry and back again as she puzzled together the answer.

"He doesn't need us anymore, is that it?" She knew it was true. It broke her heart to say it. "Was Augustus even in Rhode Island? Or was he working with your kind to dig dirt on Henry and me?"

Rathbone did not busy himself with elaboration. His face did not twitch, yet Ruth was certain his expression depressed as subtly as the wind etched grooves into rock.

"Is that it?" Ruth asked again. "You were keeping us here until you found something that would make it easy to rid yourself of us?"

Henry spoke low. "Ruthy—"

"Windom couldn't even come here himself to see it happen. Think about it, Henry. How far back's he been scheming? Having himself a honeyed chuckle over the rubes?" She squared on the gunman. "At least you're here, dirtying your hands."

"Will you come downstairs peacefully?" Rathbone asked. "Let no more violence be brought to you."

"You're already doing the most violent thing you can do to me," she said.

He sighed. "You only think that because you have a thin imagination."

A haze overtook her mind. The room expanded, and the distance between her and Rathbone grew. She wasn't moving so much as drawing away against her will. It was a temporary delirium. A trick of the mind. Any second a black hood would slip over her head and she'd hear the snap of her own neck in a noose. Then everything would go black forever. Or she'd wake in Chattanooga fifteen years younger. Or back at her family farm. Maybe she was still a girl having a most bizarre nightmare. Maybe she'd dreamt up Henry and the children and the States War. Maybe her mother hadn't fallen ill. Dreams were devils playing with time. Maybe a catnap on her front porch explained her whole life. She'd wake and join Mother to wash onions.

To her horror, the room's appearance arrived once again cold and detailed and real. She had energy enough only to ask, "Why?"

And Rathbone, glum and grumbling, only answered, "If a man doesn't pick the low-hanging fruit first, he'd starve on his way up the tree."

Had Ruth possessed a knife at that moment, she'd have punched it through the gunman's ribs and slapped the handle.

"Goddamn you. Don't pretend Henry and me ain't had no part. Don't you stand there and dare try to sever us!"

Rathbone closed in on her. He moved begrudgingly, not appearing to enjoy any part of it.

Henry called out, "Ruthy—"

"Missus Casper—"

Henry called out again. "Ruthy—"

"Don't sever us. Please. My husband and I, we *did* something. Please don't make it different. Like we weren't ever here."

"You *weren't* ever here."

There was no place left to go. The fates had cheated and discarded her in every way.

"You're a misery," she whispered.

Rathbone nodded. "I know."

She'd never given up in her life. Not when her mother was sickly, or her father stopped talking, or little Paul was born with a hole in his lung, or Henry went off to war. She never quit. She endured. Maybe she could endure no longer because of everything that had come before. Everyone is born with a limit to the fights they have in them and maybe she was, at this late hour, one shorter than she needed to be. All the lard of her past had thickened into something unmovable, and now she was stuck. All her endeavors had run their course. She'd done all a woman could do besides quit.

So now she would quit.

Except she didn't. She couldn't. An idea had come over her. Something desperate and unpolished, but it was something. Standing there with all that hate scorching up the sides of her belly, a half-cocked idea was better than none at all.

A chamber pot, teeming with their own shit and piss was right at her feet. She looked to make sure it was within sliding distance. Deciding it was, she kicked it and sent it skimming toward Rathbone. Then came the golden sluice slopping across the parquet and onto the agent's boots.

He kicked like a spooked horse, backing into the wet floor Henry had left, dropped his shotgun and fell sidelong into the pith of it.

In the time it took Rathbone to squirm himself back up to one knee, Henry moved between him and Ruth. He looked at the shotgun.

Ruth knew that if he wanted to he could have gotten it. But he stood there, not knowing what to do next. Just froze watching the agent smear around in the squash.

Rathbone was too soaked to rid himself of the dip. Half of him appeared perspiry. He moved to his shirt, having to brush each hand across his chest. The act of it enraged him more with each swipe. His face twisted and glowed scarlet.

He clutched around his waistband, not going for either pistol. He pulled out something smaller, something the size of a wrench with two knobby ends. He was back on his feet with it faster than had seemed possible a moment ago.

He jabbed the object between Henry's eyes, where it opened a squirt of blood from his brow. The pain caused Henry to wail as he reeled backward and tumbled over a footstool.

The agent's footing returned, and he moved in front of Ruth, too close for her to give a good kick.

"Stick out your thumbs," he said.

Ruth took a half-step back. She looked down at the wrench-like object he was holding. She saw now it was a double-hinged thumb shackle about eight inches long and covered in Henry's blood.

Rathbone snapped forward. With one hand, he grabbed her wrist and with the other fit the piece of iron around her thumb. The surprise of his quick movement forced her to twist into the room's center as if trying to distance herself from her own arm. She made it as far as the round mahogany center table before bumping into it and stopping her momentum. She knocked over a short spruce decorated for Christmas in tallow candles and ribbon. Rathbone tightened the thumbscrew and used it to pull her close. He finished locking her free thumb to the other end, then pushed her down until she sat on the floor, her hands locked together only a few inches apart. In her struggle, her wet hair had fallen in thick clumpy strands in front of her face. Candles from the tree dropped on either side of her. She must have appeared silly sitting there with two thumbs sticking in the air as if checking the wind's direction.

Henry made simpering sounds as he sat up, readying to stand in defense of his wife. He blinked rapidly, likely blinded by the eruption of blood brooking down his face.

Rathbone left Ruth slumped under the table to cuff Henry next. She watched him plant a boot on Henry's chest and put his weight on him. He knelt beside Henry and spoke in his ear. "Plenty of bludgeons at arm's length should I need them. Fist, foot, end table. Hell, I'll fetch that empty goddamn chamber pot and beat you into sludge if it keeps you still." He yanked another thumbscrew from his pocket and clamped it on before flipping Henry onto his stomach. "Best stay down." He huff-puffed above Henry, dripping wet dregs.

"Mister Rathbone," Ruth said, with an affected calm she couldn't be sure was convincing. "Please let him go. He raised no hand to you."

Rathbone drove a knee into Henry's back, flipped the pistol out of his holster, and held it by the barrel showing Ruth its smooth ivory grip. "Come closer or he gets the butt."

Ruth pleaded. "Mister Rathbone! Henry's treated you with respect and softness, and you know he's no kind of horse thief or no kind of criminal. He invented a brake and all we want to do is make enough money to pay back that Virginian and start a proper life."

"I said come closer."

"Henry's a gentle man. Please, don't send him to the noose." All the anger she'd felt toward Henry before Rathbone's arrival had vanished. She saw herself on that floor with the gunman's knee jammed in her ribs.

Rathbone slapped the pistol grip across Henry's temple. Henry gave out a sniveled yelp. It wasn't as loud or as pained as it seemed it ought to have been. Ruth worried he'd been knocked cold.

With the pistol butt repositioned over Henry's head, Rathbone looked at Ruth once again. "If you don't come any closer, it'll get worse. Come closer to me now."

They'd spent every last dime they owned getting here. Without having scratched the surface of what they'd hoped to accomplish, they were being ousted with nothing to show. The most she could say is that their invention had made the papers and she'd managed to gum up a

Yankee hotel with her own feculence. There would be no partnering with Augustus Windom, no sale, and, worse yet, they might both end up dead for their trouble.

"Just tell me," Ruth said, "what are you going to do with our train?"

"Windom knows it's stolen."

The room went silent. The earth stopped spinning. Now Ruth reckoned the full extent of her disadvantage. She was chilled down in her marrow at the thought that everything that had happened in the last year was common knowledge. Her head was screaming at her to run. But she didn't know if running was the smartest thing to do. Her hands were bound, Henry would be on his own, and she didn't know where she'd go. If she slipped out the door, past Rathbone, and down the stairs, she'd figure out the rest after. Her mind only raged at her to run.

Get away from the gunman and disappear. Leave Henry. Run away.

She looked over to Henry, saw his eyes flickering out a telegraph to her. Then the rest of him fell into fits. He began to writhe and buck, making horrible gurgling sounds. Rathbone struggled to stay in control, his knees sliding in the mess on the floor.

Ruth took advantage of his pre-occupation. She propelled herself up and galloped as best she could in a dress, tight shoes, and manacles.

It happened in flashes.

First, she was moving, still inside. Then the doorway. Closed. Narrow frame. She'd have to reach, turn the knob, and pull in one motion if she was to get out. Twist. Pull. Go. She was out and turning the corner. Banging her shoulder into the hallway wall opposite her room. People. A couple. Older.

Rathbone's voice rose over her shoulder. Had he lunged? Was he fast? Would he fire his pistols at her? Would he fire at the couple?

End of the hallway. Then the first step of a long staircase going down. Wide steps. Good for jumping. Tenth step. Eighth. Sixth. Fourth. Last jump. Landed hard on the floorboards. Hundreds of people in the foyer. No. Probably just a dozen. Felt like more. More shouts.

Getting to this point had felt like an epic poem, every step cut into her. Then the cold breath of the outdoors cut in.

Where were the other gunmen? There must be other gunmen.

She considered looking back but refrained. If someone tackled her, then she would know where the other agents were. Otherwise, she just had to keep running.

Above her, she heard Henry's voice and Rathbone's. Grunting. Squealing. Henry was shrieking.

She just had to keep running. *Ask your questions later. For now, keep running. Keep running.*

20

Henry wasn't sure what he'd intended when he'd feigned the seizure. Just wanted to take Rathbone's mind off Ruthy, give her a chance to come up with a plan. But no sensible person would have run. Not shackled. Not when she had no place to go. Not with her husband forsaken behind her.

She panicked, Henry told himself. *Thank God.*

Sometimes panic saves us. He'd survived the war by panicking. Panicking and retreating. Panicking and hiding. Panicking and leaving a locomotive at the Virginia border. Panic was, to Henry's way of thinking, an unfairly maligned emotion. It wasn't noble or brave nor did it aim to be. It aimed to keep you alive. Panic was the soul taking the reins of a person's life and steering it away from danger.

That's the last time I'll see her, he thought. *Running hell-for-leather from the hotel room.* Ruth had run toward the front door and Rathbone had tried to grab her. All Henry could do was kick out once more and sink a heel into the back of the gunman's knee. It wasn't much, but it was enough to buckle him and put some distance between him and Ruth.

He knew, in his heart, she'd done the right thing, saving herself. Running.

When Rathbone returned to his feet, it was as if Ruth had never existed. He'd given her no second thought. Instead, he'd cocked his fist like the hammer of a pistol and blasted straight away, cracking the bridge of Henry's nose. He stood over Henry and drove the same fist into him again and again.

There was nothing Henry could do. Couldn't even hold his arms out to defend himself. Rathbone said nothing. He barely let loose anything more than a few exerted grunts as he alternated one fist for the other on either side of Henry's skull.

Rathbone was going to kill him, Henry was certain. Henry could only hear some of the punches. The ones that made wet, cracking sounds. The rest never reached his ears.

He thought about High Bridge—the last battle he'd fought in the war. Every day he'd wondered what happened there. Had some from his side escaped, after all? He hadn't been friends with anyone left alive, didn't know who to trust so he trusted no one. He left them all there. As he burned to the end of his wick, there on the floor of the City Hotel, he could not help but wonder who he might have trusted and who he might have saved.

He thought of Ruth and the promise he'd made to her. He wouldn't run. No matter what, this time he wouldn't run.

He would run no more…forever.

21

There would be time for hating later. Ruth would stew on what rotten bastards Rathbone and Augustus and the Virginian were when she wasn't busy running for her life.

She hadn't thought further than to retrieve Wimp from the hotel livery. It was possible someone was waiting for her there. She had been right to think something bad was coming, hadn't she? No reason to doubt her feelings now.

She ran into the livery, keeping an eye out for more of Augustus's rowdies or anyone else who might be searching for her. There was a stable hand, a boy, done up in a leather apron that reached his shins. He was an unlikely threat, but she took no chances. And even if he meant her no harm, she was conspicuous. Cuffed at the thumbs. It wasn't only Augustus's killers she had to watch out for, but anyone who might mistake her for a dangerous criminal.

The stable hand had been cleaning a pile of horse brushes on the far end. She came up behind Wimp and thought a moment about how she might saddle this horse herself. There wasn't any way she could figure. She'd have to rely on the stable hand to do it.

She called to him and asked him to work hastily and, when he'd finished saddling Wimp, she reached for the saddle horn. She exposed the thumbscrew that way, showed that she was linked together like sausages. She made a sloppy mount and jabbed at Wimp's hindquarters without another word to the boy. No thanks, no gratuity. She took the weak nag from a walk to a gallop in three flat kicks and rode away from the hotel. Her slouch hat—Henry's slouch hat—tied to the girth strap, flapped behind them.

As Ruth tore northward, a sudden and disastrous thought occurred to her, so hot and beleaguering, she led Wimp into a side alley and stopped just to get a grip on it. All her belongings were in that hotel room, which the gunmen were no doubt ravaging at this very moment. They'd shuck most of her clothes and things, but she was certain Rathbone would hand over the patent renderings to Augustus. The certificate, too.

The avalanche of bad thoughts continued rolling toward her. The money Rathbone had given them each week, and of which Ruth had saved a portion, was in the same bag as the certificate. Henry had been right. They should have taken the money, returned to the Virginian and begged forgiveness.

It was no king's ransom, the money she'd saved, but it might have kept Henry from the noose. It might have bought them some time. She didn't know what would happen to him, and she started shaking at the thought of what might be the end for both of them. Small tremors quaked her chest and arms. Her blood lapped through her body with record speed. The cold evening air froze her lungs and made it difficult to breathe.

It had all gone so wrong.

She'd somehow managed to take a one-eyed cow of a life and blinded it. She sat atop Wimp gasping for breath. She had no idea where they were headed, until she realized there was only one safe place to go.

Ruth had taken an interest in the undertakeress—the one who'd been seated next to her in the Patent Office—and made a point to remember the address painted on the side of her wagon. One could walk past the old woman's shop and never notice the two-story brick building was there. Its only unique quality was that it was set further back as if losing to the other buildings in a race to the street. Ruth slid off Wimp and struggled to tie her to the hitching-post, clumsy as she was with two hands bound together. She took a long breath before giving the door's bell a stern tug. If Etta Claire Blighton was in, there was no doubt she'd hear it. The door was of solid stuff, with no small window or eyehole. Thick enough to muffle the croaked voice on the other side asking who was bothering her on Christmas.

Ruth had forgotten what day it was. "Truly sorry, ma'am. I've been through an ordeal."

"Are you dying?"

"No, ma'am. I've no place else to go."

"The only people I've ever known with no place else to go but an undertaker's have all been dead."

"Miss Blighton, ma'am, I beg your pardon. My name is Ruth Casper. We met and spoke briefly a few months ago at the Patent Office. Do you remember? My husband was sleeping upright, and you told me about your diamond-point caskets."

"Coffins," Blighton said. "Caskets aren't tapered at the heads."

"Yes. Do you remember me?"

There was no answer at first, then the distinct sound of a revolver's hammer being cocked halfway. "I remember," she called from inside. "Now, I'm going to open this door and I want *you* to remember something while I do it—that sound you just heard is a loaded derringer."

Blighton unlocked her locks. Each clacking one after the other down the length of the door. There must have been a dozen locks on the other side. The unadorned woman peeked out from behind the half-opened door. She was bedraggled and uncombed, wearing a heavy silk chemise and brogans. She had a disarmed quality—despite her having answered the door fully armed. That the door was open, and Ruth had not yet been fired upon, was the only salutation the old woman would offer. She flicked the small gun bore behind Ruth in Wimp's direction. "Is that a horse?"

Ruth nodded. "Wimp."

"That's a wimp?"

"Her name's Wimp. On account of she's wimpy."

Blighton fixed her eyes on Ruth. She looked vexed.

It made Ruth self-conscious, so she spoke again to stave off nervousness. "Anyway, it's just us two."

"Where is your drowsy husband?"

"He's been bedeviled by hired guns." Ruth lifted her thumb-cuffed hands. "So have I. But we're both innocent of what they say we done."

"What do they say you did?"

"Horse thievery. But we took that horse on loan."

Blighton nodded at Wimp. "You took *that* horse on loan?"

"A different one. And we promised to pay back the owner. Even left him my wedding ring as bond."

"Then why did he say you stole the horse?"

"Don't know. I guess my ring wasn't his style."

Blighton's brow knitted. "What's it have to do with me?"

"Nothing, except I'm innocent and I thought if anyone here might know something about scrapes like the one I've got myself into, it'd be you."

"Show me your hands, again."

Ruth raised up, fingers outstretched, thumbs attached by the iron shackle.

"That belong to a hired gun?" Blighton asked, pointing her derringer at the thumbscrew.

Ruth nodded. "And I hope to return it to him one day. And then some."

Blighton nodded. "You've got pluck, girl," she said. "But, given your circumstance, having pluck suggests you are also a bedlamite."

Ruth was caught by surprise. "Well," she said, "again, ma'am, if anyone could appreciate a bedlamite, my guess is it'd be you."

To which Blighton opened the door.

They weren't alone. A young girl with a wild tumbleweed of chestnut ringlets had been standing behind Blighton. She was tall and skinny, which muddied up Ruth's estimation of her age. She could have been anywhere between five and eight. Also, her standing there at all confused Ruth further.

"Hello," Ruth said, removing her wide-brimmed hat and squeezing it with her free fingers.

The girl didn't answer. She looked to Blighton, as if requesting permission to speak.

Blighton turned, shot the girl a sour grass look, and barked, "What are you doing up? There aren't any more presents. Christmas is over. Go to bed."

The girl turned quietly and disappeared up the stairs.

"Your granddaughter?" Ruth asked.

Blighton looked at Ruth as if she was softheaded. "Does this look like any kind of place to house a child?"

Ruth smiled. "It looks like a place housing a child at this moment, ma'am."

"She belongs to a swindler named Ditto. Who's Ditto? Don't know. Can't say. He knocked on my door a couple months ago, much like you just did, asking for work. Said he'd been working funerary establishments all his life. Knew enough about it that I believed him. Plus, he had the kid with him, so I figured how bad could he be? I gave him a stipend of a dollar a day to hammer coffins, drive carriage, sweep, and the like. How do I know he's a swindler? Because one day, after a couple weeks, half my tools were gone but the kid was still here." She opened her arms to emphasize that she meant here as in the spot she was currently standing. "Middle of the room, with her thumb in her mouth. His real name probably wasn't Ditto. The girl's dumb, hardly says a word. Now that's the best quality a kid can have, but it doesn't help me figure where Ditto went with my tools. And, to tell you true, I'm not positive she's even his daughter."

The story was troubling enough that Ruth almost forgot her own predicament. It was a welcome distraction. Somehow it had made her feel better. It was absurd. Everything was absurd since she'd left Chattanooga. She guessed that when everything in life is absurd, nothing is.

Ruth shook her head. "Kind of world is this, anyway?" She didn't know what else to say.

The open first floor was all gray decor. It wasn't brightened any by the evening's darkness. There weren't many windows. Of the windows there, each had broken pieces of furniture stacked or piled in front of it. Pine boxes in various stages of construction lined the wall like obedient schoolchildren. It was a rugged room, littered with all manner of cast-off tools but no Christmas decorations, the kind of space proper ladies would say needed a woman's touch. A cat pounced down the staircase, and Ruth guessed Etta Claire Blighton likely quartered upstairs with the girl.

"You ain't alone no more," Ruth said. Then, when she saw a look of confusion on Blighton's face, she added, "At the Patent Office, we talked about how you work alone." She pointed to the cat. "You have a girl and a cat helping now."

"Oh, I see," Blighton responded, "you're joking a little." She dug out an upholsterer's hammer from a tool cabinet against the wall, then reached for Ruth's hand and laid it on the workbench. Ruth wondered if the tool was a replacement for one stolen from her.

"So you're desperate?" Blighton asked.

"Well, I'm just—I…"

"It's fine to be desperate. I've been desperate before and I suspect I'll be desperate again." She inspected the lock. "I don't mind helping, but do not drag me into whatever mess you're in." She tossed the hammer back into the cabinet. "I'll break both of your thumbs if I use that." She looked around for a better tool.

"Well, ma'am," Ruth said. "I come hoping for more than just the use of my thumbs. You mentioned before you had a lawyer."

"A lawyer?" Blighton repeated without paying attention to what Ruth had asked. The thumbscrew had pulled all her attention. "Can you pick locks? I have hairpins and nails that might do."

Ruth shook her head.

"No. Well…" She reconsidered Ruth's hands. "We can't jam the lock and we can't bash it. But we might be able to pry both cuffs open."

"As long as I keep my thumbs," Ruth said, "I'll try anything."

"You'll keep them," said Blighton. "Don't know what shape they'll be in. If we wedge something thin into the teeth of each cuff, then pull it out…" She searched around the shop. Braces, bevels, saws, mallets, compasses, augers, metal planes, chisels, mortise and tenon gauges, rules and levels, hook pins, calipers, dividers, sash filisters, and other bits of every sort were littered hither and yon as if caught in a gust and scattered. She gripped a socket chisel, then fetched her last thought right where she'd dropped it. "If we wedge something like this into the jaws of the cuff, I'm pretty certain it'll loosen."

"Pretty certain?"

"As certain as I can be. Not knowing we'll see the morning doesn't stop us from sleeping at night, does it? Now you've knocked on my door in the waning hours of Christmas…do you want that lock off or don't you? Hunker down."

Ruth swallowed, widened her stance, and held her arms away from her body.

Blighton forced the chisel head into the cuff's teeth. The cat leapt to the workbench for a closer inspection.

"Here's the rub," Blighton said. "The chisel's going to have to catch the teeth of the lock. To do that, I'm going to have to tighten the teeth before I can loosen it."

"The cuff's already as tight as it can go. You close it any more it's gonna cut straight into my thumb."

"Yes, ma'am. You understand completely." She was close enough for a whispered voice to travel the distance between them. "So I suggest you look away and bite down on this."

Blighton held a tattered rag in front of Ruth. Ruth accepted.

"Go on," Ruth said, through the rag.

She felt the woman's touch, her hardened, persistent fingers squeezing the—

The lock clicked and scythed into Ruth's thumb.

Blinding pain. And Hell followed with it.

Ruth could not cry out for fear of Blighton stopping before the job was done. She looked down, certain the gears had dug into her flesh. Certain it had snapped the bone. Certain she was one less a finger. She forced her mouth shut, her lower teeth compacting into the rag compacting into her uppers. Had she not done this she'd instead have released a howl for the whole city to ponder.

Blighton held the chisel as if it was a knife that had just been hilted in a man's belly.

Ruth let out a yelp. Her thumb remained, but the chisel had slit her hand on the way out of the cuff. Like a well spring, blood seeped from below in a thick pool around the intruding metal. Scraping and bruising she could handle. Leaking she could not.

Blighton couldn't tell what damage she'd done through the blood. She leaned back, her hands at her side, as if she believed her job done.

Ruth grunted. "You ain't finished."

The other thumb still needed freeing. The pain was not imagined. It stung and would continue to sting. But the longer she waited to bust out her other thumb, the harder it would be to put herself through it a second time. She let out another bark. "Do the other thumb."

The old woman tightened her grip on the chisel and moved in before stopping. Her eyes widened as she looked behind Ruth. "Girl, I said go to bed. There is nothing proper here for a child's eyes."

Ruth, eyes open and stinging of salty tears, turned to see the girl, covered in an oversized, fraying nightgown. All at once, Ruth felt guilt, shame, and annoyance. This wasn't anyone's fault but her own. She hadn't wanted to involve any innocents, especially not a child. Why hadn't the girl stayed in bed like she'd been told?

"I can pick it," the kid said.

Blighton looked at the little one and then at Ruth, as if Ruth would be able to detect if the little one was lying.

"You can pick this lock?" Ruth asked, panting like a hot wolf.

The girl nodded, walking further into the parlor, past a bin of thin nails. She pulled out two. "With these."

Ruth looked at Blighton as the child went to work.

"Maybe she is kin to that chiseler, after all," Blighton said.

A few seconds later, the cuff sprang open. Blighton tossed the blood-smeared chisel onto the workbench. "Well, hell, girl," she said, "what were you doing in bed in the first place?"

Ruth wiggled free her shackled thumb and sat a long time appreciating her freedom. Appreciated, too, the pain that freedom had caused. Only then did she look down and inspect herself. Her vision was blurry from the rinse of tears. The back of her left hand was covered in blood from wrist to thumbnail, the wound originating from the meaty part of the palm. She could tell it would hurt to hold anything or grip with any force. She staunched the blood by wrapping the bite rag around her hand.

She was still breathing heavy, hunched like a birthing beast, but the roar in her head had quieted, at least. At her feet was the snapped thumbscrew. She examined it there on the sawdusted floor.

It had been somewhere between a minute and a year since Ruth had last regarded anyone else in the room. The girl was sitting cross-legged on a short stack of pallets, unshaken. Blighton sat, exhausted from the excitement.

"I'll tell you, little one," Ruth said, "it never felt so good to bleed like a stuck saint."

The girl gave no reaction as she watched Ruth panting and searching for more lengths of unused upholstery to soak up the oozing from her hand. The child looked sad. Ruth had looked the same way. *Oh Lord,* she thought, *I hope we ain't alike. Pray I'm no prophecy of this girl's future.* She sniffled, not wanting to continue with this turn of mind.

"Look here, child." She gently balled up two cords of tapestry cloth before tying a third around it, then held it up. The girl remained stone faced, not recognizing what it was Ruth was making. Ruth was no longer concerned with the slice in her hand, which had been well situated. She was fashioning something for the girl now.

"That must have been some horse you stole," Blighton said.

"We didn't steal it."

"It doesn't seem like you paid for it."

"We needed a second horse to help Wimp."

"Well, I believe that."

Ruth twisted the rest of the tapestry cords until they traveled off in four directions. It was a perfectly lovely rag doll with a frilly head and four limbs.

"Then we needed to sell the horse to afford the patent fee."

"Ah," Blighton said. "And, eventually, the patent would pay for the horse."

"That's right."

"Except selling a patent is the hardest part of the endeavor. I know this myself."

"We thought we'd stirred Augustus Windom." She nibbled around the cloth head to bring out the doll's crude likeness of hair. "He put us up in the City Hotel since October." The child watched Ruth's hands as if witnessing a fantastic display of hocus-pocus.

"You can't do much better than the City."

"It was a distraction from what Windom was doing."

"Oh, he stole your idea, I'm sure."

Ruth gave Blighton a curious look. "How'd you know that?"

"He's a scoundrel. And a cheat. Smiles big. Looks nice. Talks polite. Those are all distractions, too. Man's a serpent."

"Has he cheated you?"

"No. My lawyer has strong feelings about him, though."

"Your lawyer?"

"Yes, ma'am."

"Can I meet him…talk to him?"

"He's not the kind of lawyer you need. He doesn't do hanging cases."

"I don't need that kind of lawyer. I need a patent lawyer."

"Honey, your patent won't matter against Windom."

"A patent lawyer with animosities toward Augustus Windom strikes me as at least a good start."

When she'd finished constructing the doll, Ruth drew two dotted eyes and an upturned smiling mouth using hinge grease, then handed it to the child. "Voila," she said, recollecting one of the words translated in *The Encyclopedia Americana*'s section on the French language. The girl accepted the doll, turning it over in her hands, inspecting its every fiber. Ruth sensed a tiny glow in the little one. Perhaps she imagined it.

The blood had already spread through the fibers wrapped around her hand. It spread like drops of ink in a glass of clean water. The girl tucked the doll under her arm, took another patch of tapestry cloth, and re-wrapped Ruth's hand. The girl worked slowly, watching Ruth's face for any sign of increased pain. Any twitch or quick intake of air from Ruth caused the girl to stop moving. She wouldn't start up again until Ruth signaled her to continue.

When the girl was done, she sat back and smiled. "Fa la."

Ruth crinkled her brow, not understanding.

The girl returned the look of confusion. She motioned proudly toward the wrapped fabrics. "Fa la," she repeated.

Ruth closed her eyes and nodded.

"You mean, *voila*," she said, smiling. "Not *fa la*. But you've got the right season."

"This is the most I've ever heard this girl speak." Blighton shook her head. "All right. Tomorrow we'll go see my lawyer. You'll sleep here tonight. And I was wrong, child." She smiled at the little one. "Evidently, there were still a few presents to be given out, after all."

22

Henry Casper lay in a heap on the parquet floor of the City Hotel's Room 22. He was unrecognizable. Mangled and cold. His left eye swollen closed, leaking and misshapen from the pummeling he'd taken. Blood caked like war paint across his face. His right cheek jutted so unnaturally Augustus assumed Rathbone had broken it more than once. It didn't matter now. Looking down at the poor, heaped bastard, he saw that nothing would ever matter to Henry Casper again.

"You were not supposed to be this man's executioner," Augustus told Rathbone. He drew out each word in a show of labored calmness. His hands shook. His voice seethed. He still had the same ghostly pallor he'd had when Rathbone left him sitting in his own sick at the dinner table. Now it was Rathbone awash in feculence. "You were to put this man on a wagon to Virginia and let their marshals execute him."

Rathbone had already explained what had happened. And Augustus could see it for himself. The lake of piss, the tipped center table, the wet footprints and handprints trailing from the room's middle to the room's entrance. Henry Casper lying pulped and turgid on the floor amongst it all. Rathbone's clothes were still damp, and he smelled like sewer rat. He'd said his piece.

He'd left Henry in the hotel and returned to the Windom mansion. When Jefferson answered the front door, Rathbone did not wait for an invitation inside. He stalked down the hallway, threw open the door, and let Augustus see the mess he'd created.

"The fuck happened to you?" asked Augustus.

"Come with me and I'll tell you."

This was a lie. He disclosed only one detail—that the woman had gotten away. They completed the rest of the late-night carriage ride back to Room 22 in silence. Augustus had quickly deduced that whatever it was that had happened to his man, it wasn't likely something either of them wanted to discuss within earshot of the driver or anyone else.

Once they reached the hotel room, Augustus saw that the woman's escape was a mild inconvenience compared to the calamity at their feet. "You sonofabitch."

"I didn't mean it."

"That's twice in one night I've heard that from you." Augustus sniffed the air between them. "Is that—?"

"Yes."

"Are you—?"

"I slipped in it. Now let's shut up about it."

"Don't tell me to shut up. You bring me here—slathered in shitpiss—to show me a corpse that shouldn't be. *You* shut up."

Rathbone shot him a glare that warned of the dangers of continued sass. "If anyone looks close enough, they'll find you just as guilty as me." He tilted his head toward Augustus. "And, if need be, I'll see to it they look close enough."

Augustus let the threat soak in. They both stared down at Henry's body.

Augustus knew Rathbone hadn't wanted to wither the Caspers. Knew, too, that Rathbone believed this to be Augustus's fault. But he also knew Rathbone had lived high off the Windoms for years. He'd dug holes a lot deeper than the one in which they'd toss Henry Casper.

"He's nobody," Augustus continued. "A true nothing." Augustus watched the last of Henry's blood leak from under his hairline. "No trade. No money. He fought on the losing side of the war and performed cowardly in it. People won't know he died, because no one hardly knew he was alive."

Rathbone continued staring down at his accidental sacrifice.

"Is it more than you can bear, Mister Rathbone?"

"Most men who get done in have it coming to them." Rathbone opened his mouth to say more but stayed his tongue.

"Secession, desertion, a multitude of thievery, and general violence, Mister Rathbone. Think long enough on it, I believe you'll forgive yourself. Just as I forgive you."

An angry silence settled over the room.

"You're a hard man to bleed for," Rathbone said.

"Most men bleed for a lot less." Augustus looked down at his shoes, the acrid flavor of bile still haunting his mouth from his previous meal. "Unlock his thumbs," he said after a while. "Put him in three burlap sacks. Take each one out at separate times. The back door. Burn each sack."

Rathbone nodded as a matter of reflex action. It had become habit to do so whenever Augustus finished talking.

Augustus stepped back and regarded the two men—one living, one dead. "Does the wife know?"

"No."

"Do you know where she is? Where she might go?"

Rathbone shook his head. "I never got an inkling she knew anyone besides us in this room."

Augustus gave him another hard glance. "Close the report on the both of them. Settle up with the Virginian and buy a one-way ticket back to Tennessee. Then tell your Pinkerton friends the Caspers left on the train with that bounty paid. Mister Casper has retreated southward." Rathbone remained still, standing over Henry. "Before you do any of that, Uriah…change your clothes."

23

I'd like to introduce you to Mister Broussais Kimball," Blighton said to Ruth. The portly lawyer stood in the frame of his own front door, his shirtsleeves rolled to the elbow, exposing hair down to the second knuckle.

"Pleasure, madam," he said, looking askance at the pair. He rolled aside and allowed them to enter. "What have you brought me, Etta?" he asked as he led the two women into his office chamber.

Kimball's mansion was spacious. It was uncluttered with furniture, but what existed was heavy, with deep tufting and wide armrests. It had been confidently decorated. The windows held clouded glass. Untended hop vines crept around the edges and blocked half the light. All this suggested there was nothing more compelling outside than the business taking place inside. Tables, sofas, and settees were scattered aplenty in the office. The room's only two desks had been stored against the wall.

"No chairs," Ruth whispered to Blighton as they made themselves comfortable.

"He's too fat to fit in most," Blighton whispered back.

Kimball sat, seemingly unaware of their aside and asked, "Tell me directly why it is you are here."

Ruth told Kimball about the night they took Augustus on the train and what made the air brake valuable.

"How did you know you'd find a locomotive?" Kimball asked.

Ruth considered telling Kimball the truth but decided she had enough going against her.

"I didn't." It was truth enough and she hoped not to be asked any more questions on the matter.

"But your plan was eventually to steal an abandoned Confederate train?"

"My husband stole it," Ruth heard herself say. It surprised her. "And my husband ain't up for that particular crime. If someone wants to hang him for taking a leftover locomotive, they can get in line. I'm only considering the fights I got in front of me." She had not intended to rest the blame at Henry's feet, but there it came, tumbling out of her.

Kimball eyed Ruth. "If the Virginian never agreed to release the horse, your intention to pay him for it is inconsequential. You and your husband are horse thieves in the eyes of the law." He gave a sharp glance to Blighton. "And train robbers."

"Henry ain't up for the train," Ruth said. "The horseman offered up the stallion for ninety dollars."

"Have you paid him?"

"No."

"If killers hadn't killed, they'd be innocent, too."

"We're no killers."

"Nor are you innocents."

"Mister, listen here. The patent was how we were going to pay the Virginian."

"I don't understand."

"If Augustus Windom had licensed the patent like he said he would, my husband and I would use that money to pay back the Virginian."

"I see. But Windom is not connected to the Virginian. Those are two separate adversaries you have."

"Yes, sir."

"As far as the Virginian goes, you're guilty."

Ruth's hopefulness wilted.

Kimball shrugged at Blighton. "Are we then finished here or am I missing something?"

"Slow down," Blighton said. "We both know things are never as clear cut as lawyers pretend they are."

"Skip the Virginian," Ruth said. "Someone hands that old man his money he stops being a problem. What don't stop being a problem is Augustus Windom stealing our patent."

"Augustus Windom isn't the one slipping your husband's head in a noose."

Ruth shrugged. "Isn't he?"

"Consider the urgency of the two issues. One will not result in your husband's hanging. The other will."

"I've considered it."

"And what's your certainty Windom stole your patent?"

"What sense does it make to put us up in the City Hotel for months and then set his gunman on us?"

"Did he know you were a horse thief early on?"

"I don't believe so."

"One would assume learning that news would be dissuasive." Kimball again shrugged at Blighton. "What's the case here, Etta?"

"Do you believe this girl stole a horse because she's a lawless devil?"

"It's immaterial what I—"

"Don't speak to me in lawyer, Broussais. I'm not asking you as a lawyer. I'm asking you as a person."

"Would it help you to know the examiner what granted our patent says Windom visited him? Offered him money to reject the application."

"The examiner rebuffed him?"

"If rebuffed means 'told him to piss in the wind,' it seems so. Then Windom got him ousted."

"How do you know that?"

"The man said he strongly suspects it."

"The dismissed examiner?"

"Yes."

Kimball looked at her as if she were a unique type of stupid. He remained still, looking over the blood-soaked fabrics wrapped around her hand. "Why are you bloody?" he asked, after a moment. Ruth opened her mouth to answer, but he interrupted. "On second thought, don't answer. I don't want to know. I don't know you and I'm not sure I want to."

"That is a common reaction to her," Blighton said.

She had given Ruth a calico dress to wear in place of the one she'd bloodied the night before. At first, Ruth was wary. The dress had not belonged to the old woman in the sense that she ever wore it, but in that she stored it with other garments to dress up the dead if need be. Now she was relieved not to have to sit before Kimball in a bloody dress, appearing as if a participant in a massacre.

Blighton tapped Ruth's leg. "I met this woman at the Patent Office. She says she was granted a patent for a brake that would stop a train cold. You and I both know what kind of brouhaha the show they made with that brake on Windom's train caused. You know what kind of profit Windom would make on a train like that. You know he knows it, too, or else he wouldn't put them up at a fancy hotel and keep them there till Christmas. This woman has no reason to be in the horse-stealing business unless she has no other choice."

"She's still in the horse-stealing business. The reasons why are irrelevant."

Blighton reclined on the sofa and chuffed in frustration. "Then let me ask you this—you think Augustus Windom came up with that miracle train on his own? Mind you, you're under oath. And, mind you, I already know your answer because you've talked about it before."

"I'm not under oath, Etta. All these years, you still don't know how swearing in works?"

"Tell you what," Ruth interrupted, "let me speak to you of revenge." Kimball considered her from his damask settee. "Miss Blighton tells me you withstood a wronging at Windom's hand some months back?"

"It would be a great masterpiece of understatement to call it a wronging."

The answer suited Ruth. "Them papers got it wrong. It was our brake we took him on, not the other way around. I can't prove it, but I believe he's figured a way to build our train without us in the mix."

Kimball allowed himself a nod. "It would be simple. He'd forge his own patents. Or, even simpler, ignore your rightful claim to the machinery knowing you haven't the money to wrestle him in court."

Blighton and Ruth eyed him sidewise. He'd just articulated what they'd been trying to say.

"I hope that isn't the sum and substance of why you're here. His crime, if he indeed committed it—"

"You know he committed it," Blighton said.

"I know he's *capable* of it. Many are capable of it. Patent disobedience is not only common, it's expected. It's why you must be more careful than you were sharing your contraption. Where does the vengeance come into play?" Kimball remained reserved, but the door remained open.

"I heard what he did to you," Ruth said. "Your ousting. His embarrassing you in public. The damage to your reputation—"

Kimball smiled at her. It was a tight smile. No teeth. "Etta exaggerates. My reputation is untarnished."

"Nevertheless, I believe you share a similar outlook on the man as I do. Might be you know him to be the sort of swindler I'm describing. I come looking to you for justice and I offer justice in return."

Kimball's knee began jouncing, his interest piqued. "Have you something particular in mind?"

"In part."

"Well, will you get on with describing it or shall I have a birthday first?"

"Augustus Windom owns the biggest fleet of trains in the world."

"Yes," Kimball agreed, wondering why she was making the case *against* his involvement. His knee bobbed with greater force.

"Bigger than any other two locomotive companies combined."

"Mm-hm."

"But not bigger than *all* other locomotive companies combined." Kimball's bouncing knee stopped as she continued. "I have an idea how to turn 'em all loose on Augustus at once."

Kimball looked at Ruth as if she'd whispered some magic conjuration. His eyes searched the floor as if placing the rush of thoughts one-by-one at his feet.

"See? That's why I brought her. I like her," said Blighton.

Kimball pointed casually at Ruth. "You've thought about this?"

"I need your help."

"Yes. But what about your husband?"

"Yes. Well…" Ruth scooted forward on the deep sofa cushion. "So I have two favors to ask right up front. The first is for you to find out what they done to Henry."

"The second?" Kimball asked.

Ruth was careful to note that he had not declined the first. "The second is you loan me the horseman's money."

Kimball had agreed to find Augustus at home and Blighton had agreed to let Ruth sleep in the child's room until they figured what would happen next.

"I can't keep the child," Blighton said. "Nor can I send her away. I suppose an orphanage is the answer, but those places are indecent. I can't send *you* away, either, though I should, given that you're a thief of all manner." Ruth thanked her and Blighton swatted away the words like an annoying gnat before leaving the spare room.

Ruth didn't want to intrude on the child more than she already had. She couldn't help scrutinizing the signs of her harsh rearing. The girl wrestled off her clothes, each item shamed with holes. Traded them in for a nightgown of even more threadbare material. Ruth surveyed her worsted stockings bunched inside each street-mired shoe. Beside them was a pair of high-waisted gray boy's pants; a faded olive shirt that had not been boiled, soaped, or ironed in some time; and a wool muffler that served the duty of her coat. Given the sorry condition of her clothes, Ruth had the urge to pull back the child's lips and inspect the condition of her teeth just as she'd done with Wimp. The horse didn't like it and Ruth figured the same would be true for the child. Her hair was unbrushed and sprung from her head in every direction. The sharp protrusions of her shoulder bones called attention to her starved frame. Her skin appeared rugged and worn, older than the skin a girl her age should have. It was dry and gray at the joints.

Ruth wanted to touch her. Reach out and heal her somehow, forgetting in that moment which one of them was the injured party. Her own circumstances had returned in a flood. For so long Ruth's pain had been preserved, pickled by the loss of her own babies, still just as bitter now as it always had been. Ruth had not let a day pass without thinking of them, imagining what they'd be doing if they'd lived. Her heart had kept them alive and, with it, her own pain.

Paul was the name of her first child, born with a full mop of dark hair, dead two days later. Introductions on Tuesday, eulogy on Thursday. The next two were gone before they'd come to fruition. They hadn't made it far enough along to name. She'd always believed the second two were girls. Felt it down in her middlebones. To know nothing about them was a persistent torment. Ruth had named the other two privately and never told Henry. She'd named the second Evangeline and her third Cornelia. In her imagination—the only place the children had ever lived—she couldn't abide them carrying on without names. *Evangeline Holliday Casper*, she'd say. *Cornelia Elizabeth Casper*. She whispered them into the air just to hear them curl and bounce from her lips.

If she was not to be a mother—which seemed like a damned fateful justice given how she let her own mother wither—what was she fated to be, instead? She'd spent too much of her life caring for those she shouldn't have.

The child had heaped her clothes on the floor. She adjusted her nightgown and turned to see Ruth watching her but didn't move beyond that.

Ruth averted her eyes. "Ain't you going to sleep, little one?"

The girl looked at Ruth uneasily, then looked at the bed and finally at the blankets spread across the floor.

"Oh," Ruth said. "You're wondering if I mean to take the bed?" The girl offered no confirmation. "Way I see it, I'm the interloper." Ruth patted the bed. "Rest your sit-upon there, girl." The narrow bed sank in the middle as the girl climbed into it. She held the doll close. "The man what brung you here," Ruth asked the child, "was he your daddy?" The girl nodded, concentrating her gaze on the rag doll, as if diverting her eyes would halt Ruth's questions. "Did he tell you where he's going?"

The child gave no answer. Maybe the girl didn't know or didn't trust her enough to say.

A pair of weak tallow candles kept the room from darkness. Ruth wished it wasn't so late, wished she wasn't so tired, wished she'd thought to wash the girl's clothes in the water tub before now. Or better yet, since these were wishes, she wished the girl's father, wherever in hell he was, would come back and claim her. Or better still, that he'd never left her alone in this place full of dead things.

What she could do, however, was freshen up the girl's hair. "Well, if you ain't asleep yet, sit up." She began to use a comb to sort out the child's thick ringlets. "I've always had wispy hair. I don't know a thing about curls like you've got, but we need to do something." She stood behind the child and loosened the knots at her neck. Nearly an hour passed before all of the girl's hair had been combed out and parted to either side of her head.

Ruth brought close both candles so the girl could see herself in the hand mirror. "You like that?"

The girl shook her head.

"Well, I don't know how to fix you proper and I don't suspect Miss Blighton does either. You'll just have to live with it for now, trusting it's better than it was. Can you do that? Live with it?"

The girl nodded, though her expression suggested otherwise.

"Tell you what." Ruth pulled her slouch hat from a nail stuck in the wall. "You like hats?"

The girl considered the one in Ruth's hand and nodded. Ruth placed it on her head like a crown. Although the hat was wide, the girl's hair filled the space. It looked fanciful and striking atop her head. Its wide brim dipped just below the child's eye line, her thick hair pushed down around her ears, framing her face. It gave the shy girl an air of mystery. In the weak glow of the candles, she appeared more outlaw than child.

"Looks better on you than it ever did on me. You wear that until we can do up your hair in a way that suits." A smile appeared from underneath the wide brim. The first Ruth had ever seen from her. "I guess that means it's your hat now, girl. We'll puzzle out the rest as we go."

The child bent up the brim to see and swept her fingertips along the soft fabric. It might as well have been velvet.

Ruth returned the slouch to the wall. "This hat left the nail as mine and returned to it as yours."

The girl nodded.

"Will your pa come looking for you?"

The girl thought about it then shook her head.

"Never?"

Another shake.

Ruth straightened, bracing against the bleakness of the girl's woe.

"Now, look here. I want to thank you for your help. Saving my right hand from the fate of my left with your lock picking."

The girl nodded again.

"You ain't enthusiastic about conversation, I can tell that much." The child's gaze fled to the safety of the rag doll. "From now on, don't just nod. Say, 'Yes, ma'am.'"

"Yes, ma'am." The girl studied Ruth's hand. "Your hand feel better?"

It undid Ruth that such an unlucky child should concern herself with a stranger's well-being. She simply nodded, her wellspring of words having gone dry.

And the little wiseacre said, "Say, 'Yes, ma'am.'"

It roped a laugh and pulled it right out of Ruth, a true and deep laugh that stretched her insides and cleared her mind of all the bad things. "Yes, ma'am," Ruth said, still laughing. "I do believe you've kept me honest." It felt good to laugh. She almost asked the girl's name but thought better of it. She didn't want to know for the same reason her family never named the hogs they kept—because they never kept them long.

She took her place on the floor. She unwrapped the blood cloth. It returned her dark thoughts like thunderheads blotting out the sun. She blew out the candles, figuring the child didn't need to watch her wounds air out. "If you go wandering in the night, remember to watch your step. I'm down here, ripe for the squashing."

"Yes, ma'am," came a whisper from the bed above her.

In the dark, all her troubles returned in full. She remembered the patent and the gunman, and what had happened to Henry. What *would* happen to Henry. She remembered every decision that brought her here. She remembered that her future—*the* future—was uncertain.

There in the darkness, so the girl wouldn't notice, Ruth squeezed her eyes shut and muffled the sound of her cries with the ruddy fabrics that had lately been wrapped around her hand.

It felt good coming out of her. Almost as good as laughing.

24

The brake was being produced. At a snail's pace, compared to what Augustus had wanted, but faster than his lead engineer had guessed was possible. Augustus derived no joy from it. He derived no joy in anything. Joy was a precious metal fully mined from his life. He'd tipped off his center and, having tipped, could not regain his footing. He felt as if he'd been in a perpetual stumble for years, now culminating in his final crash in the dirt. It was him doing these things. It was him lowering costs by swapping good Windom locomotives for bad Fairbanks ones. It was him shouting at the Orange Street Club staff and members until they would no longer turn up. It was him who'd ordered his man to give over Henry Casper to the law, and it was him who'd arranged to cover up his demise.

He'd lost himself. He tried to remember who he was. What kind of man had he been before he'd been this? No kind of man, he guessed. He'd gone from boy to bastard in more ways than one.

The days after Christmas had been bloated with the comings and goings of one client or another. Henry Casper's mangled face lingered through it all in his mind's eye, the fractured body shielding half his vision. It lay always before him in judgment, speaking not a word.

The serapi in his office had worn thin from the trail of feet crossing over it to his desk. Knocks on the door, people entering, handshakes and head nods, exits. And he could not think. He could not see.

And so it continued this morning with the first knock of the day.

"Woe is the man arriving here before my coffee and biscuit."

"It's Uriah," Rathbone said through the door. "Broussais Kimball's come a-calling. He's unarmed."

"I thought it better to avoid enticement altogether," Kimball added, without invitation. "My feelings on you are not mixed, Augustus. If I am here it is because it must be so."

Augustus sat back in his chair. He let loose his wonderings about why Broussais Kimball might think this a place accepting of his visitation. A sick feeling came over him. The kind that starts in the throat and sinks into the belly. That Kimball should come to call was perhaps the most unexpected thing in a week brimming with them.

"Bring him in, Uriah. Linger just behind."

The door opened and Kimball filled the frame, only a hint of Rathbone visible behind him. When Rathbone emerged from around Kimball's great bulk, Augustus noticed his sagging comportment. He looked, daresay, worse than Augustus, if that was possible. No doubt this was the result of three days disposing of Henry Casper's body and traveling to the Virginian. He'd have sectioned the corpse and burned it, scrubbed clean the hotel, traveled to Virginia and back. It was likely, now that Augustus thought about it, that Rathbone had not slept at all.

Augustus took him in before hurling the opening salvo. "I've never been good newsed by anyone arriving unannounced."

Kimball aimed a finger at Rathbone. "Must he stand behind me? If your gutless brute listens in, I'd prefer he do it head-on."

"I thought you were here to talk to me, not him," Augustus said.

Kimball stilled himself, waiting for Rathbone to move into view. If Augustus hadn't been so curious about Kimball's presence, he might have obliged the standoff. Instead, he waved Rathbone over.

Kimball's eyes were stony on Augustus. "Where is Henry Casper?"

Augustus snorted and shook his head but offered no other response. The inquiry dropped his throat to the cellar. His mind raced to connect Broussais Kimball to Henry Casper. He couldn't have known, could he? Rathbone was careful, the most discreet of men. But hadn't it been Rathbone's misjudgment and brutality that got him stuck in this mess in the first place? And wasn't Kimball just ruthless enough to sniff out his mistakes? Kimball was ruthless, that much was certain. It would not surprise Augustus if Kimball had been following him for months.

Jesus Christ. Had Rathbone told Kimball? How quickly paranoia can take control of a man's thoughts. Perhaps Kimball had not visited on his own, after all. Perhaps it was Rathbone who'd urged his arrival.

Augustus had let too much time pass without answering. "I'm sure I don't know," he finally said. "Mister Casper and I only had the briefest acquaintance."

Kimball nodded at Rathbone. "Does he know?"

Rathbone didn't answer. Kimball's question encouraged Augustus. Perhaps he and Rathbone had not conspired after all.

"What concern of yours is Henry Casper?" Augustus asked.

"As it happens, I've come to ask you the same thing. It is my understanding you put Mister Casper up in the City Hotel."

"Yes."

"For several months."

"Yes."

"And on Christmas Day you expelled him."

"Well now, who told you that?" It took a mule's stubbornness not to glance in Rathbone's direction.

"Do you deny it happened?"

If there was one man with whom Augustus had not wanted to parry and joust, it was his father. But if there was a second, it was Kimball. "I won't deny it, no. Mister Casper turned out to be a poor investment."

"Was he?"

Augustus shrugged. "Good investments don't get drummed out."

"Mister Casper has a patent on the very same air brake you've been credited with having invented yourself."

Augustus felt his face redden and warm. He could not guess what Kimball knew or did not know. But now, suddenly, that gap-toothed patent examiner came to mind. He might have been the connector. Or the Casper wife. Perhaps, if not Rathbone, it had been her to compel Kimball here. Though her connection to Kimball was as much a mystery as anything else.

"If you know that, counselor, perhaps you know that I, too, have air brake patents. Had them first, in fact." Kimball gave no sign he'd heard. Augustus continued. "Are you Casper's lawyer?"

"If he were my client, I suppose I'd already know where he is. But I don't. And so I ask again, do you?"

Augustus could not tell the truth, of course, and did not know what parts of the lie Kimball would recognize. Unprepared to take either action, he stupidly took both. He smirked and shrugged, the most gutless admission of guilt possible. He immediately regretted his bungled reaction and aimed to rally. He couldn't afford the conversation about Henry Casper to continue. It must become about himself and Kimball.

"The last time we spoke you—"

Kimball interrupted. "I know when we last spoke."

"Then you understand my confusion as to why you'd come here."

"Where else am I to find you? I'm disallowed at the Orange."

"You should consider yourself disallowed from my presence no matter the location."

Kimball gathered himself up. "So then you do not know where Henry Casper is?"

"I've already told you I do not."

"You've told me, yes. But perhaps you've not made mention of everything you know. It's not inconceivable one would leave something out. I, for instance, have not mentioned everything I know."

"No?"

"I've not mentioned the Virginian's bounty on Mister Casper for borrowing a horse."

"Borrowing? Is that what Henry Casper told you?" Augustus had become invested in his own deceit. He'd momentarily forgotten that Henry Casper couldn't have told Kimball anything.

"So you know about it?"

Augustus was in a tight spot. "Horse thievery is a fine reason to disemploy anyone, isn't it? Kingdom save you from having to defend that poor bastard."

"Skip the Kingdom. A much smaller sum will save Mister Casper. Just tell me where he is." Kimball stabbed a look at Augustus meant to bleed out an answer.

"I don't know where he is. He's gone."

Kimball's attention turned to Rathbone. "If either of you has him, turn him loose or prepare to join him wherever it is he's stowed."

Augustus came out with it. "We already paid the Virginian." It sprung from him like a throat clear. "And my man put Mister Casper on a Tennessee-bound train just three days ago."

"Who paid the Virginian?" Kimball asked.

Augustus's eagerness left him. "It came from my coffers," he said. "Mister Rathbone returned just late last night."

Kimball looked on in suspicion. "Do the Pinkertons know this?"

"It's early yet," Augustus said. "My intention was to alert them of that very fact later today. Once I learned the man was a charlatan and a criminal, I was compelled to cut him loose. And, once loosed, I had to tie off the remaining limb to ensure his gangrenous crimes progressed on me no further."

"Are you suggesting Henry Casper was as vital to your business as a limb is to your body?"

"It is eight o'clock in the goddamn morning, Broussais. I'm sorry my poetry suffers from the same early morning delirium as the rest of me." Augustus was keen to see Kimball out of his chamber. "Now, I've answered all the questions I care to."

"You've already said more than I thought you would."

What a sneaky bastard, Augustus thought. To play with him in this manner. He had come asking little and saying little. He was here to shake him. To show him there was more of Kimball left.

Kimball stepped forward. He was deliberate. His movement sent Rathbone's hands to his holsters and Augustus into a clench. Augustus hated that his first reaction was to tighten, but he covered it well. His face did not change, nor his posture. He'd appeared bored when Kimball started moving and bored when he stopped.

"If that's the story you swear to in court, I'm going to spread it on toast and make you eat it." He turned to Rathbone. "The smartest thing you could do is unholster those irons and paint me in scarlet right here. But you won't do it because you were a Pinkerton and Pinkertons don't get to be Pinkertons unless they have a conscience." He looked Rathbone over from top to toe. "Hidden away by time as that conscience may be. So I will repeat quietly and hope it reaches whatever small part of you is still decent—where is Henry Casper now?"

Augustus did not interrupt because Augustus wondered the same thing.

"Home," Rathbone said. "Sent on a train intended for Chattanooga."

"And his belongings? He had clothes and a patent in a haversack."

"His property went with him to Chattanooga," Augustus said.

"Given his leave-behinds, that strikes me as unlikely."

"What leave-behinds?"

"His wife, Augustus. She remains. I doubt he'd leave her behind. That he did suggests he left against his will. And, if he left against his will, it's unlikely he packed up his possessions. Especially the one I believe you stole."

"All right, then," Augustus said, having danced as close to the fire as he cared to. "If there's one thing I like about you, Broussais, you know when to leave a room."

A silent stare passed between them before Kimball smiled and left without another word.

25

When Kimball arrived at Blighton's shop, it was darker than usual. Ruth was busy helping her construct a regiment of coffins, enough to form a blockade of light before each window.

"Have you ever considered adding a window or two to this cellar?" Kimball asked. "Just because your customers live in eternal darkness does not require you doing the same."

"The sun at the window is not my concern as much as the paying customers at the door," Brighton replied as she moved to a tool cabinet and rooted in one of the square shelves for nails. She inspected each and threw the bent ones to the floor. "And, if I want to keep the customers at the door, these pine boxes need hammering along with a dozen other things. My energies have been too divided of late." She stole a glance at Ruth and went on rooting.

"You talk to Windom?" Ruth asked.

Kimball nodded. "Before the popinjay barred me from the Orange, I'd told him he was not to be voted in as a board member in place of his father. The reason, as it was explained to him, was because he'd accomplished nothing on his own. If he'd been developing your train brake then, I am quite certain he'd have trumpeted it that day before the board. I'm certain now that you've got month-old patents that are real and he's got year-old patents that are fake."

"And what about Henry?"

"Augustus paid his bounty. Didn't want the Virginian drawing attention to his own crimes, is my guess. They put him on a train to Chattanooga three days ago."

Ruth stopped. Henry was alive and free. She'd stopped listening to Kimball. What was it she was feeling now if not relief?

Blighton snorted. "How do you know they ain't lying about Henry?"

"I traveled from Augustus's mansion to the Baltimore police bureau to verify the claim," Kimball said. "Seems he's telling the truth. The warrant only named your husband and it had been lifted earlier this morning."

"Only Henry?" Ruth looked disappointed. "I was the one aiming the damn rifle."

Kimball shielded himself with his hand. "I don't want to hear any more."

Blighton tisked. "I don't know if I'll ever understand you, lady," she said. "You're the only fool I've ever met sad her name was free and clear."

"What name?" Ruth said, louder than she intended. "That old pisser was too embarrassed to admit he was taken by a woman and so he did what everybody does, he cut me out of it."

"Missus Casper—" Kimball said.

"You both have your name printed on the side of your buildings. Me? I can break the law without a notice. You'd be ornery, too, if no one took notice of you."

Neither Blighton nor Kimball knew what to say, so they let a respectful moment of silence pass.

"Augustus's position, Missus Casper, is that he has no business with you and no earthly idea why you credit yourself with having invented the Windom Air Brake."

"The *Casper* Air Brake."

"That *is* what we're fighting to determine."

"We?" Blighton said. "So is she your client?"

"I believe her. I also believe Missus Casper here has a fine plan in place. Let us band together now in battle with the men who hate Augustus Windom as much as you or I."

"So I'm your client?" Ruth asked. She needed to hear him say it.

"You are my client. And, more importantly, I am your lawyer. So you will do what I say and when."

"That's not how I featured it."

"Madam, I will front you the cost of my services but, in so doing, I'll not give a good goddamn what you feature. We will leave by my personal passenger train in three days. We'll likely be gone two months or more, depending on the necessaries of my other clients."

"Well, if we're setting conditions, I have only one. I insist on Blighton and her stripling coming on the expedition with us."

The old woman sat up straight. "Now, wait a minute," she protested.

Kimball did not let her continue. "We'll have to impose upon nine companies in seven weeks and prepare for each one."

Ruth nodded. "That's why I want them in tow."

Blighton turned now. "I said wait a minute. No one asked my position on the matter. If I close shop for a month, I might as well close up forever."

"What if I paid your way?" Ruth asked.

A rude little laugh came burping out of the old woman. She didn't need to explain why. She stood and retrieved a flask from one of the square bins. Ruth had not known Blighton to be a tippler, but the week had been long, and a person could only take so much.

Ruth pushed on. "When this is over, I'll be flush. Whatever you lose, I'll pay it twice over."

"You're a little early on the promise making," Blighton said.

Kimball focused on Ruth, agitation in his voice. "I will pay for travel and board and two outfits befitting business acquaintanceship. If Etta and her orphan decide they want to come, that is for you to straighten with them."

"Thank you." Ruth understood all at once that he was offering her more than anyone else would have. She decided his grudge against Augustus must have been as powerful as her own.

"It is a loan only, madam," Kimball said. "I will recoup every personal cost to me immediately following a legal victory."

"What if there ain't one?"

"I never concern myself with that possibility." He opened the front door. "Meet me Friday morning at the Centre Street depot. Six o'clock."

"You're leaving already?" Ruth asked.

"Would you prefer I sip tea and hammer on coffins or pull together an expedition?"

"Well, *I* wouldn't mind you hammering a coffin," Blighton said.

Kimball let go of something close to a smile. A smirk, perhaps. Then he was gone.

"He's never in one place for more than a short while," Blighton said. "As inflated as that man's belly is, he gets around like a rabbit." Having found all the necessary straight nails, she emptied them into an unfinished coffin, save for the one she pounded into the pine.

Ruth watched her. Even though she could see every hammer whack coming, each one made her blink. She felt herself getting agitated and spoke through the hammering. "Tenderness ain't where I'm comfortable. Just the same I want to thank you. For opening your door to me and for everything else."

"What?" Blighton said through her own hammering.

"I said I want to thank you."

"So thank me."

"I mean I want to show my gratitude."

Blighton looked at Ruth as if she'd just been insulted. "You haven't two coins to rub together. Show your gratitude by doing for yourself."

"My, but you are sour. I'm trying to thank you."

"Sourness is what's kept me from sleeping on people's floors. You'd be good to catch a little sourness yourself."

"Most people think I'm plenty sour."

"Well, none of those people are here now, darling."

It surprised Ruth how little she cottoned to being called darling. "So you won't come with me?"

"No, thank you. But, if you come away a richling, I would not turn down a generous donation." Ruth watched her go on hammering. After a few more nails, Blighton stopped. "I appreciate your inclination. Don't let my refusal convince you otherwise."

Ruth nodded.

"If you wanted to do something now, you could look after the child."

"What?"

"She's taken a liking to you and I believe you to her, if I'm not mistaken."

Ruth hadn't considered how the girl might have felt about her. Only how she felt about the girl. She nodded at Blighton's appraisal.

"Now, I've heard you tell that girl that wobbling your head up and down is no kind of answer."

Ruth answered properly. "Yes, ma'am. You're right. About the girl and the head wobbles."

"All right. So, take the girl. Free up my spare room again."

"Is it right to just take her?"

"Hell, honey, the child's daddy left her here." Blighton tossed the hammer into the coffin and traded it for her flask. "What's right got to do with it?"

Ruth had found a spot on the floor to stare at and escaped into the recesses of her imagination. "What do you suppose is harder? Hoping he returns or knowing he won't?"

Blighton tipped back the flask in full. She'd finished it without sacrificing any to Ruth. "That's some question there, isn't it?"

"What kind of man puts such worry on a child?"

"Listen here. You've got no call to be this woebegone. That kid's going to be peaches. Maybe a bit more hardscrabble than a well-reared girl, but she'll live a life worth living."

"I can't figure how a man leaves a child to grow up poorly reared, knowingly missing what he could have been there to see."

"For some people, a child isn't what makes life worth living."

Ruth looked at Blighton and remembered who she was talking to. She refrained from comment.

"If the lawyer will have the girl and you'll have the girl, take her. She's better off with you than me." She quieted her tone and peered up the stairs to ensure the child wasn't within listening distance. "If we're being most truthful, I wouldn't mind losing the weight from my shoulders." She escaped within herself for a moment, stood unmoving as if the operator of her body had left his post. When she returned, all she said was, "I lack the ache of motherhood," before continuing to hammer her coffin.

It was the only divergence in Ruth's admiration for her.

Ruth spent the afternoon deciding whether she wanted to take the child. Having decided she did, she spent the evening figuring how to extend her the invitation. She was embarrassed. A grown woman hemming and hawing over an orphan's approval. She began to gird herself against the possibility the girl would not want to go. It was a probable and understandable outcome.

They were preparing for bed again. The child tucked into the cot and Ruth laid out across the planks. They'd been sprawled for a few long minutes before Ruth sat up and filled the silence.

"I'm leaving, little one. Couple days."

The girl did not move. "Where?" she asked.

"You ever ridden a train?"

"No, ma'am." The soft rustle of the girl's pillow suggested she was shaking her head.

"Well, look here, Miss Blighton can't keep watch over you. Or don't want to, it's uncertain. You come with me, I'll watch over you. See you get fed proper. Maybe make you another rag doll on a slow evening. You'll stay with me for safekeeping. That fine by you?"

From what Ruth could see in the low light, the child appeared frozen. Eyes open. Thinking.

"That's fine by me," the child said, finally.

"Now, I ain't forcing you to go. So, if come tomorrow you find yourself having a second thought, I won't be cross. Just know that I'd like some company while I'm gone, and you'd make a fine companion." She said this into the darkness about where she guessed the girl's face still rested.

"Yes, ma'am."

"Good. I'll tell you the rest in the morning. The wheres and the whys. For now, drift off to sleep thinking about what you want to take along with you. Not that your choices are plentiful."

The girl's meagerness had the surprising effect of spiriting Ruth. That this child had so little was a reminder that life could be worse and would become worse if Ruth gave up. As long as she drew breath, there was something left to do. Some new reason to care.

What happens is, pieces of a person's dignity get nicked—embarrassments, flinches, concessions, negotiations, broken promises—each indignity chips away at the whole. A person doesn't know how much has been chipped away until there's nothing left. Ruth stayed awake on that floor thinking about the indignities and how much of her was left.

Her time with Henry had been more bitter than sweet. He'd become a reminder of the life she'd never live. When the war separated them, Ruth called on her imagination to keep her company. She'd spend the late morning talking with the ghosts of her three children or singing to an empty room at night. She'd pass the choring hour telling an empty room the story of the great cypress stand behind her father's house. A part of her knew she hadn't really shared those songs and those stories with anyone. But only a part. At times, it felt someone else had heard it, that it mattered to someone besides her. She'd pleaded with the logical part of her mind to withdraw and leave her to her reverie. Occasionally, she'd travel too far into delirium. She'd believe she heard a question arise from a dark corner or she'd hold out a rag for someone to take from her, leaving it dripping. She often frightened herself with how counterfeit she'd allowed her world to become.

And when her imaginings hadn't run away from her in full, they were cruel. She imagined the children with Henry and—when Henry would return inside or walk past the window or sit beside her—she'd believe, for a moment, the children were there, too. A hopeful flash followed by sorrow. A bird's chirp might sound like a distant giggle. Rabbit feet across the porch echoed the *tip-tip-tip* of a cup 'n' ball game. Her mind had its own cypress grove to wander through. She imagined those children everywhere, conjured them in the periphery of every glance. A million little letdowns every day. Always. They'd lived a hundred lives in Ruth's mind and not one on Earth. There was no defense against it. It twisted her soul in a way that wrung all the life from it. They would never be there with her. They would never trail behind her like ducklings in a pond. Never appear beside Henry's silhouette in the distance. Babies had a fresh scent she'd never smell. She'd never understand the melt a child's hug could give her heart. Never know what her children's giggle sounded like. Was it high and silly or short and from the gut? No sniffles or first words or first steps or first birthdays even. She would never see them learn, and never learn from them in kind. She would never show them what a strong mother could do. She would never be able to prove she was a better mother than her own had been. And maybe she wasn't. Her own sickly mother had, at least, borne three children. What had Ruth done?

She'd done none of those things. She'd only imagined them.

When Ruth opened her eyes to a new day, the child was sitting feet a-dangle on the bed looking down at her. She'd hatted herself and gripped the rag doll, adorned in the same tatter-cloth dress she'd worn the last two days.

"Ready," said the child.

"And eager, I see."

The child nodded before quickly adding a "Yes, ma'am."

"That hat sure does add an air of pride to you, little one."

Ruth rinsed her face in the wash basin, chewed a fingerful of mint, and scraped a brush through her hair before folding up her blanket. "Now, listen here, girl. We don't leave just yet, but we are going to do some shopping today. Will you come?"

"Shop for what?" asked the girl.

"A dress that hasn't belonged to a hundred dead women before me." The girl didn't understand the explanation and nodded absently. "If you're still planning to leave with me, before you go, you'll need to give your thanks to Miss Blighton for sheltering you as long as she did. There's not much kindness to go around so, when you get treated to it, it's best not to let it go unnoticed. And don't start in silent nodding, either. You say warm words to her. She coulda done you worse. You don't have to tell her just yet, but I smell breakfast and she might give you one extra strip of bacon if you do."

"Ain't you coming?" asked the child.

"Soon enough. I'm to write a fast letter, first." Ruth watched the girl go. "Listen here, little one." The girl spun back like an indecisive gust had taken hold of her. Ruth pointed to her hat. "You tie the string up tight once we're outside. Mind me, now. I've seen plenty hats take to the wind."

They arrived at C. Wm. Easterday's dress shop. Easterday was a handsome man without humility. He turned up his nose at Ruth, Blighton, and the child as they entered. They asked him about business-appropriate garments. He believed them neither moneyed enough to afford his prices nor sophisticated enough to require such finery in the first place. They were grubby, certainly, and could not approach the refinery common to the boutique. So it was quite a thrill for Ruth to hush the rude clothier by unfolding the banknotes Kimball had loaned her and laying them one by one on the glass display case. Easterday played along, after that.

Moved now by the sight of money, the clothier asked, "Is it a party you are attending?"

"No," said Ruth. "I'm rousing men to do battle."

The clothier had no reaction to this or, if he did, he kept it to himself and rephrased his question. "How do you want people to react to you?"

Ruth had no idea. She hadn't considered it. No one had ever asked such a simple question in such a straight-ahead manner. It set her on her heels not to have a ready answer. She did not know who she was or how she wanted others to see her.

Blighton interjected, "How about the exact reverse of how you reacted to her when we walked in?"

Ruth thought a bit more. "If given the choice between crossing an emperor or crossing me, I want them to prefer crossing the emperor."

With Blighton's encouragement, Ruth chose a crimson, ball-fringed Zouave jacket and black taffeta dress. Since the child had laid claim to the slouch hat, Ruth replaced it with a chestnut hair net and a feathered short-brimmed topper.

She did not enjoy trying on each garment and stood before the young girl and old woman with as much enthusiasm as a tired goat. She would neither twirl nor point her toe to lengthen her leg. She stood without smiling, her hands stuck on her hips.

"There you are," Blighton said in mock sincerity. "I guess parading in frippery has been your true calling all along."

Ruth felt embarrassed by the comment, knowing Blighton didn't mean it.

"You look mean," the girl said.

Ruth stood straight. She could not recall the last time anyone had appraised her appearance. The description pleased her, and she gave the girl a thankful smile.

"The girl's right," Blighton said. "You look tough as a twice-hammered nail." She retrieved a silver chatelaine from a nearby table and held it against Ruth's hips for size. "She needs to look like a killer. How's this look around her middle?" she asked Easterday.

"It's used in England for clipping one's pertinents to the end of each chain for easy reach," he said.

"I know what it's for. How's it look?"

All four studied the intricate belt and the thin chains hanging from it.

"You'll jangle," the girl said, meaning it as a positive thing.

"It'll free your hands." Easterday shrugged. "They'll be unbound."

"I'll take it, then. And let no one mistake you for a poor salesman, fella." Easterday nodded and moved toward the glass top counter. "Now," she said, halting his progress, "I suspect I have money to spare, so what have you got in the way of dresses for the little one? And you might add in some underthings and new boots for the both of us."

26

Kimball's six-car locomotive paced beside the Delaware River toward Philadelphia. Wainscoting bedecked the warm interiors and gilt molding framed the curved entrances.

Ruth and the child shared a train bench while Kimball sat across from them jabbing greasy pieces of gizzard into his mouth with a fork. The child had fallen asleep against Ruth. She snored, letting out darling little cuts of air through her nose until Ruth nudged her into a quieter position.

Kimball looked on, curious if the nudge would lead to quiet. He fed himself another hunk of slick meat and spoke with his mouth still chewing. "Does she speak?"

"Not as much as I'd like. Maybe more than you'd like."

It was the first inquiry he'd made about the girl. He'd been in her company a full day and he'd neither spoken to her nor stuck out his tongue, nor wiggled an ear in her direction. He did nothing to endear himself to her. It was as if, to Kimball, Ruth had not boarded with a girl, but with a kitten and his only concern was whether it would scratch the furniture.

"Do you have a plan for the girl?"

"I arrived at Blighton's without fully knowing what I'd do, and I haven't caught up since. A made-up mind don't allow for choices, I guess."

"Etta says the father absconded weeks ago and hasn't returned."

"Etta's not even sure he was the child's real father. The little one says he was, but I can't see how a man could ever leave his family."

She expected some sassy retort. Instead, he watched her from the corner of his eye. "Have you written your husband?"

"Yes, sir. Should arrive to him by the time we leave Iowa."

"He'll need to turn up. He's the patent holder and we can't bring about infringement charges without him." Ruth said nothing. She let the truth of the spot they were in settle over. Kimball glanced at her sidelong. "I assumed his absence would torment you more."

"Let that be your last assumption about me." Ruth's temper was darkening. Kimball had misjudged the distance remaining in her patience. It made her speak more candidly than she might otherwise have. "It's better Henry's out of it. He'd just slow us up."

Kimball only nodded. It was the cruelest thing he could do, leaving her with the noise of her own thoughts.

Before Augustus or the Virginian, it was Henry's sheepishness that derailed her. It was a helpless feeling. It made her feel small. And dimwitted. As if all the planning in the world couldn't make up for shortsightedness. A smarter person might have planned better. A smarter person might have known how to change Henry for the good. And when the mind takes to that line of thinking, there's no relief from it. *You're just too careless to prevent bad things from happening. If you were smarter, you'd live better. You're only bright enough to know how much brighter other people are.* It was a hopeless feeling that only comes after trying.

Some people live simple lives of neither risk nor reward. Nothing ventured, nothing gained. What about those who venture without gaining? Stories are written about victories following struggle or struggle following victories. Ruth could not think of a single story that didn't follow one of those two patterns. There was success somewhere in every tale.

Except hers.

No one writes about the woman who tried and tried and died a pauper anyway. Struggle following struggle. The end. That story—her story—had never been written. Would never be written.

She looked at Kimball now. She supposed there'd be no shortage of people wanting to write his story when it was all over. Or Augustus Windom's.

She'd lived more than half her life already without anything to show for it. She stroked the girl's hair, which she'd managed to keep unknotted, though far from tidy. She examined each root, each strand, each subtle change in hue. She did this while listening to Kimball chew.

"Is it a good plan, Mister Kimball?" she asked after a while.

"Pardon?"

"Tell me truly. Is there a hope of this plan working? All my life I've had ideas and no way to know for sure which ones were any good."

Ever the lawyer, Kimball only offered, "I smell blood. I *do* smell blood." He fed himself another greasy slice of gizzard and watched the land outside the window zip by. "The daily papers all agree. Windom orchestrated a public spectacle, employing a daredevil to dash a specially rigged Windom locomotive through the city streets. That is the record."

"That's a gob of cow shit."

"Anything can become fact when it's printed. And Augustus is happy to oblige the cow shit version." He trapped another cheekful of meat and began chewing, each bite making a wet squish. "And we'll have to be careful, because the other version is you and your husband are horse thieves, train thieves, kidnappers, assaulters, and patent forgers. He wouldn't be incorrect in any of those assertions but the last."

Ruth quailed. The taste of unadorned truth was like soot in her mouth.

"You read it yourself in the newspapers," Kimball continued. "Your husband worked for *Windom*. The romp through the city was a public spectacle that *Windom* orchestrated. And I'm certain he's readied himself against you pursuing acknowledgment or payment for your patent. It happens more than you think."

"Goddamn pinchbeck." It was all Ruth could do to keep from somersaulting the contents of her stomach. She couldn't look at Kimball's plate of meat. "Henry invented the thing. We both built it. It was us who shot Windom through the city. It was us changed what trains could do. I've got witnesses."

Kimball shrugged. "Witnesses to what? No one in this world saw you or your husband sign a contract, which is a shame for you because your claim sounds ludicrous as I sit here reciting it."

He returned to his dwindling plate of giblets, picking up a wet ropey piece and tossing it in his mouth. "You brought Windom his air brake—"

"*My* air brake."

"—Plunked it on his lap and waited to hear from him. Does that sound believable? Because it certainly does not *sound* smart."

Ruth didn't know how to respond and sat like a dull-eyed parochial, her brow furrowed and her mouth open.

"The Patent Office will vouch for the filing's authenticity," she said.

"The fact that your particular patent examiner—whom you say hurried your application through—was ousted does not look good. It makes it look as if your patent was obtained in an irregular manner."

"What's the point of a patent if the thing's not patented?" she said, setting her jaw.

"In a court of law," Kimball said, "it would appear laughable, Windom making unwritten promises to you and you believing him. This is not Chattanooga. You and your husband abducted the president of Windom & Fairbanks Locomotive Works, then you forged his patented documents. You've also broken, entered, brandished fists and feet, and made threats. What you have not done is sign your name to any written agreements of any kind. Nor has your husband. That is the version Windom will use to fight you in court. What I've got to puzzle out is how to frame your version."

"My version is we invented the air brake and took an advance on a horse exchange."

"Yes. Your version is that the Tennessee Caspers are casual thieves and fools. And here's another part of it—where did you get the locomotive in the first place?"

She searched for some reasonable reply, some bullet of truth to shoot into the hollow of his chest. Nothing came to her. The chamber was empty. Only limp, formless excuses. She'd gone full red.

"We're not on trial for a stolen locomotive."

"If I were Windom, I'd move the trial to a southern court, paint your husband as a thieving deserter, and watch how fast a jury ignores anything I've got to say." Another bite of meat separated an old thought from a new one. "We'll have to fight for this not to go to trial."

"I understand."

"No, I don't think you do. For us to avoid trial, we'd have to walk up to the wealthiest man in Baltimore and threaten him so thoroughly that he falls down right there in front of us without hazarding a fight. Our aim cannot simply be to absorb any punches Windom throws, but to convince him not to throw any."

Ruth watched the child sleep and moved the stray hairs from her face as she began talking. "You can't outrun a threatened rattlesnake," she said. "Come across one, you have two choices—one, light a fire and scare it off, or, two, hold dear your antidote and hope it endures the poison."

"You can also shoot it," Kimball said.

"Can we shoot this one?"

"No, ma'am."

"Well, I guess then we light that fire."

PART III

January-April 1866

27

It was an exhausting series of visitations. Kimball remained unto himself during the long, dull train rides. He spoke with Ruth only when necessary. Were it not for the girl, Ruth would have gone days without speaking.

At the outset of the excursion, Kimball had instructed Ruth to interject only when explaining to the men of Philadelphia's Juniper Locomotive Company details of the brake's function. "But no improvising," he'd said.

Juniper's president—a round pug of a man—was tickled to meet Kimball, shaking his hand enthusiastically and praising one courtroom tale or another. He regarded Ruth as a mere clerk or other non-entity and directed her to squat along a bench outside the room.

Kimball had to quietly correct him, explaining that Ruth had a unique understanding of the apparatus they'd come to discuss. Before the man's possible embarrassment overtook him, Kimball moved the conversation along. He was masterful at both creating tension and alleviating it.

When Ruth explained the brake's function to the roly-poly, he listened patiently. One hand framed the side of his face as he leaned on his elbow and waited for her to finish. When she did, he perked up and addressed Kimball again as if she'd never spoken. Ruth guessed the company president had made up his mind before they arrived. He was curious about the brake, but not enough to quell his fear of Augustus Windom and the cost to his business of losing the gamble.

"Every yes we get improves the odds, sir," Kimball said.

It was not compelling enough, and they were dismissed without success.

"You happy at least that I didn't improvise?" Ruth asked, defeated and sullen, as they carriaged back to the train. "It doesn't surprise me now that Windom's made a meal of Juniper. It's a wonder that company isn't flat broke for all the interest its president showed in building a better locomotive."

"Not everyone is a cutthroat," Kimball said. He'd used the same dismissive tone with her as had the Juniper president. "He likes me. I'll write him in a month. See if he'll reconsider."

"We better not rely on people liking you," Ruth said. "Only takes but a minute to figure out that you ain't likable. These men need a better reason."

Kimball grinned. "Increasing their company's value isn't enough?"

"Not from the looks of Mister Juniper back there. Not for the war we're asking them to fight. I know cowards in war, Mister Kimball. They run. All the glory and honor bunkum leaves 'em and they hide. Only way they stay is if it's personal. We need to make these men feel wronged by Augustus Windom. They can't be doing us a favor. They have to want his blood. Got to want it more than we do or they'll retreat. They'll leave us bare-assed before every lawyer Windom cares to throw at us."

There wasn't a man they planned to speak to who hadn't been wronged by the Windom family. A popular saying about the Windoms was that they were friends with everyone except their enemies. If you were their competitor, you'd been cheated, taunted, spurned, or rallied against, and you could be sure it had been done successfully. These company presidents were the only ones guaranteed to loathe Augustus as much as Ruth and Kimball did. They had to be persuaded, not only of the air brake's value and their plan to wrestle it away from Windom, but that Windom was someone susceptible to punishment.

Before their Chicago arrival, Ruth urged Kimball to rejigger his approach. He didn't refuse, but Chicago came and went without Kimball altering anything. And, for the second time in a row, they'd failed to convince a Windom enemy to help them. From what Ruth had come to understand of Kimball, he'd earned his success navigating the world as his own guide. It would be difficult for him to abandon his instincts and follow a woman.

As the two of them shuffled into the cramped Cooke Locomotive Manufacturing Company office in Cincinnati, Ruth whispered to Kimball, "Improvise more."

The meeting began as had the others. Kimball gave an even and well-considered preamble. He stated how Cooke would stand to profit from the Casper Air Brake and how they envisioned sinking Windom. And the president, along with his menagerie of lawyers and engineers seated around the periphery, nodded. They asked cautious questions and Kimball provided clever answers and no one in the room felt anything.

Then Ruth cleared her throat.

She spoke with sober purpose. She did so with vigor and animus, leaning forward. She spoke of Henry not as her husband, but as a cheated inventor. She took the Lord's name in vain, as was customary among men of this stripe when the situation required urgency. And she never spoke in long stretches. Her interjections landed like jabs. She said her piece and leaned back, letting Kimball smooth it over with logic. Then, as soon as he had, she'd find another place to jab again. Poking and punching and creating something that stuck with the men in the room. Ruth and Kimball's patter had a rhythm, a drumbeat to which they both danced. And, when they finished, the room fell silent, until a voice rose from the corner.

"If you're inclined to draw and quarter Augustus Windom, I'd gladly take a leg."

Every head swiveled toward the man who'd spoken. He introduced himself to Ruth and Kimball as Caldwell Begone. He was a thin man, with uneven features. On the near side of elderly. His smile was slight, but it was all teeth. Lupine. It made him appear more menacing than pleasant.

"If there's one thing I've learned about the Windom family," he said, "it's that they relish putting their boot to you. If there's something else I know about that family, it's that they underestimate a man's resilience."

Ruth did not recognize him. She had not yet learned that he'd traveled to Baltimore months before to view Leopold Windom's dead body. Didn't know Augustus had rebuffed him from doing so. Didn't know he'd been embarrassed in front of hundreds. Didn't know he'd been a former engineer whom Leopold had intimidated. Didn't know the glee behind the man's off-putting grin. He delighted in their presence. Salivated at the prospect of dismantling the Windom family.

It seemed from the reaction in the room, that no one else had known about his history with the Windoms either. "The man's father embarrassed me once, years ago, and when I called on him to answer for it, he refused to fight. Instead, he crept close and recited the names of my daughters. That sonofabitch. He had never met my children nor had any occasion to know their names. It still chills me to think of him sitting down and taking the time to learn such details. And for what purpose? Perhaps to protect himself against that very situation. I don't know."

"I'd have killed him where he stood," said another Cooke engineer sitting along the room's periphery.

"I might have done the same," Begone said, "had he not also recited to me in which room of my home each of my daughters slept and suggested any pain to him would beget pain to them."

"My god!" exclaimed the Cooke president.

Begone did not appear to revel in the story. In fact, the fear of that moment nearly twenty years ago appeared on his face all over again. "I've spent more hours than I can count imagining the unique brutality of a man playing a game made up of those rules. It took me years to sleep soundly again."

The room had imperceptibly slumped. No one spoke until Ruth asked, "How'd he come to know that about your girls?"

"Leopold Windom employed more outlaws than Samaritans, I'm certain. But how he *procured* the information isn't nearly as helpful to you as how he *remembered* it." The room held its breath. Ruth felt her own breath catch. "Under his employ at the time was a woman who served as his private clerk, an amanuensis, so to speak. Quite irregular to have a woman employed in that way, but I understand she had a unique understanding of his ways. She was at his funeral, and so I have no doubt she was under his employ right up until the end. She kept the strictest of records. Not just figures and dates, but people, places, facts. She whispered in his ear the things he needed to know the moment he needed to know them. I've no doubt she had records. A woman cannot remain beside a man like that for long unless she's as sharp as a scythe. Knew every stitch of business in which the Windoms were involved. If you were to locate her, she could tell you if the Windoms were building an air brake last year."

"You know her name?"

"Beryl. Beryl Gerry."

"By Augustus's own tongue," Kimball said, "Leopold had overseen the air brake and its patent. If this was true, the secretary would have some memory or record of this."

"And, if she has no recollection," Ruth said, "it'd go a far sight to proving the patent's false."

Begone nodded. "She was loyal to Leopold. I've since come to learn, however, that Augustus did not keep her in his employ after his father's death. Therefore, I don't imagine her loyalties run as deeply with the son as they did with the father."

The Cooke president had fallen rapt. So had everyone else in the room.

"I hated the father, you understand," Begone said. "I would spare as little mercy on his child as he threatened to spare on mine."

"I'd like to drown that bastard, myself," said another lawyer sitting opposite Begone.

The Cooke president said nothing but shook his head.

"Yes, sir," Ruth said to the room. "I believe your help would be most welcomed." She looked at Kimball out of the corner of her eye.

He sensed her looking at him, she was certain of it. He shifted in his seat to avoid her excited, smirking gaze and her delight in being correct about the effect passion would have on these men. He simply refused to look at her but conceded to the briefest of nods. She looked away but not before she'd scorched him with the full heat of her triumph, her subtle wordless exclamation: *I told you so.*

Ruth wrote Henry three times during the expedition. She wrote to tell him of what Augustus had done to hurt them and what Kimball had done to help. She also wrote to tell him what would happen next and where he could find her. She kept each letter short and wrote with a dispassionate pen. Each night, at every hotel, she'd asked the clerk if any letters had arrived for her. None ever had.

At best, the letters were slow moving. At worst, Henry hadn't received any of her letters because he was not where the gunman said he'd be.

Her concern grew with each unanswered letter. So did her relief. She could neither explain the existence of these opposing feelings nor deny them.

As the weeks progressed, Henry grew more distant in her mind. Of course she still thought of him—he was the inventor of the contraption they were traveling from city to city to sell to people, after all—but he had become an abstraction. The way men are spoken of a hundred years after their deaths.

Several cooks, an aide-de-camp, and two maids had accompanied Kimball on their expedition. Ruth figured one of the old maids could fashion the girl's hair properly. They braided and knotted it in a decorative way far more pleasing to the child than the slapdash manner in which Ruth had fixed it. What's more, they taught Ruth how to do it for future endeavors. Even with her hair tamed, though, the girl wore the wide-brimmed hat everywhere. It may as well have been armor.

Kimball's traveling staff looked after the child whenever Ruth left the train for meetings with company presidents. Otherwise, she was under Ruth's care and Ruth accepted the task with surety.

After several weeks and many miles together, the child still rarely spoke. Ruth continued to make an effort. She often gibbered about nothing in particular just to get the girl talking back. She asked the girl questions about her memories or about what she was thinking. Where her abilities to articulate these things fell short, Ruth nudged her along. She made guesses on her behalf or gave the girl choices of appropriate answers. No one knew the girl's age. The discovery depressed Ruth twice over when she realized it meant the girl had likely never celebrated a birthday in any memorable way.

It was a peculiar thing that had happened. Ruth had spent years imagining herself teaching her own children their letters, their figures, how to tend fields, and otherwise live in the world. She'd imagined learning them and lettering them. It would be slow going at first, but they'd pick up. She'd never imagined the predicament she found herself in now. With a girl partway into her learning and no way for Ruth to know exactly how far. There was no map for where the girl had come from or where she needed to go next.

Equally peculiar was the comfort they brought each other. Ruth found herself distressed whenever she left the child. She'd depart the train distracted by worry on the girl's behalf. Had she been situated properly? What had the girl eaten so far that day and what would she need to eat while Ruth was away? Did the child trust Ruth would return to her? What trouble could she get into? Was it possible for the girl's father to track her down and take her away after all this? No matter the number of weeks passed since leaving Baltimore, Ruth still feared losing the child somehow. It was an increasingly horrid fiction getting done in her mind, thinking of one day finding the little girl gone.

She requested another advance on the loan from Kimball to buy the child an orange and a toy wagon. Passing a mercantile on the way to a meeting in Plymouth, Kimball dodged Ruth's request the first time. He tried to resist on the return journey, too. Ruth threatened to poke fun at Kimball's weight in front of the Plymouth president if he didn't loan her the money. He knew it was no idle threat. She'd started in on such ribaldry at his expense during their stop in Cincinnati. The men of Cooke had been made giddy by the humbling Kimball was forced to endure. Everyone enjoyed watching big men get knocked down a peg—especially, it seemed, by a woman. Kimball had not been in a position of power and so had to bite his lip and take the titters at his expense. And, if he didn't loan Ruth money for the child's gifts, he'd have to do the same in the next five cities.

He acquiesced. Or rather, he handed Ruth a note to cover the cost and groused in the carriage while Ruth made her purchases.

She hid the presents from the girl until Camden, where they were to stay hoteled for five days while Kimball attended to business for a number of other clients. She had spirited away the child's rag doll, sat it upright in the wagon with the orange, and wheeled it behind her into the room where the girl was finishing up her bath. Her long eyelashes held dewdrops of water and twinkled in the lamplight.

The girl didn't notice the wagon until Ruth stepped aside to make it plain.

"These are for you."

The girl gaped as if the stars had rearranged themselves in the night sky. She remained motionless, her eyes trained on the wagon.

Ruth feared she'd erred in her judgment and felt the disturbance of tears coming on. She so thoroughly wanted the girl to accept the gift. "Penny for your thoughts?" she said, her voice so timid, it almost didn't register.

"What?" asked the child.

"I said, 'penny for your thoughts.' I'll pay you a penny to tell me what you're thinking."

"Are oranges called oranges 'cause that's what color they are or is it the other way around?"

Ruth raised an eyebrow, then held out a one-cent coin to the girl. "I can't help but feel swindled for that penny." It was shiny, untarnished. "So, you like the wagon then?"

The girl answered, "Yes, ma'am. I love it." She nodded. "I love it."

Ruth turned on her heel and moved down the hallway, out of sight from the child, feeling a bout of weeping taking hold.

She walked down the hotel hallway to Kimball's room and knocked on the door.

When it opened, there stood the lawyer, shirtless, an expression of harassment across his face.

"Have you an allergy to shirting, Counselor?"

"It binds my girth," he said. "Why are you banging on my door?"

She'd used Kimball's loan to buy a second orange and showed it to him now. "It's Sunday. The day for kindness and charity."

"And so you present me the orange I paid for?"

"The orange I picked out special. There were a lot of duds in the bunch, I assure you."

Though he could have bought the store's full stock if he'd wanted, Ruth guessed it was not so dark inside him that he'd miss the flicker of kindness on display.

He took the fruit and gave a tiny bow. "Thank you, madam."

"And thank you, Counselor. I heckle you plenty, but I'd be dead now if not for you. I'd like to think this helps you, too. Maybe, when the maneuvering's done, you'll find yourself a member of that men's club again."

Kimball dismissed this. "No."

Ruth blinked. "No?"

"They all retreated inside." He looked down at the orange as if reading it. "Windom shamed me in the street and every member stood there. They obliged him, the other members, by returning to the club."

"They were likely just in shock. Not knowing—"

"They could have stopped him right then and there. They didn't. Each one walked up the steps and went inside and they did it because they thought following him was smarter than not. I'll not forget that. So, no. Justice is not returning to the club. Not for me."

Ruth traded a throat-clear for a few extra seconds to think. Eventually, she nodded.

"Everything else though, it's gone damn well, hasn't it?"

"Indeed. Fine progress."

She nodded uncomfortably. "Deal's in the offing, isn't it? After all this time traipsing about, an accounting is coming, I do believe."

"If we continue as we have, yes."

"Victory's a conclusion I thought limited to people of a different station."

"My station, yes," Kimball said. "Lucky I'm here."

"Yeah, I owe you. Won't be long before I'm able to repay my debts to you in full."

"You may be correct."

"Then what's another loan thrown on the pile?"

Kimball narrowed his eyes. "We're not done with the day's charity portion, are we?"

Ruth came right out with it. "I want you to give me one hundred dollars."

The request loosened Kimball's grip on the orange and he dropped it at his feet. He held the door in preparation of slamming it in her face.

"Wait. Now, I aim to bring Henry back. He doesn't have anyone else. I'm scared what's come of him. Scared he's hurt. Scared I'm the one hurt him the most by running. If I send him one hundred dollars to return to Baltimore, I'd feel better. As good as everything has gone, I haven't felt right about that part of it."

Kimball studied Ruth but offered nothing.

She pointed to the floor. "If you say no, I aim to reclaim that orange."

His expression had not changed, though he did glance at the orange.

Ruth continued. "Is it because you're in love with me? Is that why you don't want my husband around?" Ruth had been under the impression she'd already seen his darkest glowers, but her last comment brought out one darker.

He dug into his pocket, retrieved several notes, and handed them to her. "If it takes this to assure you that I'm not in love with you, then it was money well spent. Happy Sunday to you." He plucked up the orange and closed the door.

28

R uth and Kimball had garnered the favor of Augustus Windom's remaining enemies. When they returned to Baltimore, they were fat with excitement.

She described every part of it to Blighton, despite expecting the old woman to lose interest halfway through. When she and the child had arrived back at the undertakeress's and rung the bell, Blighton answered with a grim expression. It was gray and drawn, as if some terrible woe had afflicted her since they'd been gone.

"You're back?" she asked. Ruth nodded. "Victorious, I hope?" Her words were hollow. They'd left her mouth as if by ceremony, having no purpose or direction once out.

"What is it, Miss Blighton?"

Blighton told her to sit. Ruth obliged and searched her friend's features. "Well, come on now. What is it?"

Blighton came up with a bundle of letters, all twined together. They were dirty and dog eared. They looked familiar. All at once Ruth knew why Blighton had looked so glum. They were the letters she'd written to Henry.

"Where'd you get these?"

Blighton didn't answer at first. She held them out for Ruth and let her take them. "Postman came along four or five days ago with the bundle. I didn't open them, of course, but I did notice two of them were in a different handwriting than yours. I suspect they might offer some clue."

Ruth did, indeed, spy two letters she hadn't written. One with a return address from the Ooltewah station in Tennessee.

"Maybe the one from Tennessee is from your husband," Blighton said.

The address on the envelope had not been written in Henry's hand. Ruth did not want to open it. It must have showed in her face because Blighton looked at her and shook her head. "You'll have to do it sometime."

Ruth slid her thumb underneath the letter's buff wax seal and began reading to herself.

Mar. 12, 1866
Missus Casper,

I hope this letter finds you in good health. I write to you fearful for Mister Casper's well-being. After receiving your letter regarding any mail received here for you, I sent my son out to visit your homestead as he had other errands to run out that way. He went out first on Mar. 5, whereby he knocked on your door and called your husband's name. He received no answer after a patient wait and tells me that he saw no signs of active life about the place. Two days later, he returned to your cabin again, called out and again found all was as still as a held breath. This time, Lord forgive him, he let himself in. Please take no offense in my saying that my son reports your house has taken on a grimy appearance. He insists there exists no sign of anyone having been inside (except for himself) in quite some time.

I send this letter and the bundle of mail that has been waiting for your husband here at the Ooltewah post office all these long months. There are four letters excluding my own, three in your own hand and a fourth oddity. It is not lettered in your hand and carries an odd protrusion. Your letters remaining here at the post office for so long without being retrieved has worried me and I was glad to get your letter enquiring after them. I don't believe Mister Casper is where you think he is, namely at your cabin.

If I have overstepped my duties, ma'am, I do apologize. I intended no meddling or confusion, and in the proceeding have, myself, become more curious about your husband's state of affairs than pen can paint out.
I wish a happy outcome to you and yourn.

Respectfully,
Carroll Klondike
Postmaster, Ooltewah Post Office

Ruth closed the letter and stared at it folded in her hand. There was no recognizable emotion present in her. She felt neither sadness, nor worry, nor anger. It was as if all the news had unpacked inside her mind and shuffled around, seeking the right place to settle.

He never returned to Tennessee. The sentiment repeated in her head. *He never returned to Tennessee.* The thought formed a circle and started over again just as soon as it ended. *He never returned to TennessHe never returned to TennessHe never returned to TeennessHe never...*

Even as it revolved over and again in her head, she knew it wasn't quite accurate. It wasn't that he never returned, it's that they never sent him.

"What's it say, hon'?" Blighton asked.

"They never sent Henry home," she said.

Blighton's expression shriveled like a salted slug. "What?"

Ruth shook her head but elaborated no further. She leaned forward to hand Blighton the letter.

The room hung in silence as Blighton read it to herself.

Ruth still had the Virginia letter. The one the carrier described as having "an odd protrusion." By now she was frightened to open it.

She opened it. It didn't appear anything was inside at first. She felt a small lump in one corner of the envelope. She upturned it and let the contents fall into her open hand. It was her wedding ring. She stared down at it in disbelief. She'd forgotten all about it and had to retrace almost a year's worth of living to place the last time she'd held it. The ring looked worn and chintzier than she'd remembered. It was like a small, sick thing that was begging for her help. She held it to the light. She did not put it on.

"What's that?" the girl asked.

"It's my wedding ring."

Blighton looked up, her brow pulled low as if staked by tentpoles.

"Can I see?" the girl asked.

Ruth did not answer. She did not, at that moment, know the answer. Could the girl see it? What harm could it do? Her brain was racing. She needed the world to slow down and let her think. "Be gentle with it," Ruth said and slid the ring along the table toward the child.

An odd sensation chilled her spine. In the months past, she'd gotten used to Henry's absence. Somewhere in her gut, she'd known he was gone, had accepted it. She'd even felt whole in some ways, not having to worry about some other part of herself wandering without her. Only part of her sadness was due to Henry being done in. The other was because she didn't miss him.

Blighton folded the letter. Her expression of woe had hardened into anger. "The world has no shortage of hardships, does it?" Ruth shrugged. Blighton continued. "That's why Windom paid the Virginian, isn't it?" She did not specify what she meant by "that's."

Ruth nodded. They would wait until the girl was out of earshot to acknowledge out loud that Henry was dead.

29

The first floor of the Orleans Vinegar factory held a legion of oak barrels. Hundreds laid end-to-end across the great expanse, fouling the air with their putrid rot. The second floor was little more than a ruddy confluence of catwalks. They, along with hundreds of long-necked funnels, hovered above the barrels, swinging and dripping tart runoff.

"I won't make that climb," Ruth said, chin raised, gazing at the ladder climb toward the catwalks. She looked Kimball up and down and regarded the weak ladder once more. "And Lord knows you won't make it, either."

Kimball, too, trained his eyes at the catwalks. "Well, now. Do you propose we shout our business at her from down here?"

"We can shout our intention to speak to her," she said. "Save our business for when she comes down."

They were watching Beryl Gerry—hair netted, smocked, and carrying a thin ledger. The bottom of it was wedged into her hip as she scribbled on its pages. She was unaware of the two below watching her. No one had been aware of their arrival. They'd not announced themselves and no one had been introduced to them to do the announcing on their behalf.

It had taken Kimball weeks to figure out what had become of the woman after her dismissal from the Windom family. A woman resistant to house chores and seamstressing would find few choices for work. In Beryl Gerry's situation, tabulating output in this hothouse stink-factory was as good as it got.

Ruth felt tied to the woman, already. She was certain of her strength, without having yet met her. A place like this—a factory sweating alcohol out of bungholes—had burned the insides of Ruth's nostrils after three minutes. She couldn't imagine what the woman above her must endure. Twelve hours daily swimming in eyewatering, gag-inducing air. And for what? Had Augustus Windom even given her a reason for ousting her? It was a good bet that woman up there hated Augustus Windom maybe more than anybody and Ruth aimed to do anything to air those feelings out in public.

Anything except climb up those rickety goddamn ladder steps to get her.

"Beryl Gerry!" She cupped her hands around her mouth and yelled, hoping to cut through the frantic hum of the cloud of insects above, fighting their way past the spigot netting.

Everyone on the ground floor turned in the direction of the shouting woman. Even the foreman above leaned over the catwalk rail to determine if these were a woman's shouts they could ignore. But the woman doing all the shouting was unfamiliar to everyone and so they did nothing. They waited for her to shout again, which Ruth did because the only person in the entire goddamn factory not to have heard her shouting was the one person to whom Ruth aimed her voice.

"Miss Beryl Gerry! Former assistant to Leopold Windom!"

That caught her attention. Didn't recognize her own name, but the name of her former employer perked her up like a dog with the scent of raw meat in her nose. She leaned forward as if an extra foot was what muddied her vision and not the rest of the distance between them.

Kimball cupped his hands around his mouth, too, and joined in. "Miss Gerry, may we speak to you? One minute just?"

The woman looked down the catwalk to her foreman, either for clarity or permission, Ruth wasn't certain. Nor was Ruth certain if the foreman stepped aside to let her through out of obligation or curiosity.

The sight of the woman climbing down unclenched Ruth from the terror of having to climb up. Gerry approached with solemnity, as if at any moment she might make a sharp turn and spring away. But she pushed on until she was close enough that none had further reason to yell.

Kimball tipped his hat. Ruth remained still.

"Miss Gerry," Kimball started, "My name is Brou—"

"I know who you are," Gerry said and looked Ruth up and down as if to say *But I don't know you.*

"Ruth Casper, ma'am."

Gerry's expression did not change, nor did she offer any warm words of greeting. Nor should she, Ruth guessed. If she was being honest.

The woman was both young and old in appearance. Dark rings anchored her big eyes. Her clear skin was also quite pale. She looked like a child overdue on sleep.

"Why are you here?" Gerry asked.

"We'd like to speak to you of revenge," Ruth said. It was the line she'd spoken to Kimball and every one of the railroad men after Cincinnati. Everyone likes a little give-back when it's them doling it out. Ruth knew it had worked here, too, because Gerry held her tabulations book at her side and waited for the two of them to continue. "Tell me, is there any amount of washing that can get the stink of this place out of your clothes?"

Gerry looked cautiously from Ruth to Kimball and back again before answering. "It's my hair that seems to hold the stench most."

"Do you enjoy it here?" Kimball asked.

Gerry stole a glance behind her in the direction of her foreman. He'd followed her down and was drifting ever closer, trying to listen in. "Very much," she said. It was a dull delivery. It suggested she'd never disliked anything more in her life than recording malt levels and batch weights.

Kimball nodded. "We're here because of Augustus Windom."

Ruth pointed at Gerry. "You're here because of Augustus Windom, too, I hear." Gerry appeared more inclined to listen than to speak. "Miss Gerry, what did Augustus Windom tell you when he severed his tie with you?"

"He didn't say anything," Gerry said. "He had his man do it. And why it happened I'm sure I don't know."

"You were given no reason?" Kimball asked.

Gerry straightened. "Men of that station never give reason for anything."

The foreman had closed in. "Miss Gerry," he said, with no intention of saying more.

"Yes, sir." She took a step away from Ruth and Kimball, almost as if she'd ceded control of her feet. "Say what you've come to say."

Ruth stepped toward her to cover the distance. "We understand you're reliable with paper and ink?"

The foreman gave a throat clear. "Beryl. The south end bungholes all need checks."

Gerry took a few more steps away. "I'm sorry."

It wasn't clear who she was apologizing to. Everyone probably. The way Ruth saw it, this was a woman who apologized to everyone as a matter of course.

"Nothing to be sorry about, Miss Gerry."

Kimball moved in just behind Ruth and spoke softly. "We believe we can retaliate against Augustus Windom's many egregious acts, including your severance. And we believe you possess notebooks that can help..." Kimball thought of the most appropriate word. "... hasten such a retaliation."

"I don't pay her a wage to speak," the foreman said to Kimball. "Especially to people off the street."

Ruth skittered toward the foreman. "You don't pay her to click her heels, either. My guess is you pay her just enough to keep her from taking up with a dress shop or an apothecary. My guess is you pay her, what? A dollar a day? A dollar and a fifth? If you were to hire a man, you couldn't get away with less than three. And you'll not let her loose because she's never been your problem and she's not your problem now. I'm your problem. And I'm not the one can do you any real damage. The fat tub behind me's the one can really go to work on you. So, you're gonna climb back up them devil's steps and wait for Miss Gerry to rejoin you. You're gonna be patient and kind when she returns because she didn't ask for us, we asked for her. She's not your problem, but you know as well as we do she's been your solution for months. So shut up and bring no more agitation upon any of us three."

She waited. Everyone waited. The factory had ceased all action. The sticky sloshing of the fermenting acid tinkled all around them, waiting for the world to spin again.

"Two minutes," the foreman said to Gerry. "Any more than that," he pointed to Ruth, "I'll hire this one to replace you." He spun on his heels and stomped right back up the ladder rungs like Ruth told him to. He gave them all a glare as he did it, but nothing more.

Ruth returned to Gerry. "Don't think, ma'am, that we ain't ready to fight."

"Miss Gerry," Kimball said, "we only ask that you point us in the direction of Augustus Windom's crimes. It doesn't have to be all of it. We know there's a fair amount to choose from."

She shook her head lightly. "I carry no warm feelings for the son. But what of the father?"

Ruth and Kimball traded glances. "You know better than us, Miss Gerry, what the Windom family was up to."

"And so I ask it again," Gerry said. "What of the father?"

"What of the contents of your records, Miss Gerry? You can say better than us if we can stitch up the son without pricking the father."

She considered this, her slender hands in front of her, one wringing the other. "I just don't believe Mister Windom, Leopold Windom, should be painted with the same brush as his son. They are different."

Kimball did not move. He watched the woman a moment longer. "No, I don't believe they are."

"He allowed me to work. Paid a fine wage and taught me some. Protected my father's business. And, in turn, I gave him all."

"All what?" Kimball asked.

Gerry looked into the middle distance, considering how to answer. She shook her head when no proper words came.

"Everything she could," Ruth said. She stepped closer to Gerry. "She helped him build something."

She considered this. "If you delegitimize him, you delegitimize me."

"Augustus already delegitimized everything his father built. I'm sorry, but it's gone." Kimball crossed his arms as best he could around the wide cage of his belly. "We've come offering you a chance to punish him for doing it."

Gerry had been studying the cold expression pressed into Kimball's soft features. Now she looked at Ruth. Ruth could see Gerry was pained. Not in the moment, exactly. This was a deeper pain. The roots having grown strong from underneath.

Ruth moved close enough to whisper and did so just then. "You can still leave a mark," she said. She wanted to touch the woman, which was not a compulsion that overtook Ruth often. "It's just that this mark is going to be bloodier than the one you thought you'd leave."

The woman searched Ruth's face, for what Ruth didn't know. She kept still. Allowed Gerry to find whatever was there.

"Will you accompany me home at seven?" Gerry asked, finally. "I'll provide you what I can."

30

The Orange Street Club was only half full. It had been thinning steadily over the last six months. There had been no discernible change to the grand old club's edifice. From all outward appearances, it had weathered the upheaval of Augustus's reign. Once inside, however, one would not hold the same opinion.

Frank Marcy stood beside the crackling fireplace repeating himself for the third time. "We won't have half the trains you want in the time you want them."

Rathbone was on guard outside the room, seated in the club's loneliest chair, between the closed Regency Room doors and the drawn anteroom curtain.

Marcy had been hostile to the Windom Air Brake, never having gotten a straight answer from Augustus about where it came from or why he'd not been included in its development.

"We can't build more than ten trains by summer's end," Marcy said. "Not with the new brake."

Augustus sniped. "Both *before* Christmas and *after* Christmas you promised you could build one new train a week. It is now—what day is it?—the eighteenth of April. That's fifteen weeks between now and August to deliver fifteen trains. It was fifteen four months ago when we discussed the order and two months ago when I confirmed the order."

"It's ten now."

"Then why did you agree to fifteen?"

"I agreed suppositionally."

"Suppositionally?" Augustus looked at Marcy as if he was decomposing in front of him.

"Yes."

"Well, suppose you were someone who solved problems. What would you tell me then?"

"I *am* someone who solves problems and I told you that, to get fifteen trains by August, I need more men. To get fifteen with only the men I have, I need more time."

"Then why, when asked before, did you agree to a train a week?"

"Because I thought you were giving me more men. You've asked me to move mountains, but you're my only mountain."

"You're peppery today."

"It's what you get when you grind down a peppercorn."

Augustus smiled, moved to a threatening distance, and kept his voice low. "Listen to me now. The men drilling the steel plates, what happens after they're done?"

"That has no bearing on—"

"They stand idle is what happens."

"They're instructed to stand idle after a run of two hundred. If they kept going, they'd exceed the amount of product the floor can hold."

"So they're standing there when they could be assisting the smithers. And if not the smithers, then the foundry men."

Marcy was insistent. "That's not how it works. You've announced that the new Windom trains will be the safest in the world, but they won't be safe if they're rushed through production and built by drillers doing something other than drilling or millers doing something other than milling. They'd be the world's least safe trains."

"I promised reliability, not safety. Having fifteen trains when I promised fifteen is reliable."

Marcy took a thick book from under his arm and set it on the table in front of Augustus—two hundred pages of approved manufacturing designs for the air brake with a simple binding. He pointed to it. "I showed you these plans. You didn't look at them. You didn't do your job."

"*You're* paid to look at them," Augustus said. "*I'm* paid to hire the best qualified men to do the looking."

"If you'd have looked at these plans, you'd have seen they required more men to deliver in the time you asked for. You'd have looked at them and we'd have had this discussion in January. Now it can't be done."

"It has to be."

"Why?"

"Because the Union Pacific is a quarter way through Nebraska."

"I don't know what that means."

"Yes, you do. The Transcontinental will be completed through Nebraska this time next year and the Utah territory the year after. Every year that goes by, I'm going to need to supply more trains to the construction effort. If I don't, and the Union Pacific goes to some other company, we will find ourselves in desperate straits. Do you understand? We won't weather it. So I need a fleet. And you need a fleet. And the fleet starts at fifteen. If I don't have it, we will have squandered the moment the United States connected two oceans. The Transcontinental will attract every eye and, goddammit, there had better be nothing but Windom air braking trains for those eyes to see."

"Then give me more men. Extra labor won't cost a fraction of what you'll recoup once that fleet heads westward."

Augustus leaned in to the engineer and whispered, "I cannot afford it."

Marcy leaned away to get a full look at him. His face wrinkled in confusion. He believed Augustus Windom could afford anything.

"Not now," Augustus said. "Not after the Fairbanks sale. And not after the money I sank into this fucking place."

"Why you bought this place still eludes me," Marcy said. "Followed swiftly by my bewilderment that you bought it and then left it to wither."

Augustus nearly pulled a muscle straining for calmness. He imagined popping Marcy in the mouth with his stupid book, imagined the man holding closed his mouth full of rearranged teeth. But he needed Marcy and so he remained silent.

"The club is in rot," the engineer continued. "The voting board avoids this place altogether. Several of them are prepared to resign if they haven't already. Without a voting board, the Orange will fall deeper into stasis. Dues have not been renewed, which means supplies are lagging, accouterments are spare, and your standing throughout the club is flagging. Now, having done all that, you tell me I cannot have more men because you've tethered your spending to this place? It's unfathomable."

"Your fathoms will not change the certainty that building fifteen trains now is the only way we can build fifteen after."

A knock came from outside. Augustus left Marcy to swing open the door. It was Rathbone.

"What?" Augustus asked.

The agent motioned to the door valet standing beside him, looking worried.

"Yes? What?" Augustus said to the valet.

"I explained to them, sir, that they were not allowed on these premises."

"Who?"

The valet bit his lip, hesitating.

The expression stirred the silt in Augustus's stomach. He straightened his back, preparing for whatever was coming. "Out with it, goddammit."

"Broussais Kimball, sir. I told him he wasn't allowed and, if he persisted, I would have to announce his arrival to you."

From inside the room, Marcy called out. "Augustus, we should revisit the idea of refortifying the old trains with the new brake."

"Not now, Marcy," Augustus snapped. Then he turned and closed in on the valet. "What did Kimball say when you told him you'd alert me?"

The valet drooped. He did not relish the part of messenger. "He told me to do it. Said do it quickly."

"He...he used the word *quickly*?"

The valet nodded.

In truth, Kimball's return had felt inevitable. Augustus had been waiting for it, though he didn't know exactly what he would find when it arrived. It was exhilarating. He no longer had to fear this day. The day was here. Augustus left only an intimate distance between the valet and himself. He spoke in a near-whisper. "Where is he?"

"They are in the drinkery, sir."

Augustus blinked at a thought. "You said *they* are in the drinkery? They?" He wrinkled his brow. "Well, who else is with him?"

"A woman."

Augustus exchanged a singular glance with Rathbone, and they were both on the move. Behind them both was the valet, uncertain about the necessity of his involvement.

They appeared in the bar's archway. To Augustus's amazement, Kimball and the Casper woman were seated along the bar. The bartender poured two glasses of rye and slid one before each of the interlopers.

"Rye is not your drink," he heard Kimball tell the woman. "But today you'll want a rye."

She squeezed her nostrils before upturning the glass. "Oh, that's awful."

"Yes." Kimball nodded. "Now have one more."

Augustus cleared his throat, which attracted the woman's attention. "Women are not allowed in the Orange Street Club nor are fat sacks of pompous fuckery. I believe the rules are unmistakable about both."

Ruth tightened at the sight of Rathbone resting a hand on each of his revolver grips. Kimball hadn't yet turned around.

Rathbone thumbed both hammers. "Are you here for vengeance?" he asked.

Kimball turned on his stool. "I'm here for justice."

"Justice is pulling the knife from your back," Ruth said. "Vengeance is stabbing the guy who put it there. I'm here for both."

"Talk like that is a fast way to a justified shooting," Augustus said.

"Believe it or don't, popinjay, our presence is a courtesy. And if you shoot us dead here on your flooring, it won't stop what we've come to warn you about."

"Well, go ahead and warn me then. I don't admire coyness."

"You'll not want this conversation in the open." Kimball rose from his stool and opened his coat to show Rathbone he had no hidden weapons. Rathbone scrutinized his middle. Next, he looked upon the approaching woman who had a chatelaine clasped around her waist.

From the belt hung five thin chains, which fell in front of her like a chainmail apron. At the end of each chain were clasps holding a variety of items: a ring, folded papers, and the gunman's broken thumbscrew.

Rathbone studied her weaponry as she jangled nearer like a marauder with her implements of torture. "A handbag wouldn't suffice?" he asked her.

"Turns out I prefer my hands free," she answered.

She unhooked the gunman's broken thumbscrew from the chatelaine and dropped it at his feet without spending another word.

Rathbone picked it up. Twirled it once in his hand.

She had a nasty little curdled grin ready for the agent. She was all mirth from the nose down, but her eyes were stony on Rathbone. "Did you put my husband on a train to Tennessee?"

Rathbone's face matched hers for grimness. "I did."

Ruth leaned closer. "Waved goodbye when he left the station, did he?" She studied his eyes.

Rathbone didn't move.

Ruth was a foot away from his face and spoke barely above a whisper. "Tell me more lies, man." She lifted a chain in her chatelaine, at the end of which was her wedding ring. "Tally them up and fling 'em."

His eyes flickered with recognition before he doused their light. "If you have that, you've evidently spoken to your husband."

"How you figure?"

"Because it was your husband to whom I mailed that ring."

"You sent this ring to my home, not my husband. And there, in my empty postal box, it sat. But you already knew that."

"I didn't."

"I've done my share of lying. I know its face."

"It's not enough to say it. You have to prove it."

Ruth shook her head. "This is what happens. You don't get away with it." She looked him in the eye and inched up under his chin, whispering, "You lie and you cover and it's just not enough and you don't get away with it after all."

Rathbone moved to the window looking out onto the Orange Street Club's grand front steps. "I've been threatened before," he said. He drew aside one half of the curtains and rapped on the glass before turning back.

Augustus knew what was coming.

Rathbone pointed at Kimball and continued. "What was it you told me to do next time Augustus saw you? Have forty of me standing behind him?"

As if carefully practiced, the club's front doors split open and a crush of Rathbone's operatives stomped up behind, readied for blood. Not quite forty men, but still a damn fine showing.

Kimball and Ruth studied the sudden crowd in front of them.

Augustus was uncertain what Kimball and the woman had come for, but they appeared certain in themselves, undeterred by the crush of gunmen. The two of them had entered the Orange knowing it was unlawful to do so. He was hoping they'd miscalculated and that he'd be nimble enough to regain the advantage. Goddamn Kimball. Staring down two dozen guns, they were as calm as if they'd been offered a warm meal.

"I know it might not appear this way to you just yet, Augustus," Kimball said, "but these boys only complicate things for you. I still advise you to adjourn with us in private."

Augustus surrendered to something inside himself and waved them to all follow him. As he drew closer to the Regency Room, he whispered to the valet. "Tell Mister Marcy to wait until I finish here."

The valet nodded and skittered ahead as Ruth, Kimball, and Augustus entered the Regency. Rathbone and his legion waited outside.

31

The muscles in Augustus's jaw tightened. He struck a relaxed posture, but a flexing jaw always tattled on a man's nerves.

"So, which one of you is here to shoot me?" Augustus asked with cheek.

Kimball made no movement. The woman shook her head and answered in kind. "Bullets aren't what you ought to fear now."

Augustus stepped inside, watching Kimball sink into his old chair. It was the chair Augustus had chosen for his own in Kimball's absence. It was the largest chair. The widest. Accommodating to both Kimball's girth and Augustus's nature. Kimball watched Augustus's reaction as he sat.

"What ought I fear now, Missus Casper, if not a bullet?"

"You've debts to pay, sir," she said. "To Mister Kimball, to me, and especially to my husband."

He felt a tightness close around his chest as he sat across from them. He'd always suspected Kimball would come, especially after the surprise arrival at his mansion a few months before. The woman, though, he'd never expected to see again.

He could not be certain, at that moment, which of the two unnerved him more—the silent lawyer or the blustering woman. He supposed that, if he must choose, he'd select the woman. She seemed at ease. Certainly not panicked and fleeing as had been Rathbone's last view.

The chatelaine tinkled as she crossed her leg at the knees. The thick material of what appeared to be a newly acquired taffeta dress and jacket rose with her leg and draped over her with crude wrinkles.

His gaze oscillated between the two, the false front of his pleased demeanor sliding away.

"You've come to deliver a message. Get on with it."

"You stole my husband's patent," she said.

"No, ma'am," Augustus said, his smile setting further below the horizon every second. "You've got that quite wrong."

The woman unclasped the folded papers from her belt. "I've got two letters." She held out the first. "I'm hoping only to hand you this one."

He took it from her and unfolded it. It appeared to be an agreement with space for three signatures. Kimball and the woman had already signed it. The open space awaited his own mark.

"It's a statement," she said. "Says you claim no rights in any part for the Casper Air Brake. You read through, you'll see Mister Kimball here let you off the hook for the forged patents."

Kimball had appeared to stop listening. He leaned far forward, lifted Marcy's large book left on the table and leafed through it. Augustus watched him and became rigid. He took in a breath of air and readied to object, but the woman reclaimed his attention.

"Where Mister Kimball gets you is in admitting any patents *you* have infringe on the patents *I* have. In regular speak, that means we'll pretend you didn't do anything, so long as you stop doing it." She turned to Kimball. "That about cover it?"

Kimball nodded.

"I believe you misspoke just now," Augustus said. "The only air brake is the *Windom* Air Brake."

"That's fine," said the woman. "Now we both know where we stand. You know I know what you're up to. And I know you plan to sit there and lie about it. Is this how you and your daddy made your pile? You stole it all?"

Kimball sighed but remained mute, flipping through Marcy's manufacturing designs.

"Paper threats, madam." Augustus tossed the letter to the ground, where it caught a small updraft before sliding across the floor.

"Paper threats are as good as promises when they're written by Broussais Kimball." She leaned over to retrieve the paper from the floor. "I expected you to know that."

She waggled the letter in front of him once more to see if he'd changed his mind.

He remained still, indicating he hadn't.

"All right, then." She re-folded the unsigned paper before clipping it onto her chain belt. "I never figured it to go any other way."

"What way has it gone?" Augustus asked. "I've done nothing unwarranted."

She held up the second document. "Since you last spoke with Mister Kimball, he's been traveling. And I along with him. Do you believe it?" Augustus said nothing. Ruth continued. "Uh-huh. Fast friends, the two of us. Been to New Jersey, Massachusetts, Iowa, New York," she recited slowly, not breaking her stare with Augustus. "Pennsylvania, Ohio, and Illinois. Do you know why?"

He broke from her glower to spy Kimball, who continued flipping through the book as if alone in a library.

"I said do you know why? Because your competition is in those states." This reclaimed Augustus's attention. "Juniper, Cooke, Baldwin, Bailey, Dickson, Richmond, Plymouth, Sterling, and Kingston. Met with all nine, we did. And they asked us to give you a message." She leaned on the table and tossed the second letter in front of him. He peered down as if he expected it to open itself. "And that message, Augustus, is *run*."

Augustus wondered why Kimball had still not said a single goddamned word.

"Juniper, Cooke, Baldwin, Bailey, Dickson, Richmond, Plymouth, Sterling, and Kingston are suing you. Filed a case against you under Equity Rule 48. Ever heard of it?" Ruth asked.

Augustus gave a demure shrug. He thought it better not to pit his possible knowledge against the woman's certitude.

"I hadn't heard of it either," she continued. "Mister Kimball's been helpful on that point. The clarifying, I mean."

Kimball smiled and closed the book but did not return it to the table. He held it in his lap as if he was its new owner.

"The rule allows similar cases to be bound together and tried as one," Ruth continued. "If enough people file the same complaint against the same defendant, all those smaller cases join to make one *big* case. In this case, Mister Windom, that defendant," she said, aiming a pointed finger at him as if about to fire a bullet, "is you."

Augustus looked at Kimball. *Why won't the prick say anything?* is what he thought. What he said was, "What is it these companies claim I've done?"

"The same thing *I'm* claiming you done," Ruth said. "You stole the Casper Air Brake." She appeared to enjoy the theater of it. It was as if disorder invigorated her.

"What have those other companies got to do with it?"

The woman smiled.

Kimball smiled.

Everything within Augustus that could drop, dropped.

"Well, see, I licensed the Casper Air Brake to every one of them. Every one of them agreed to share the license on the same condition. Do you know what that condition was?"

Augustus stared dead eyed at her, waiting for her little show to wind down.

"The condition," she continued, "was that your company would not be allowed to have the device. They didn't mind sharing it betwixt and between them, but they mind you having it. And since you're claiming not only to have it, but that it's yours..." Ruth made a meal out of it. She looked at Kimball, who appeared to be ignoring her. "Well, none of your biggest competitors cottoned to that. So, it's not me alone suing you, see, but me and every lawyer your competitors have. Think of them all as the orchestra and Mister Kimball here as the conductor."

"And you?"

Her smile widened. "It's my stage."

Augustus unfolded the letter and read it. He felt a tightening around his forehead, an immense pressure that drummed at both temples. Though he remained still, his thoughts were popping like skillet grease. He re-folded the letter. To Kimball, he said, "How will you litigate all this when you've been shot for trespassing on private property?"

"Look here." Ruth snapped her finger. "*Here*. You've looked over me, through me, past me, around me, behind me. Well, now's a good time to look *at* me, you motherless bastard." She delivered the words without affectation. "You ever seen a battalion of lawyers? They look a lot like the gunmen waiting for us outside, only our guys can bleed a lot more than a body. All your men can do is end my life. But my men, they can end yours and your dead father's and any kin you ever plan to have. It took me my entire life to have nothing, they can make sure you have it in a month. They start digging, day in, day out, picking through the old bones of your life. How sure are you they won't find anything?"

Augustus looked at Kimball only briefly until the woman shook her head.

"You keep looking at him like he's gonna help you," she said. "That first letter was your help. Your choices now are surrender or fight. And, since you seem to enjoy a fight, let's start there. Say you keep up the lie and defend yourself against half the states in the union. Maybe you'd win if you had five years, but you'll be bankrupted in two. The legal hang-ups alone would put a Vanderbilt in the poorhouse. And that's not good for you because the Transcontinental's getting built with or without you. If you're cinched up in court, it'll go on without you. And if it goes on without you, your company will unravel like a loose sweater. That, Augustus, is what fighting'll get you."

She swung off the chair. Her chatelaine clinked like a wind chime as she moved to the fireplace and leaned against it. Ruth tossed the first letter into the fire and watched it shrivel into black ash. For a moment, the fireplace flared behind, giving her a ghoulish appearance.

"Your second choice is quitting. And quitting means your trains will be the only ones still taking a thousand yards to stop. Means your old locomotives'll still chew up the track, still maim everything in their path, still haul only half as many cars as your competitors. How long do you think you'll stay in business? The men you've fought hardest against will all have what you have, except they got it legally, and for only a fraction, to boot. Obso...uh...obsole— What's the word?"

"Obsolescence," Kimball said.

"Yes," Ruth continued "That's what *not* fighting will get you. I'd prefer to see you go this route, myself."

"This is fucking collusion," Augustus squalled.

"Well, but you'll have to take us to court to prove that out," Ruth said. "Do you want to add that to the pile? *Can* you add it to the pile, even?"

"You think this is the first threat I've had to weather? You think I'll fall over at the first slow wind? I'll out gut you. You've no idea what I can endure."

Ruth snickered.

Kimball reached inside his shoe to rub his ankle but otherwise did nothing.

Augustus looked like a man who had miscalculated himself. But it was not in his nature to collapse and expose his belly and so he spoke deliberately. His tone was stiff, as if reciting a monologue he'd only tenuously memorized.

"If a tiger is whipped when he moves left and whipped when he moves right and whipped when he remains still, what is the tiger to do but go after the fucking whip?" He pointed to Kimball. "You won't make it out the front door without shackles. And you," he said, turning to Ruth, "you have a record of thievery. You stole my train and that Virginian's horse before that. I will send you back to Tennessee just as I sent your husband—"

"You killed the only Casper the authorities wanted. No warrant on my head, Jack."

"I will return you south and those secesh barbarians will not bother with a trial. They will shoot you dead at your front door and leave you there for the pickings."

The two sat listening, unmoved. Something ragged had come loose in him.

Kimball straightened. "Your father was never satisfied weakening a man," he said, finally. "He aimed to destroy him."

"Do not tell me about my own father."

"I will tell you whatever I damn well choose and perhaps a bit more than that. And do not again threaten us with violence from that pack of corrupt gunmen out there. If you had the sand to have us murdered, it would already have been done. You are a wanton milksop son to a greedy cynic of a father."

Augustus's face glowed like the end of a hot poker. His shout of "Mister Rathbone!" caused the doors to crash open and the man to appear tussle-ready with one of his pistols already aimed. Behind him, filing into the room one by one, were the rest of the gunmen, until there was no room left to pour in.

Kimball spared only a glance at Rathbone before returning to Augustus. "You'll not command a killing until I've had my say because you're a sneaky, snooping little devil's prick. You still, despite all else, want to know the full sum and substance of what we've come to say." He pointed at Rathbone. "You've already searched us, halfwit. Point your pistols elsewhere."

Rathbone thought a moment, then aimed his gun at Ruth.

"You've got no right to plug me, either," she told him.

"You soaked me in piss and worse. I've got the right to crack your noggin as many times as it takes to tire me out."

Kimball, concentrating on Augustus again, broke in. "Your contemptuous father aimed to destroy men but didn't always do it."

Augustus slammed the table with his fist. He was corpse pale and just as drawn. "Only you enjoy the sound of your own gibbering," he protested.

"You spoke like him, moved like him, and you've erred like him. You both believed you'd vanquished your victims without ever ensuring the bodies were cold. You never finished them off," Kimball continued.

Augustus dared not respond.

"Your father left records, dimwit. And it baffles the mind why you'd not thought to collect them before someone like me could do it."

Augustus fought against his nature to rebut. He felt baited to speak. As if any response would play into one of Kimball's waiting traps. The tiger was coiling, evaluating how it might move to spare a whipping.

"Records, notations, marginalia. It was all written down," Kimball went on. "Books of it. Page after page. All untouched. You didn't finish them off. And I mean to tell you, having read through those records, they're enough to put your father's legacy in the ground with him and put you in chains for the rest of your days. Your hired rowdies shooting us dead where we sit won't stop those books from an open airing. It would only hurt your case more." Ruth nodded along. Kimball shifted his attention to Rathbone. "You should know, I've requested that an investigation be opened on the disappearance of Mister Henry Casper. Missus Casper and I have told the Pinkertons everything we know. I suspect they'll visit you both soon enough. And I tell you that so you'll consider this—how might it look if the two people to have opened the investigation are found dead at the hands of the two prime suspects?"

"Are you gonna have enough lawyers to cover all the open cases against you, Mister Windom?" Ruth asked.

Dark rings formed around Augustus's eyes. He looked stricken with misery. "I'm going to come for you," he growled.

"You've already said that. Surely you understand our presence here is a signal that *we've* come for *you*," Kimball retorted. Looking at Augustus but speaking to Rathbone, he said, "Point that pistol at the floor and do not raise it to me or Missus Casper ever again in your life." His eyes still fixed on Augustus, he spoke *sotto voce*. "Now I want you to turn and watch all your men lower their pistols. And, when they do, I want you to consider what it means for you."

It was belittling for Augustus to turn around. It was belittling for him to remain still. He was caught on the horns of these bastards and did not know how to loose himself.

Rathbone holstered his pistol.

The others all did the same.

At the sound of every pistol sliding into its rawhide holster, a smile formed on Kimball's fleshy face like rising dough. "Order them out of the room."

"No."

"They are all witnesses to anything you say. And I think you're going to want privacy from here on out."

Augustus knew Kimball was right. He hated to admit it and tried to concoct a better alternative, one that did not find him obeying the man. "Stand just outside, Mister Rathbone," he said after a while. "Close the door after your last man exits."

The men filed out in seconds. Was that eagerness to leave Augustus detected? Rathbone was last out and, when he closed the door behind him, Augustus saw that he did not look back.

"You could only have gotten those records from one person," Augustus said. "And those were not hers to give."

"We've no plan to submit any Windom records in court. Only to use them to point me to people who can prove the things the notes claim. Which brings us back to a man who asked that I send you his regards—Mister Caldwell Begone. The name does ring familiar, yes? He was once an engineer, now works for Cooke as a lawyer." He didn't wait for Augustus to answer. "You spoke to him at your father's funeral. He had some stories about your father's dealings. More than a few. And his storytelling inspired others to tell their stories and then others to follow still after. Augustus, it's clear now the hard part won't be uncovering your crimes but *organizing* them all. And not only your company, but you. And your father. See here, that's the trick with stabbing people in the back like your family's always done, you can't see their face to know if they're really dead."

Ruth cut in. "Your mistake was not understanding what the patent meant to me. It's all I got."

"But you don't *got* it."

"Excuse me?"

"You have no claim to any patent. Your husband does. You're going to need to find him, ma'am, because you cannot license something you do not own. And if you want a hundred lawyers to prove ownership, the first thing they'll need is the man claiming I've stolen from him. So where is he?"

Ruth looked at Kimball. Kimball did not return her glance.

"And if your husband does not turn up," Augustus continued, "how far do you think your little scheme will take you? You two sorry sacks of pig shit are holding airless balloons. You've come into my place with knives out. You took your swipes, but you missed. And now I'm going to send you both out of here without heads."

"Will it be a problem, Augustus?" Kimball said. "Finding Henry Casper?"

He shrugged. "Not if you go to Chattanooga."

"You don't seem concerned about Mister Casper turning up," Kimball said.

"Innocent men aren't concerned by false accusations."

A chuff of laughter escaped Kimball's nostrils. "Months ago," he started, "I asked you to name the men who helped Gutenberg build the printing press."

"Yes. And no one could. Because you think they were unimportant."

"I've changed my mind about this. I used to value the owner of things over the maker of them."

"Now you don't?"

Kimball shook his head. "I can't be sure what Gutenberg's role in the printing press was."

"So you value no one?"

"I value the printing press." Kimball rose from the chair and buttoned his jacket. "I'll understand, of course, if you keep your soft spot for the forgotten men, Augustus. Because when we're through with you, you'll be one of them." He dropped the hefty manual with a bang on the table and moved toward the door.

"Imagine if we were on the same side, Broussais."

"His imagination's not that nimble," Ruth said as she exited the room close behind Kimball. Neither Rathbone, nor any of the other hired guns, did anything to stop them from passing.

The pop and crackle from the fireplace were the only sounds and movement in the room until Marcy returned. "Augustus?" he said with as much urgency as was possible in three syllables.

"Sit, Frank," Augustus said. "Give me a moment." He opened the lawsuit complaint against him and stared at the signatures, the last of which was Ruth Casper's.

Frank sat and immediately started. "About how we can meet the demand by—"

Augustus waved him silent and squinted hard into the scratched paper. It was written in ink, a blotch at each period. Full recognition filled Augustus's eyes. He'd been outplayed.

"All is lost," he muttered.

"You're talking about the trains?" Marcy asked.

"That, too."

Augustus slipped the note in the book of Windom Air Brake plans and held it in front of him like Yorick's skull. Then he pitched it into the fireplace.

32

They calmed themselves with another rye in the tippling room—or, rather, Kimball calmed himself while Ruth watched. She'd never developed a taste for spirits, which Kimball suggested was a good thing in the long run. He dumped the brown contents down his throat, then said, "It went as well as can be expected."

"Did it? Windom said he was going to fight."

"He won't."

"But he said—"

"He also said we weren't going to walk out of here with our heads and here I am still pouring rye into mine."

"But what about the other things? We're never gonna find Henry's body."

"My condolences for that, Ruth." He had never said it before. "But I do believe," he continued, "the Pinkertons will out enough evidence to show Rathbone was the last one to see Henry's body alive."

"That won't bring him back."

"It will bring justice. And vengeance. You'll find those two to be the next best thing."

"Meanwhile, we lose time waiting for proof that Henry's dead. No one can represent Henry's patent and Windom goes on building his own air brake and no one can do anything about it. How am I supposed to live tomorrow and the day after? I've got nothing."

Kimball upturned his glass and swallowed another drink. He eyed his empty glass as if contemplating filling it up again. Instead, he set it down and gestured for her to follow him, then they climbed the grand staircase.

The club was dark, but the late afternoon's russet light poured in through the windows. The churchwarden pipes appeared as if licking flames. For a moment, Ruth was in love. The place was even better than she'd imagined a place like this could be. The smell of tobacco and tanned leather filled her nostrils. She smoothed her hand along a wingback as she passed, feeling the coolness of each buttoned tuft. Had a woman ever been present as a guest before? She plucked a pipe from one of the countless tin tongs mounted on the low ceiling. She inspected the bowl and spun the fragile thing slowly in her hand. It was the lightest clay pipe she'd held. Delicacy was surprising in such a place. She wondered what Henry would think of it. Probably not much at all, she decided bitterly.

Kimball led her to the second-floor balcony. They watched the city's bustle rise and fall just below them along the street. Kimball had gone quiet. He leaned over the balcony rail, lost in a memory he had not cared to narrate to Ruth.

She retrieved her pouch of tobacco and stuffed the pipe, lit it using the taper light just inside, and puffed until it was sufficiently kindled. "I don't know what to do with myself," she said, breaking the silence. "Spent so much time preparing for this moment, I haven't hardly thought about any of the moments after."

"Will you return home? Is there a chance Windom really did send your husband there?"

Ruth gave him a look that begged him to be serious.

She joined Kimball in peering down onto the street. She did not know how to answer. The reply was, yes. Of course she would return to her home. But what was there for her? More than anything, she wanted to return to the floor of Blighton's shop and wake up beside that precious little near-mute child.

Kimball scoured her face and made his own deductions. "I see," he said, and let rest anything else he might say. He pulled out a letter that had been tucked inside his vest. "This is for you." He held it out and waited for her to relieve him of it.

She looked at his face to get some hint at the letter's contents. Was it good or bad or what?

"Haven't we already spread around enough letters for one afternoon?" she asked.

"Before we started the expedition, I struck up a correspondence with a judge friend. He agreed to look into the matter of wardship."

Ruth opened the letter and couldn't fully understand its meaning. "Wardship?"

Kimball nodded. "Over the child. I provided the judge the circumstances and put in a favorable word on your behalf."

She skipped around the letter's scribbling, looking for a string of words that made sense. "It's all written in lawyer," she protested. "What's it mean?"

"It means that, if you want, you can be the legal caretaker of that girl. She would be your charge until adulthood."

The letter no longer held words. It became a blank parchment with only the girl's face on it.

"I'd be something like her...her...?" The word *mother* hung on her tongue, so fragile she dared not speak it.

"If that's a pleasing circumstance to you, yes. I've never seen another woman more determined to mother someone through this world."

"I..." No useful words arrived to her. "Does the girl know?"

"It's your news to share with her, no matter which way you share it. Either she'll remain in your care or be placed in an orphanage."

Ruth let both choices simmer.

Kimball watched her from the corner of his eye. "I hope I've not overreached."

Ruth shook her head. "I've never wanted anything so much without knowing it beforehand."

Kimball allowed himself a grin. "Good."

"Except..." Ruth said.

"Except?"

"Well, this makes my gift to you of an orange look downright paltry by comparison."

Kimball nodded. "It certainly does."

There on the bed was the little girl, studying a book—a simple thing with large pictures and small sentences.

The child looked up and smiled, then returned to the book. When they'd first met, the girl had looked at her with skepticism. That the child was happy to be herself now, and calm in her presence, made Ruth quiver with pride.

"Those letters making sense to you, girl?"

The girl nodded. "Yes, ma'am."

"Not a month ago that same book appeared all a-jumble, didn't it?"

"Mostly. I can make it out now, though."

Ruth made a great task of unclasping her chatelaine. She yanked off her boots, unpinned her hat, and freed herself of her jacket. Anything to stall the next conversation she needed to have.

She sat on a chair watching the child, still unsure how to start the talk. During the ride back to Blighton's in Kimball's carriage she'd tried to plan out how she'd bring up the subject of wardship to the little one. It was a tricky parlay and she didn't know how to start. She still hadn't figured out how to broach the subject. She believed once she began, it would come naturally, but how did one begin to tell a child that they were to be family? Maybe telling her wasn't the right measure. Maybe, instead, it would be better to ask the child what it was she wanted.

Never before short of words, she had none now. She simply did not know how to start the talk. She inhaled and spoke, but what came out surprised even her. "My husband has died, little one."

The girl mirrored her surprise. She seemed overmatched by the statement, as if it was required to show deference to its power. She returned her gaze to her book, but it was clear she no longer paid attention to it. She would wrestle with too many thoughts without any weapons to beat them back.

"You needn't say anything, dear," Ruth continued. "Sitting here now, I'm not certain why I told you. I'd suspected him gone for a while. I had readied for to never see him again. But suspecting and readying aren't the same as living it out."

The girl's eyes had sunk below the book to her own lap. She seemed ashamed at not having any of the right words to offer.

"Was he nice?"

"That's all he was, little girl." Ruth had been staring at her own hand but looked now at the child. She wondered what went through such an innocent mind at times like this. "If you were to never see your father again, child, how do you think you'd feel?" The girl did not move her eyes from her lap. She shrugged after thinking about the question. "Well, let me ask you. How've you felt riding around on trains with me? Sleeping in hotels?" The girl's eyes remained low. Another shrug. "More good than bad, I hope?"

The girl nodded. At least that.

Blighton shambled into the room with a letter in her hand.

"I've come with a delivery from the Patent Office. I angled to see about getting another copy of the patent. They were real excited that I'd asked about it."

"A delivery from who?"

"Your examiner, I guess. Before he was ousted."

The old woman's exertions on her behalf were too much to bear and Ruth began to tremble. Her chest felt heavy. "You didn't hafta do that, Miss Blighton. That's—"

"I know what I do and don't have to do. But, I'll tell you, it's a good thing I went 'cause they were holding a letter for you."

"Another letter?" It was a damned unwelcome thought, slitting open another letter and bearing the words inside…until she saw the handwriting. It was Henry's. Sent from the City Hotel.

Her mind raced. For a moment she thought she was holding proof of ghosts until Blighton snapped her back into the present. "The examiner said he didn't know where to find you to send it. Henry sent this letter to you and another letter to your ousted examiner. Man at the Patent Office said he'd be surprised if they didn't say much the same thing."

For the few seconds it took to unfold the correspondence, Ruth was riveted with confusion.

She opened the letter and noticed right away that it was dated a day before Christmas.

Dec. 24, 1865
My Dearest Ruth,

I last wrote you as a soldier stationed at Fort Cass. You were miles away from me then. As I write tonight, you are a mere few feet away, sleeping soundly.
And since you won't likely read this unless something has happened to me, let me say this for the record—no one is just one thing or another. I lived my life with both clever bits and foolish and I wish I had more control of it all. I am ashamed not to have given you a proud life. I'm scared of things moving and you're scared of them standing still. I know I've disappointed you. The world, up to the writing of this letter, has disappointed you.
I can just hear you telling me to button up and quit simpering, so I will. I have decided to heed our patent examiner's warning about A. W. fixing to steal away my patent. I remain uncertain we are at war with the man but, in case we are, I'd prefer us safe rather than sorry.
It's clear A. W. doesn't see you as the hard-headed deadeye that I know you to be. I know that irks you, but it may work in our favor. If he decides to take aim on us, there is a chance he'll go only after me and spare you.
That, above everything else, is why I have written the statement below and sent a copy of it to our beloved examiner. I trust he will see to its execution.

I, Henry Barlow Casper, sound in head and heart, give equal rights and credit of the Casper Air Brake patents and licensing to my cherished wife, Ruth Judith Leigh Casper. This change is to have immediate effect.

This brake came into being for reasons owing more to you than to me. It's only right your name go right alongside my own.
Let nothing else that has happened or will happen confuse the only thing I know is true: I love you. I've always loved you. And I will love you in the hereafter forever and ever, amen.

In eternal love,
Henry

P. S. Make it count.

She inhaled, letting Henry's words sink into her bones. She folded the letter as the girl and Blighton looked on in conspicuous curiosity, Blighton sitting on one end of the bed, the girl on the other.

Ruth had believed, despite all their efforts, the plan would fall through. They'd have no case without a live and present patent owner. Henry was the missing piece, both literally and figuratively. She knew they'd never find Henry's body and therefore never prove he'd died. Without such proof, the rights to the patent would never revert to her and Augustus Windom would have his way.

But not now. Now she was the patent holder. Not simply the handler of Henry's estate, but the right and lawful co-inventor of the Casper Air Brake.

She would come for Augustus Windom. They would all come for him.

For a man who'd formerly been unable to give her anything, Henry had just given her everything. She remembered their life in Chattanooga, their three departed children, their poverty, the lonely nights she spent waiting for the war to end, waiting for her life to begin. She had imagined Henry returning from the war and rejoining the East Tennessee, or making a modest profit on a small invention, or finding a job in a factory and working his way to respectability. She'd considered a hundred things Henry could do, never once imagining it could be her doing them instead. Never understanding that she'd been removing herself from her own future. Nothing Henry could have done would have improved her station because in every instance it would have been Henry at the center of the doing.

She felt this before she understood it but, when her mind came to understand what she'd done to herself, she became overwhelmed and moved to kneel between the two women. To the two most favored women in her life. She reached out for them.

"Is it more bad tidings?" Blighton asked.

Ruth shook her head and gripped both of them around the shoulders. Pulled them close. She held the child until the child decided it was easier to join Ruth on the floor than to continue teetering over the bed's edge. Unable to squeeze the girl any tighter, she pulled Blighton closer. She forced a surprised grunt out of the old woman. With each squeeze that drew them closer, so, too, did Ruth's weeping grow stronger.

"What's wrong?" asked the girl, fear mingling with the curiosity in her voice.

"Nothing's wrong. All is right for once." The girl nodded, forgetting herself. Ruth did not scold her. She squeezed her. "And you need a name, girl. What did your daddy call you?"

The child did not answer right off. She imagined the girl had forgotten, or never knew, or perhaps she'd simply never been named.

"Evangeline," the girl said in a whisper.

Evangeline. My god. Ruth could hardly believe the fluke of it. It was a name her soul had whispered ad infinitum. Evangeline. Paul, Evangeline, and Cornelia. How long had Ruth wanted to speak these names out loud and hear someone respond? How many fantasies of her children—breathing and vibrant in front of her—had she imagined? There in the dimming light, still woozy from a vengeful day, Ruth spoke into the soft fabric of the child's nightgown.

"I'll call you Evangeline. My Evangeline."

And that was how Ruth started the talk.

33

December 25, 1867

The Pinkertons spent eighteen months tracking down every last passenger on the Tennessee-bound train on which Henry had supposedly traveled home. Questioned every rider about who they saw, who they sat near, and who got on and off. There were three passenger cars transporting sixty-one men, women, and children, all of whom could remember details that aligned with others on the same train. Each rider corroborating the stories of someone else. No one remembered Henry Casper or anyone matching his description. Pendants had been recalled. Hats, beauty marks, snippets of conversation, distinctive laughter, persistent coughs and sneezes, nervous toe-tapping, rambunctious children, sweat stench, breath rot, beards and mustaches. Anything that could be recalled had been recalled. No one remembered seeing a bloody man who was without his boots or a jacket in December, who might have been unconscious. Not one person. When Rathbone testified that he set the unconscious body of Henry Casper in the rear car, propped against a window, Ruth's team of lawyers narrowed down the witnesses to nineteen people and had them testify to having no recollection of any such man.

The lawyers, for their part, scoured every acre of Hamilton County, near the Casper homestead, not only for Henry Casper, but also anyone who'd seen Henry Casper since Christmas. No one had. Only a few knew who he was, but many knew the overgrown property at the bend in the Tennessee River. They all repeated some version of "As flowered as the fields had become, no one could live there in that condition if they wanted to. And why would anyone ever want to?"

It was a question Ruth couldn't herself answer. She'd put off thinking about it. She focused only on trials and licensing agreements. And Evangeline.

But she returned to the home she once shared with Henry one last time.

She was never certain she would and, when the notion took hold, it surprised her.

They'd taken a train from Baltimore to Chattanooga Station, rebuilt and opened five months before. In hindsight, she supposed paying for its reconstruction was itself a signal she intended to return someday.

Ruth arrived by a four-horse carriage. She insisted on driving it herself. Her new churchwarden pipe was squeezed between her teeth, smoke splitting around her face like opening curtains. They traveled around the familiar bend in the Tennessee River and onto the meadow. The trail from the station was unchanged. Nature, of course, took longer than two-and-a-half years to grow unrecognizable. Familiarity, even in unloved places, stirred warm feelings in her belly.

The homestead, however, was utterly wild. Right off, she noticed that any signs of crop rows were long gone, and the barn had collapsed. The meadow was flat and motionless. The wind seemed to move with caution, as if maintaining a quiet respect for the dead. The horse path had grown over, too. When she got close enough, she cut straight through the dried-up weeds and browned sprout grass.

She saw that the cabin's catawampus door had fallen to the porch, taking the hinges right along with it. There was now no separation between the cabin's interior and its exterior. She imagined the family of wild animals that had made a life for themselves in her home.

A thought sprang into her mind—*Maybe Henry's been here all along. Maybe Carroll Klondike, and the Pinkertons, and the lawyers were all mistaken. He fell, maybe. Still woozy from Rathbone's blows to his head. Or he starved and died in his bed.* She thought of him lying dead inside the cabin. Long dead, perhaps. And her, in her adornments and fine patterned garments, arriving to find her husband rotten and peeled away.

She slowed the horses and called out, "Hold up." Nothing inside the cabin moved. She tapped her pipe empty and set it on the bench beside her.

Henry trundled from inside, through the busted front door and onto the porch.

"Ruthy?"

"Yes, Henry Casper. It's me. Frozen solid and bearing gifts."

He made his way to the carriage with ease. His beard was bushy and combed. It had widened his face. He was thicker now, not fat, but he was no longer gaunt. His skin had a pleasant pinkness to it rather than the ashen gray she'd remembered.

"There he is. Mister Quiet Desperation." She flung the reins over the rear horses, dismounted, and landed with a bounce on the frozen ground.

Ruth waved toward the carriage. "You oughta meet somebody," she said, though it was unclear if she was speaking to Henry or to whomever was in the carriage.

The door swung open and out stepped Evangeline, slightly fuller in the face herself. Her chin had begun to dimple. She blinked at the change in light before climbing down the coach's single step. She still wore Henry's old slouch hat pushed back on her forehead.

"Is she wearing my hat?" Henry whispered under his breath for only Ruth to hear.

"No. It's *her* hat," Ruth whispered back. She put her arm around the approaching girl. "You believe I lived here ten years, little girl?"

Evangeline shook her head. "No, ma'am."

"Not too many good memories. Wouldn't trade our lives for this one, that's for sure."

The girl looked all around her as if every new vision was a fresh horror.

Henry looked at the two of them. "You're in your imagination again, ain't you, Ruthy?" Ruth nodded. "I'm not here?" She shook her head. "Was this how it was with Paul and the girls?" Ruth nodded.

Henry smiled. "Do I often find my way into your imaginings?" he asked.

Ruth shook her head. "I'm sorry."

Evangeline took a half-step away from Ruth to get a better look at her. "Sorry for what?"

Ruth blinked herself back into the present. "For bringing you here. It's no place for young ones. We won't stay long."

"S'okay, Ruth."

Ruth pointed to the barn—or what was left of it. "Will you gather me five solid boards from yonder? And anything you can find to hammer them together?"

The girl nodded and set out.

"I like her," Henry said.

Ruth nodded.

"You think Windom'll ever pop out again?"

"I don't see how. He's only worth a sliver now. And Rathbone disappeared," Ruth said. "But I'm keeping an eye out for them just the same."

"I heard about that young man from Pittsburg. Westinghouse?"

Ruth shrugged. "Everybody claims they invented the first air brake. You're the only one ever put it on a train and rode around on it."

Henry gave a nod of appreciation. "It's a damn hard world with no soft edges. I ain't sorry to miss it."

"And anyhow," Ruth said, "if all else goes to pot, Evangeline just inherited an undertaking business from a departed friend. We'll survive on that."

Henry didn't know what to say and Ruth let it sit between them, suggesting there was nothing more needed saying.

"The girl," Henry said.

"Evangeline," Ruth corrected. They watched the girl gather proper planks. Not too long, nothing split or splintered.

"Evangeline. Yes. Why is she herding together them boards?"

"You need a grave marker, Henry Casper. We come to build you one."

Henry nodded. "What's it gonna say?"

Ruth shrugged. "Been wondering that myself."

She couldn't shake the memory of her mother's grave marker. *Be ye also ready.* It would be just as appropriate for Henry as it was for her mother.

"I'm sure it'll be fine whatever it is," Henry said.

Ruth's lip quivered, but her eyes were dry. "I'm sorry our last words to each other were angry ones, Henry." Henry nodded. "This wasn't how we were supposed to end up."

"There's no supposed to, I guess. Life goes and we go with it."

Ruth sighed. Shook her head. When she looked over at Henry, he was watching the girl. She'd found enough wood for the grave marker.

"I'm sorry I ran, Henry."

He smiled. "You are not."

"Well, I'm sorry for my sour words to you at the end."

Henry nodded.

"I reckon it'll be a fine marker. I thank you."

"Least I could do. I owe you that much. Something to prove you were here. That you mattered."

"Did I?"

She studied his calm face. "You left something behind, even if I'm the only one who knows it."

"It's like that poem. The one that goes, 'For them what never sing, they die with all their music in 'em.'"

Ruth gave a chuckle. "That's you, for certain."

The girl stood straight, her arms filled with equal sized boards.

She yelled from the barn. "I've got 'em, Ruth!"

Ruth raised her hand and walked toward her. Henry did not follow and when she looked back toward the carriage, he was gone.

They constructed a crude grave marker and planted it at the spot the bear trap had once been. The spot the Casper Air Brake had been born. Ruth spent a half hour etching the eternal message into the wood.

Henry Casper
b. 1827
d. 1865
He kept his music inside him

THE END

HISTORICAL NOTE

The months immediately following the end of the Civil War were a conflicting time of moral courage and human decimation, blood and bewilderment. The North's victory was bitter. The feeling across the country amounted to "What now?"

It is during this wound-licking, dust-settling, dead-burying moment in our nation's history that I wanted to set this story. The country had to destroy itself to survive, and it would survive. But first there would be chaos—a mad scramble among the survivors to mark their place in the country's new history. Both Ruth Casper and Augustus Windom are a part of the same scramble, albeit starting from starkly different places.

This book itself had two different starting points that I didn't initially realize would be connected. The first was Ruth. Before there was anything else, there was a woman with limited resources in a broken land who refused to accept her position in the world. *Never Walk Back* is a Western in spirit, but one that demanded a heroine who was more than a damsel and who couldn't rely on murder as her means of revenge. I built Ruth using countless personal and historical resources. Karen Abbott's *Liar, Temptress, Soldier, Spy: Four Women Undercover in the Civil War* (2014) provided a baseline cleverness and toughness for the females of this story. Erica Armstrong Dunbar's *Never Caught: The Washingtons' Relentless Pursuit of Their Runaway Slave, Ona Judge* (2017) is a tremendous story of desperate survival and helped provide guidance on how a person could keep moving against overwhelming odds. Chris Enss's *The Pinks: The First Women Detectives, Operatives, and Spies with the Pinkerton National Detective Agency* (2017) was another useful book that helped me define Ruth's spirit, drive, and gumption.

This book's second starting point came while reading Ted Franklin Belue's *The Long Hunt: Death of the Buffalo East of the Mississippi* (1996), which illustrated how the westward expansion of rail decimated the American buffalo. The details it described showed me how essential, yet reckless, railroad travel had become midway through the nineteenth century. The construction of the Transcontinental Railroad spurred inventors, investors, and engineers to chase innovations that were nearly as dangerous as the trains themselves. Men risked their reputations, fortunes, and lives to make railroad travel safer and paradoxically faster. I wanted in on that chase. Ruth wanted in on that chase. And so we entered it. My time at the Union Pacific Railroad Museum in Council Bluffs, Iowa was an indispensable immersion into train activity—including how they operated, where they operated, and the types of people doing the operating.

While reading was a large portion of the research done for this book, I relished any opportunity to visit museums and historical sites to more emotionally absorb the feel and function of various locations included in the story. When describing the minutae of life in 1865, I took much from my time at the South Park City museum in Fairplay, Colorado. Everything from the mortuary tools and the floor plan of the Virginian's house to businesses in the abandoned mining town of White Cake was available to me there. If I could live in that museum, I would. The Orange Street Club is fictionalized, but the original Odd Fellows Hall in Baltimore and the famous Keens Chophouse in New York were direct inspirations.

T. D. Griffith's *Deadwood: The Best Writings on the Most Notorious Town in the West* (2009) helped me find the right tone for the letters written throughout the story. Kenneth D. Ackerman's *Dark Horse: The Surprise Election and Political Murder of President James A. Garfield* (2003) was my "Bickering Bible," greatly helping me establish the way powerful enemies like Augustus Windom and Broussais Kimball would talk to one another, especially when they couldn't say exactly what they felt.

All of the primary characters in this novel are fictional. However, I've done my best to insert them into a world that very much existed. Leopold Windom's funeral was carried out with similar gravitas to Abraham Lincoln's funeral procession. George Westinghouse's air brake was patented two years after the events of this novel—just enough time to suggest another fight Ruth may have engaged in after *Never Walk Back*. That said, the activities I describe involving Lincoln, Westinghouse, the Pinkerton Detective Agency, the United States Patent Office, the Confederate and Union armies, and any other historical figures or entities, are wholly products of my imagination.

A painstaking amount of effort was used in creating the Caspers' path from Chattanooga to Washington, D.C., as well as the navigation through Washington and Baltimore. In addition to pulling a lot of period-specific journey insight from Mark Twain's *Roughing It* (1872), I also used more than forty maps available through the Library of Congress that highlighted overland routes and city streets in Tennessee, Virginia, West Virginia, Maryland, and Pennsylvania. I estimate a quarter of the creation of this book was spent staring at minute details of trails and rail lines originally printed over 150 years ago. Believe it or not, this is an incredibly fun way to spend time.

Alas, nothing's perfect and I apologize for any inaccuracies the reader may uncover.

ACKNOWLEDGMENTS

No one writes a book alone—or shouldn't, anyway. More than a few people influenced the outcome of this book in some essential way. They deserve much more than thanks. Unfortunately for them, thanks is the only thing this section provides. I hope it's better than nothing.

First and foremost, I owe my editor, Emily Victorson, a thousand kudos for every time she turned something false into something true. She saw what I saw and helped me see it clearer. The entire process of putting a novel into the world was an absolute pleasure. I thank her for her commitment, vigilance, and compassion.

It took four and a half years to outline, write, edit, and publish this book. Throughout that time, my writer's group was an invaluable resource. I paraphrase Springsteen when I say I learned more from a three-hour session than I ever learned in school. Thanks to Dan Bacarella, Rachel Baker, Michael Devens, Traci Failla, Michelle Finkler, Dan Finnen, Jason Runnels, and especially Jaclyn Hamer who introduced me into the group in the first place and gave my first draft the kick in the rear it deserved.

I'd also like to thank my friends who provided indispensable feedback on various drafts. They helped clean up more than a few literary messes. Jason Lukehart, Ryan McGuire, Kathryn Mendes, Sam Nekrosius, and Robbie Ocampo. I've thanked them before, but I cannot thank them enough.

My family never made me feel silly or self-centered for writing and if they had, I may very well have stopped doing it. I'm grateful to my mom, dad, sister, and extended family for their unwavering support.

My wife, Emily, read early drafts of this three times before anyone else read it once. She took the time to articulate the myriad reasons my first instincts were wrong (they were wrong often) and provided the opposing perspective every time I needed it. Thank you. You were right.

I should also thank my daughter, Eloise. If she hadn't been such a good sleeper, I'd never have finished this thing. She's my absolute favorite part about being alive.

ALSO PUBLISHED BY
ALLIUM PRESS OF CHICAGO

Fiction with a Chicago Connection

Visit our website for more information:
www.alliumpress.com

THE EMILY CABOT MYSTERIES
Frances McNamara

Death at the Fair

The 1893 World's Columbian Exposition provides a vibrant backdrop for the first book in the series. Emily Cabot, one of the first women graduate students at the University of Chicago, is eager to prove herself in the emerging field of sociology. While she is busy exploring the Exposition with her family and friends, her colleague, Dr. Stephen Chapman, is accused of murder. Emily sets out to search for the truth behind the crime, but is thwarted by the gamblers, thieves, and corrupt politicians who are ever-present in Chicago. A lynching that occurred in the dead man's past leads Emily to seek the assistance of the black activist Ida B. Wells.

◆

Death at Hull House

After Emily Cabot is expelled from the University of Chicago, she finds work at Hull House, the famous settlement established by Jane Addams. There she quickly becomes involved in the political and social problems of the immigrant community. But, when a man who works for a sweatshop owner is murdered in the Hull House parlor, Emily must determine whether one of her colleagues is responsible, or whether the real reason for the murder is revenge for a past tragedy in her own family. As a smallpox epidemic spreads through the impoverished west side of Chicago, the very existence of the settlement is threatened and Emily finds herself in jeopardy from both the deadly disease and a killer.

◆

Death at Pullman

A model town at war with itself . . . George Pullman created an ideal community for his railroad car workers, complete with every amenity they could want or need. But when hard economic times hit in 1894, lay-offs follow and the workers can no longer pay their rent or buy food at the company store. Starving and desperate, they turn against their once benevolent employer. Emily Cabot and her friend Dr. Stephen Chapman bring much needed food and medical supplies to the town, hoping they can meet the immediate needs of the workers and keep them from resorting to violence. But when one young worker—suspected of being a spy—is murdered, and a bomb plot comes to light, Emily must race to discover the truth behind a tangled web of family and company alliances.

THE EMILY CABOT MYSTERIES
Frances McNamara

Death at Woods Hole

Exhausted after the tumult of the Pullman Strike of 1894, Emily Cabot is looking forward to a restful summer visit to Cape Cod. She has plans to collect "beasties" for the Marine Biological Laboratory, alongside other visiting scientists from the University of Chicago. She also hopes to enjoy romantic clambakes with Dr. Stephen Chapman, although they must keep an important secret from their friends. But her summer takes a dramatic turn when she finds a dead man floating in a fish tank. In order to solve his murder she must first deal with dueling scientists, a testy local sheriff, the theft of a fortune, and uncooperative weather.

◆

Death at Chinatown

In the summer of 1896, amateur sleuth Emily Cabot meets two young Chinese women who have recently received medical degrees. She is inspired to make an important decision about her own life when she learns about the difficult choices they have made in order to pursue their careers. When one of the women is accused of poisoning a Chinese herbalist, Emily once again finds herself in the midst of a murder investigation. But, before the case can be solved, she must first settle a serious quarrel with her husband, help quell a political uprising, and overcome threats against her family. Timeless issues, such as restrictions on immigration, the conflict between Western and Eastern medicine, and women's struggle to balance family and work, are woven seamlessly throughout this mystery set in Chicago's original Chinatown.

Death at the Paris Exposition

In the sixth Emily Cabot Mystery, the intrepid amateur sleuth's journey once again takes her to a world's fair—the Paris Exposition of 1900. Chicago socialite Bertha Palmer has been named the only female U. S. commissioner to the Exposition and she enlists Emily's services as her social secretary. Their visit to the House of Worth for the fitting of a couture gown is interrupted by the theft of Mrs. Palmer's famous pearl necklace. Before that crime can be solved, several young women meet untimely deaths and a member of the Palmers' inner circle is accused of the crimes. As Emily races to clear the family name she encounters jealous society ladies, American heiresses seeking titled European husbands, and more luscious gowns and priceless jewels. Along the way, she takes refuge from the tumult at the country estate of Impressionist painter Mary Cassatt. In between her work and sleuthing, she is able to share the Art Nouveau delights of the Exposition, and the enduring pleasures of the City of Light, with her husband and their young children.

◆

Death at the Selig Studios

The early summer of 1909 finds Emily Cabot eagerly anticipating a relaxing vacation with her family. Before they can depart, however, she receives news that her brother, Alden, has been involved in a shooting death at the Selig Polyscope silent movie studios on Chicago's northwest side. She races to investigate, along with her friend Detective Henry Whitbread. There they discover a sprawling backlot, complete with ferocious jungle animals and the celluloid cowboys Tom Mix and Broncho Billy. As they dig deeper into the situation, they uncover furtive romantic liaisons between budding movie stars and an attempt by Thomas Edison to maintain his stranglehold over the emerging film industry. Before the intrepid amateur sleuth can clear her brother's name she faces a serious break with the detective; a struggle with her adolescent daughter, who is obsessed with the filming of the original Wizard of Oz movie; and threats upon her own life.

◆

Death on the Homefront

coming in Winter 2020

With the United States on the verge of entering World War I, tensions run high in Chicago in the Spring of 1917, and the city simmers with anti-German sentiment mixed with virulent patriotism. Shockingly, amateur sleuth Emily Cabot is present when a young Chicago woman, who is about to make a brilliant society marriage, is murdered. Was her death retaliation for her pacifist activities, or was it linked to her romantic entanglements? Emily has a personal connection to the woman, but she's torn between her determination to solve the murder and her deep need to protect her newly adult children from the realities of a new world. As the country's entry into the war unfolds, Emily watches with trepidation as her sons and daughter make questionable choices about their own futures. Violent worker unrest and the tumultuous arena of automobile racing provide an emotionally charged backdrop for this compelling mystery.

THE HANLEY & RIVKA MYSTERIES
D. M. Pirrone

Shall We Not Revenge

In the harsh early winter months of 1872, while Chicago is still smoldering from the Great Fire, Irish Catholic detective Frank Hanley is assigned the case of a murdered Orthodox Jewish rabbi. His investigation proves difficult when the neighborhood's Yiddish-speaking residents, wary of outsiders, are reluctant to talk. But when the rabbi's headstrong daughter, Rivka, unexpectedly offers to help Hanley find her father's killer, the detective receives much more than the break he was looking for. Their pursuit of the truth draws Rivka and Hanley closer together and leads them to a relief organization run by the city's wealthy movers and shakers. Along the way, they uncover a web of political corruption, crooked cops, and well-buried ties to two notorious Irish thugs from Hanley's checkered past. Even after he is kicked off the case, stripped of his badge, and thrown in jail, Hanley refuses to quit. With a personal vendetta to settle for an innocent life lost, he is determined to expose a complicated criminal scheme, not only for his own sake, but for Rivka's as well.

◆

For You Were Strangers

On a spring morning in 1872, former Civil War officer Ben Champion is discovered dead in his Chicago bedroom—a bayonet protruding from his back. What starts as a routine case for Detective Frank Hanley soon becomes anything but, as his investigation into Champion's life turns up hidden truths best left buried. Meanwhile, Rivka Kelmansky's long-lost brother, Aaron, arrives on her doorstep, along with his mulatto wife and son. Fugitives from an attack by night riders, Aaron and his family know too much about past actions that still threaten powerful men—defective guns provided to Union soldiers, and an 1864 conspiracy to establish Chicago as the capital of a Northwest Confederacy. Champion had his own connection to that conspiracy, along with ties to a former slave now passing as white and an escaped Confederate guerrilla bent on vengeance, any of which might have led to his death. Hanley and Rivka must untangle this web of circumstances, amid simmering hostilities still present seven years after the end of the Civil War, as they race against time to solve the murder, before the secrets of bygone days claim more victims.

THE HANLEY & RIVKA MYSTERIES
D. M. Pirrone

Promises to the Dead

As Chicago recovers from the Great Fire of 1871, the Civil War continues to haunt its residents. What begins for Detective Frank Hanley as the simple case of a missing railroad clerk quickly escalates into something much more complex. Ezra Hayes, who has made a daring escape from forced servitude on a Louisiana sugar plantation, brings to Chicago proof of nefarious doings in the South. His information implicates the missing clerk's employer, a major shipper of sugar. As Hanley struggles to untangle the web of circumstances surrounding the railroad's role in the clerk's disappearance, Rivka Kelmansky faces her own personal struggle. Her brother is pressuring her to marry a young man from her tight-knit Jewish community, but she still dreams of forging a new life with Hanley. When her mulatto sister-in-law is wrongfully accused of murder, Rivka turns to Hanley for help. Facing opposition on multiple fronts, they must race against time to save Ada's life and uncover the shocking truth.

Set the Night on Fire
Libby Fischer Hellmann

Someone is trying to kill Lila Hilliard. During the Christmas holidays she returns from running errands to find her family home in flames, her father and brother trapped inside. Later, she is attacked by a mysterious man on a motorcycle. . . and the threats don't end there. As Lila desperately tries to piece together who is after her and why, she uncovers information about her father's past in Chicago during the volatile days of the late 1960s . . . information he never shared with her, but now threatens to destroy her. Part thriller, part historical novel, and part love story, *Set the Night on Fire* paints an unforgettable portrait of Chicago during a turbulent time: the riots at the Democratic Convention . . . the struggle for power between the Black Panthers and SDS . . . and a group of young idealists who tried to change the world.

◆

A Bitter Veil
Libby Fischer Hellmann

It all began with a line of Persian poetry . . . Anna and Nouri, both studying in Chicago, fall in love despite their very different backgrounds. Anna, who has never been close to her parents, is more than happy to return with Nouri to his native Iran, to be embraced by his wealthy family. Beginning their married life together in 1978, their world is abruptly turned upside down by the overthrow of the Shah and the rise of the Islamic Republic. Under the Ayatollah Khomeini and the Republican Guard, life becomes increasingly restricted and Anna must learn to exist in a transformed world, where none of the familiar Western rules apply. Random arrests and torture become the norm, women are required to wear hijab, and Anna discovers that she is no longer free to leave the country. As events reach a fevered pitch, Anna realizes that nothing is as she thought, and no one can be trusted...not even her husband.

Honor Above All
J. Bard-Collins

Pinkerton agent Garrett Lyons arrives in Chicago in 1882, close on the trail of the person who murdered his partner. He encounters a vibrant city that is striving ever upwards, full of plans to construct new buildings that will "scrape the sky." In his quest for the truth Garrett stumbles across a complex plot involving counterfeit government bonds, fierce architectural competition, and painful reminders of his military past. Along the way he seeks the support and companionship of his friends—elegant Charlotte, who runs an upscale poker game for the city's elite, and up-and-coming architect Louis Sullivan. Rich with historical details that bring early 1880s Chicago to life, this novel will appeal equally to mystery fans, history buffs, and architecture enthusiasts.

◆

The Reason for Time
Mary Burns

On a hot, humid Monday afternoon in July 1919, Maeve Curragh watches as a blimp plunges from the sky and smashes into a downtown Chicago bank building. It is the first of ten extraordinary days in Chicago history that will forever change the course of her life. Racial tensions mount as soldiers return from the battlefields of Europe and the Great Migration brings new faces to the city, culminating in violent race riots. Each day the young Irish immigrant, a catalogue order clerk for the Chicago Magic Company, devours the news of a metropolis where cultural pressures are every bit as febrile as the weather. But her interest in the headlines wanes when she catches the eye of a charming streetcar conductor. Maeve's singular voice captures the spirit of a young woman living through one of Chicago's most turbulent periods. Seamlessly blending fact with fiction, Mary Burns weaves an evocative tale of how an ordinary life can become inextricably linked with history.

Where My Body Ends and the World Begins
Tony Romano

On December 1, 1958, a devastating blaze at Our Lady of the Angels School in Chicago took the lives of ninety-two children, shattering a close-knit Italian neighborhood. In this eloquent novel, set nearly a decade later, twenty-year-old Anthony Lazzeri struggles with survivor's guilt, which is manifested through conflicted feelings about his own body. Complicating his life is a retired detective's dogged belief that Anthony was involved in the setting of the fire. Tony Romano's delicate handling of Anthony's journey is deeply moving, exploring the complex psychological toll such an event has on those involved, including families…and an entire community. This multi-faceted tale follows Anthony's struggles to come to terms with how the events of that day continue to affect him and those around him. Aided by a sometime girlfriend, a former teacher, and later his parents—after long buried family secrets are brought into the open—he attempts to piece together a life for himself as an adult.

◆

Sync
K. P. Kyle

Every day we each make thousands of decisions. Sometimes it's the big ones that change our lives, sometimes it's the tiny ones. What if all the choices not made led to billions of alternate realities where different versions of our lives unwind? On a cold and rainy night in New England, the paths of two strangers collide—a young man fleeing from his past, and a forty-something woman dreading what her future holds. When his past catches up to him, the two of them embark on a journey of danger, adventure, and self-discovery. Ultimately, they each need to face the question, How far would you go to help someone in need? K. P. Kyle's debut novel is a riveting technothriller/road trip/parallel universes combo with a healthy dollop of romance. It will keep you hooked until the very end and make you ponder the choices you've made in your own life.

FOR YOUNGER READERS

Her Mother's Secret
Barbara Garland Polikoff

Fifteen-year-old Sarah, the daughter of Jewish immigrants, wants nothing more than to become an artist. But as she spreads her wings she must come to terms with the secrets that her family is only beginning to share with her. Replete with historical details that vividly evoke the Chicago of the 1890s, this moving coming-of-age story is set against the backdrop of a vibrant, turbulent city. Sarah moves between two very different worlds—the colorful immigrant neighborhood surrounding Hull House and the sophisticated, elegant World's Columbian Exposition. This novel eloquently captures the struggles of a young girl as she experiences the timeless emotions of friendship, family turmoil, loss...and first love.

A companion guide to *Her Mother's Secret*
is available at www.alliumpress.com. In the guide you will find resources
for further exploration of Sarah's time and place.

◆

City of Grit and Gold
Maud Macrory Powell

The streets of Chicago in 1886 are full of turmoil. Striking workers clash with police...illness and injury lurk around every corner...and twelve-year-old Addie must find her way through it all. Torn between her gruff Papa—who owns a hat shop and thinks the workers should be content with their American lives—and her beloved Uncle Chaim—who is active in the protests for the eight-hour day—Addie struggles to understand her topsy-turvy world, while keeping her family intact. Set in a Jewish neighborhood of Chicago during the days surrounding the Haymarket Affair, this novel vividly portrays one immigrant family's experience, while also eloquently depicting the timeless conflict between the haves and the have-nots.

A companion guide to *City of Grit and Gold*
is available at www.alliumpress.com. In the guide you will find resources
for further exploration of Addie's time and place.

Made in the USA
Monee, IL
30 March 2021